RoseHill Manor

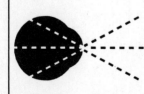

ROSEHILL MANOR

SHAROL LOUISE

THORNDIKE PRESS
A part of Gale, Cengage Learning

Detroit • New York • San Francisco • New Haven, Conn • Waterville, Maine • London

GALE
CENGAGE Learning·

Copyright © 2010 by Sharol Louise Schell.
Thorndike Press, a part of Gale, Cengage Learning.

Thorndike Press® Large Print Clean Reads.
The text of this Large Print edition is unabridged.
Other aspects of the book may vary from the original edition.
Set in 16 pt. Plantin.

LIBRARY OF CONGRESS CATALOGING-IN-PUBLICATION DATA

Louise, Sharol.
　Rosehill manor / by Sharol Louise.
　　p. cm. — (Thorndike Press large print clean reads)
　ISBN-13: 978-1-4104-3520-0 (hardcover)
　ISBN-10: 1-4104-3520-2 (hardcover)
　1. Young women—Fiction. 2. Aristocracy (Social class)—England—19th century—Fiction. 3. Country life—England—Fiction. 4. Large type books. I. Title.
　PS3612.O82R67 2011
　813'.6—dc22　　　　　　　　　　　　　　2010045465

Published in 2011 by arrangement with Tekno Books.

Printed in the United States of America
1 2 3 4 5 6 7 15 14 13 12 11

To Tomás, life partner *extraordinaire:*
Thank you. It's been
an incredible journey.

ACKNOWLEDGMENTS

I gratefully acknowledge those who supported the adventure:

Pat Mack
Linda Hoversland
Mary Nicholson
Lynette Alison Young
Jeff Schell
Jennifer Vlasman
Juanita Stave
Susan Elizabeth Groves
Carolyn Frilot
And my patient editor, Alice Duncan

CHAPTER ONE

RoseHill Manor, England
The doors blew open under the stormy force of a taffeta cyclone.

"Constance, I need your help!" Lady Larissa Wakefield burst into the library, fuchsia skirts still in motion, ebony curls bouncing.

"Good morning, Larissa." Without turning, Lady Constance Chambreville continued to layer mugwort and lavender stems in a heavy crystal vase.

"Please promise you'll help me. Quickly, before it is too late."

"Mugwort," mused Constance with a frown as she twirled a woody stalk. "Who dreams up these unattractive names?" She wedged the purplish-red spear into the arrangement, then glanced over her shoulder in time to see Lady Larissa slump gracefully onto a sofa. "Do you suppose it's the same person who came up with the name

9

'Wormwood'? Or 'Constance'?"

Larissa, her face buried in delicate hands, dropped them and looked up. "I'm to become a prisoner," she whispered hoarsely. Her large, sapphire-blue eyes brimmed with tears. "I am practically a grown woman and I'm being imprisoned."

Constance carried the vase to a large walnut desk that squatted near terrace windows. "Larissa, what scheme are you about this time?" She returned to the gilt-wood side table, scooped up leftover lavender branches, and brushed them from her hands into the fireplace. A stray branch fell on the marble surround, and she bent to pick it up.

Noting her friend's uncustomary silence, Constance glanced across the room, then quickly carried the amethyst stem to the sofa and took a seat close to the young lady. "Larissa, you're so pale. What is it?"

"It's the very worst luck you could imagine." Springy curls swung merrily as she shook her head, in contrast to her somber tone. "My brother has returned from his commission early. And he's convinced Aunt and Uncle I've become much too wild under their guardianship." Her eyelids narrowed. "Here I was anticipating the three of us would remove to Brighton, or perhaps to

Bath for the summer. Yet suddenly my brother arrives and begins ordering everyone about as if he is still playing the commanding officer. And now, instead of an exhilarating summer, he insists I rusticate in the country. Like you. Oh!" Her cherry cheeks burned a shade more scarlet, and she reached for the other young woman's hand. "Constance, I didn't mean that. I know there is a reason *you* do not go about in society."

"I'm not offended." Constance squeezed Larissa's hand. "Truthfully, I prefer the quiet solitude of the country. I find . . . rusticating —" She grinned, showing a brief dimple. "— suits me."

It had been almost three months, Constance realized in surprise, since she'd fled from London in the wake of her brother's scandal. She'd chosen to retreat to their country home, while Alec thought it most prudent he leave England's shores posthaste. Now she wished she'd followed him to the continent. This waiting and worrying wore upon her; a dozen times a day she wondered if he was safe.

The single dry stalk of lavender snapped in her fists, returning her attention to Lady Larissa. She caught only the last word. "Did you say 'tyrant'?"

11

"Yes. He was a tyrant before he left, and seeing the world has not improved him one whit. He is still a tyrant. Perhaps worse." Larissa puckered her smooth brow. "What is worse than a tyrant?"

"A dictator?" offered Constance in the dry tone she'd learned so well from her Aunt Agatha.

"Precisely." Larissa nodded primly. "A dictator, then. Lord help the woman he should deign to marry — if ever, that is, he should find one perfect enough to match himself." She jumped up and paced, wringing her small hands. "He will lock her in the pantry, I am sure, and only allow her out on social occasions." She spun to face her friend, eyes wild. "Constance, he'll lock *me* in the pantry, and for the entire summer."

"Larissa, sit down and calm yourself. Mrs. Dewberry will be in shortly with tea. You're getting yourself worked into hysterics." She watched the young woman continue to pace. "Besides, how could *I* possibly help?"

"I have an idea."

Constance groaned. She'd learned to fear these four words over the years she'd known Lady Larissa Wakefield. Whenever Larissa was in a bind she would draw upon the heroines of her novels. These wild schemes might work in a world of fiction but were never practical — or successful — in reality.

Hearing the cantering of a horse upon the long gravel lane, Constance turned her head.

"He's here!" Larissa turned white and looked about to faint.

"Who is here?" Constance stood and glided over to peer out the bay window. She pulled the sheer curtain to one side and craned, but Larissa grabbed her by the arm, pulling her away and out of view.

"My brother. But I left hours before him." She lowered her voice, but it was intense with urgency. "Constance, quickly. We are out of time. Do give me your word you'll help."

"Larissa, you're not making sense. And why are we whispering? What is it you expect of me?"

"It's just . . . I thought . . . if I must be locked away in the country, then perhaps I could spend the summer with *you*. You certainly have the freedom to do as you please. We could amuse ourselves with out-ings and picnics. Perhaps a trip to London."

"That would be fun. I'd love —"

"And Aunt and Uncle agreed before leaving on their trip. You know how they love you like a daughter. We all three agreed it would be delightful, and that I should stay with you for the summer. The whole summer. It was quite settled."

Constance bit back a smile. "Well, I'm glad everyone has settled the arrangements. Less work for me."

"But that's why it is so desperately unfair." Larissa still whispered. "He's come home, and now they've taken the opportunity to visit Cousin Ruth for several weeks — though I'm sure it was just an excuse to escape from my irritating brother." She frowned. "They left in such a hurry. And now he's about to ruin everything."

"Never tell me they forgot to tell him about your plans before they left? And their approval?"

"They did tell him that I'd be staying safely at RoseHill Manor." Larissa dropped onto a nearby settee, her shoulders sagging along with the cushions. "But he started interrogating me again this morning, almost as soon as their coach rolled past the gate. I know him. He's searching for a reason to cancel any enjoyment I might chance to find." She cast a brief look up at Constance. "He doesn't believe in having fun, you know." Larissa glanced nervously toward the window.

"He can't hear you," said Constance. This

14

time she did smile, but Larissa didn't seem to notice.

"I repeated to him, I am sure it was for the second time — or was it the third? — about RoseHill Manor. All of a sudden he snaps his fingers. 'Chambreville,' he says. 'Is this family connected to the Earl of St. Edmunds? Alec Chambreville?' "

Constance stiffened. "Did he? And what else did he say?"

"Nothing more about your brother. But of course, I immediately realized he would make an issue of the scandal that's befallen this house. As I said, he's sifting for an excuse to deny me. Any excuse. So I blurted the truth: that Lord St. Edmunds was currently on the continent, and absolutely not in residence. Not even in England. And that this was simply a house belonging to a distant member of the family —"

"A distant member! A sister and brother?"

Larissa bit her lower lip. "Constance, he made me so flustered. And he's such a stickler for propriety. I was afraid to admit that Aunt and Uncle agreed I'd be staying with *you* . . . with St. Edmunds's sister." She avoided looking at Constance; her gaze slanted to the hearth. "I'm sorry. What with the scandal and all." She shrugged prettily.

Constance sat down beside Lady Larissa.

15

"You chose not to tell him you'd be staying with me — with Lord St. Edmunds's sister?"

Larissa's black curls nodded and she dismissed the question breezily. "I told him that the house had been generously offered. To Aunt and Uncle and to me." She leaned forward and confided, "I told him you were in Italy."

Constance's mouth dropped open at yet another of Larissa's tales. "But . . . but he certainly wouldn't allow you to stay here at RoseHill Manor by yourself, even if your aunt and uncle had agreed."

Larissa's blue eyes were innocently wide. "Oh no, of course not. He knows I won't be staying here alone. He just doesn't know that you are . . . who you really are."

Constance put a hand to her temple. "I didn't have a megrim this morning when I awoke. What did you just say?"

"I said that I told him *you* were in Italy. And he knows I'm staying with *you,* but he just doesn't know who *you* are. Which is why he insists upon meeting you, before he tells me no." She pouted. "I know he will say *no.* He will deny me this."

Studying her friend closely, Constance spoke slowly. "Larissa . . . then who, exactly, am *I,* if I am still in Italy?"

16

"Why, you're the companion we hired." Larissa beamed.

Constance looked at her friend as if she'd grown an extra nose. "Your aunt and uncle would never have approved of that outrageous scheme."

Larissa laughed. "Of course not. They left happily secure I'll be with my best friend, Lady Constance Chambreville, whom they love and approve of." She nodded primly. "In spite of the scandal, I am pleased to add. For they are not judgmental, such as some people we know." She glanced toward the door. "But *he* doesn't know that you are Lady Constance. I told him they'd already arranged for a proper companion to stay with me at RoseHill."

"Your brother believed this?" asked Constance in skeptical surprise. "That your aunt and uncle would allow you to stay at this house, with a stranger — a paid companion? For much of the summer?"

Larissa leaned forward again, angled her head confidentially. "I told him they had already interviewed you and that you had *impeccable* references." She giggled.

Constance choked.

Larissa talked faster now, glancing nervously toward the threshold. "And I told him they also agreed because they know all the servants here."

"What?"

"Well, perhaps not *all* the servants. But their own Jefferson is related by marriage to your James. Besides, this is such a short ride from Amber Crossing. I explained to Marcus they were comfortable because I'm practically in their paddock. Just a short visit away."

"Practically in their paddock?" repeated Constance. "We are practically in the next village. This is impossible to believe." She shook her head gently, tiptoeing around the headache.

Larissa's mouth turned down. Rising swiftly, she continued to pace. "He said the same thing. He insists on rescinding their agreement now they are gone. Which is so very unfair!" This final remark was accompanied by the stamp of a tiny foot.

Constance sighed, watched her friend stride nervously to the window. "I hate to state the obvious, but perhaps if you had told him the truth? He might have agreed immediately. Allowed you to stay with me — the real Lady Constance — not with a stranger. He would understand why your aunt and uncle gave their approval in good faith. And you wouldn't be in this brine. Perhaps the fact that Alec is my brother would have counted for naught. So why not confess and tell him the truth now?"

Larissa spun toward her and gasped. "Admit I fibbed? Oh, no. Noooo. He hates dishonesty above all else. He'd surely lock me up for the entire summer. In the pantry," she added.

"Perhaps I agree with your brother. Staying here alone —" As Larissa opened her mouth in protest, Constance held up a hand. "— or with an unknown companion, at your age. . . . This might do irreparable damage to your reputation, Larissa."

"How can it? I'll actually be with you, not an unknown companion."

"Oh. That's true. I see." Constance shook her head. "No, I don't see. I'm still confused."

Larissa rushed over to take her friend's hand. Pulling her to her feet, she said, "But there isn't time to explain more. Please, Constance, you don't know what an ogre my brother is. All you need do is pretend to be a proper lady's companion and then he'll leave, and I'll be free for the summer, and we'll have the most splendid time together. Please, Constance, please, please, please." Again, tears looked on the verge of spilling from Larissa's dark blue eyes.

"I wouldn't even know how to pass for a

lady's companion," declared Constance in consternation just to turn the subject.

Larissa perked up. "Why, you'd be perfect for the role. You're proper, you dress simply, and . . . I'm sorry, but . . . but look what you're wearing right now."

Constance looked down at the faded green muslin skirt, recalling she had matched it with one of her oldest white cambric blouses; so old, the fabric was soft and a bit too sheer. "I was dressed for working in my garden," she scolded. "And not expecting guests, I might add." She held out her hands to the room, palms up. "Yet here it appears I have a circus going on."

At that perfect timing Mrs. Dewberry opened the door and announced crisply, "His Lordship, Marcus Wakefield, Earl of Havington." Mrs. Dewberry spoke quickly, with barely enough time to move out of the way before Lord Havington strode past the small woman.

Constance could see her housekeeper was as shocked as she, that a visitor would barge in without being settled in a sitting room. Yet here he was, filling the doorway with his huge frame.

With dark hair like his sister's, there all resemblance ended. Larissa was short and soft with a pert little nose and rosy cheeks.

The earl had no softness to his face or his lean military frame, and no rosiness in that dark face. He stood over six feet, noted Constance, who was tall herself.

Well, she was not intimidated by large men, especially not in her own domain. And she did not particularly care for that pinched crease above his brows.

"I beg your pardon —" began Constance frostily.

"Marcus," interrupted Larissa, "I didn't expect you so quickly." She turned to face Constance. "May I present my brother, the Earl of Havington? Marcus, this is . . ." Larissa faltered for a half second, her back still to her brother. "My companion —"

Constance saw her friend's brow clear the moment inspiration struck.

"— Miss Violet," Larissa blurted, holding her hand toward Constance as a conjurer might. "Miss Constance Violet," she announced a bit too loudly, her pleading gaze focused on her friend.

Constance blinked, taken aback. Miss Violet, indeed! Goodness, where did Larissa's imagination stem from?

Ignoring the lie a moment, Constance debated how best to handle her friend's brother. She'd been taken by surprise when Larissa, flustered and speaking rapidly, had descended upon her. And Constance had fully planned to say *no* to this absurd scheme. In fact, she ought now to expose Larissa's game, establishing herself as the lady of the house.

She knew that. Every instinct told her so in the few seconds she delayed.

Constance regarded Larissa's worried face — eyebrows framing such sad and panicked eyes.

She looked over and met the earl's steely eyes. A face that could have been handsome, if not for its sternness. Was he judging her? As he'd judged her brother, according to Larissa? His arrogance of manner triggered a reaction that held her tongue.

If she ignored the mis-introduction, it could not be the same as agreeing to the lie. She tilted her chin up slightly; did not hold out her hand, as the man obviously had no manners. Folding her hands carefully on her skirt, Constance nodded her head, saying crisply, "My Lord," with the tiniest of curtsies.

Lord Havington continued to frown.

Marcus could not help staring at the young woman. Larissa had assured him their aunt and uncle had already approved of a suitable companion, so he was of course expecting an older woman.

She didn't necessarily need grey hair, but it would have been a plus in her favor, instead of this mass of sun-streaked hair falling in obstinate curls. And she did not necessarily need a large, stout figure, but it would have helped intimidate young men who might think to show interest in his sister.

Plain features would have been very desirable; not exotic eyes that were a mix of emerald green and grey. Companions he'd met were homely spinsters of impoverished noble families, skeptical toward the respectable intentions of gentlemen. That bitterness would have helped keep improper beaux a good distance away.

A prune face might also have helped, he decided. Yet this young chit didn't even have one wrinkle, let alone enough to fill a prune.

Except, he now noted, that one wrinkling frown above her eyebrows. Perhaps she was nervous about the coming interview. She was right to be; her job was about to end before it had begun. He wasn't about to allow his sister to remain in this house for the summer. Nor would he entrust his sister's reputation to someone so green, even if he had not already made up his mind to squash the silly scheme.

"Miss Violet." His nod was curt. "Lady Larissa has informed me your references are impeccable. However . . . I find you are perhaps a bit young. I trust you will forgive a brother's concern."

Constance visibly softened. "You are forgiven, my Lord," she replied with generosity.

"I was not asking your forgiveness, madam," he said with impatience. "That was a figure of speech."

Constance turned pink, and it was not the becoming flush of embarrassment.

"You will excuse us, brother?" Larissa took her friend's elbow, glancing over her shoulder toward Marcus as she steered Constance forward on wooden legs.

They stood by the glass terrace doors, and Larissa whispered, "Please, Constance? Do you see now how he is? Please do not antagonize him. You only need deal with him this afternoon and he'll be gone. If you refuse to go along with this, then I shall be confined with him all summer, under his constant critical eye at Amber Crossing." Larissa gripped Constance's arm as if she were drowning.

Marcus watched the ladies conferring by the window, their heads close. As Constance shifted, backlit by the window, his eyes widened. He could not help but stare at the perfect figure so clearly revealed by her sheer blouse.

Of a sudden, she turned her head his way. His eyes snapped to her face, and he tried not to look guilty as he cleared his throat. In a brisk, husky voice, he said, "Miss Violet, you will now excuse my sister and me, as we must confer."

"As you wish, my Lord." She walked across the room and, placing her hands on the desktop, leaned over to smell the lavender arrangement.

He cleared his throat impatiently. She spun around, eyebrows lifted.

"Miss Violet," Lord Havington said slowly, as if speaking to the village simpleton, "I wish privacy while speaking to my sister. Perhaps you might find a ladies' room and wait until your attendance is requested?"

Constance hid balled fists behind her skirt. "Excuse me, my Lord. I shall be happy to leave the two of you together." As she marched toward the door, she said clearly, without looking back, "Though this actually is a lady's library."

"One moment," Marcus ordered.

She turned a look of cool disinterest toward the earl. "Yes, my Lord?"

"Do you really think this to be a lady's

library?" His voice echoed his skepticism.

Constance glanced at Larissa, who appeared to be holding her breath. She turned to Lord Havington and calmly asked, "And why would you suppose otherwise, my Lord?"

"Well, this is obviously a room belonging to an orderly mind." He gestured around the neat room. "Ladies usually have books of pressed flowers lying everywhere. With delicate little writing tables, not sturdy walnut desks such as that one. And," he continued, proud of his keen observational skills, "small tapestried stools placed near the window, with sewing baskets upon them."

"Sewing baskets?" Constance enunciated clearly, as if she had misheard. "It may surprise you, Lord Havington, to know there are some ladies who —"

"Who keep their sewing baskets even closer at hand," filled in Larissa. "Miss Violet keeps her sewing basket with her at all times. Don't you, Miss Violet?"

Constance stared at her friend for several ticks of the clock before answering. "Of course," she said smoothly. "That is, when it is not beside my bed. I find it very comforting to have it at my fingertips. One never knows when a button will pop off unexpectedly or a stitch will slip." To Lord Havington she added, in bland tones, with eyebrows raised, "And sometimes I dream about exciting embroidery patterns and wake up determined to capture them while they are fresh in my mind."

Marcus nodded approvingly, distractedly, as he picked up a title on a nearby shelf. "*Sir Anthony's Book of Animal Husbandry?* Really, Larissa, how unsuitable for a young lady." He held the book out toward his sister. "Is this the type of reading you would pursue all summer without proper supervision?"

"I must agree with the earl." In three strides, Constance grabbed the book midair, drawing a look of shock from her visitors. "As your companion, I insist we dispose of this book, Lady Larissa." She held the offensive material — one of her favorite books — at arm's length between two fingers, dangling it as if it were a piece of last year's rancid cheese. "In fact, I think we should lock up the entire room for the summer. Else, this library will have to be most carefully examined. We shall have to go through every single title on these shelves, and box up the inappropriate books, delegating them to the attics.

"Lord Havington," Constance continued,

looking at him from under long lashes, "would you be willing to inspect these books for us?" She gestured to all four walls covered with books from ceiling to floor. "As a companion, I would be most uncomfortable with the phrases that could be lurking in this room."

"But . . . there are hundreds of books in this room." Marcus looked dazed as he surveyed the four walls. His eyes came back to Constance and held her gaze.

She blinked those long lashes innocently. "I shall leave you now, as you so politely requested, my Lord."

She floated out of the room, closing the twin doors silently behind her with a grand gesture.

CHAPTER TWO

Larissa sat in the library facing her brother, back straight, hands folded primly in her lap. Lord Havington sat brooding behind the large desk, his boots propped upon its surface and his elbows resting on the arms of the chair, fingers steepled.

He stared at his younger sibling.

"Larissa." He finally broke the silence. "Why? You know I cannot possibly allow this. Why are you pursuing this nonsense about a summer on your own?"

She flinched slightly, her blue eyes swimming with moisture.

Marcus sighed with disgust. "By next spring you'll enter your first Season in London. You'll have whirlwinds of parties, a circle of beaux at your beck and call. All the frivolity you could desire."

She swallowed and focused her gaze on the lavender floral arrangement perched on one side of the desk.

"Further," he continued, "I am confident that within the year you shall marry, and you shall then be in charge of your own household." He ran long fingers through his dark hair. "A real household. Instead of playing at keeping house, away from your family. I've never heard of anything so ridiculous." He slammed a hand on the armrest. "So what the blast does this streak of summer independence mean?"

She looked down at the handkerchief she twisted in her lap.

He waited for an answer.

"Marcus . . ." Her eyes met his. "I beg of you to understand. I know I am not as smart as you. I fear I do not have the words to explain." When he did not respond, she continued in a desperate voice, "I was so hoping for this one summer. One last summer before I must put upon the responsibilities of a wife. One last summer before I must face the Season. And you do not know what a Season is like. My friends tell me I shall be watched and judged and condemned by a thousand eyes — every movement, every utterance. Worse, I'll be under Cousin Elsbeth's chaperonage. She's a dragon of a paragon. Last time I visited London, she was so very critical of everything I did. Or did not do. I know she

30

dislikes me.

"And my reward for all of this misery and inspection? To submit to a husband, a stranger. I will become a piece of *his* household. I'll be Lady such-and-such. I shall no longer know who I am. Please, brother, just one last summer? I am so afraid of the Season! And I am afraid of becoming a wife." Her handkerchief was twisted into a tiny corkscrew by now.

Marcus wished to reach out, to calm his young sister's agitation. But he did not. She seemed afraid of him; when had this happened? Didn't she understand he only wished to protect her? It hurt as well that she feared her wifely role. Knowing of men's baser instincts, her maidenly fears touched him deeply.

"What of your reputation?" he asked. "It was irresponsible of our aunt and uncle to have agreed to this outlandish scheme."

"But how could my reputation be hurt? Who would know? And I would live so quietly here — more quietly than a field mouse. It is the last summer of my youth I shall ever remember. I spent many wonderful weeks here during my girlhood, with my dearest friend Lady Chambreville and her great-aunt. I feel a great peace in this home. Please, just grant me a few more weeks of

31

that serenity. I beg you, brother." She bit her lip, which trembled uncontrollably. "I'd already convinced Aunt and Uncle," Larissa said quietly, in resignation, her eyes downcast. "This is so very unfair." Her shoulders shook as she brought the crumpled linen to her mouth.

Marcus swore softly. He'd been fearless in his military escapades but was afraid of his own sister's tears. So much for the brave Major Lord Havington, he thought with disgust.

He took a deep breath and considered. He could easily keep an eye on her if she were sequestered here for a very short period of time. Not the entire summer, of course. Perhaps a month at the most. It would cost him a few weeks of his own freedom, but — she was right — what harm could befall her in the quiet countryside? She knew the staff here. She'd stayed here before, many times, when the lady of the house was in residence. And his aunt and uncle had been comfortable enough to grant her this retreat. None of their London circle need ever know. Drat the silly coddling of his aunt and uncle, to have encouraged her, and to now put him in this ridiculous situation.

He exhaled noisily. He sat up, drummed

his fingers on the solid desk. "All right, Larissa, I am willing to consider this hare-brained scheme — but only because this commitment was foolishly made to you by Aunt and Uncle."

Larissa froze, as if afraid to breathe.

"But only to *consider* it," Marcus said. "And it will *not* be for the entire summer. One or two months. No longer."

Larissa's eyes lit up, and he held up a cautioning hand, adding firmly, "I shall give you one chance. Only one."

Her curls bobbed vigorously as she nodded her head, holding the wrinkled handkerchief to her chest with tightly praying fists.

"However . . ." Marcus drew out the three syllables. "Should your companion prove unsuitable, or should I even *suspect* this was an unwise decision upon my part, I will not hesitate to cut this escapade short, and you will be sent home to Amber Crossing without notice. Do I make myself clear?"

He composed his sternest look, the one that cowered the troops.

"Marcus!" she gasped with a sob. She jumped out of her chair and ran around the desk, throwing her arms about him and threatening to topple him backward. "Thank you, thank you, thank you."

Marcus sighed in exasperation as the tears

he dreaded began to fall anyway, wetting his new vest. But it was a half sigh, as he wrapped an arm about his young sister and hugged her protectively, a lopsided smile upon his lips.

CHAPTER THREE

At daybreak, two cloaked figures slipped out the kitchen entrance.

Tugging the heavy oak door closed, Constance paused. She ran her hand over its painted panels. Even in dawn's soft light, the deep rose color was discernible. A smile tugged at her lips and she was ten years old again, walking with Aunt Agatha along their favorite path.

"When I am mistress of my own home," *Young Constance pointed at a clump of brilliant foxgloves, "I shall have a cottage with a door this exact shade."*

A silly notion, forgotten until a few days later when they strolled toward the manor following their daily walk. The young girl stopped and clapped her hands over her mouth. Even from afar, one could not help but notice the brilliant plum-rose door at RoseHill's kitchen entrance. Barrows and Mrs. Eldridge could be seen peeping out the kitchen window, craning their necks to catch her reaction.

"Perhaps it is a bit too colorful?" Constance looked guiltily at her guardian.

"Child, I believe it suits the two of us perfectly," Aunt Agatha said. "This whimsical reminder of our walks and the delightful foxgloves in bloom. And whom else should we care to suit, if not ourselves? See now, here is Barrows at the window. He insisted upon painting the surprise himself, so we'll not let him know it's a bit bright, shall we?"

Constance now peeked in at the very same window where the butler and cook had stood as she continued along the paved pathway with Larissa. Every one of its many square panes reflected the amber warmth within the great room. One could see the flickering from the huge fireplace and the servants already bustling about in the kitchen. Blue smoke lifted lazily from the dozen twin chimneys, and dawn painted the distant gatekeeper's thatched cottage with peaches and roses.

This manor now belonged to Constance, given to her in Aunt Agatha's will, and Constance loved every stone, every tree.

Just thinking about Aunt Agatha still brought moistness to her eyes. A year and a half had passed since her great-aunt had died, just a fortnight before Constance's eighteenth birthday; just before her first planned Season. Instead of a rainbow of ball gowns, the dressmakers had busily stitched a black and somber wardrobe to fill her closets.

A few months ago fate dealt its next cruel blow.

Thankfully, her great-aunt was not alive to witness Alec's scandal. Though perhaps Aunt Agatha's connections would have put a stop to the nonsense; perhaps Aunt Agatha would have helped Constance face the gossipmongers. But there was no wise woman to counsel and protect her, and Constance had chosen to flee London rather than fight. Well, she was home at RoseHill now, safe from the stares and the whispers. And here she would stay, most likely in seclusion the rest of her life.

"Come along, Constance, I can't wait!" Larissa paused with one hand on the stable door, unintentionally striking a charming pose in her riding habit. The yellow pelisse over the heavy ivy-green skirt set off her creamy complexion and dark curls to advantage.

Constance motioned her friend to precede her. She'd promised their first adventure this morning: a ride at sunrise to see the ancient burial grounds overlooking the coast.

Before entering the stables, she looked down at her own serviceable costume. Smoothing a hand over her skirt, she recalled its once plush chocolate velvet. Now it was a dull brown, with the nap flattened in several spots, particularly where she sat her horse. She'd topped it with a clean ivory military blouse. Granted, the style was a little outdated, but they weren't riding in Hyde Park, after all.

They stepped inside the cavernous stables but did not need to accustom themselves to the dark. Young Tommy and his father Tom were already busy, sitting astride hay bales, repairing harnesses in the warm lantern light.

"Good morning, gentlemen," greeted Constance.

They jumped to attention, tipping their caps, father and son two peas in a pod.

"Larissa wishes to choose a mare, Tommy. Would you assist her?"

"I've a couple in mind, m'lady," the boy said as he ducked his head. "Right this way, if ye please." He led Larissa toward the stalls.

"Tom, Cook just made some fresh crossed buns, and I thought you might enjoy a bite before breakfast." Constance passed her small basket to the stable master.

"Why, thank ye, m'lady. I knew I smelled somethin' wonderful. Would those be her currant and spice buns?" he peeked under the checkered cloth. "Mmm, smells to be." Tom gingerly fished out a roll with his gnarled hand.

Wandering over to join the others, Constance found Larissa stroking the neck of a dappled mare.

"Constance, isn't she wonderful? I feel we're already friends."

The mare whinnied, as if in agreement.

"Good choice, Tommy. Appleby will be perfect." She grabbed her friend's hand. "But come along, Larissa, and see Jasmine. She's *my* baby." Constance tugged Larissa toward the back stalls, where Jasmine nickered as she recognized Constance's voice approaching. The beautiful chestnut horse raised her head, settled her eye on Constance and her friend, and bobbed her mane in greeting.

"Oh, she's beautiful," Larissa said, standing aside as Constance placed an affectionate hand on the large mare.

Constance unlatched the wooden gate and allowed young Tommy to lead Jasmine back toward where his father was readying Appleby's saddle.

"What smells so wonderful?" asked Larissa.

The elder Tom turned to retrieve the basket from the hook where it hung, safe from many of the barn critters. "It be Mrs. Eldridge's specially baked rolls, my Lady." He shuffled over to offer it to Larissa.

"Ah, not so fast." Constance laughed and reached out her hand for the basket. "Now, Larissa, you must play a game Cook and I enjoyed when I was young. You must close your eyes and guess what spice is in the buns. Close your eyes," said Constance, demonstrating as long lashes shuttered over her eyes. "And, put the basket under your nose, then lift the cloth quickly, like this."

Constance brought the steaming bundle close to her own dainty chin, then lifted a corner of the cloth, letting it drop again.

"Mmmm," she hummed.

"Mmmm," repeated a deep voice.

Constance's eyes flew open in time to see an arm lifting the basket from her hands. She spun and faced Lord Havington.

"I believe it's cardamom." He inhaled, his eyes closed and the basket dangling directly beneath his regal nose.

Larissa giggled and old Tom and his son smiled the same crooked smile.

"What do I win, Miss Violet?" he asked in a teasing voice, looking directly into her green eyes.

"You, sir, win nothing since you guessed incorrectly." She tugged on the basket.

To her surprise, he quickly trapped her hand in his and said, no playfulness in his voice any longer, "For a companion, you are quite bossy. Do you plan to boss my sister thusly, or merely to set bad examples for her?"

Constance was mortified. The very idea he would dress her down in front of her servants. Yesterday she'd assembled the staff, letting them in on the "game" they were to play if the earl should return to RoseHill. She assured them it was not at all likely he should appear again. However, she had carefully explained to the attentive staff, it was important his Lordship believe that his sister, Lady Larissa, was the lady in charge at the manor. Constance would pretend to be Larissa's companion.

They looked at her and then at each other with confusion on their faces and expressions of disbelief. Constance repeated the explanation a second time, and then a third, slowly and patiently. Finally, looking at the faces surrounding her, she threw up her hands, claiming they should never mind, as it was unlikely the earl would appear at RoseHill again.

Yet here he was.

Young Tommy and his father now stood with their mouths open, looking from Lord Havington to Constance.

Checking her pride, Constance bit her lower lip and murmured, "Excuse me, my Lord. Of course you are welcome to a treat." With a slight pout, she avoided his gaze as she released the basket handle to his large hands.

Lord Havington stared at her lips a moment too long, then passed the basket to his sister.

Larissa closed her blue eyes, sniffing through the cloth, seemingly unaware anything had passed between her brother and her friend. "Cinnamon and cloves?" She inhaled again.

"Very clever, Larissa," said Constance stiffly, making an attempt to compose herself. "Help yourself to a bun, and then let's leave them to the gentlemen, shall we, while we go for our ride?"

"Allow me to help you choose a suitable horse, sister," Lord Havington ordered rather than offered as he headed to the stalls.

Larissa drooped with obvious dismay.

"But Marcus, I had my heart set on Appleby. Young Thomas helped me pick her out." Approaching the mare, she held out her hand for the gentle animal to snuffle.

Appleby whinnied as the young woman stroked her cheek.

"Well, I must admit Thomas has chosen well," said Lord Havington in an approving tone.

Tommy beamed. And Constance fumed.

How dare he play the master of the castle, taking that approving tone with my servants? She realized with a tinge of guilt that his approval was better than a reprimand. She should be happy Tommy glowed with the compliment. Yet, why did it make her angry? Why should she be jealous if her staff reacted to the self-appointed oaf?

Shaking her head behind his back, she marched off past him to retrieve her own horse. The sooner they got away from under big brother's cardamom-smelling nose, the sooner they could enjoy their independent adventures. Poor Larissa. It was obvious if she were at home she would be stifled by his constant supervision.

Though . . . wasn't Larissa now at Rose-Hill, and wasn't she still under his scrutiny? Constance turned to ask Lord Havington what time he'd left Amber Crossing in order

43

to appear here at dawn. She caught him looking down at her worn riding habit, where the smooth nap clung to her hips, and shiny where it got the most use. His eyes quickly moved up to meet hers.

"Tommy, please saddle Jasmine," she snapped.

Moving quickly to obey her sharp command, the boy grabbed the halter a little too suddenly, and Jasmine reared and complained with a spirited retort.

"Stop! What are you thinking?" demanded Havington, striding to where the young man stood. "This is not at all a proper horse for Miss Violet. Return that one to its stall, and we shall find another more suitable."

"What?" squeaked Constance, pale-faced. Advancing upon young Tommy, she intended to grab her horse and set everyone straight.

But Lord Havington grabbed her elbow instead as she stomped by. "Can you not see how wild that mare is, Miss Violet? Besides, it is several hands too high for a lady. Allow me, madam, to assist you in selecting a gentler mare." He gallantly took her hand and placed it in the crook of his arm.

Larissa was in front of Constance in a trice. "Constance, you must agree this is most generous of Lord Havington. To take the time to assist us, so that we may be on — our — way." The last three words were pointedly emphasized.

Constance heard the nervous plea in her friend's voice and once again weighed the wisdom of this farce. But what peeved her most was the fact young Tommy had turned Jasmine and was already leading the mare back to her stall. She swallowed any reprimands and turned to face Lord Havington.

"It is indeed most generous of you, my Lord," Constance said chillingly. "However, I must politely point out that I have quite a good seat and I can easily handle a mare of that size."

"Nonsense," he corrected her once again in front of the stablemen. "Madam, you will allow me to direct you in this as, I assure you, I am a much better judge of horseflesh and lady's seats."

This last was met with silence in the barn, and a slight blush touched his cheeks. He frowned, looking away, and quickly pointed out the first small mare he saw to old Tom.

"Saddle this one for Miss Violet," he snapped the order.

"Biscuit, sir?" queried old Tom dubiously.

"Biscuit?" echoed Constance. "We are going for a ride, sir, not out to pasture."

Lord Havington raised an eyebrow at Constance and then looked at Tom, who appeared to be enjoying the discourse, but now jumped to execute his Lordship's order.

"Constance," said Larissa at her elbow, "my brother is indeed an excellent judge of horses, and he has only our safety and enjoyment in mind."

Constance stared for several seconds at Larissa; blinked; debated giving her traitorous "friend" a response. But seeing the nervous glance Larissa threw her brother, Constance softened ever so slightly. It's only for one morning's ride. *And it's only for a few weeks,* became her calming mantra to herself. She would honor her agreement to Larissa, and the summer would pass quickly. And they would have fun — just to spite the earl if necessary.

She looked back up at the man who still had her hand captured against his side. "Thank you for your concern, my Lord. I should be happy to take your advice." This said as demurely as she could manage without a sarcastic edge. *I should be happy, that is, only if I were a complete and utter fool,* she consoled herself by adding the words aloud in her head.

She was pleased with her humor, but only

until the earl announced he would accompany them on their ride.

CHAPTER FOUR

Constance rolled up the raspberry sleeves of her India muslin blouse and grabbed one of the heavy white aprons hanging on S-hooks beside the kitchen door.

Learning to bake in the kitchen alongside Mrs. Eldridge had been one of her favorite pastimes as a child, most likely because of the secrecy attached. While Aunt Agatha approved of cooking and gardening, she warned young Constance that society did not: "Just thinking about dirt and flour might give one unclean fingernails."

Constance chuckled at the memory. The frightened orphan had taken Aunt Agatha so very seriously on every subject when she and her brother arrived at RoseHill. She feared displeasing yet another relative, feared being turned out again, until she began to discern the irreverent tone behind the words and the twinkle in her great-aunt's eyes.

Mixing flour, leavening, and a sprinkling of salt for this evening's dinner rolls, Constance replayed yesterday's drama in the stables. Lord Havington had ordered her about like a servant. She stirred the mix more vigorously, until she realized her wooden spoon was flinging flour right out of the bowl.

How odd. Cooking was normally quite relaxing.

She paused, holding an egg on the edge of the thick crockery bowl as she pictured the earl forbidding her to saddle up her own horse — *her* horse! She brought the egg down with an angry motion. Eggshell pieces flew everywhere, and the yolk and white dribbled down the outside of the bowl. *This is all his fault,* she realized, as she hastened to wipe up the sticky mess. She carefully plucked a few stray pieces of eggshell out of the batter.

As if that weren't enough, young Tommy had witnessed everything. His father, old Tom, had continually peeked his head around the tackle room, tipping his cap back to get a better look at the goings-on.

Being the true friend to Larissa that she was, Constance had bitten her lip as her friend's brother had lectured her on the dangers of riding a horse too big and too powerful for her capabilities. While Old Tom, who had often witnessed Constance recklessly jumping gates, wore a toothless grin that nearly split his face in half. When Constance glowered at him, saying, "Don't you have a harness to mend, sir?" he bobbed his head, touching his fingers to his cap, and ducked back into the tackle room.

Lord Havington had studied her without another word. She knew he thought her bossy and churlish.

Sighing, Constance tipped the contents of the bowl out onto a floured board and began kneading. As she grabbed another handful of flour to sprinkle onto the dough, she shook her head in frustration. Punching down the dough as Mrs. Eldridge had taught her was very therapeutic just now, as she pretended it was the man's smug face. Punch, punch, punch. Folding the dough in half, she punched it again and again. Punch, punch, punch.

"Heavens, my Lady, why are you already punching down the dough when it hasn't even had its first rising yet?" Mrs. Eldridge had come to stand at Constance's elbow.

"Goodness, I guess I was just daydreaming." Constance blushed, thankful that Cook could not read her mind.

"Daydreamin' about his Lordship, I suppose," Mrs. Eldridge observed, proving that she could read minds, as Constance had already half-suspected as a child.

"I'm not sure what to do, Mrs. Eldridge." Constance pulled and pushed the elastic dough, kneading it properly again. "I do believe poor Larissa will not enjoy a moment's freedom unless I go along with this for a bit." She sprinkled a little more flour over the wooden surface. "Should I play along? Doesn't she deserve to have a taste of the independence I've treasured for years?" When Cook didn't answer, Constance continued thoughtfully, "The only danger, of course, is should he ever learn the truth. Larissa says he values honesty above all else. Wouldn't he be furious to know he'd been duped!"

She smiled an evil little grin. Lord Havington would soon realize Constance could not be bossed, bullied, or banished.

Barrows smiled as he passed the kitchen, for laughter bubbled out. He backed up a few steps and peered through the archway. A handful of the staff gathered around their mistress.

Whenever Lady Constance was in the kitchen the room became twice-warmed: warmed from the great chimney with its open hearth for baking, and warmed from her presence and the camaraderie.

Mrs. Eldridge used a corner of her apron to wipe tears of laughter from her eyes. When she dropped the apron and looked up at Barrows, he noticed the flour she had accidentally smeared onto the tip of her nose and her chin. In fact, flour even circled the eye she wiped, as if she were an owl.

Barrows laughed, more of a one-note cough as he entered the kitchen, a laugh that shocked everyone. Barrows was the most proper of butlers, serious and formal. The staff exchanged surprised glances with one another. However, looking toward Mrs. Eldridge soon made apparent what Barrows found so humorous.

Mrs. Eldridge had no idea what everyone was laughing about; she just loved to laugh. Her laugh was so contagious, they could sometimes continue laughing and crying until no one even remembered what had set them off to begin with.

The more Mrs. Eldridge laughed tears, the more often she wiped her face with her apron, and the more the flour dust powdered her merry face. This, of course, set everyone off into fresh gales of laughter. Constance had a twinge of conscience for laughing at Mrs. Eldridge's expense, and reached up on tiptoes to grab one of the shiny copper pots hanging just out of reach.

Barrows, noticing her struggle, reached up past her slim figure and easily put a hand on a pot. Constance nodded toward Mrs. Eldridge, who was watching them curiously, and Barrows winced, but honorably walked over and held the pot up to the cook. Mrs. Eldridge would now see her reflection in the mirrored copper surface.

"Oh . . . oh!" She huffed. Another small exclamation of surprise escaped.

Constance suspected if Mrs. Eldridge did not have a bit of a tendre for Barrows, it might not have bothered the cook so to see Barrows unbend his stiff and stuffy self — only to make fun of her.

Without hesitation, Mrs. Eldridge dipped her pudgy hand in the flour bin and flicked her hand in front of the butler's nose, which sent flour dust onto his face. A snow of it floated down to dust his dark vest. His eyes went wide, and everyone stilled. The man prided himself upon appearance and dignity.

And then, Barrows did what no one could ever have expected: he grabbed his own fistful of flour and flung it right back at Mrs. Eldridge. And he barked a laugh.

The fight was on. They both grabbed handfuls of flour and chased each other in a circle around the massive butcher block like young children. Dodging one way, then the other, it was obvious Mrs. Eldridge would tire first, not being able to keep up with the wiry butler.

Constance came to intervene between them, to end the fight while it was still playful. At that moment, however, the two realized they could just as easily fling the powder across the cutting block at one another. Just as the powder flew, Constance stepped into clouds of flying flour.

The room came to a shocked halt. Constance looked down at herself, covered in white. She laughed, precipitating nervous giggles.

"What is going on in here?" came the cold demand from the doorway.

The kitchen troupe turned as one to face the doorway where Lord Havington filled the frame, a hand above his head on each doorjamb and a stern look to his face and mouth.

When his gaze rested on Constance as one of the culprits under a coating of flour, his eyelids narrowed. A chill descended to replace the warmth in the room.

Fearing the earl was about to give her a dressing down on proper behavior in front of her kitchen staff, Constance arched her flour-coated eyebrows and raised her dusty chin in the air as she imperiously exited past the staff.

Passing the flour bin, she let her hand trail behind her skirt, and grabbed a good fistful. She marched toward Lord Havington in the doorway.

"Let me guess, my Lord," she said quietly, her shoulders stiff. "We need to have a little talk."

"Yes." He dropped one arm, watching her, allowing her barely enough room to pass.

As she squeezed past him, Lord Havington glanced back at the staff members who still stood frozen. Constance turned and quickly flicked her hand at his dark coat. To her satisfaction, a river of flour streaked down his broad back, from his shoulder to his waist. She wiped the remaining powder from her hands onto her apron.

As Havington turned his back on the staff, Constance stood on tiptoes so she could see them through the doorway.

Noticing the flour on his back, their eyes became saucers. Then, seeing their mistress's mischievous farewell smile, their heads dipped to hide uncontrollable grins.

Lord Havington stood as the ladies entered the parlour. "May I pour you a glass of wine, Larissa? Miss Violet?"

"Please." Both nodded at the same time.

He turned toward the small liqueur cabinet. Larissa inhaled sharply at the powder covering her brother's jacket, but Constance caught her friend's eye, then shook her head quickly just before Havington glanced up. Larissa looked innocently at him and smiled crookedly.

Constance hadn't told Larissa any of what had happened in the kitchen, nor the blistering lecture Lord Havington had delivered afterward. She'd come dangerously close to tipping her hand when she called him "Your Grace," but he was too pompous to realize it for sarcasm. She'd focused on her shoes during his speech and thought of punching down dough.

Punch, punch, punch.

Silence? Had the man finally stopped? She looked up demurely and said, "Forgive me, Your Grace."

And he had softened. How odd. This was the first time she'd seen any softening in those steel grey eyes and that stern countenance. For a moment, a different man appeared: one capable — possibly — of being a caring brother.

And her heart began to thaw, just a little.

Just a little, that is, until he broke eye

contact and curtly said, "Dismissed." Did he think she was a bloody soldier? And it was *her* library.

As the ladies now crossed the room to sit on the tiny sofa, Larissa raised questioning eyebrows at her friend. Constance, however, could not keep the wide smile from her face, so she kept her chin down, thinking it would be better for him not to see her reaction.

When she finally glanced back up, he was approaching her, glass in hand.

My God, thought Marcus, *the woman is transformed when she smiles.* He pictured the hoyden he had apprehended in the kitchen, then the humble penitent he had taken to the library to lecture on the inappropriateness of ladies' companions mixing with hired servants. And now she was dimpling beautifully.

But she suddenly looked guilty as he approached with her drink. She licked her lips nervously, then looked away as soon as he handed her the goblet. He stared a moment longer at the lips she had just moistened with her tongue, but was recalled by a question from his sister.

"Did you enjoy your stroll, brother?"

Marcus, still puzzling over Miss Violet's reaction, realized Larissa awaited an answer.

"Yes, you are right about RoseHill. Very tranquil. I was quite relaxed upon my return. However, I then had to deal with an unpleasant staff situation. But I believe we all understand each other now." He looked at Miss Violet, whose head snapped up at his words.

He caught a hint of it again — the daggers with emerald hilts hiding in her green eyes. But, as usual, it disappeared so quickly as she lowered her long-lashed eyelids, he had to wonder if he'd imagined it. Except he was sure his imagination could not have conjured up green lightning bolts in such otherwise clear eyes.

In truth, he felt like a cad in bringing up the subject again, especially since Miss Violet had apologized so prettily.

Perhaps he hoped to see that same docile lady who'd bent her golden head, bowing to his wishes, and then looked up with soft green eyes and whispered, "Forgive me, Your Grace." Of course, he'd been forced to explain to her that he was an earl, not a duke.

He'd also found himself wanting to lean forward and cup her floured chin in his hand as he wiped the flour dust away softly and explained, but that led to the thought of bending his head and kissing her half-pouted lips. He cleared his throat and rose, signaling he was ready for dinner.

In the dining room Constance aimed for the head of the table, arriving at the same time Marcus rounded from the other side. They came face-to-face and her eyes widened in surprise. He motioned with exaggerated patience toward the seat on his right, as his sister settled into the chair at the down end of the table. "May I seat you?" he asked, in the tone of a tutor.

"I shall seat myself, thank you." She pursed her lips primly.

Marcus was once again baffled by the young chit. How could she possibly mix in society? She was definitely an "original," though others might choose an even less flattering label. She'd be the talk of the drawing rooms — mixing with the lower echelons of the staff; not knowing the strict seating order between men and women of rank; not knowing what was appropriately modest attire to wear in the company of gentlemen. She obviously had a lot of schooling left unfinished. And, remembering her soft green eyes looking up to his in the library, Marcus found himself wistfully wishing he could be her teacher.

Of course, he would only be doing it to help his sister, he rationalized. It was important for Larissa to have a companion above reproach. He applauded himself for his brotherly motives and reached for the peas.

Dinner was companionable, and the conversation never lulled once they began discussing books. Marcus pointed with his roll, engrossed in their debate on the merits of Defoe. He broke the roll, spreading butter on the soft pillow as he finished his thought. "Mmm, these rolls are unusually delicious."

"Thank you." Constance beamed. And immediately she turned pink and focused on her plate, chewing busily.

Marcus simply looked down the length of the table at his sister and frowned, implying her hiring skills left much to be desired.

He swiftly excused himself after dinner. Not even staying to have port, he was anxious to reach his club in London, where he would be meeting Allermaine.

The earl found himself whistling as he jogged up the steps of the venerable building. Still enjoying memories of dinner, he looked forward to sharing the details of his silly sister's indulgent exploits. He could trust his best friend not to let others know of the unusual arrangement. As he glanced around for Philip's sandy hair, the thought of Larissa's unpolished companion made him smile, though Lord knows why it didn't infuriate him instead.

Philip Thorne, Duke of Allermaine, raised his chin in greeting as he saw the earl striding toward him.

"My, you're in an unusually good mood this evening, Havington."

"Evening, Allermaine," he acknowledged, then turned slightly to order a bottle of hock from a passing servant. "It's been a long ride," Marcus continued, "and I'm not up to making the rounds, unless I stop by the townhouse to freshen up. How about some cards, and just relaxing here by the fire?"

"You read my mind," the duke replied. "Don't happen to have a cigar on you, do you, Havington? I'm fresh out."

On a table a few feet away, Marcus spied a cedar box. "Let me just grab a few, though they won't be up to your usual brand, I'm sure." He stood and turned, stretching over to reach the table, grabbing two dark cigars.

"I say, Havington, whatever happened to your coat?" exclaimed Allermaine.

"What?" asked Marcus, looking down the front of his dark coat. He had worn it most of today, hadn't bothered to stop at his townhouse to change. But he couldn't see anything amiss.

He looked up at Philip, who motioned with his thumb to a glass lining the wall behind them. Marcus strode to the wall, still saw nothing, and turning around craned his neck over his shoulder.

From his shoulder blades to his waist, a long streak of powdery grit stood out against the dark fabric of his coat. Marcus couldn't imagine what it was. He had no recollection of leaning against any walls or dusty fences. He reached a long arm over his shoulder and brought some of the dust up to his nose, then tasted it. It tasted like flour.

Of a sudden, he remembered being in the kitchens this morning and bringing a halt to the food play. But he had never even entered the room. This flour could not have accidentally rubbed off while he was there. There was too much in volume — more like a generous handful.

And then he remembered the unrepentant gleam in Miss Violet's eyes as she haughtily marched past him. He remembered her closed fist.

When he turned back to face his friend, Philip realized the earl was no longer in a good mood.

Havington's expression was black and his

jaw was tightly clenched. In fact, he looked as if he were about to challenge someone to a duel.

CHAPTER FIVE

Absorbed in the ledgers, Constance barely noticed the small tapping sound.

She glanced up at the door. It certainly wasn't Mrs. Dewberry's firm knock. And Larissa would have flown in without knocking.

"Yes? Mrs. Dewberry?" Constance queried. No turning of the knob, no response from the other side, so she called again, more clearly, "Yes? Do come in."

There it was again: a small tapping, but this time she realized it was not coming from the direction of the door. Constance turned around — and jumped. Outside her library window she could make out a person's outline through the lace curtains. Constance strode to the window, grabbed the edge of the curtain, and yanked it to the right.

On the flagstones outside the library stood Larissa, shivering in the cold.

Constance unlatched the brass fixture and swung the French door inward. "Larissa, come in this instant. It's freezing cold on this side of the house. Come over to the fire, quickly."

Larissa stepped inside, shivering in her thin morning dress. Her arms were wrapped tightly about herself.

Constance urged her to a chair in front of the fire. "Larissa, what were you doing outside?"

The young woman perched on the edge of the chair and turned toward Constance. "C-C-Constance, my brother is here," Larissa chattered through blue lips.

As if that explained everything. Actually, thought Constance, perhaps that *was* an explanation of sorts, for it seemed every time Larissa's brother showed up on their doorstep, Larissa began panicking and acting illogically. And — Constance wondered ungraciously — why *was* Larissa's brother showing up so much of late?

Most likely he was not assured his sister was being companioned well. Forgetting she was not really a companion did not make her any less angry. She could be an impeccable companion, oh yes! That is, of course, if she chose to be.

"Constance, he is come looking for us. I

heard Mrs. Dewberry ask him to wait in the parlour downstairs. He said he preferred Mrs. Dewberry find me directly, or he would find me himself."

Larissa was still rubbing her frozen hands together, but it seemed to Constance her friend was also wringing them in helpless despair.

"I don't understand why my brother can't behave as a proper guest and allow himself to be shown to the morning room, while he is then announced."

"That, dearest Larissa, is because — as you surely must know by now — he thinks of himself more as your father, not as your brother, and certainly not as a guest. In fact —" Her voice rose. "— I'm sure he pictures himself lord of this and every single manor, and does not believe social niceties even apply to him. Larissa, have you ever hinted to Lord Havington how you expect him to deport himself in *your* home?" Constance knew sarcasm was lost on sweet Larissa.

"No," confessed Larissa. "He rattles me so. I'm afraid if I give him instructions on how I expect him to behave, he'll send me to my room without supper. At least, that's how he makes me feel."

"Humph." Constance tapped her foot on the hearth, angry again at the arrogant earl.

"Larissa, you still haven't said what you were doing outside."

"Well, I was in the piano room when I heard Marcus commanding Mrs. Dewberry. So I let myself out the window and I ran along the terrace to your library." Larissa's blue eyes cleared, and she smiled, having given a satisfactory account.

"And," prodded Constance, "why didn't you just go to your brother and bring him here? Through the hallway. You know the hallway — that corridor that joins all the rooms?"

Larissa's eyes widened. "I wanted to warn you! I was afraid if he found you at your desk, going over ledgers, it would look suspicious."

As she said this, Larissa jumped up and raced to Constance's desk and slapped closed the large book. Carrying it to the nearest shelf, she struggled until it was inserted between two other large volumes.

Constance watched with a smile. Silly Larissa. Always worrying how the companion is perceived by her brother. *And why not,* her devilish side argued, *when it ensures a carefree summer for Larissa at the expense of my own identification and freedom.*

Constance had just returned to stand beside the cleared desk when they heard

67

heavy steps, and the doors were thrown open.

Marcus walked in, surveying the room and each of them in turn: Constance by the desk, and Larissa standing with her back against the bookshelves, as if protecting the volumes. They both flushed, as if caught drawing on their school desks.

As usual, Mrs. Dewberry flew along in his wake like a small skiff being towed behind a massive sailing ship.

"I'll get tea, my Lady," she apologized.

"Thank you," said Larissa and Constance at the same time. Stricken, Constance looked quickly at Larissa, and they both looked to Lord Havington to see if he'd noticed.

"Marcus!" croaked Larissa, "how wonderful to see you . . . again. I mean, so soon. Not that you're not welcome, it's just . . . it's so soon . . . but it's also wonderful," she said, nodding foolishly.

Lord Havington glanced at Larissa, ignoring her prattling, then settled his scrutiny on her companion.

Constance reluctantly dropped her gaze. *When this summer charade is over,* she fumed, *you shall be given a ripe piece of my mind.* The satisfaction of the direct cut he would be given made her raise her chin and smile.

The perpetual frown between his eyes cleared for a moment as he smiled back. In spite of the vertical creases in both his cheeks, however, the smile did not seem to reach his grey eyes. Constance felt there was a gauntlet being thrown here, yet there was nothing on the carpet between them. *What a fanciful imagination I have,* she thought to herself, but could not help glancing nervously down at the tapestry beneath her feet.

"Why do I always find you at that desk, Miss Violet? Could it be our companion is really a bluestocking governess in disguise?" he teased.

Constance considered telling him she was in fact a "bluestocking," and quite proud of the fact.

"Miss Violet is so generous in helping me with my correspondence," offered Larissa.

His measuring gaze moved back to his sister. "I am impressed. But surely there is not that much dictation to be done?"

Constance stepped in with what she believed would be an innocuous explanation. "My Lord, I have many dear acquaintances of my own, and I enjoy writing to them of this beautiful summer retreat."

Larissa chirped, "They also enjoy hearing

about the educational books Constance and I are studying in the evenings, as we work on our embroidery."

Constance moaned inwardly; as if they could embroider and read at the same time!

Marcus, however, became surprisingly animated. "Ah, that is wonderful to hear, sister. I expect, then, my errand will be deemed fruitful. I was going through Uncle's library, and I found some books I thought should provide suitable reading for you this summer. This will keep your mind properly engaged, rather than taking a chance at the unsuitable books contained on these shelves."

Constance did not think any of her books unsuitable. She bit her tongue in the familiar grooves formed this past week.

"I think," Lord Havington continued, "this would be the perfect opportunity to take advantage of improving your mind. In feminine matters, of course," he amended, adding explicitly, "such as etiquette, and menu selection, and furniture placement."

Constance barked a short laugh, but when his eyes snapped to hers, she covered her mouth and leaned against the desk, forcing a slight coughing spell. She sucked in her lip to contain the smile that threatened to escape.

He crossed to the bell rope and pulled authoritatively. When Barrows appeared in the doorway, Lord Havington commanded, "There is a crate in my carriage. Please have it brought in." Turning back, he said, "I included an especial surprise for you, sister."

"A surprise — for me, Marcus?" Larissa's eyes lit up.

Constance could see how badly Larissa needed just a few crumbs of approval from her demanding brother.

"I think you will be pleased," he said. "I know I've been skeptical of your being alone, far from close supervision during the summer weeks, but then I realized you can practice a domestic task or two, as you assist Mrs. Dewberry with menus and household directions. This could be the perfect training prior to entering your Season."

Rather than pleasing his sister, Constance could see the reminder of the Season and its dreaded outcome had just the opposite effect. Constance reached out and touched Larissa's hand in sympathy.

Marcus didn't even notice. He was rolling up his white shirt sleeves, readying himself for some physical task. Barrows came struggling into the library with a crate, and Marcus dismissed the man as he lifted the crate from Barrows's straining arms.

Constance couldn't help notice that while Barrows had been bent and huffing, Marcus took the box as if it were weightless and bore the burden easily across the room. She stared at the muscles of his forearm, clearly outlined beneath his rolled-up sleeves. When he placed the box on the desk beside her, he looked up to catch her staring at his arms. She colored, stepping farther away from the desk, and from his closeness.

Larissa came forward to peer into the box, hoping to catch a glimpse of her "surprise."

Both ladies watched as Lord Havington lifted out one book after another, reading each title aloud to them. He was concentrating on the contents within, and so did not see them making eye contact over his back. Larissa looked desperate, Constance mutinous.

"This book is the latest, I am informed, on embroidery patterns." He picked out yet another, reading, "*Herbal Remedies and Poultices.* Ah, and here is one on *Watercolor Techniques.*"

He glanced up, cocking an eyebrow at Larissa, who instantly transformed her expression to one of polite interest. "Perhaps Miss Violet would be willing to work with you on improving your painting, and could assist you in improving your drawing skills," he suggested, turning his head with a questioning look to Constance.

Constance avoided Larissa's gaze to keep from smiling, since they both knew Larissa had already surpassed Constance in both drawing and watercolors. In truth, most young women within one week of their first lesson had most likely surpassed Constance in those skills.

Still, she decided to do justice to the question. "Of course, my Lord. I should be delighted to oblige." She smiled broadly at Larissa, whose eyes were round. "As long as there will be none of those insipid little puppies that all women draw," she threw in cleverly.

"My mother drew those insipid little puppies, madam." The cold grey storm was back in his eyes.

Constance did not feel so very clever. It seemed his lack of manners was surpassed by his lack of humour. She simply stared at the box pointedly, waiting for him to continue, so that he could leave.

As he droned on, Constance thought it inconceivable that for every boring topic there had been at least five boring books written on the subject. She had to stifle a yawn, merely listening to the ridiculous titles.

Just as she'd begun to fear this was a magic box with no bottom, Marcus leaned in and extracted the final item, which was large and heavy. Turning to his sister, he grinned and held it out for her inspection. Larissa leaned forward on tiptoes, craning her neck sideways to read the gilt title.

"And this, my little sister, is my personal gift to you —" He paused dramatically. "— a very hard-to-find, autographed edition of *Mrs. Carver's Hints for Young Ladies.*"

He beamed, holding his treasure out to Larissa.

It hurt Constance to watch the spark in Larissa's eyes dim, and to see her friend struggle to paste a pleasant smile upon her face.

"Oh, Marcus, this is so . . . special!" Larissa said.

Lord Havington was obviously quite proud of himself. He turned his head to include Constance in the celebration.

Struggling to find a polite comment, Constance asked, "So, this book is autographed by Mrs. Carver herself?"

"Yes, as a matter of fact." He sounded unbearably smug.

"I am happy you were able to meet her personally," Constance said, "to obtain her signature. It sounds as if you both have much in common in your views on etiquette and propriety. I am sure she must prove to be the woman of your dreams. You will make a grand pair, sir."

Marcus appeared flustered. "I did not say I was interested in pursuing a relationship with the author. Besides, I did not obtain her autograph myself. It was already in the book. This is an old, rare edition. The woman could be in her sixties by now, or even her seventies."

"Then all the more proper she must be. How wonderful for you." Constance nodded once, approvingly.

"I am saying, Miss Violet, I have no idea how old she is. And, she is already titled as 'Mrs.' Surely you noticed."

"But she could be widowed, sir! And isn't it true that gentlemen of the *ton* prefer widows?" Constance asked with wide-eyed innocence.

Marcus blushed, saying gruffly, "I'm sure I don't know."

"Oh. Of course not. I beg your pardon. I forgot, your sister says you are a paragon of morality and decorum. But, I'm sure Mrs. Carver is also a stickler. You two should deal very well together, my Lord."

"But she is most likely dead by now."

"Oh." Constance sighed as she moved to

the door. "Well, then she is beyond indiscretions, isn't she? The perfect wife." She excused herself with a brief curtsy, and left Larissa to her brother's company.

CHAPTER SIX

The apricot-washed walls of the breakfast room shimmered with reflections of early sunlight. Constance savored this room in the summer when early sunbeam prisms angled through the glass.

Picking up a plate from the sideboard, she lifted the lid from the first serving dish. A waft of citrus rose with the steam as she spooned a small square of lemon-laced baked egg and curds pudding onto her plate.

This morning she had dressed carefully. One no longer knew when company would arrive on the doorstep at dawn, or would come bursting into the library. Lost in thoughts of Lord Havington, she slid the flat silver spoon under another small helping of eggs and aligned it neatly next to her first serving.

Its color, palest citron, reminded her of her dress. She'd chosen a butter-yellow morning gown. The square neckline was a bit low, but cleverly woven with white satin ribbon. The bodice was gathered tightly against her ribs with rows of matching ribbon. She glanced down at the yellow slippers peeping out beneath the flounced hem.

Oh, my. She also looked straight into the deeply cut bodice. She'd forgotten to tuck in the white satin fichu that modestly filled the gap. The first thing she'd do after breakfasting would be to retrieve it from her dressing room. Without it, this muslin dress was a bit too revealing, and even with higher necklines, she preferred a small scarf or fichu against her throat in the morning. As she dwelt on where she'd placed the bit of cloth — she'd had it in hand at one point this morning — she absent-mindedly slid the serving spoon under another square of custard, forming a neatly edged row of yellow squares on her plate.

It's been two days since the last visit from Larissa's brother, she realized. It had been the same number of days since she'd been able to exercise Jasmine. Hopefully Havington would leave them alone for at least one more day. The mare had been a gift from her brother Alec, who said the pretty filly reminded him of his sister: a trifle too much spirit. Constance blinked back tears. Through the wet haze, too many egg squares

78

on her plate swam into focus.

"Hungry, Miss Violet?" came an all-too-familiar voice behind her back.

If the earl hadn't been there, she'd have quickly spaded all the little squares back into the chafing dish. But to do so now would appear she took direction from him. "Quite, thank you," she said, not turning toward him, but proceeding to the dining table.

Lord Havington helped himself to two moderate spoonfuls of eggs, two plump sausages, and a bit of kidney pie in rich gravy. He picked up two steaming berry muffins in one huge hand, and came to sit across from her. Setting down his plate, and depositing the muffins on a small bread dish, he slid into his chair. He lifted his napkin, flicked it halfway open, and laid it on his lap. While doing so, he looked up at Constance — and froze.

From his taller vantage point, she realized he was being treated to quite an expanse of bosom. She watched his eyes follow her exposed curves down into the dark hollows of the yellow dress. When he looked back up at her face, she pinned him with a glare. He had a manly flush above his starched white collar as he cleared his throat.

Constance closed her eyes briefly and

cursed her absent-mindedness. It could no longer wait until she breakfasted; she must return briefly to her room. She was about to rise and excuse herself when he cleared this throat once more.

"You wish to say something, my Lord?"

"Miss Violet," he began. He picked up his teacup, staring at her eyes — just her eyes — over the rim.

He has beautiful eyes, Constance observed. *But this is ridiculous. Is he using the bone china to avoid staring at my bodice?*

"Miss Violet," he repeated, speaking behind his teacup. "I don't know how to say this."

"Perhaps if my Lord were to put down his cup, I could hear what he was trying to say."

"Perhaps if madam were not half-dressed, his Lordship would be less distracted."

Constance went pink to her hairline. She was not about to return to her room now for the fichu; oh, no. She set her fork down and daintily wiped her mouth with a snowy napkin, as she tested one retort after another.

"I cannot believe his Lordship does not see women at evening functions who wear less. Further, I cannot believe a gentleman's wits become scrambled when women wear low gowns, else the entire *ton* would be in a constant state of bedlam."

"There is a great distinction in decorum," he said, "between demireps of the night, and modest women in the sanctum of the breakfast room in broad daylight."

Marcus stifled a groan.

He couldn't believe he was saying something so stuffy. Lord, he sounded like his father. This wasn't what he'd meant to say. It was the companion's fault he wasn't making sense. He'd been doing his best not to stare at what lay beneath her beautiful white throat. He'd been acting the perfect gentleman, using his teacup to block out her lush upper torso.

Her green eyes smoldered. "What I choose to wear, sir, should be of no concern to you."

"Madam," he began, in his sternest vicar's tone, "you will not be escorting my sister while indecently exposed. In the mornings, I will expect you to wear a . . . a . . . whatever you ladies call those . . ." He finished lamely, waving his hand in front of his chest as he stumbled for the correct term.

In the mornings? What if she went out in the afternoons or in the twilight, with her beautiful bosom on display for those lecherous acquaintances of his in the *ton?* Or on display for the local gentry? "And, of course," he amended, "later in the day and evening as well. I believe a companion must be a paragon of virtue."

There was a full minute of silence as she ignored him, and both stabbed noisily at their plates.

Constance set down her fork with care. "I shall make you a deal, my Lord." She looked down at her plate, as if weighing each word carefully. "I shall endeavor to be the paragon you desire for your sister." She glanced up at him quickly through her lashes — to catch him staring again?

He was relieved he'd not taken advantage to ogle her, as he'd wanted. He concentrated on direct eye contact.

Her lips parted, and she licked them, as if contemplating her next words. He found it almost as hard to concentrate as before, watching her delicate open mouth. He snapped his eyes back to her eyes. "Yes? And the deal?"

"You, my Lord, shall honor social rules as pertain to visiting your sister."

"What the blazes does that mean?"

Ticking off upon her fingers, she commanded, "You will announce yourself to her staff upon arrival. And you shall wait in the guest parlour until fetched to her Ladyship's presence."

The nerve of the chit! The companion who carried herself as a duchess. He snorted loudly.

"Snorting is not proper at the breakfast table," she reprimanded primly.

"Madam," he enunciated crisply and loudly, "snorting *is* allowed at the breakfast table when excesses of cleavage are displayed in the morning."

Neither had noticed the butler entering, but both were aware at the same time that Barrows had heard this exchange of etiquette wisdom. With a blank expression, Barrows unobtrusively refreshed their tea, then left the room.

Constance followed the butler's exit with her eyes, then grinned at Lord Havington. "Did you read that in *Mrs. Carver's Hints for Young Ladies,* my Lord?"

Marcus chuckled. "I expect you shall now read it word-for-word, if only to be able to contradict me, madam."

Larissa entered, in time to find both parties smiling. "La, it is wonderful to see my two favorite people getting along so cordially!"

Silly darling, mused Constance.

Silly chit, thought Marcus.

■ ■ ■ ■

"I love this drawing room, Constance. I still remember when your aunt Agatha allowed the two of us to choose the wall coverings. And the drapery." Larissa twirled upon entering the room, arms spread like a turnstile.

Her wave took in daffodil-hued draperies, fabric walls striped in yellow, and white wainscoting. Across the large windows Greek cornices marched, covered in the same bright yellow damask. White silk curtains hung from the cornice and pooled on the floor.

Constance looked up from her reading and surveyed the warm room. "Yes, I remember that very day." She lowered her book as her friend took a seat. "Now that I recall, you and I decided to do the room in warm colors because it was always quite chilly when we sat in here to read, until —"

"Until we finally realized the chill was coming from the doors! Yes, I remember now," Larissa said. "It was that gap where the French doors join."

Constance looked at the guilty doors. "We really should have chosen a sitting room on the warmer south side of the house."

"Ah, but this was our domain." Larissa twisted to gaze at the room, resting her arm across the back of the settee. "Your aunt Agatha always made us feel so grown up. Remember when she would 'meet' us in here for tea? And we would take turns pouring, as if we were the hostesses." She turned back. "I loved your great-aunt, Constance."

"We were both lucky, Larissa, for I feel affection toward your aunt Marguerite as well. And your uncle Nigel is so gallant and charming. Do you remember when I'd come to stay a few nights, and your uncle would escort us both into the dining room, as if we were princesses, one on each arm? By the way . . ." Constance closed the book on her lap. "When do you anticipate their return?"

Larissa stared hypnotically into the hearth flames. "They mentioned staying a few months with Cousin Ruth, but . . . with Marcus home to stay . . ." She swallowed. "Constance, I'm so afraid that when they return they'll shortly relinquish the house to him and retreat from Amber Crossing. It does belong to him, after all, and there'll be no reason for my guardians to remain now that he's home. He swears, though, that they've agreed to stay on until I am married off." Larissa looked up. "I couldn't bear it if they were to leave. I'd want to go with them! I hardly know my own brother, and . . . he frightens me terribly." Larissa looked downcast.

"They won't desert you, Larissa. Your aunt Marguerite is a mother hen when it comes to your happiness. Look how they agreed to your spending the summer here, knowing they would miss your company."

Larissa visibly relaxed.

Constance, though, continued to think about Lord Havington. It was no wonder he intimidated a nervous sparrow such as his sister. Constance thought about how he'd criticized her *own* manner of dressing. Then she thought about his reprimanding her over the silly kitchen staff incident. And she was reminded of his particularly odious choices of "summer reading material."

Constance had been reclining in the overstuffed chair, in her favorite curled-up reading position, but straightened with excitement. "Gracious! Why didn't I think of this before?" She jumped up determinedly. "Larissa, I have the perfect use for that ridiculous etiquette book."

She marched to the tulipwood table where Marcus had enshrined the precious tome. She grabbed it by its edges and struggled to lift the heavy book, while Larissa watched curiously. Constance was able to get her hands under it and raise it to waist-height. Turning, she let it drop to the floor with a dusty, reverberating thunderclap. Larissa stared round-eyed as Constance bent down and put her hands on its gilt edges. Leaning over, she began pushing the heavy book ahead of her, across the carpet, to the far wall. She picked up speed and did not stop until the massive volume butted up against the terrace doors. It covered the small crack where the doors met the floor.

Constance stood and dusted her hands together in satisfaction. "There. I believe that should keep the draft out quite nicely."

CHAPTER SEVEN

Wispy fog hugged hills and valleys in the early dawn. A soft gold tinted the white haze, trying to warm it away.

Much more like autumn than summer, thought Constance as she stretched lazily. This was her favorite type of morning, with a crisp coolness in the air and sunlight drifting through oaks and poplars.

If it were fall, she'd rise early and go for a hike in the woods, crunching through dry leaves. But on this unusually cool summer morning it would be marvelous to slip out into the chilly sunrise, wander down by the stream bed, and practice her angling. She jumped out of bed. No reason to have a fire lit in her room this early, as she would not be lying about sipping hot chocolate. She'd dress quickly, and pack a bite to take with her. She would most likely be back before Larissa, who was a late sleeper, finished breakfasting.

The room was cold, so she removed her chemise quickly, dropping it on the counterpane, and hurried past her armoire to a plain seaman's trunk beneath the window. This was where she often sat and read, but not today. She tossed the bench cushion to the floor and lifted the lid to rifle through the trunk.

Alec had brought this chest home from one of his journeys, and in it she'd secreted a handy wardrobe for these special outdoor adventures. Constance pulled out a pair of her brother's outgrown breeches and a soft linen shirt. Next, a thick pair of warm woolen socks, and a sweater she'd made for him when she was fourteen years old. It was terribly misshapen, and one arm was noticeably longer than the other. Alec had appeared not to notice, as if it were quite the dandiest gentleman's clothing he'd ever worn.

She held the sweater closely for a moment, remembering Alec wearing it as he rode off to the village. She'd been so proud . . . and he'd been so wonderful, unconcernedly pushing up one sleeve where it covered his hand on the reins.

Where was Alec right now? Why hadn't she heard from him?

After a moment Constance tugged the

sweater over her head and bent to pull her long hair through the neck. Bouncing back up, she dove into the chest to rummage for gloves. Quickly twisting her long hair, she held it high as she dug in the chest, then jammed it beneath the large knit cap she surfaced with.

Looking in the cheval glass, she laughed at the small, slim lad who stared back at her. Ah, if Lord Havington thought her gardening clothes were unsuitable, wouldn't he just choke if he saw her fishing outfit. The smile on her face turned to a frown. To think he acted the lord of *her* manor made it worse. She made a face at the mirror and felt much better, then spun and left the room.

Constance stopped in the billiard room, where her fishing rod leaned alongside the many cue sticks. Her wicker tackle box was in a lower cupboard of the gun cabinet, where she'd left it after her last outing. One of her greatest pleasures was to come home and sit by the fire, tying feathers and tiny pieces of fluff together to make new lures, while Cook put the afternoon's catch, coated with flour and ground cornmeal, in a pan to sizzle in a spoonful of fat.

Peeking in the kitchen, she spotted Mrs. Eldridge rolling out pastry for meat pies.

"Morning! Might I grab a few bites for a picnic breakfast, Mrs. Eldridge?"

"Heavens, my Lady, you gave me a start! I thought one of the village urchins had crept into the house."

"Come, I don't look *that* scruffy, do I? I rather fancied I could pass as a young lord." Constance leaned jauntily against the butcher block.

Mrs. Eldridge raised both eyebrows in answer. "Well, let's pack a lunch that will put some meat on those bones, or you won't have enough energy to win a tug-o'-war with a guppy on your line."

Constance laughed, watching as Cook quickly packed one of yesterday's crusty loaves, some sheep's cheese, two crisp apples, a lamb pasty — "Stop! If I eat that much, I'll do nothing but sleep in the sun all morning."

Mrs. Eldridge wrapped a linen drying cloth around the food, tied it with a knot, then helped Constance sling it over her shoulder.

"Thank you, Mrs. Eldridge," said Constance, leaning sideways to give the woman a quick peck on the cheek.

"Bring back some trout for tonight's dinner, lad," Mrs. Eldridge winked, "and we just might offer you a permanent position

91

in the household."

"Don't you think we had better ask his Lordship's approval first?" asked Constance, and got the reaction she hoped for as Mrs. Eldridge puffed out her round cheeks, and turned and huffed off with a shake of her head.

An hour or two later, Constance added an iridescent trout to the line holding the other four fish. By transferring the fish quickly from her hook to the line, her day's catch would stay fresh as it lay tethered in the ice-cold stream. Time for a bite to eat, she thought with satisfaction.

This was heaven on earth: a forest dappled with early morning sunlight, and a few leaves spiraling lazily to the stream, where they were whisked away by the soft current. She stretched, picking a spot on the grassy bank at the stream's edge where she sat with her picnic feast.

She knew the water would be cold, even in the summer, but she couldn't resist the temptation to dangle her feet as was her habit. Removing the sturdy half boots, she unrolled her wool socks and stuffed each into an empty boot. Then she rolled her pant legs up until they bulked just below her knees, and slid forward, dangling her feet and legs over the low bank's edge and into a clear side pool formed by the rocks. The water was not as cold as she'd expected, but then the current was also slow in this protected little pool.

Marcus rode toward the manor, trumping up an excuse for yet another sojourn to check upon his sister. Of course, he felt justified; it was for her own safety, wasn't it?

If that were so, why did the companion's face keep coming to mind?

He seemed to have a hard time lately keeping Miss Violet from intruding in his thoughts. He'd picture her slim but gently curved figure and clear green eyes with grey specks. But when his imagination slipped down below her eyes and her pert little nose, all he saw was the familiar frown . . . or her lips pressed together sanctimoniously . . . except for that smile she'd granted him in the library. He'd no idea what that was about, but it had warmed him for days.

Why must she always purse her lips, like the vicar's righteous wife?

As Marcus came over the rise he saw the manor perched on the hill ahead. He had to admit it was a beautiful setting: smoke curling from the chimneys, and the dark greens of the forest a striking backdrop. Down to his right, at the base of the manor's hillock ran a wide river. Hardly a river, actually; more of a deep stream, reflecting the sunlight back at him in brilliant twinklings as it . . . Marcus spied the horse in the distance.

It was tethered at the edge of the meadow sloping down to meet the river. From here, it looked to be the same coloring and size of that horse Miss Violet insisted on riding against his explicit advice.

Miss Constance Violet *appeared* malleable. But Marcus was convinced a hint of insurrection hibernated just below the companion's calm surface. He'd seen the smoldering in those green eyes just before she lowered them. When she raised them to meet his again, they'd be calm and clear. He rather liked the smoldering green. It reminded him of mossy weeds waving just below the surface of a clear brook.

Before he realized, he reached the oaks at the meadow's border. And — just as he'd suspected — it *was* the chestnut mare he'd forbidden both his sister and Miss Violet to ride. Tightening his fist on the reins, he jumped off his horse and tied the stallion to a nearby tree, then went stalking down to the water to apprehend the transgressor, with not much success at keeping his temper in check.

Much to Marcus's surprise, neither his sister nor her companion was at fault.

It was just one of the stable boys trying his luck with a fishing pole. Lord Havington realized with a start that he was a little disappointed. He'd actually looked forward to a verbal fencing with Miss Violet.

The boy slid back from the bank, where he'd been wiggling his feet in the water. As the lad stood up, Marcus noticed his wet calves. Not the skinny calves of a young boy, but lightly muscled calves with a pronounced curve. Marcus narrowed his eyelids, and moved in for a closer look.

The boy looked up at the clouds, his navy cap tight on his head, and then stared across the river, stretching sinuously. Actually, more sensuously than sinuously, Marcus realized. Something was not quite right. Marcus advanced slowly forward, studying the figure in the bulky sweater that ended just at the hips. He couldn't help following the sweater's ragged edge down to curves displayed in snug breeches, and on past rolled pant knees, to those shapely calves, trim ankles, and delicate pink feet.

The lad edged his toes to the bank's edge, and peered at something just over its lip. He leaned a bit farther, went up on his tiptoes. The action of rising up on his toes seemed to accentuate the curves of his calves and the roundness stretching those breeches. Marcus felt disoriented.

"Hallo," greeted Marcus in his baritone, from just a few feet away.

The boy spun around, his eyes wide as barrel hoops. He stepped quickly backward as if Marcus meant to do him harm.

Unfortunately, he went right over the bank's edge, arms flailing, and with a high-pitched screech.

Constance fell with a splash into the pool and ended up sitting on the sandy stream bed. She sucked in her breath as the cold water trapped the air in her lungs. Up to her neck in water, she immediately looked up at the bank to see a tall figure outlined there, backlit by the bright sunlight, looking like an avenging angel. Constance groaned. She knew it was more of an avenging devil, and the devil's name was Lord Havington.

She panicked as she began mentally ticking off her multiple transgressions: her unladylike clothing, her unladylike hobby, and — oh, Lord — she'd ridden Jasmine down to the stream.

"Are you all right?" he asked the capped head sitting atop the water.

Her mind whirred. *Perhaps he won't realize it's me.* If I don't talk, if I sit here mutely until he's gone . . .

The earl reached his hand toward the stranded youth.

Well, thought Constance, *so much for sitting here until he's gone.* She couldn't ignore the outstretched hand. She put her hands on the sand, and gathering her feet beneath her, she stood.

As she did so, the water-drenched clothing sucked up out of the water and clung and outlined her entire torso. Constance looked down and screamed, plopping back into the water. The sweater ballooned with air and settled down around her.

She hazarded a glance at Lord Havington.

"Miss Violet?" he asked in an awful tone.

"Yes, my Lord?" Her tone was imperious, as if she always received social callers while sitting in the river with a knit cap upon her head.

"What exactly are you about?"

"Do you mean: why am I sitting in the water, my Lord?"

"That might do for a start," he began softly, but his voice continued to rise with each question. "And then, please explain why you are wearing boys' clothing. And then, if you'd be so kind, explain why you

97

are sitting by an angling rod, as if you did not know such a manly activity is not typically pursued by proper companions. And —" He was roaring now. "— kindly explain why that blasted horse is here, which you have been forbidden to ride!"

Constance started with the worst offense, deciding to work backward to the piddling items.

"Actually, my Lord," she began, licking her lips, "the stable boy rode Jasmine down here. To bring me a picnic meal." *Lord forgive me, I sound just like Larissa,* she realized, but couldn't stop now. Was this how her friend ended up in such ridiculous spiderwebs?

"And?"

"And?" She splashed the water with studied nonchalance, though her toes were feeling numb from the cold.

"Where is he, Miss Violet? Where is this stable boy?"

Constance looked around as if she expected him to appear shortly. "You will not believe the luck, my Lord, but *my* horse panicked at a snake and ran off. So he has gone to fetch her." She looked around again, impatiently. "I wonder what is keeping him?" she muttered, almost below her breath.

"Your horse panicked. At a snake," Lord Havington repeated in a skeptical tone.

"Yes, that is what I said." She looked up at Havington and said sweetly, "You *do* remember Biscuit, don't you? My mare?"

"As I recall," Marcus said, "Biscuit is so near death, she wouldn't see a snake if it twined itself up her leg."

Constance bit back a smile. "Ah . . . but as you can see, she did, and she panicked, and thus — I am simply waiting for them to return. So . . ." She splashed the water on each side. "Please don't bother yourself about me. I'll just sit right here and wait until he returns." A little more splashing. "But . . . thank you for your concern." She tried a tentative smile.

"And the angling gear, madam?"

"His." Her answer was swift, delivered with conviction.

"The stable boy's."

"Right." *Goodness,* she thought, *I must tell Larissa I understand now. This fabricating does indeed get easier as one goes along.*

"Of course," Lord Havington said, looking around. "He could not take his gear with him if he were chasing down a runaway horse, now could he?"

"Exactly. Very perceptive, my Lord." She nodded her approval dismissively, and looked around for the stable boy and Biscuit, masking the slight shaking of her chilled shoulders.

Marcus didn't ask about the clothing.

He already knew Miss Violet did not know how to dress properly. Perhaps she didn't have the necessary funds. He'd been remiss on discussing this with his sister, but he intended to provide for a proper wardrobe if Constance were to be accompanying his sister to London for the Season, in the place of his aunt, after this summer silliness.

And then he would order the maids to remove every last stitch from Miss Violet's cupboards, and consign them to the kitchen fires.

Picturing the vision that rose out of the water only minutes ago, he found it hard to think of Constance wearing proper clothing. He turned to the manor, hands on hips, as if he were searching for the missing stable boy, whom he very much doubted had been here at all. He did not wish Miss Violet to note the effect her wet clothing had.

When he turned back, he said, "So, madam, as the boy will soon be returning . . ." Marcus raised an eyebrow as he surveyed the surrounding hill. "Gallant and I shall walk Jasmine back to the stables, and you may have the lad escort you back. On Biscuit." He enjoyed her indignant reaction, and waited several moments before adding, "Or . . . I suppose I could give you a ride back with me, and let your boy bring Jasmine in later."

Her shoulders shivered noticeably. "I . . ." Her teeth chattered. "I would appreciate a ride back to the manor, Lord Havington." She crossed her arms, tightly grasping her chilled shoulders. "However, may I ask that you turn around, and wait for me to gather myself?"

There was a gleam in Marcus's eye, but he turned and walked toward his stallion, with a curt, "You have exactly one minute, Miss Violet."

Constance stood and wrung out as much water as she could from her clothing. She held the clinging material away from her body, shaking it to allow some air to circulate and to keep it from forming to her curves.

Making certain his back was still turned, she grabbed the leader of trout hidden under the ledge of the bank, and scrambled up the bank and hurried to her fishing basket. She quickly crammed the five live fish in and let the lid drop. Slinging it over her shoulder, she came up behind Marcus, who now sat atop his stallion.

"You may assist me, but do not turn around, sir."

Marcus bristled at her imperious tone. He ought to gallop off and leave the hellion to freeze. But he was sure she'd jump upon Jasmine, and he could not allow that showdown of wills. Without a word he reached down his hand, sliding free his boot so she might use his stirrup.

Gallant stood tolerantly as the wet miss grabbed the earl's wrist and boosted herself up behind him. She came down on the saddle with a loud, wet plop, and water flew onto both horse and rider from her dripping clothes.

As they started off, the fish started flapping in the wicker crewel. Flap, flop, flop.

"What's that?" demanded Marcus.

"I don't hear anything, my Lord."

Flap, flap. Constance coughed loudly, then cleared her throat. Soon, the dying fish would stop flailing around.

Marcus, however, no longer heard the noise. All he could think about was Constance sitting against his back in her wet, clinging outfit. He slowed Gallant to a walk. He didn't know which was worse: the torture of a long walk back, with this image plaguing him all the way, or a quick gallop with the delectable Miss Violet bouncing against him.

As they rode along, Constance pulled off the wet woolen cap, shaking the water from her mane. She removed the wet sweater and pulled and fanned the linen shirt away from her body.

It was a bit drier by time they approached the stables.

"Lord Havington, could you please allow me to dismount on the west side of the stables? I'd prefer not to be seen by the staff."

Marcus thought about the request a long moment. He ought to drop her off in the most visible spot of foot traffic he could find. On the other hand, he thought about Tommy and his father and any other stablemen seeing as much of Constance as he had seen at the river, and immediately turned Gallant to where Constance had suggested.

Of course, he himself had ogled her, but fortunately that twinge of conscience passed as quickly as it came.

"May I dismount first and assist you, madam?" he asked huskily, taken with the vision of putting his hands around the sheer wet fabric of her waist, lifting her down.

"Absolutely not!"

Marcus, expecting this exact reply, continued to look forward and once again held his hand out to his side to aid Miss Violet in dismounting. As she slipped down from behind him he felt a draft, realizing how wet his back was.

"Hmm, first I'm coated with flour, and now water. I suppose all I need next is a little salt on my back and I'll soon be sprouting loaves of bread," he muttered.

Constance shook her tangled mass of hair. As she ran her hands through the curls, lifting them to dry, she looked up at him and chuckled. "Very clever, my Lord," she saluted him, and crossed his path as she hurried toward the house.

Marcus observed that while her shirt and hair had dried somewhat, her breeches were still soaked and clinging provocatively. He further observed it was fortunate he had not dismounted; he'd have been tempted to give her a wet companionable smack as she departed.

Good Lord, what am I thinking? He frowned.

Dinner that evening was again excellent, realized Marcus. The trout was tender and flaky and accompanied with a tart lingonberry sauce. When he took his first bite of the fried fish he actually closed his eyes in culinary appreciation. And when he opened them, Miss Violet was watching him with a look of anticipation and an attractive glow behind her smiling eyes.

Marcus smiled back. He was coming to enjoy these companionable dinner sessions more and more. It seemed unnecessary to dine at his club, when the cook at RoseHill Manor was so skilled. And Miss Violet provided an additional feast for his eyes in the soft candlelight.

Marcus had to admit the unconventional miss was coming along well under his guidance. It had been some time since he'd been forced to match wills with the stubborn companion. (Well, he reflected, perhaps it had only been since this morning at the stream . . .)

Still, he believed his constant supervision was making a difference for both his sister and Miss Violet, and this made him feel quite magnanimous toward both young women.

"And how goes your studying of *Mrs. Carver's Hints for Young Ladies?*" inquired Marcus of his sister.

Larissa choked briefly on a bite of bread and picked up her water glass, sipping as she glanced at Constance over its rim.

"Well," Constance said with sweetness and

wide eyes, "we've learned how to deal with drafty rooms. We could not have managed *that* without your book, my Lord."

Marcus beamed.

CHAPTER EIGHT

A handful of days passed with no visits from Lord Havington. Constance had begun to hope her ruse could be dropped. Not only did she find it inconvenient, her staff found it confusing.

And yet, here he was again: sitting in the parlour as if it were his own. He poured himself an after-dinner port, not even bothering to offer a glass to Constance. Wouldn't he be shocked to know she and Aunt Agatha usually had a sip of port before bedtime, and tiny glasses of sherry with afternoon tea.

Larissa escaped to her room to retrieve her embroidery.

Constance strove to think of a safe topic to explore with the stuffy earl. "May I ask what games you play, my Lord?"

Marcus looked at her and replied in a sincere tone, "I am not at any game, Miss Violet."

Constance laughed, but caught herself at his expression. "I meant, do you play cards, or chess, or . . . ?"

"Ah! A bit of both."

"Cards? Wonderful! Would you care to place a wager, my Lord?"

"Ladies do not wager, Miss Violet."

"Perhaps *ladies* do not, but I am a mere companion, as you've pointed out to me many times, Lord Havington." Her voice was laced with lassitude.

"If you desire to continue in your career as my sister's companion, madam, I would strongly recommend you not wager."

"So," she pursued, annoyed once again with his interminable threats, "let me get this right, my Lord." She picked up the deck of cards on the nearby table, and began to shuffle as she chose her words.

"Yes, Miss Violet?"

She noticed the change in his voice, and glanced up. He had a playful look — perhaps it would be prudent not to spoil the man's good mood. She hesitated . . . no, she decided, she would much rather torment the sanctimonious earl.

"So, Lord Havington, if a *man* makes a bet, it is considered very sporting. If he should lose that bet and show good form, he is admired as a gracious loser. If, on the other hand, he wins the bet and does not gloat but accepts his winnings modestly, he is admired as a gracious winner. Do I have the right of this so far?"

She caught him watching her lips. His own twitched.

Slowly, his grey eyes met hers. "Yes. You have the right of it, Miss Violet. However, may I ask where this argument is leading?"

She smiled saucily, which dimpled her cheeks. "Then, my Lord, whether he should win or lose, betting is a test of his mettle as a gentleman. A show of comportment, if you will."

"Mmm." He held her gaze in an overly bold fashion.

She returned his stare. "But a lady must not bet a'tall?" She lifted her brows, waiting for a reply.

"Of course not," he said, lowering his brows as he always did when lecturing.

"Posh! Do you not believe women play cards?"

"I am sure they do."

"And what do you suppose they use for ante?"

"I don't know. Buttons? Pieces of chocolate?"

"Humph," she snorted. "What if I were to tell you they bet their pin money?"

"Then I would suppose their quarterly allowance a bit too generous."

"Ugh! You are impossible." She continued shuffling the cards. "Lord Havington, what if you and I were to make a bet?"

"That would not be proper."

"Who is here to say it should not be proper?" She waved the cards in her hand around the empty room. "I do not see the oh-so-correct Mrs. Carver. And Larissa would neither know nor care."

"*I* am here. I should know, and I should not approve. Moreover, I should feel badly taking away whatever little spending money you have."

"*What?*" she squeaked, her voice rising an octave. "You odious man, what makes you think you would win? You make me insane, Your Grace."

"My Lord."

"What?" she said.

"Why do you insist on addressing me as Your Grace, when I tell you I am a mere Lord?"

"It is so refreshing to hear you admit you are a mere anything, sir."

"I suspect that was not a compliment . . ."

"We need not bet for money," she baited. "Would it then be proper? A *friendly* wager? One could hardly even call it a bet if it were not for money, now could one?"

He raised a brow. "And what would be the prize, Miss Violet?"

She shuffled the cards once again, ready to set the trap. "We shall play a game of cribbage, sir. If I win, then I am allowed to ride your stallion, Gallant."

"Absolutely not!"

"Well, perhaps not *your* stallion, my Lord. All right, let us agree: if I win, then I am allowed to ride a different stallion, one of RoseHill's stallions. I am a very good ri—"

"No." He locked gazes with Constance, and there was no longer any playfulness.

She sighed theatrically, then looked down. "Well, then, perhaps a mare. But one with just a tiny bit more spirit than Biscuit?" She studied the cards nonchalantly. "I find myself particularly drawn to that chestnut mare with the white fetlock. I believe her name is . . . Jasmine?"

"I believe you refer to the horse the stable boy rode down to the river. Fishing."

She peeked up at Lord Havington through her lashes, to ascertain his mood. She smiled, wondering if the man was intentionally displaying a bit of wit. "Yes . . ." She drew the word out. "Assuming, of course, the stable manager Tom were to approve. *Only* with the condition that he approve."

Wistfully, she added, "Just one brief outing on a different mare. Perhaps a short, sedate walk through the lower meadows. Assuming, that is, that I were *able* to win a round of cribbage."

Marcus visibly relaxed. "All right. I believe that to be a fair wager."

Constance suppressed a smug smile, for it had been her intent to wager a ride on Jasmine at the very beginning. As simple as taking sweets from a child, she complimented herself. "Then it is a bet!" She smiled charmingly, and began shuffling the cards in earnest.

"You forget one detail, Miss Violet."

Her hands stilled on the card deck. "Yes, my Lord?"

"We have not negotiated what *my* winnings will be."

Oh, breathed Constance, *is that all?* She supposed she must acknowledge the possibility, however unlikely. The cad would most likely ask for a kiss. Her chin rose a bit higher. "And . . . what might that be, sir?"

"If I were to win, Miss Violet, I should wish to have you recite a selection to me."

"A selection? Poetry?" Her brow wrinkled in surprise.

"I was thinking more of a selection from

Mrs. Carver's Hints for Young Ladies. Perhaps a dialogue on . . . the evils of gambling?"

Constance frowned. Reading a passage from that stuffy book might be worse than being kissed by the stuffy earl. She replaced this image quickly; she focused instead on a reckless ride against the wind, her hair flying as she took jumps, riding bareback astride Jasmine. Besides, she did not plan to lose. She opened her mouth to agree. "I —"

"When I say recite, I mean . . . by memory, of course."

Havington stared at Constance, without the slightest expression, and she stared stonily back.

"Cut," she ordered, pushing the deck across the table.

The very next dawn, Constance woke and stretched her arms and toes as far as she could, yawning. She jumped out of bed, as she planned on being on top of the hill as the sun rose. On her very own Jasmine, of course.

Still smiling as she dressed, she recalled last night's game of cribbage. Lord Havington had been a gracious loser, she had to admit.

She, on the other hand, had *not* been a gracious winner.

She'd jumped up and twirled around, laughing merrily. But when she caught his eye as he sat calmly studying her, she simply hugged herself and plopped back down in her seat.

"Forgive me," she said. Her effort to be sober stressed the dimples forced by her tightened lips.

Abruptly he laughed, and his laugh was contagious. "Forgive you for what, Miss Violet? For winning? Or for gloating shamelessly?"

"That really is awful of me, isn't it? It's just that I *never* seem to win at cribbage. . . . Did you lose on purpose, my Lord? Did you play so I would win?" she asked with wide eyes, and one extra blink of her long lashes.

Lord Havington eyed her speculatively, as if reading her very thoughts. Finally, he said, "Actually, Miss Violet, what if I told you I did indeed play poorly — with a mind to seeing you allowed to win?"

"The devil you did!" she exclaimed with indignation.

He laughed again. "No, madam. I concede that was well played on your part."

She wasn't sure to what he referred, and how much he intuited. She thought it safest not to reply.

The earl stood and, taking her hand,

114

bowed over it. He raised her hand to his lips as he watched her with those grey eyes, and he placed a soft kiss there. "Well done, madam," he repeated, then nodded and left the room.

Shaking herself back to the present, Constance let out a breath, remembering what his touch had made her feel last night. She continued dressing, blaming the goose flesh on the cold room.

She'd soon be dashing across the countryside on her beloved Jasmine.

Still, she might have shown a little more restraint and less of a victory celebration. Perhaps the next time she beat the earl at a game, she would attempt to gloat less. And there *would* be a next time. She knew it as well as she knew the sun would appear this morning, for the earl had been a fierce opponent last night. It was obvious he was every bit as competitive as Constance herself. He played his hands thoughtfully and intelligently. There were even a few moments, looking at the hand she'd been dealt, when she was fearful she would be memorizing a passage out of that foul book.

Well, it had come to nothing, hadn't it? She pulled her hair back with a ribbon, and lastly pulled on her soft kid riding boots. Constance smoothed down her butternut riding skirt, and looked in the mirror. She looked decently attired, for once. If she were alone on her estate, with no fear of brotherly earls popping in unexpectedly, she would have pulled on a pair of her brother's old breeches.

However, the thought of Lord Havington arriving for breakfast and catching her in such attire had been enough to change her mind. When he'd caught her at the fishing pond, she'd found him staring at her tightly clad legs once too often. Thinking about it brought a soft flush of color to her cheeks as she looked at herself in the mirror.

She did not plan on allowing the earl's gaze to wander intimately over her figure again. The man had no manners. She spun in front of the mirror, checking out her fashionable outfit from several angles. Most likely he would not even appear today, she thought.

She would not admit to herself she had taken especial care as she dressed, hoping otherwise.

The stable door creaked as Constance swung it open. It was still quite dark inside, even with daylight openings cut in the rafters above. However, Constance could maneuver through the building blindfolded, so familiar was she with these beloved stables. Finding her way to Jasmine's stall was easy. It was a miracle she had not worn a smooth path to it in the old floorboards.

She was exhilarated, flushed with expectations of the ride with Jasmine and longing to see the sunrise from her favorite hill. Jasmine nickered, and Constance answered just as sweetly. Leading the mare out of her stall, she brought her to the front of the stables where a bit more light filtered through the open doors. As she reached for the saddle she heard steps upon the floorboard, and recognized Old Tom by his bowlegged gait as he hurried over, still scratching his neck and yawning.

"Mornin', my Lady. Here, let me get that saddle for you."

"Not *that* saddle, Tom," came another voice.

"Drat!" hissed Constance under her breath, before she turned to greet Lord Havington. "My goodness, my Lord, you are up early."

"I am always up before sunrise, Miss Violet."

"Even after staying up late last night? Drinking, nursing your sorrow over your loss at cards?"

He flashed a white smile in the dark, and

said, "If you were a gentleman, Miss Violet, you would definitely *not* be admired as a gracious winner. I see we must have a rematch, or I shall have no peace."

She had to smile. So, his majesty did have a sense of humor. And their easy bantering of late was enjoyable. However, this did not excuse his ruining her excursion. She looked at Tom with annoyance, as he had already swapped her favorite saddle and was cinching on a lady's sidesaddle.

"Speaking of bets, Miss Violet, I believe we agreed Tom would first approve of your choice of Jasmine as being a safe ride for a lady?"

Now Constance swung toward Tom, so Lord Havington could not see her expression. She stared meaningfully at Tom, as she said, "Why, of course I asked Tom for his approval on riding Jasmine, my Lord. Tom assures me that riding Jasmine is well within my ability as a horsewoman. Isn't that correct, Tom?"

Tom looked at her blankly, and then at Lord Havington, who stared at him, waiting for a response. "Oh! Well, yes, of course, yer Lordship. I do approve. Jasmine is just the right horse for m'lady." He raised bushy eyebrows at Constance, looking very pleased with himself.

Constance groaned inwardly. Subtlety would have been nice.

"I am pleased to hear that," Havington said to the stable master. "Then, Miss Violet, you most likely do not need my chaperonage."

She swung around to say, "No, of course not." Just a little too quickly and fervently.

"But, I assume you would also not object to my accompanying you? For your own safety?"

"No-o-o," she drew the word out slowly, but it sounded more like a groan.

She could forget galloping wildly. She could forget riding astride. She could forget jumping hurdles, she could forget viewing the sunrise in quiet solitude.

She could forget making that same bet again.

CHAPTER NINE

The glazed sapphire urn she and Aunt Agatha had brought from Italy was now freshly planted with trailing rosemary. Tiny blue flowers against the green foliage offset the blue pot like miniature jeweled stars. The pungency of the narrow leaves she'd crushed while tamping the soil brought vivid flashbacks of their walks through sunflower-heavy Umbrian hill towns.

Constance stood in the sun surveying her handiwork.

The pot was ready to be moved to its final spot, at the corner of her herbal knot garden. Swiping a dirt-stained glove across her forehead, she bent over and pushed against the container. It barely budged. She'd not given thought to how heavy it would be, and realized it might have been wiser to plant it closer to its final location.

"Here, allow me to help you with that, Miss Violet."

She stood and rolled her eyes before turning around. *Wasn't the man here just two days before?*

It was unfair, really, the sacrifices she was making for Larissa! Briefly, she considering telling Lord Havington *no.* First of all, this garden was *her* domain. Second, she was not about to listen to his lectures on why ladies should not work outdoors in the sun. Third, why, just look how the man was dressed. How could he possibly lift a finger without soiling his stiff white shirt and vest?

He must have heard her thoughts, for he unbuttoned his vest and shrugged out of it. Looking around, he advanced to the low-limbed pear tree and draped his vest over the nearest branch.

He rolled up first one shirt sleeve and then the other, methodically, folding each roll carefully and evenly. Constance was mesmerized by his forearms: dark hair, and skin a deep walnut color. And nicely muscled.

Havington, his face still down, glanced up beneath his dark lashes and caught her focus. "Have you any brothers, Miss Violet?"

Constance grew wary. Had the servants accidentally revealed her identity? Did he know about Alec? "Why do you ask, my Lord?"

"It would seem you'd never seen a man's

arm before, is all."

Her cheeks warmed in a trice. "It is just . . . I . . . I could not help noticing how brown your skin is. . . . Surely you must realize most gentlemen do not labor in the sun? In my experience," she added with a bit of disgust, "men of the *ton* — which is to say men of leisure — may be spotted as they approach one in London at night by their glowing, pasty skin."

The earl laughed. "I have this image of ghostly white strollers. No, the men in my family have always had dark tones in the skin. In my case, because I enjoy sports, a little sun quickly darkens it several shades. Some gentlemen do enjoy the outdoors, Miss Violet, even though you may think we are all lazy, pasty-skinned idlers. Surely you yourself can relate to that, with your love of gardening and fishing?"

She saw he watched her closely . . . she did not know whether he expected a confession or an apology, but he would receive neither. "Ah, but I am a mere companion, sir, so I may do as I please." Constance turned to address the heavy pot again. "In fact, I may garden in the sun as much as I wish, Lord Havington. So if you will please excuse me, I am quite busy."

Dismissing him thus, she grabbed the top

of the pot with each hand on an opposite side of the rim, to try rolling it into place.

Lord Havington stepped to the opposite side, bending down and lifting the pot effortlessly.

"Where would you like this to go?"

Down in the village, she found herself tempted to tell the show-off. Instead, she pointed at a spot a few yards away. "At that corner of the herb garden, if you will."

He placed it where she specified, with no obvious effort.

She smiled, pleased with the addition to the knot garden. It gave just the formal touch she'd planned. "Thank you."

"That will cost you another game of cribbage, Miss Violet."

"Oh? And are your stakes the same, my Lord?"

"Yes. I find it pleases me very much to contemplate hearing you recite Mrs. Carver's sensibilities."

"Would this be about the evils of gambling, or would it now be a tyranny against gentlewomen gardening in the sun?"

Marcus squinted up at the sun with a grin, as he contemplated this. "Gambling," he decided crisply, addressing the sky. Looking back at her, he offered, "I find no fault in your gardening, madam. I think every lady should be so charming with a dirt smudge across the bridge of her nose."

"Oh!" Constance reached her gloved hand up and swiped. This only added more dirt, as her glove was the culprit.

"Allow me," said the earl. Removing a square of linen from his pocket, he stepped dangerously close to her and put one hand beneath her jaw while he gently wiped her face with his handkerchief.

Constance froze. Once more she found her breathing irregular and her senses scrambled as he stood so close.

"And what would your winnings be, should you win our wager this evening, Miss Violet? Another ride on a mare such as Jasmine?" His eyes moved from the handkerchief to her eyes.

"No," she answered with a sigh, standing obediently still as he finished wiping.

Marcus stopped wiping, but did not step away. His hand still held her jaw. "Then what would you desire as a reward, madam?" It was a husky whisper, his eyes moving to her mouth.

Constance jumped at the thrill the whisper sent along her neck and stepped back, trying to concentrate on the question. What *did* she desire?

To see a less autocratic side of the earl,

for one thing. The playful side she thought she spied now and then. The human side. Yes, something to make the earl more personable and less like a king.

"Do you know any of your staff, my Lord?" she asked on a hunch.

Marcus took a half step back. "Are you asking if I am acquainted with them? I should hope so, since I myself interviewed most of them, following their hire."

"And their names? What is the name of your maid in your London townhouse?"

He concentrated on stuffing his handkerchief back into his pocket. "How should I know each servant by name? My butler knows all their names."

"So, your butler's name is the only name *you* know."

"And my valet, of course."

"Has your valet any brothers, my Lord? Are his parents still alive? Does he ever suffer from the gout? How old is he?"

The earl looked impatient and opened his mouth to speak, but she interrupted. "I have decided upon my wager, my Lord," she said, folding her arms. "I shall wager, if you were to lose our game, sir, you need to undertake talking to two of our servants at RoseHill."

Marcus tilted his head to the side, as if to make sure he heard her aright. "I am simply to converse with two of the servants?" he asked, not without some suspicion.

"Not just talking, as in 'How do you do?' You must learn their Christian names, Lord Havington, *and* you must learn something — just one personal fact — about each of them."

She saw his brow wrinkle; saw him trying to make sense of the wager, searching for a motive.

"Ah. I now see. We are dealing with the progressive ideas of a blue-stockinged companion, aren't we? Of course. You must think equality is just a matter of address, and thus friendliness will undermine the entire social class structure, centuries in the making. Your naiveté makes me smile, madam. All right." He shoved his hands in his pockets. "Then I must change *my* bet, Miss Violet. If I should win, you shall memorize Mrs. Carver's esteemed views on the impropriety of a gentlewoman becoming overly familiar with the servants."

What an odious snob! she thought.

However, he was not about to win. Perhaps a little humility and graciousness shown to her servants by the earl would be worth the distasteful risk on her part.

"You, sir, have a bet."

126

CHAPTER TEN

"By the way —" Larissa peeked over the top of her book as her friend entered the parlour. "— Marcus insists on escorting us to Baroness Montague's country dance."

"What?"

"I couldn't tell him no, Constance. He seemed so pleased with his offer."

"Certainly he is pleased," Constance said with a hint of asperity. "Because it means he can dream up new ways to follow us around while being bossy."

"But he could so easily have forbidden our going. I was quite surprised he delivered the invitation at all. Even though the baroness is an especial friend of Aunt Marguerite's, he might have torn it up and I'd have never known. He does not approve of country parties, you see. So I was trying to be agreeable and appreciative. I do believe I was successful, as we will now both be going . . . with Marcus," she added dolefully.

Constance smiled gently. "A country party and a country dance are not at all the same, Larissa. A country *party* is an event that may stretch out over several days. Men tend to see these as a chance to single out a woman's company over several nights, if you take my meaning. All sorts of naughty dalliances can occur at country parties, and your brother is likely suspicious of those because he's attended them himself."

Larissa missed the sarcasm as her eyes widened in fascination.

"The Montagues', Larissa, is a country *dance*. We are there to enjoy one single evening. Heavens, it is possible the baroness may not even allow a waltz. Even your brother could hardly balk at the innocence of a simple country dance."

"It isn't just country parties he disapproves of —"

"I find that difficult to believe," muttered Constance.

"He has also expressly forbidden me to attend any masquerades when he is not escorting me."

Constance wrinkled her nose. "Why not? Masquerades are ever so much fun." Perched on the edge of the settee, she warmed up to her subject. "And so romantic and mysterious. Women dress in costumes, which may be as demure as an abbess or as shocking as a courtesan. You see, you pretend to play a role. You'd be excellent at that, Larissa. And even when not dressing in costume, one wears a masque, as is done during the carnival season in Italy." Constance touched her fingertips together, forming a mask over her eyes, peeking between her fingers. "If ever I go to a masquerade, I already know what my masque will be: I plan to wear a white satin masque, as delicate as a swan, with glittery white plumes. You would be amazed, Larissa, but without seeing all of one's face it is hard to recognize even people you know. That's half the fun!"

Larissa surprised Constance by making a stern face, bringing her eyebrows as low as she could, and, tucking her chin down toward her chest, saying in a ridiculously deep voice, "You will *not* be attending any masquerades during your upcoming Season. I expressly forbid it. Wearing masques is an excuse for licentious gentlemen to take advantage of innocent women. Actually, women of virtuous character would not attend a masquerade in the first place, I am sure. At least, *you* shall not, and that is the end of this discussion. If you will only read the book I have recommended, I am sure you will find the impeccable Mrs. Carver would offer exactly the same advice."

Constance laughed at the excellent imitation of the earl, but the laugh ended on a sigh. Constance had looked forward to this upcoming dance. She had planned on being introduced as herself, not playing the role of meek companion. If Lord Havington were to attend, she would have to remain the oh-so-correct Miss Constance Violet. Drat!

"Larissa, dear, perhaps we should bring our charade to a close." She regretted her words instantly, as Larissa's lower lip begin to tremble. "I mean, wouldn't it be better to be honest with your brother? Certainly by now he will allow you to stay on as my guest. You've been here three weeks, and we've toed the line on every single directive he's dreamt up. And surely, now he knows me, he would not consider you marred by my brother's scandal."

Larissa blinked back a tear, but her blue eyes filled with water anyway. "But if he finds out I fabricated all of this, he will not hesitate to send me home in punishment. I'll miss the dance, I'll miss our outings, I'll miss the entire summer! I know him, Constance. He values honesty above everything."

Constance could not help the outburst of a laugh. She tried to choke it down immediately. "Larissa, you have been nothing *but* dishonest from the moment this whole charade started. Not about this home, not about my identity, not about my name, not about my horse, not about your intentions —"

"I realize that," interrupted Larissa. "I can't help it, it all sort of slips out. But it's really only one transgression, with a few minor embellishments."

"Embellishments? Minor?" Constance did not mean her voice to hit such a high note.

"Constance, I am truly sorry," Larissa said. "This must be awful for you. I cannot imagine why he is always around! I wanted a summer of freedom, but I've seen him more in the last few weeks than I did in the prior ten years."

Constance sat a few moments in silence. She could make this easy for Larissa and declare it to be not such an inconvenience. After all, when Larissa left, the household would be back to normal and Constance would be its independent mistress once again. *La,* perhaps she would even miss these theatrical summer antics.

And yet . . . no, she should not let Larissa off the hook so easily. Her friend needed to understand the frustration, the great sacrifice, required on Constance's part.

Besides, Larissa needed to start questioning her brother's right to exercise overbearing authority. How was Larissa to train her future husband if she couldn't even handle her own brother?

And why did the earl act thus? Larissa was the most gentle, malleable creature alive. Constance wanted to shake some sense into her friend. Worse, this nonsense affected Constance's own lifestyle.

"Larissa," she stood to pace as she chose her words, but bit off the intended lecture in frustration. Larissa waited. This is impossible, moaned Constance. How could her sweet friend be cut from the same cloth as that barbarian? How to make her understand?

"Larissa, listen to me. Perhaps we needed a nanny when we were young girls, but we are now grown women. I for one no longer need one — especially not a nanny who wears breeches and disguises herself as an earl. An earl, one would assume, with responsibilities. Yet one who strangely has nothing better to do than follow us around as if we were attached to his leading strings."

Larissa's eyes grew wider. She sat stiffly straight, attentive. Constance took this as a positive sign. Putting a hand on her hip for emphasis, she pointed the other hand toward Larissa. "If his Highness — I mean his Lordship — had himself been invited to the dance by our hostess, then it would be acceptable for him to attend."

Larissa bit her lower lip and shook her head to the negative, very slightly.

Constance continued with a tilt of her head, "Or, if his Grace — I mean his Lordship — desired to accompany us as our carriage driver, or lackey, I would even grant we might allow the hired help to dance. But —" She ignored Larissa's look of shock. "— if he thinks we need a nanny, then he shall be set straight right away."

Constance noticed Larissa no longer watched her, but stared at a point just above Constance's head. She felt her insides go cold. Or perhaps there was an iceberg behind her with the chilliest of winds about to descend.

Just to cover her suspicions, she added, "That is, of course, with his wise counsel and consensus."

She spun around and ran into a faceful of wool, finding herself up against Lord Havington's chest.

"Forgive me," he said. "It is just your lackey, come to see if I might bring you ladies some tea."

Constance looked down at the hem of her gown, but decided she would stand by her words. Perhaps humor would help the situation? "But you did hear me say, my Lord, that even the hired help would be allowed to dance."

"Do you include companions in that category?" he hissed.

Constance turned pink.

She glanced at Larissa, who sat frozen, mortified. Constance took a deep breath. Once more, in wearisome sacrifice, she would not hurt her timid friend. "Please forgive my outburst, my Lord," she said. "I have not been myself today. I suppose I am not used to having the benefit . . ." She gritted her teeth and continued. ". . . or the wise counsel of an older brother such as yourself."

"I daresay you've never received direction from *any* male, including your father," observed Marcus with a frown.

Constance bristled. She'd swallowed her pride for Larissa's sake, but she refused to have it jammed farther down her throat. Further, as she thought of her wonderful father, the room began to shrink and blackness surrounded her. She was no longer aware of the presence of the other two. As hard as she tried to grasp and trap the memories, her father's face and his voice had both slipped away from her. Forever.

Determined to escape before she broke into tears or said anything more she would regret, she slipped quickly by Lord Havington. His arm shot out, and he trapped her wrist gently in the powerful grip of his hand.

He leaned toward her and whispered, "And I'll take that dance you promised, Miss Violet."

Yanking her arm away, Constance flew from the room.

Marcus watched her go, then nodded curtly to his sister and made to leave.

Larissa's soft voice detained him, though she spoke barely above a whisper. "Marcus, that was so unkind."

He frowned. "Asking a companion for a dance?"

"No. About her father."

Larissa's throat tightened in anguish, but she forced her voice to remain steady as she informed him of the tragic circumstances that had robbed Constance, a young girl, of both her parents.

Constance pulled her wrap closer against the chill as the wind whipped across the flagstone terrace. Standing against the wall with her elbows on the capstone, she appeared to be staring at the moon, but in reality focused on nothing. All her focus turned inward as she thought about her parents, trying desperately to remember them.

She didn't know at what age she could no longer remember their faces, but she'd cried more on that day than she had on the day they'd died.

She thought they'd always be with her if she could just remember their sweet faces and their loving voices.

Her father was now just a tall grey shape, and she could no longer put a voice to the shape. Her mother was a pair of arms holding Constance's small body close. At least she could remember the hug, but there was only a shadow where her mother's face should be, and there was no voice. None at all.

She didn't remember much before Aunt Agatha came to "take her home," but she knew she loved them and they loved her. Her youngest years were now just a series of flashbacks, and these were dimming with time.

Her earliest full memory was her parents' funeral. She was five years old when they both died in the carriage accident.

Their country home was near the coast, and they'd been returning from a party at a neighboring estate. The road was icy and the carriage slid over the cliff before they could escape. Her parents and the horses died when they hit the rocky beach below. Only the driver had been able to jump in time. When they found him unconscious, lying in the muddy road, they said he had barely a scratch on him. Of course, the fact he was drunk probably helped his limp body take the impact of the fall, and saved him from suffering any broken bones.

He had no broken bones — yet her parents' bodies were crushed so badly, the caskets were sealed as they lay in state.

Would they still be alive if the carriage driver had been sober? She would never know, as he disappeared forever the next day, most likely fearing a reprisal. Her parents were loved by servants and tenants alike.

But this was told her by others, many years later. All Constance remembered was standing in the hushed parlour, then being pulled forward by her cousin's wife, who intended to approach the bodies hidden in sealed caskets. Constance hadn't wanted to approach the twin coffins looming high above her head. But the woman held a tight grip on her wrist and pulled her closer. Constance tried to dig her heels into the dark carpet.

Everything was dark in the room, or so it seemed in her memory. She could still see the dark wine carpet, the windows hung with black satin bunting, and the blur of guests in dark somber outfits. Even nature seemed saddened, as no light filtered through the rainy gloom outside.

Constance didn't understand the significance of the boxes; their size dwarfed and frightened her. Cousin Elsinore reached out to touch the black casket on the left, which held her mother.

"Kiss the wood, Constance," she commanded coldly as she pushed Constance up against the rough surface. "Your mother lies in here. And your father is there." She lifted her shawled arm to point to the other wooden coffin.

Constance obediently puckered her tiny lips and planted a child's loud kiss on each box. Then the tiny five-year-old looked up at her cousin and asked in a pleading voice, "Mama sometimes has nightmares. Could we please put her in the same box with Papa so she won't be afraid?"

A female guest sobbed with a sharp intake of breath. Her cousin was displeased with her audacity. She scowled and sharply pulled Constance away from her parents.

Forever.

Wracked with tears and bitter memories, Constance buried her face in her arms, leaning for support against the cold stone wall.

She did not want to remember her cousin and his wife Elsinore, who'd been cruel. Then why was it still so easy to hear their ugly voices, scolding and criticizing — and not the loving voices of her mother and father? Had ugly memories used up too much precious space in her head, to edge out those of her parents?

She still remembered when her cousin and his shrewish wife turned her over to her spinster great-aunt Agatha in disgust, feeling they'd done their share. They believed the seven-year-old was useless; Constance believed it by then as well.

Aunt Agatha had come to retrieve her, and her life changed. All thanks to the kind-hearted woman.

And now Constance had lost her loving great-aunt also. She had an unreasonable fear of losing her memories of the grand woman, as she had of her parents. It seemed everyone she loved deserted her forever.

No longer sobbing, feeling quite drained, she turned her head sideways on her arm.

The tears threatened to continue down her cheek and into her ear. Constance stood upright and sniffed twice as she felt in her pocket for her handkerchief.

"Here, please — use mine," came Lord Havington's voice.

She wouldn't turn around; didn't want him to see her tear-streaked face, so she reached one hand behind her, not trusting her voice.

Marcus pressed the large square of cloth into her palm, using his hands to curl her fingers around it. Constance blotted her eyes, then blew her nose loudly.

"Thank you," she acknowledged in a hushed voice, turning just slightly. But Marcus was at her side, peering around at her face. He took the handkerchief from her and, holding her face with one hand, dabbed the path of tears on her cheek, then where they'd run down below her jaw.

Reminded of the morning in the garden, Constance tensed at the electricity of his touch in the hollow of her neck.

Misunderstanding her body language, Marcus swore at himself for the distaste she must feel. He was the reason she cried, here on the cold terrace, alone in a strange house without family. The brave little companion

140

who had no money and no future, except to wait on others. How could he be such a cad?

"I . . ." He didn't know what to say. He was not accustomed to apologizing.

Constance raised her eyes to his, and he noticed her long lashes still trapped tears. And her moist eyes were the most beautiful he'd ever looked into. Marcus didn't realize he still held her face cupped in his large hand as he looked into her eyes, and said, "I'm sorry, Miss Violet." It came easily.

He could not believe how easily he did the next thing that came as naturally: he bent his head and kissed her.

Constance didn't breathe until he broke the kiss. She took a step backward and fled toward the light through the terrace doors.

Much later, Marcus sat in the dark leather chair pulled close to the library fire. *Damnation,* he thought, *why did I do that?* I don't even care for the woman and her airs. And I hate apologizing. Though he certainly hadn't hated the kiss. And what of the promise to dance? It seemed of late the oddest things slipped from his mouth, including that kiss.

She was a minx in the disguise of a companion. This brought to mind her inappropriate outfits. What would she wear to the upcoming dance? Did she own a gown?

Perhaps this was why she didn't wish Marcus to accompany them . . . of course. She must be mortified.

He got up and helped himself to a third glass of brandy, then rang the bell. He would inform Barrows he needed to speak to his sister at once.

He would inform Larissa he intended to pay for a gown for Miss Violet for the upcoming dance. He pictured Constance floating in an apple-green confection hugging her slim figure. Her eyes would be dark emeralds against that color. Perhaps a single emerald hanging upon a golden chain, dropping down into the valley, suspended just before plunging down, drawing his eyes to the inviting crevice.

Blinking, he pushed the image away, swallowed and fortified himself with another swallow of brandy. Now he saw the others at the dance. Those lecherous fellows stood staring and ogling Miss Violet in the revealing gown.

No, this would not be an appropriate fashion for a country dance. The local gentry would be too swift to appear at Rose-Hill in the following days, and he had to think of his sister's safety. He might not be around to keep the wolves away.

Perhaps it would be best to choose a dress

as no-nonsense as she. Something rather high-necked, which would draw attention upward to her green eyes. He gulped the remainder of his brandy, feeling much more comfortable for some reason.

He would instruct his sister to convince Constance it was Larissa's idea and generous gesture. The companion must never know he was behind it. This should be easy. He had no doubt whatsoever his sister would obey him, as expected.

Larissa clutched her stomach, laughing. She could barely continue. She sat on the bed in Constance's room, where she'd immediately sought her out.

"And this is why he reasoned you were hesitant to have him attend us. Because you do not have a suitable dress in your wardrobe to wear to the dance." This set Larissa off in a fresh cascade of giggles. "And," she went on, once she caught her breath, "he therefore insists upon having a gown made for you." She laughed, until she realized she was laughing alone.

"He wouldn't!" Constance's eyebrows knit together. "Larissa, you've got to stop him. I've already planned what I'm wearing to the dance. I have the most beautiful, diaphanous green silk. If your brother were to choose a dress, I'm sure I'd be a twin to the vicar's wife, dressed in the heaviest of wools. Please be a dear, and let him know first thing tomorrow that I really do have my own wardrobe."

And with that, Constance considered the subject of the gown to be closed. Just as she considered the subject of the kiss to be closed. She'd been victim of a vulnerable moment; that was all. No need to tell Larissa, since it really meant nothing at all.

But she fooled herself. She could not stop thinking about the kiss.

Constance massaged her temples as she slipped into the library. *Perhaps I'll sit by the fire and relax,* she thought. Of late, the strain of playing a role and heeding her every conversation weighed upon her.

What an arrogant man. Thank goodness she had her loving brother Alec as a different male to measure others by. Lord Havington was exactly the same as every other male of the *ton* she'd met . . . one more reinforcement of her decision never to marry.

How unjust that Alec should be ostracized because of a misunderstanding, while men in the ilk of Lord Havington, who thought nothing of stealing kisses from innocent women, should be allowed to roam free.

The room was deep in shadows, the walls flickering softly with reflections of firelight. Out of habit, Constance stopped first at the liquor cabinet and poured a stream of claret-colored port into the shallow bowl of a delicately carved glass. Rubbing her neck, she took a sip and walked to the welcome blaze set in the hearth. Two large armchairs faced the fire, and Constance chose the right. Mesmerized by flames, she moved by memory.

And sat down, ending right in someone's lap.

To her amazement, she did not scream. She jumped up, mortified to find she had sat right atop Lord Havington.

The earl looked just as surprised as she.

Of a sudden, Constance realized she held a glass of port in her hand. "My Lord," she stuttered, "I . . . I wished to surprise you. I poured a glass of port for you." She held her arm out stiffly, as if she couldn't stand far enough away from the offending snifter.

"I already have a glass, madam." Marcus's expression was unreadable as he watched her, his eyes hooded.

"So I see." She swallowed nervously; her throat was dry.

Constance imagined herself raising her glass in salute, tossing the hot liquid down her throat in one gulp, and smashing the glass cavalierly into the fireplace just before she marched out of the room.

"What are you smiling at, Constance?"

Constance. He'd used her given name. And she definitely had not given him leave to use it! Did the man think by kissing her, he could now take all sorts of improper liberties? Think again, sir.

His slurred words replayed in her head. She noted the empty decanter at his elbow and the strong, sweet smell of liquor surrounding him. Ahh, the man was in his cups.

"I was smiling at . . . nothing. Just a rather pleasant thought . . . Marcus." *Let's see just how far in his cups he is,* she thought. *Perhaps I'll even have a little fun.*

"Did you just call me Marcush?" he asked slowly.

"Oh, no, my Lord. I would never be so presumptuous. Good night, then."

She didn't lie. She had called him "Marcus," not "Marcush."

CHAPTER ELEVEN

Huddled in concentration over the book on her lap, Constance was unaware of Lord Havington as he peeked into the room. She sat on the velvet sofa with a pool of books on the floor at her feet.

He paused a moment at the threshold, drinking in the tranquil scene. It was a vision for a painting: The sunlight slanted in, golden highlights shimmering in her curls. Her lemon morning gown hazily reflected the soft light and her white-stockinged legs were tucked beneath her. With a soft maize ribbon pulling the curls up, away from her face, she could have been a young schoolgirl. He tiptoed in and came around behind the sofa, attempting to peek over her shoulder to discern what held her so transfixed.

Constance looked up at the empty doorway. Mentally shrugging, she bent to her book, but a shadow fell across its pages. Gasping, she twisted quickly toward the window. Marcus blocked the light.

"Lord Havington! You gave me an awful fright! And what are you doing sneaking up on me?"

"I do apologize, Miss Violet." He laughed. "You were so engrossed in your book, I must confess I was hesitant to disturb you. But, now I see I have done just that."

Constance nodded, accepting his apology, and filing the information away for later digestion. The earl apologizing yet again? *Well, well.* Plus, he did seem in an unusually good mood this morning.

He stepped closer, peering. "May I inquire what you are reading that is so fascinating?"

"It's not Mrs. Carver, my Lord," she answered in a bored monotone without looking up from her book.

Tilting his head, he attempted to read the cover. Constance closed her book with a sigh and handed it up to him.

"*The Compleat Angler,*" he read aloud. "By Isaak Walton, Esquire."

She tilted her chin a bit, waiting for the judgment guillotine to fall. But it did not. He perused the table of contents, flipped to where her ribboned marker rested, and appeared to be absorbed. Constance cleared her throat.

Sheepishly, he handed it back to her. "I've

been wanting to read this very book. May I borrow it when you've finished?"

"Certainly," she drew the word out cautiously.

He came around to the front of the sofa, and picked up a book from the pile on the floor. "*Tretyse of Fishing With the Angle.*"

Squatting down, he became absorbed in other titles. "Miss Violet . . ." He looked up; they were practically eye-to-eye. "You have chosen some excellent books from the library. Is this an interest of yours?"

"Yes," she drew out her answer again, not ready to admit these were her own books. "Are you an angler, my Lord?"

He chuckled, and said with an attractive modesty, "I *attempt* to angle, but I must admit it is not one of my more polished skills. However, I do enjoy practicing the technique."

Constance enthused, "And to tie your own flies?"

"Yes. Do you tie your own, as well?"

Constance unfolded her legs, ready to jump up to retrieve her gear and to pursue this discussion of one of her favorite hobbies.

"But . . ." He stretched out his hand, signaling her to stop. "Please don't get up, Miss Violet. Perhaps another time. That is not why I came in here, actually."

"No? Did you seek me out for a purpose then, my Lord?"

"I most certainly did." He was unusually cheerful. Crossing the room toward the door, he smiled over his shoulder. "Would you mind if I invited my sister to join us, Miss Violet?"

"No, of course not." She determined to be as friendly as she found the earl today. Was he going to make an announcement? Had he come to a conclusion about leaving his sister in her care? My goodness, and it was about time. The earl had been practically living on their doorstep for almost a month now.

Havington exited and was back only minutes later with Larissa. He beamed at them both.

Larissa laughed. "My goodness, brother, I cannot remember the last time I've seen you in such excellent spirits. Is this a special occasion?"

"Yes, sister, it is, and I have a very special treat for you. In fact, I find I can barely contain my own excitement, and *I* already know the surprise."

Larissa clapped her hands together, exclaiming, "I love surprises!"

"Another autographed book of Mrs.

Carver's?" asked Constance, but felt churlish on seeing how her comment deflated Larissa.

The earl appeared not to have heard. He motioned Larissa to a chair with a sweep of his arm.

Larissa hurried over to an armchair and sat with her hands clasped expectantly on her lap.

"Now —" said Lord Havington, "— I shall sit . . ." He glanced around briefly. "Here." And he lowered his tall frame into a deep armchair. "Ah. Quite comfortable."

Both women looked at each other, and Constance grinned and shrugged. They turned back to the earl, awaiting the next unfolding of the plot.

Lord Havington, however, simply turned his head and smiled broadly at Constance. She raised her eyebrows, still smiling.

When still nothing was offered by him, Larissa prompted, "Yes? Marcus, what is this about?"

Without looking at his sister, Havington watched Constance as he announced, "Miss Violet has a special treat in store for us, Larissa."

Constance, still smiling, said, "I'm sure I do not know what his Lordship is alluding to."

151

"Mrs. Carver? Does that ring a bell, Miss Violet?"

The smile immediately disappeared from Constance's face.

"What, Constance? Do tell!" encouraged Larissa.

"Allow me, Larissa," her brother began. "Miss Violet has graciously offered to recite for us. She has chosen a passage from . . . let me see, I believe it was to be from *Mrs. Carver's Hints for Young Ladies?* Do I have that correct, Miss Violet?"

Larissa looked stunned.

Constance's brows came together. "Yes." *How unsporting.* She finally lost a game in their cribbage series, and he intended to extract his winnings in front of her friend.

"I believe Miss Violet has found an especially appropriate selection she desires to share." He held out a hand, palm up, toward Constance.

"I don't know that we agreed upon *publicly performing* our little verse, Lord Havington," Constance said. "What was it you pointed out to me? About winning graciously?"

"Come, come, Miss Violet. Let's not be petty. I just assumed this would be edifying for my sister. And you know how much *I* adore Mrs. Carver."

Constance gritted her teeth. He'd lost the

152

first two games, but won the third. All right. She would show him just how gracefully she could accept the terms of their agreement.

She cleared her throat, rolled her eyes, and spoke from memory in an extremely bored monotone:

"A young woman who marries and assumes management of a household is always aware of her comportment and appearance. Appearance is everything. She is, after all, an adornment to her husband's properties. In dealings with the staff, she is also a representative of her husband's authority. As such, she is careful to remain on the highest level, and to keep a social distance between the staff and herself. She may converse with the governess on matters pertaining to the nursery, and she may converse with the cook on matters pertaining to the pantry and the menu. Thus should she limit any conversations with those below her station."

Staring at Marcus, she was quite in a temper to see him grinning.

"Well done, Miss Violet, well done! Charming!" He laughed.

They were interrupted as Barrows

knocked and entered. "My Lady," Barrows turned to Constance, but remembered his role and turned, flustered, to Larissa. "My Lady," he began again, "Per Lord Havington's suggestion, I took the liberty to inform Mrs. Dewberry we shall serve tea in here, shortly." As he spoke, he advanced to spread a crisp white table linen upon the tea table nearest to Larissa's chair.

"That would be fine, thank you," answered Larissa with a measure of shyness.

He turned to leave, when Marcus stopped him. "Barrows —"

"Yes, my Lord?" Barrows turned attentively toward the earl.

"How is your niece's cold? I believe her name is Amy?"

Barrows smiled, obviously pleased the earl remembered her name. "She is doing much better. I thank your Lordship for asking."

Mrs. Dewberry chose that moment to bring in the tray, and Barrows moved to assist.

As the housekeeper busily moved about, Marcus commented, "Thank you, Mrs. Dewberry. As usual, everything looks delicious. Are these the scones," he asked, "from that special recipe you gave Mrs. Eldridge? The recipe handed down to you by your grandmother?"

Mrs. Dewberry flushed with pleasure. "My goodness, my Lord, you do have quite a memory. Yes, they are. Since you said you liked them, I asked Cook to bake a fresh batch. With currants. I do hope you enjoy these with the currants," she twittered.

Bobbing a quick curtsy to Lord Havington, she exited the parlour, followed by Barrows.

Larissa sat in her chair and looked dazed. Constance reciting Mrs. Carver? Her brother knowing the names of the staff? And chatting personably with them? In spite of what Mrs. Carver said about being overly familiar with the servants? Larissa was sure the world had just turned topsy-turvy.

Constance, on the other hand, was most pleased. The earl was, after all, impressively sportsmanlike. Not only had he extracted *her* payment from their bargain, he had clearly paid his own dues as well.

If he forced her to recite in front of Larissa in order to have fun at Constance's expense, he'd at least been gracious enough to let them have fun at his own expense as well.

Lord Havington glanced at her across the room, and she nodded her approval with a dimpled smile. When he winked in return, however, her eyes flew first to Larissa, who thankfully had not noticed, and then to the

155

tea set so he would not see her embarrassment.

Humph, she snorted to herself. Should she remind him what Mrs. Carver would most likely say about gentlemen winking at ladies?

She had half a notion to look it up, and recite *that* to his Lordship! Of course, this would only give the man satisfaction, so she quickly discarded both halves of the notion and moved to help Larissa serve.

CHAPTER TWELVE

Mrs. Dewberry responded to the ringing at the servants' entrance and opened the door to find a gangly youth, cap in hand, and a sway-backed horse tied to the nearby post.

"Good day, mum." He bobbed his head and held out an elegant envelope that looked out of place in his grimy hand. "I's supposed to deliver this to Miss Violet. Be she here, mum?"

Mrs. Dewberry reached for the missive, but the boy snatched it back, holding it to his chest.

"Are you Miss Violet, then?" he asked with skeptical inspection, still trapping the envelope.

"I am the housekeeper, young man," Mrs. Dewberry lectured in her sternest tone, "and I will see that her Ladyship — I mean, Miss Violet — receives this letter immediately." And on the last word she snatched the letter from the unsuspecting lad.

"But," he whined, "I was told I was to give it only to Miss Violet, directly-like, and if I do, then there's another shilling waiting for me at the Inn."

"Well then, for heaven's sake, tell your benefactor . . ." Mrs. Dewberry turned it over and scrutinized the wax seal. "Tell his Lordship you gave it directly to Miss Violet, then."

"But . . ." The lad still looked upset. "Begging your pardon, mum, but his Lordship says he will be expectin' a description from me to verify I delivered it right and proper. And he says she's quite young . . . and . . . er . . . not at all plump, begging yer pardon." He colored from his homespun collar to his hairline, waiting to see if the stout woman would box his ears.

Mrs. Dewberry harrumphed.

Remembering a comical instance Constance had confided, she added with an evil twinkle, "If you want to earn that shilling, you must tell his Lordship that Miss Violet is most beautiful, with hair the color of honey. And be sure to add she was wearing a very gauzy morning dress, which was cut much too low for modesty's sake. You can bet your boots only then will he believe you. Now be off with you."

With that, she shut the door on the cheeky

ragamuffin.

"My Lady, this was just delivered by a young lad up from the village."

Constance took the sealed envelope from Mrs. Dewberry. On the front, in a bold script, it read "Miss Constance Violet, Rose-Hill Manor."

Constance turned it over and recognized the Havington imprint in the maroon wax. Before breaking the seal, she glanced up to find Mrs. Dewberry standing on tiptoe, craning her neck to see what new turmoil his Lordship would wreak upon their household.

Constance couldn't fault the woman's curiosity. Life at the manor used to be so simple. Now there was a new pretense or a new crisis to deal with every day since Larissa and her brother had descended and taken over her home. Still, Constance raised her eyebrows at the housekeeper, in the gentlest of reproofs. Mrs. Dewberry pivoted her eyes up and to the side, as if she hadn't been snooping at all, and turned and left the parlour.

Constance carried the envelope to her favorite chair and sank down with the unopened missive in her hand. She hesitated, not ready to open it.

My goodness, I feel I need a brandy . . . not that I'm allowed to drink in my own home anymore. What does that insane man want now?

With a burgeoning resentment, she ripped the envelope open a bit more roughly than necessary and scanned the small enclosed note card:

Madam, I require your discreet presence, as we have a business matter to discuss. Attend me at the Toad & Tackle as soon as you receive this.

M.

She did not care for his high-handed tone. Constance perused the note a second time, to be sure her resentment of the earl didn't paint it to be more strongly worded than it was. But no, it was in fact a royal command, worded exactly like every other sentence that came out of the man's mouth.

And what did he mean by *discreet presence?* Was he afraid she would turn up wearing her fishing outfit, for goodness' sake? Or — the truth struck her — did he fear she would tell his sister of this mysterious rendezvous?

She jumped up from the chair, determined to march right to Larissa and show her the note.

Midstride she paused. Perhaps he wanted to surprise Larissa. Perhaps he decided to leave the area, allowing his sister to enjoy her time in the country in peace. But if so, why not tell Larissa himself? Ah — she brought the note up to her face for a third scrutiny: *"We have a business matter to discuss."* That explained it. Constance was an employee; he would first want to tie up all loose business ends, etc.

This brought a smile. How very typical of the overly efficient man. And — one must be fair — how generous to think of the companion's welfare before removing himself from the county.

The village was not a long walk away, and it was a nice day for a stroll. Besides, it might do the earl a bit of good to learn that not everyone took off galloping when he commanded. On the other hand, she was sorely tempted to put a saddle on Jasmine. She pictured herself innocently explaining that Jasmine was swift of hoof, and he had himself stipulated "as soon as you receive this."

I really am unrepentant, she thought with a sigh. It seemed she delighted in thinking up ways to foil the dictator at every opportunity. She asked one of the younger footmen to attend her, and set off walking for the village inn.

Marcus drummed his fingers on the smooth table.

He'd positioned himself in a private corner of the inn, from where he could keep an eye on the entrance. With a fire roaring on the opposite wall and clean straw covering the cold stone floor, the room was cozy and draftless. The beeswax candles and copper lanterns gave a honeyed warmth to the room, inviting intimate conversation and camaraderie.

But Marcus took no notice of the candles or the lanterns. His temper rose as he tallied up every transgression Miss Violet had ever subjected him to.

First, she should have been here by now. He purposely chose an inn in the nearby village, which should have taken a matter of minutes by carriage. He knew she'd received his summons; the lad had collected the remainder of his promised fee. In fact, Miss Violet should have been able to arrive before the errand boy, if she'd promptly sent to the stables for the carriage, as she should have.

Second, the boy's confirmation had not improved the earl's mood. He could still hear the lad's embarrassed description of how he'd found the young woman dressed when he delivered his note. The boy could not even look up from his toes to meet Marcus's eyes, as he informed him that she was a beautiful young lady. And, he stammered on, she wore a thin morning dress, and left quite a bit of herself exposed, if his Lordship knew what he meant.

By God, his Lordship did know what the lad meant. Marcus still hadn't erased the vision of Constance at the breakfast table leaning forward for the sugar bowl.

It also meant the woman still disregarded his instructions. His jaw clenched. So, she demurely acknowledged his commands, but when he was out of earshot and eyeshot, she snapped her fingers in dismissal of his wishes.

In as long as he could remember, he had no experience of his authority ever being questioned. As an officer, the men he commanded jumped instantly at whatever Marcus voiced aloud.

Aye, even when he whispered — especially when he whispered — they obeyed without question. Since he'd come into his title, he could not think of a single servant ever blatantly disobeying. If they had, they'd have been booted out the door by Marcus himself, and with no references. In his mind, a companion was still hired help. Granted, she might be a genteel lady of noble background. But she sought employment, which made her an employee. And he was the employer.

Third — there was the matter of that horse he'd caught her with down at the river. She'd denied it, of course. Lord help her if she arrived here today on that horse . . . Jasper, or Jance, or whatever its name was.

The door opened, casting afternoon light across the threshold.

His head snapped up, and with a quickening in his chest he saw it was Miss Violet. She was breathing a little too deeply, and he tried not to notice the rise and fall of her exquisite bosom in the fitted walking outfit. The dark gold velvet of the spencer was a perfect foil for the gold highlights of her disheveled mane. She must have run to her room to change out of the revealing clothes. She must think him the gullible fool.

Marcus took his own deep breath. He must calm down, or he'd frighten her away.

She started across the room. He would offer her a mug of cider and lure her into a sense of ease. He could afford to play a steady hand, and delay interrogating her as to her lateness. In fact, he found himself looking forward to her latest Banbury tale.

Constance let the door close against the bright sunlight. She squinted as her eyes adjusted to the shadowy inn. She spied the earl in the far corner, in an alcove that looked a little too private for propriety's sake.

She instructed the footman to wait outside the inn. She hadn't hurried; why was her heart beating so rapidly? Acknowledging the innkeeper with a nod in Havington's direction, she made her way to the table, breathing deeply in an effort to calm herself.

Lord Havington stood and made an elegant bow. Constance, surprised, responded automatically with a simple curtsy. He reached out his hand, palm up, and she placed her fingers on the edge of his hand. Instinctively his fingers curled around hers. With his other hand he gestured for her to sit.

Constance, disoriented by the electric response of his grasp, allowed the touch longer than was appropriate. Abruptly she pulled her hand away and sat down a little too quickly on the hard bench.

The glow of the candles and the fire left pools of welcome warmth where they filled the hollows of the earl's face and neck. He smelled of horse and leather. Constance found herself peeking at his broad shoulders as he sat in the warm room without his jacket. It was obvious he was a gentleman and a man of authority.

And, she reminded herself, he was a man about to make a generous gesture for his sister. How had she never seen this noble, handsome side to him before? She smiled dreamily up at Lord Havington as he retook his seat.

"Yes, my Lord?" Her voice was soft, docile.

Havington returned her smile hesitantly. "Miss Violet, thank you for coming . . . though, a little tardily, I might add."

Her smile thinned and her chin went up slightly, but she said nothing.

His eyes were intense as he watched her. "Did it take such a long time to change your outfit?"

Constance stiffened. "I beg your pardon?"

"Come, come. You know exactly what I mean, Miss Violet."

"I am afraid I do not." Her voice snapped with impatience. "I haven't the slightest idea to what you refer. Nor is it an appropriate topic of conversation between us, my Lord."

She noted the tick in his jaw just before he looked away. When he looked back, his eyes were mild. "As you say. Let's not waste our time arguing, shall we, Miss Violet? I'd prefer a quick and successful conclusion to this meeting." He forced a smile, though to Constance it looked more like he was baring his teeth.

"That sounds sensible," she said. "One of us has duties to attend to." She straightened her skirt prissily.

Again she noted the grimace of white teeth. "I asked you here to inform you . . . of late, I have been remiss in my business duties."

"Is it because his Lordship is constantly dawdling at RoseHill Manor?" she asked sweetly.

"Why I have been remiss should be no concern of yours, I assure you."

Noting another tensing of his jaw, she decided not to bait the man. She feigned a bored expression and waited for him to continue.

"I find my presence is now required in London."

She worked hard at maintaining her mien air of blandness, when inside she felt a stab of dismay. *This is absurd,* she thought, analyzing the melancholic twinge. *I should be ecstatic the man will finally be leaving. It is exactly as I anticipated from his note. I should be happy for Larissa, not selfishly saddened.*

"I should leave immediately," continued Lord Havington. "However, this evening I plan to remain and shall escort both of you as promised." He looked at Constance with his brow lowered, as if daring her to make another petty remark about his accompanying them to the dance.

She wisely recognized the look, and sat quietly with her hands folded primly on the table.

"In the morning, I shall be on my way to town. As I expect to be solidly occupied while there, I desire to tie any loose strings at RoseHill before I go."

Constance's heart sang. She was right; he was taking the leash off Larissa. She brightened in anticipation, and even considered telling him the truth about her identity. But no, it must come from his own sister. Larissa would have the opportunity to tell her own brother tonight — or in the morning, if she so chose.

Looking down, playing with a well-groomed thumbnail, he began, "After this employment, Miss Violet, what does the future hold for you?" He glanced back up, waited for her response.

She smiled. It touched her that the earl worried about her welfare, and her next "assignment." Knowing it to be bratty, she queried softly, "Is it possible . . . could his Lordship see to providing me with a written reference?" She made her eyes large, and hoped she appeared feminine and helpless.

The earl smiled in return. *Why was she reminded of a hunter who had cornered his prey?*

"Why, I think that could be arranged. You have *certainly* been the epitome of a proper companion . . . except, perhaps, for your immodest mode of dress? And, of course, there is that impertinence in your eyes that tells me you do not take direction well. Also, now I think of it, you appear to disobey the most specific —"

Constance coughed, covering her mouth with a fist. Looking down to hide the simmering in her eyes, she pretended to be embarrassed. *Just one more day,* she said to the tableware as she unclenched her hand and joined it to the other.

Her head flew up when Lord Havington reached over and covered her clasped hands with one of his. "Forgive me. That was unkind. I was merely teasing you, Miss Violet. Of course I should be happy to provide you with a reference. With my comital seal upon the document."

Constance looked at his large hand covering hers. Was this why men and women were not to hold ungloved hands? His hand on hers made her toes tingle. Though it was not an unpleasant tingling. She turned uncomfortably pink.

Lord Havington released her hand and signaled the innkeeper for another tankard of ale. "And a cider for madam," he said, when the man hurried over.

"I prefer lemonade, thank you," Constance corrected.

The round, aproned innkeeper turned his head inquiringly toward Lord Havington, waiting for approval.

"That's fine." Havington dismissed him.

Constance glared at the proprietor's back as he walked away to do the earl's bidding. "And did he intend to force me to drink cider, I'd like to know, if you had not given your approval?" she sputtered. "Are all males in a conspiracy, or do they truly believe women have no more brains in their heads than a wheel of cheese?"

The earl laughed. "I shall miss your quick temper, madam. And your observations. London will be so boring — beautiful women, but no thoughts in their heads. Now I shall picture myself dancing with wedges of cheese for the next few weeks."

"Are they . . . ? All?"

"All what?" he asked.

"Extraordinarily beautiful?" She couldn't stop herself from wanting to know.

Lord Havington squirmed. "That's not what I meant to say. That was rude of me." He studied her. "You've never had a Season, have you?"

"No." She looked down. "Perhaps it's for the best, if I would have stood out to a disadvantage." When he hesitated, she knew his response could not be honest. "It's of no matter, my Lord. I did not mean to appear petty. It was a silly question."

"You don't know, do you?" He waited until she glanced up. "You would be a jewel among them, Miss Violet."

"Of course." She looked her amusement at his attempt at gallantry. "Shall we return to the business at hand?"

Lord Havington cleared his throat. "As I began to say, madam —" He paused as the innkeeper arrived to bang the heavy mugs on the table and scurried away. "— I can no longer afford the luxury of waiting upon my sister, every day, in order to keep a brotherly eye on her."

"Nor should you," chimed in Constance in beaming approval.

"Nor should I. Exactly. I'm glad we see eye-to-eye so far." In spite of his words about eye-to-eye, he lowered his gaze, staring at his mug. "I'm not aware of what my sister has promised you in salary . . . but I'm offering you the chance to *double it.*"

This makes no sense, thought Constance. *Why is he offering more money?*

The earl looked up as if reading her thoughts, and said in a firm businessman's tone, "In addition to the money, I can promise you an excellent written reference."

She looked down at the lemonade, suspicious someone had drugged her. Then she looked back up, waiting, hoping he would soon make sense.

"All you have to do, Miss Violet, in order to earn the extra income — *and* the reference — is to convince Larissa this summer adventure should now come to a close. Tell her you have recalled other immediate engagements — or some such. I don't care how you do it, but you must persuade her it is time for her to return home, to Amber Crossing."

Constance's dainty chin dropped, leaving her small mouth gaping. "I do not understand." She shook her head. "Why? Whatever would be the reason for encouraging Lady Larissa to return home, when she is enjoying herself so very much?"

"Come, Miss Violet, I believe I've made

myself extremely clear. Let's not have theatrics. This is a simple business deal. It is time to stop this charade."

Her heart stopped. *Did he know?* "What charade?" Guilt flashed across her face.

"Enough, madam. You think to increase the ante, is that it? All right. Though I must tell you I'm disappointed in your greed."

"What?" Constance no longer knew what the earl was talking about.

"I've told you," he said, a cold edge to each word, "I am leaving for London, and I intend to see this business wrapped up. I want Larissa to end this spoiled game, and I want her home. Now. I do not intend to spend my time in town worrying about her. She is simply using RoseHill as her giant dollhouse, playing at dressing up and being lady of the house. I expect you to convince her this little tea party is over." His eyes were as cold as his voice. "In exchange, as I've indicated, you will be extremely well compensated. I will *triple* —" He enunciated the word clearly. "— whatever she offered you. And you will have a reference that will open any exclusive doors to you, as either a governess or a companion."

Constance's first reaction was relief as she realized he had not uncovered her role playing.

Her second reaction was fury. His meaning sank in: He wanted her to betray her best friend. Not only that, this was his own sister he connived against. Constance finally understood just how autocratic the earl could be. Larissa was correct. The man was a dictator, a bounder.

The emerald cyclones forming in her eyes delivered an early storm warning. Her hands balled into white fists, and she shook visibly as she asked in a strained voice, "And . . . you actually thought I would help you in this?"

"Come now, Miss Violet. Everyone has their price. Are you being coy so you can squeeze more money from me? I offered to double your salary, and that obviously had you grabbing for more. If tripling isn't enough, then let's cut to the chase." He leaned forward, impatiently asked, "How much did you think you could extort? Don't you realize I could end this on my own, this minute, without paying you another shilling?"

"I don't want any of your money," she whispered fiercely, afraid someone might overhear and misunderstand. Though he might as well be propositioning her; he made her feel so unclean. "I'm not a . . . a lady of *that* profession," she continued her thoughts out loud. "So don't suppose you can buy me as if I were."

"No, it's obvious you're not." Lord Havington scoffed. "I'm offering to pay you more handsomely than a prostitute would expect, and for considerably less of your time and attention."

She flinched at his coarseness.

"You're more the price of a demanding mistress," he pressed, "but without any of the benefits."

Constance colored. "Well, you ought to know the bartering rates, sir. I'm sure with your odious manners, you're forced to pay for women's favors." With this, she put her hands flat on the table, intending to push herself up.

But he was quicker. He clamped a vice on her wrists, holding her down, and said dangerously, "Sit."

They glared at each other across the short distance.

Havington released her. "If you cross me on this, Miss Violet, understand: Larissa *will* be coming home, regardless. I plan to return to RoseHill in approximately a sennight. If you have not been successful, then I will take her home myself and you will be out on your ear. Without an extra shilling. And," he added pointedly, "without a reference."

"You, sir, are the worst cad. I cannot believe you would do this to your own sister, and all for the convenience of no longer desiring to spy upon her. You should have trusted her and returned to London weeks ago, instead of subjecting her to your suffocating control. And I cannot believe you think I would go along with this underhanded scheme. It is unfortunate you carry a noble title, for you are not noble at all. You are certainly not even a gentleman."

The earl, red in the face, raised his voice to say, "If you were a man, Miss Violet, I would challenge you to a duel for those words."

Constance stood slowly, to look down at him with as much disdain as she could muster. "And if I knew how to use a weapon — any weapon, my Lord — I would challenge *you* to a duel, in defense of your helpless sister." She stiffened her shoulders, and turned her back on him.

"Remember, Miss Violet: if you fail, there will be no reference."

"Enough!" She turned and leaned toward him slightly, to make sure he would hear her, but that others nearby should not. "You — may — take — your *bloody* reference, Lord Havington — *and* your sharpened quill — and put them —"

Havington jumped to his feet, and she spun and fled.

CHAPTER THIRTEEN

Marcus sat in shock. Well, he'd seen the lady's true nature rise to the surface. And it was what he'd waited for all this time, wasn't it? She had the mouth of a lass born in the stews. He'd always suspected a wild banshee hid behind that gentle facade.

But he didn't feel smug with the discovery, nor did he feel triumphant. Nor did he feel at all good about himself.

She was right: she had acted with more honor toward his sister than he. Miss Violet — a mere companion — had been willing to defend her charge's happiness, even if it meant turning her back on a small fortune. She'd done it out of goodness and honor. If she were a man, he could not have admired her more. He was proud of her, as if she'd survived a test. And she had.

But he also realized she would now have time to think about it, and the financial reality would hit. And money was all women cared about in the end, anyway.

No, that wasn't fair. She was not a greedy miss of the *ton*. She was a woman who must survive on her own wits. Honor was not something she could casually afford.

Perhaps I should have offered her a Season, he thought. I can easily foot the bill for both ladies, and Larissa appears to treasure Miss Violet's company. He envisioned the two young women together, attending a glittering affair. Men flocked around the companion, just to peer down her ridiculously improper gowns. A faceless stranger danced too closely with Miss Violet; perhaps they waltzed. It seemed the waltz was now acceptable at every *ton* soiree. The man pulled the companion against his chest, too closely, an unyielding arm around her slender waist, leading her with his leg brushing against her skirts.

"No, a Season is out of the question," Marcus swore to an almost-empty tankard of ale.

He tipped it up for the last swallow and his chuckle echoed in the empty pewter mug. A sharpened quill? He thought of her wild curls as she'd leaned forward to give him the parting shot. He smelled the herbs and flowers released as her massive locks had dangled close by.

She'd be gone soon. In the next couple of days she would think about his offer, and he knew which way she must decide. In the meantime, he had a score to settle with her for her impertinence, and a dance to claim. He looked forward to seeing her again tonight.

Lord Havington chuckled again, stretching out his booted legs, and signaled the innkeeper for another ale.

Desperately in thought as she walked back to the manor, Constance forgot about the footman who followed a discreet distance behind. Her eyes again widened in shock at how she'd spoken to the earl. Good mercy, she didn't even *have* a temper . . . at least, she hadn't had one before she'd met Lord Havington.

What was she to do? It did not appear she could protect Larissa from her brother's scheme. Nor could she dissuade Lord Havington. Larissa was correct about one thing: If they confessed the ruse at this late date, the outcome would be the same. He'd yank his sister back to Amber Crossing. Sooner than expected. Larissa's summer adventure would end immediately. Now.

And what if Constance had truly been a simple companion? Poor Larissa would not have stood a chance at the mercy of someone who desperately needed the money. Thank goodness the earl didn't realize Constance was immune to his bribery and his threats. She was not about to end Larissa's holiday one day earlier than need be.

What to do in the meantime? Should she tell Larissa the truth the moment she returned, and see her heart broken? Well, he would break it himself in seven days' time. Perhaps she wouldn't tell her friend just yet. Perhaps instead, Constance could begin preparing Larissa with gradual hints.

What if she were to take Larissa on a holiday — say, to Bath? It gave her shivers to contemplate something so bold, so risky. The thought of the earl tracking them down made her heart palpitate; Bath was out of the question.

She should face reality and inform Larissa of the truth as soon as she reached the manor. They would still have a number of days to enjoy one another's company. And he said he'd be in London, so she could guarantee his sister the freedom to finally do as they pleased, for one entire week.

But could Larissa enjoy herself with the threat of early return to Amber Crossing? She'd dwell on the coming sojourn under her brother's thumb, with no Aunt Marguerite and Uncle Nigel to buffer the unbearable atmosphere.

Should Constance keep her friend ignorant for another week, shopping and picnicking without a care?

With the gatehouse in sight, Constance was no closer to a decision than when she'd set out from the inn. Seeing the tops of the chimneys of RoseHill always lifted her spirits, reminded her of coming home to her great-aunt. What would Aunt Agatha have done?

The grand woman possessed marvelous good sense. She also nurtured a circle of friends who confided in one another and sought each other's counsel, a luxury Constance did not have. That is what Aunt Agatha would have done. She would have sought the counsel of trusted friends before coming to her own decision. Unfortunately, Larissa was Constance's only close friend, and she couldn't very well ask Larissa for advice on what to tell herself.

If only, Constance wished, *I had an older, wiser friend such as Aunt Agatha had enjoyed.*

That was it! What about the Dowager Duchess, Lady Amelia? She'd been one of Aunt Agatha's closest friends. Perhaps she would be willing to offer advice. It would be worth a try. Constance could promise Larissa a shopping trip to London, where the dowager duchess would be in residence.

Constance felt much better, now having a solid plan of attack. She would say nothing to Larissa on this day, allowing her friend to enjoy tonight's party. In the morning, after Lord Havington left, she would announce plans to visit London to do some shopping. All they need do was be sure they avoided the earl, which should not be difficult in so large a town. Then, while she left Larissa for fittings, with a footman to watch over her, Constance would slip away for an afternoon visit with the dowager duchess.

She'd pen a letter the moment she returned to the manor.

She no longer felt so alone. She enjoyed the sparrows darting in and out of the thorn hedges along the lane, and the warm sunlight filtering through the sycamores.

One cloud remained as her thoughts turned again to the disgusting interview at the inn. If only there was some way to get even with the man. She would *not* give him the dance they'd discussed, this was certain. She'd secretly looked forward to it, the physical nearness of his tall figure, the thrill of his low voice as he leaned toward her. The memory of his kiss. . . . Her heart hardened. No, she would not dance with the earl.

She admitted she'd pictured herself being swept into his strong arms for a waltz, glissading to the crescendos of the orchestra. She could see it so clearly now, hear the music . . . and then, with a cacophonic whine, the instruments came to a discordant halt as the earl stopped the dance, informing everyone in the room that waltzing was inappropriate for young ladies, according to Mrs. Carver. The guests and the band disappeared from her imaginary ballroom.

She was certain the waltz must be on Lord Havington's tireless list of unacceptable activities for young la — she almost stumbled upon the stairs of the manor, as she tripped upon a sudden idea.

She knew now what she could do to get even, in the tiniest of ways, but enough to give her a sense of satisfaction. And she would do it, just to spite him. As the footman opened the door she hurried breathlessly through the house.

She found Larissa in the yellow parlour.

"Larissa, I have the most wonderful surprise! But you must promise not to breathe a word of it to your brother."

Larissa looked up with a slight fear at the idea of crossing her brother. But her love of surprises was greater and she held her breath, waiting to hear her friend's news.

Constance came over and gave her a fierce hug, then stepped away so she could enjoy her friend's expression. Slowly, she announced, "Larissa, you and I are going to host a masquerade ball."

CHAPTER FOURTEEN

Larissa sparkled, chatting with animation. Constance couldn't remember the last time she'd seen her friend this carefree. Well, on second thought, yes she could. Larissa had always glowed, before her brother had returned home to Amber Crossing. Lately she'd been more like a rabbit, startled at every odd noise. But tonight she shone, a glimpse of her old self.

The earl would be arriving soon to escort them to the Baron and Baroness Montague's, and even his appearance could not seem to dampen Larissa's mood. She was beautiful, flushed with anticipation. Her lavender silk gown complemented her dark hair and her ivory skin. The fan she held was a darker shade of purple, as were her slippers. Her hair was done up in curls and several fragrant lavender and pink blossoms were tucked into her upswept hair.

Constance wore a fern-green silk. A little

daring perhaps, for a country function, she had stipulated the dress be patterned in the fashion of a Grecian lady. It was comprised of several diaphanous layers, which shimmered in straight lines from the high waist to the tops of her matching slippers. Draped over one shoulder was a sheer panel, flowing behind as she walked, secured with an emerald and diamond brooch. This left the other shoulder bared, though if it were cool she could always bring the silk panel up and across, to use as a light stole to keep out the breeze.

Her honey-striped hair was held back from her face with intertwining strings of crystal and emerald drops, and cascaded down her back. She was satisfied with the dress, but sighed at her looking glass. Rather than the perfectly groomed Grecian chignon she desired, her wild mane already sprung loose curls.

As the ladies admired each other's outfits, it was announced that the earl had arrived downstairs.

Constance pulled on one long, pastel green glove, carefully stretching and smoothing it up to her elbow, as Larissa hurried ahead, fearful of keeping her brother waiting.

Constance followed in her friend's wake

and descended the stairs carefully, concentrating on tugging and coaxing on her other glove. She didn't miss a step, and when she reached out for the banister and lifted her eyes, she found Larissa and her brother waiting at the bottom of the stairs.

Marcus crossed the hall to wait for the ladies at the foot of the stairs. He chose not to remove his hat and gloves, as they would soon be on their way. Knowing some ladies dawdled, he would not tolerate that sort of missish behavior — not from his sister, and certainly not from her companion.

Footsteps approached the upper landing. He saw Larissa and his heart swelled with brotherly pride at her elegance. Upon reaching the last step, she hesitated, and the earl gallantly bowed to his sister, smiling his approval.

Straightening, he looked up in impatience, waiting for her companion. As Constance descended the circular stairway his breath stopped. The lady was beautiful. Enchanting was more exact, resembling a fairy of the forest, sparkling and filmy. Filmy? His eyelids narrowed at the sheerness of her gown. This was definitely not the dress he had described to his sister for procurement for tonight's outing. He'd specifically asked

Larissa to have a dress made for her companion at his expense, and suitable to her station.

A low-cut bodice might be in current fashion among the *ton,* but this was not appropriate for a companion escorting his sister. Once again he pictured a crowd of gentlemen all standing suffocatingly close to his sister, attempting to enjoy Miss Violet's graces.

His good mood soured with each silent descent of her slippered feet. He began tapping his evening cane against the calves of his boots as she approached, revealing more with every step. No wonder she did not dare to meet his eyes. The earl was tempted to forbid her to go.

When she reached the bottom of the stairs, she glanced up briefly and curtsied. The curtsy was his undoing, for she displayed everything he had imagined, now he towered over her. He recalled the morning at the breakfast table. His memories were not exaggerated.

He pictured sitting across from Miss Violet in their carriage as the coach jostled them along the country roads. . . . Well, perhaps not allowing her to come was a bit too strong. After all, he was their escort. All he need do was hover nearby, to ensure no local rakes would be ogling her.

And, of course, she would be so disappointed if he did not allow her the dance he had promised.

This made perfect sense. He found his mood improving already.

The threesome in the coach made an odd trio. Larissa was a canary, chirping merrily as the countryside flew past. Lord Havington, sitting at his sister's side, conversed easily with her, and they both attempted to draw Constance into their conversations.

Though Constance answered Larissa directly, warmly, in a quiet voice, she avoided the earl's gaze. It was as if there were a solid divider in the carriage.

When the earl addressed a question to her, she answered with a minimum of words, staring out the window as she did so; as if she found the darkening scenery extremely fascinating.

The more she persisted in this tactic, the more Lord Havington made it a point to draw her into conversation. Soon, not a sentence came out of the man's mouth, but that he would add, "Don't you agree, Miss Violet?" or, "And how do you feel about that, Miss Violet?"

Her answers became more clipped, her

tone frostier.

"You must have excellent vision," he said. "I swear it's now pitch dark outside, and I for one cannot see what you find so fascinating."

"Perhaps his Lordship is a little short-sighted," she declared, continuing to stare out the window.

"I believe you meant to say near-sighted, madam?"

She stared right through him. "Did you think so?"

They arrived at Baron Montague's residence.

As the footman opened the door and offered a crimson-uniformed arm, Larissa exited. Before Constance could follow, the earl barred her way with his arm and jumped out. He turned to assist her. She could not avoid reaching for his gloved hand.

Again he moved more quickly, putting both hands on her waist as he lifted her down. Slowly.

She pushed away from his shoulders, afraid others might notice. But the coachman pointedly looked away, and Larissa had already started toward the entrance, practically skipping.

Lord Havington leaned toward her and

whispered, "And I will take that dance, Miss Violet."

Constance stamped on his boot, forgetting her thin satin slippers, which met with stiff leather. "Ow!"

He grinned, white teeth flashing in the dusk. "Don't think you can get out of dancing with me by intentionally hurting yourself."

Inside, the baron and baroness stood at the top of the ivory staircase. The spacious room behind them glittered as hundreds of dangling crystal prisms reflected the candles layered in the chandeliers.

The earl of Havington's presence caused a noticeable stir. It was obvious their hosts considered it quite the coup to have the earl and his sister attending their local assembly. Constance was simply introduced as Miss Violet, companion to Lady Larissa Wakefield.

When Larissa breathlessly asked whether there would be waltzing, the baroness leaned toward her conspiratorially and said, "The baron insists this evening be limited to the cotillion and the quadrille, but he indulges me and is allowing one waltz — at the close of tonight's festivities." Both women giggled.

As Constance followed Larissa farther

into the room, Lord Havington startled her by tugging her dance card from her light grasp before she had secured it to her wrist. Holding it in the air, away from her reach, he penciled in his name and handed it toward her with a smile and a bow.

Constance snatched it. "That was most presumptuous. As it happens, I do not care to dance with you tonight, my Lord."

"Ah, and yet you lecture me on honor, Miss Violet. Does this mean you will not make good your promise to dance with the hired help? That would seem most cowardly."

She sputtered. "I am not the least bit cowardly. And *I* for one do honor my word. Unlike others I know."

"Then you must *honor* your promise to dance." He stressed the word.

She deliberated, as she secured the card to her wrist, then bit out, "All right. You shall have one dance." Glancing to be sure he had penciled in *only* one, her eyes flew open. "No. This is unacceptable. *Not* the waltz," she said with a firm shake of her head. "You must choose another."

She did not think her sensibilities could stand being held so closely by Lord Havington, knowing the feelings a simple touch of his hand could invoke. Especially as she noted how devastatingly handsome he appeared in the candlelit ballroom in his dark evening attire.

"As my sister's companion, it is not seemly you should dance the waltz at all, Miss Violet. So, if there is to be a waltz tonight, you shall be properly escorted by me, your employer." With this no-nonsense edict, he bowed curtly, thus graciously excusing himself to all appearances. He turned and made his way toward the opposite end of the ballroom.

Constance stood frozen, flustered, furious with his high-handedness. And furious with herself, because her insides hummed at the thought of dancing the waltz in the earl's arms. How could she be so disloyal to Larissa? But — couldn't she plot against him tomorrow, and enjoy just this one night?

What kind of a friend are you? she berated herself. *You cannot dance with him. He is the enemy.*

She bit her lower lip as she watched him strolling across the room, turning feminine heads as he towered above the other men, dark and resplendent in elegant formal wear.

All right, she thought with a sigh. *I will make certain not to dance the waltz with him tonight. I will not dance with him at all, out of loyalty to my friend. The things I do for*

Larissa.

The clock began to strike, signaling the final dance of the evening: the waltz promised by their hostess.

Constance had been blissfully unaware of the earl, once having decided she must have nothing to do with him.

He, however, was constantly aware — of where she was and with whom. As she promenaded and laughed with partners, the tall earl easily kept her in his sights. His eyes sought out her graceful figure whenever the music began. He found himself listening for her laughter, often to the distraction of his partners.

Now a general sigh whispered through the hall, as guests realized this successful night would soon end.

Constance gasped as she realized with sudden panic that she must not be found by Lord Havington for the final dance. Like Cinderella, she picked up her silken skirts and dashed for the closest exit as quickly yet as unobtrusively as she could manage. She slipped out the patio doors and found herself alone on the terrace. Her racing heart drowned out the excited buzz on the dance floor. Taking in deep breaths, she sidled along the wall, distancing herself from the bright light spilling out onto the tiles, covering herself within deeper shadows.

The opening strains of music came floating out, and she found herself regretting the promise made to her conscience. She leaned back, her elbows on the stone wall behind her, and stared up at the stars. In the country, the constellations were spectacular. She could lose herself in staring at the stellar diamonds for hours at a time. She hummed the sweet notes of the waltz. *Blast,* this was one of her favorites.

A hand grasped hers and she almost screamed.

In the shadows next to her stood the earl. "I assume you lost your way to the dance floor, Miss Violet. Or, perhaps you were enamored with the stars and did not hear the opening of the waltz?"

Constance looked down at the slate tiles at her feet. In a soft voice, she heard herself say, "I am sorry, but I cannot dance with you, my Lord." Thankfully, she couldn't see his usual frown.

But he sounded more amused than angry. "Why not?"

"Because my conscience has forbidden it. As you know, I have not yet followed your instructions to remove your sister from

RoseHill. Nor do I intend to." She lifted her chin, surprised to see his teeth flashing white in the dark. "I therefore realize you will soon be dismissing me and will be in no mood to partner me."

"Shhh," he whispered. "Let's declare a truce for this one night, Miss Violet," he said softly, mirroring her own earlier wish. Stepping in front of her, he drew her away from the wall. "Dance with me. Please."

Constance's conscience screamed scoldings, but her heart and feet refused to listen. She stepped away from the wall and into his open arms. His hand clasped hers warmly, as she placed her other lightly upon his shoulder. They floated, two silken feathers across the smooth patio, the pressure of his hand circling her waist, guiding her expertly in wide, sweeping circles to the swelling music.

She was shocked when he more than once guided her with his leg, his thigh brushing her own through the thin silk layers of her gown.

All of a sudden her steps faltered, as she murmured, "The music . . . I believe it's stopped."

Lord Havington halted, staring down, still holding her in a pose as if waiting for another waltz to begin. Suddenly, he brought their clasped hands down and pulled her closer, bending his head slowly to take her lips in a kiss.

She allowed it. As she allowed him to deepen the kiss. When he forced himself to break it, he held her slightly away. They both breathed shallowly, their eyes locked.

Constance recalled the last time this had happened, when she'd broken away in confusion and panic, escaping another patio a long time ago. But this time her body did not move from his arms. It refused to move. This time, she realized helplessly, Lord Havington would have to be the one to break the spell.

And he did.

Taking hold of her shoulders, he said in a low voice, "It's time we return, Miss Violet. Before I do something I regret." He dropped one hand to the small of her back, steered her gently toward the open doors of the ballroom.

As they walked slowly across the smooth stones, Constance was too aware of his hand at her waist. She could not help asking, "You do not already have regrets?"

He stopped her by encircling her waist from behind, and tugging her up against him. As he buried his head in her hair, he whispered against her neck, close to her ear,

"None whatsoever."

She started to turn around, into his arms, when she detected movement by the doors. Two other couples were strolling out for a last bit of air now the evening was winding to a close. Lord Havington immediately released her and they continued on to the double doors.

Once inside, Constance turned sharply to her left and quickly walked away from the earl. No one would suspect they'd been together.

She bumped into Larissa without seeing her.

"I've been looking everywhere for you. Are you ready to go? Did you have a perfect time?" Larissa's pink face was flushed with excitement.

Constance nodded, still in a daze. She allowed her friend to lead her to the entry, where they queued up to await their carriage. Owing to the earl's prestige, his carriage moved to the front of the line, and Larissa and Constance hurried down the steps to the open doors. Inside they found lap robes warmed by hot stones, thoughtfully provided by the earl for the late ride home.

Lord Havington jumped into the carriage

a half minute later, taking a seat next to his sister.

He and Constance made eye contact across the small space, without embarrassment, evaluating one another.

"Thank you for your consideration in providing the blankets, Lord Havington," Constance murmured.

"My pleasure, Miss Violet," was all he said, but his voice was husky as he drawled out the word *pleasure.*

Constance's cheeks warmed, and a sweet, matching warmth stirred deep within.

But it soured as she glanced across at her best friend, whom she had betrayed shamelessly this evening.

CHAPTER FIFTEEN

At the strike of the hour Marcus turned over again like one of his chef's basted chickens, but still sleep eluded him. He lay awake marking each half hour, his body uncoiling and turning as regularly as the clock springs.

Lying on this side, he watched the slight red glow of banked coals in the fireplace. Staring at the fading circle, he again relived the dance on the Montagues' terrace. Where his hair touched the pillow he could still smell a trace of Constance's fragrance, and closed his eyes to focus on the coveted scent.

She'd seemed frightened at first, her heart beating like a small wren's. He had to fight an urge to crush her close, capturing the fragile bird gently in encircling arms. He could feel her delicate hand responding to his touch as he led her in graceful circles on the terrace.

He'd wanted her tonight. He was an expert at eluding the eligible ladies of the *ton,* not to discount sidestepping their aggressive mamas. He tried replacing her face with any one of the more eligible London debutantes, but it was to no avail. All he could think of was the simple companion.

Simple? He snorted. For an individual in a position of humility, it was obvious no one had informed her of the protocol. The woman had pride. And honor, though she could afford neither. Marcus had no doubt if he'd handed her the money at the time of the bribe, she would have flung it into the mammoth fireplace at the inn . . . or, more likely, in his face. He chuckled in the quiet dark, remembering how indignant she'd been as she left him at the table. Of course, at the time he wanted to throttle her. Challenge him to a duel, would she? He smiled at the image. He should have taken her up on it, if only to see how she would fill out a pair of fencing breeches. Memories of fishing breeches had certainly not faded with time, and he recalled them clearly now, then shook the image from his mind's sight.

Miss Violet was also impertinent. With those clear green eyes giving away her every emotion, she would never succeed at humility. No, she'd finally lost her temper and, therefore, the entire battle, in their meeting at the inn. He'd suspected a tempest brewing in those eyes since the first day he met her. And he found he loved stirring the air between them, just to see the tempest swirling so attractively.

But now she'd made it clear she wanted nothing more to do with him. Marcus felt a chill; the fire burned lower. He pushed aside the covers, stood and approached the wood-box. Dawn illuminated the edges of the heavy drapes. Almost morning, and he hadn't slept. In town, he usually kept these post-midnight hours, then slept until day's bright light burned the edges of the curtains. But staying in his massive bed this dawn would not satisfy his need for sleep. She'd denied him that antidote.

Perhaps he'd light the chimney lamp on the desk and bury himself in his books.

He added two dry logs on the grate, then eased into a chair facing the hearth. He sat in the firelit dark, his thoughts slumbering to his sister's upcoming Season. Larissa would be engaged before the final ball of her first Season, he had no doubt. She'd marry a gentleman of his acquaintance and approval, and she would be protected and financially cared for the remainder of her days.

But what of Miss Violet? What did she have to look forward to as the years spun from one season to another? Another and yet another companionship — perhaps next time to a tedious old woman? Or she might take a post as governess, with her sharp mind. Would she find herself helplessly at the mercy of the lord of the manor? He'd heard too many tales of governesses who were penniless and powerless, forced to share their days with the children in the schoolroom, and forced to share their night beds with the master of the house. Marcus clenched his fists. Over his dead body!

He snapped out of his daydream with the realization *he* had nothing to say about her future. Or her fate. Most likely, after he returned his sister home in Miss Violet's company, he would have no cause to ever see the companion again.

But he wanted to. That thought stayed with him.

CHAPTER SIXTEEN

Constance sat back on her knees in the garden and swiped a gloved hand across her brow, leaving a thin smudge of dirt just over her right eyebrow. She wore a straw bonnet, more serviceable than fancy, just enough to protect her complexion from this morning's strong sun. Her sturdy half boots were already caked with dirt, as was her long white apron.

A feeling of contentment washed over her. It was a beautiful morning and she had her favorite trowel in hand. The soil was rich in this patch of ground she'd composted regularly over the years. When she sought to relax or to focus her thoughts, there was nothing as healing as the garden.

And, she thought, smiling, she did not have to worry about being caught in her favorite faded gardening clothes. Lord Havington was firmly ensconced in London for at least the next seven days. There was nothing more she could do at present for Larissa. Everything in her power had been set in motion.

She'd written her note to Lady Amelia, explaining she desired an audience with the dowager duchess when Constance and Larissa arrived in town. Hopefully her great-aunt's friend would agree to see her.

If, on the other hand, her brother's scandal had closed too many doors to her, then so be it.

She calculated a reply should arrive today or tomorrow, assuming the dowager duchess deemed to respond. If a note did not arrive prior to their London shopping trip, then Constance would have to decide whether to risk appearing at Lady Amelia's doorstep uninvited — and face the likelihood of being snubbed.

She dug below a deep weed with her trowel. She would cross that bridge if need be, but would not worry about it today.

The plans for the masquerade ball had been put into motion, and Larissa was coming through splendidly as a hostess, coordinating everything with a fine eye for detail. Constance played the role of mentor, delighting in Larissa's natural abilities and her flowering confidence.

Larissa consulted Constance on the menu

for the buffet. She then discussed it with Mrs. Eldridge, who was just as excited, and who assisted in hiring extra help from the village. Larissa followed her list religiously: the flowers, the decorations, the invitations, the extra footmen, the lighting, and so forth. The whirlwind of activity she'd been orchestrating gave her energetic friend a center of focus, something Constance hoped Larissa would treasure when this summer visit ended.

When Constance had entered the yellow parlour this past hour, she'd found an exhausted Larissa slumped in a cozy armchair, her book open in her lap but her eyes closed. Constance threw a light wrap over Larissa and slipped out to the garden, which she'd been ignoring of late.

She pulled a few more weeds and dropped them onto the tarpaulin. It was almost full enough to pull the corners together and drag to the compost pile.

A shadow fell across the tarp.

Constance glanced up, squinting, expecting to see Larissa's outline against the harsh sunlight. Instead, a much fuller figure stood over her. Constance dropped her trowel in the soil and stood, brushing her hands and removing her gloves as she did so.

And came face to face with the Dowager

Duchess, Lady Amelia.

Constance opened her mouth in shock, then closed it in mortification as she realized how ill-dressed she was. She reached for the apron strings. "Your Grace, I am so sorry to be greeting you like this." She struggled to untie the apron, which felt to be knotted.

"Nonsense, child! I did not tell you I was coming, so I am the one who should be apologizing. Here now, let me look at you."

Constance glanced down at her filthy apron, brushing it with her hands, which then strayed to her loose locks as she tried tucking willful curls behind her ears.

Lady Amelia had tears in her soft blue eyes. "Constance . . . you look so like your dear great-aunt, and I miss her so! I usually found her in the garden too." She chuckled. "Your butler wanted to fetch you, but I would not allow it. I would not have missed this sight for all the crystal in the cabinet." Lady Amelia hugged the young woman to her ample bosom.

Constance spied the dirt smudges on Lady Amelia's cream-panelled traveling dress. "Oh! Look what I've done to your outfit. Please, let me run to the house and get something to sponge that for you. I'm so very sorry." The situation was getting worse by the minute.

But Lady Amelia laughed and scolded, "Now stop that, miss. I'm not afraid of a little dirt, and if I wish to give you another hug, I shall. Dirt, or no dirt." To prove it, she did.

"Yes, Your Grace," said Constance obediently, with relief. "Shall we go in, and I'll arrange for tea?"

Lady Amelia looked around. "Actually . . . whenever I came to see Agatha, she would have tea sent there — to the gazebo. Would you mind, dear? It would bring back so many memories, and make a silly old woman very happy."

Constance could have hugged her again, this woman was so wonderful. "I'll only be a moment. I'll let the staff know," she said over her shoulder, scurrying off toward the house.

When Constance came striding back, the duchess was slowly ascending the gazebo steps, arriving inside just ahead of Constance.

"I haven't been in here myself for ages," said Constance, as she looked around the small sunny space, thankful the pine floor was swept clean and the white arbor posts appeared spotless. Even the small wooden table in the center of the gazebo looked scrubbed, she noticed gratefully.

Barrows appeared, having hustled out with linens. He flicked a starched, snow-white square over the round table, placed pastel napkins, then discreetly disappeared.

The dowager duchess seated herself, unfolding her napkin methodically. "Constance," she scolded gently, "you should never have run away. I was so upset. Imagine. Facing your brother's scandal alone, and with your great-aunt Agatha gone." She lay the partially folded napkin on her lap. "I sent one of my staff with a letter to the townhouse. But you'd already disappeared to the country. I cursed myself for not having brought it myself immediately, but my granddaughter Marianne had just given birth the week prior — her first, you know."

Barrows reappeared with the footman and the tea set. Constance poured a cup for her guest.

As Lady Amelia stirred in a lump of sugar, she continued, "Well, as you can imagine, when I received your letter this morning, I threw the staff into a to-do, commanding we had precisely one hour to be packed and in the carriage. I was determined not to make the same mistake twice, you see."

"I don't know what to say, Your Grace . . ."

"Well, do say Amelia, child. I feel we are family."

"Yes, Lady Amelia," Constance said as a compromise. "I . . . I panicked, I suppose." She stared off toward the river, remembering that day. "I even thought to follow Alec across the channel when I saw the note he'd scribbled. I knew the scandal would break quickly. I also knew Alec wasn't capable of what they said he'd done, but I was afraid. Afraid of being questioned, afraid of hearing him accused . . . I was afraid of hearing him condemned." Shaking her head, Constance brought her gaze back to the dowager duchess's. "I — well, no longer showing my face in London is not a problem, not for a country mouse such as I."

Lady Amelia raised her brows. "A country mouse? Do you not own a looking glass, child? Your dear great-aunt was a similar emerald when I first met her." Amelia's eyes twinkled. "Between the two of us, we had *all* the local boys in our basket, Agatha and I. We both made excellent matches — we'd made a pact to only marry for love, you see, and fortune was good to both of us."

The ladies sipped their tea.

"I was afraid to ask you for help," said Constance. "I didn't want to violate the memory of friendship between you and

Aunt Agatha." Looking down, she said, "I was afraid the scandal might leave its ugly stain on anyone I touched."

"Nonsense! I would have stood behind you, child, exactly because of my love for your great-aunt. And I shall tell you: a duchess at your side is a powerful deterrent to gossip. I for one let it be known that I did not believe a word of the *on-dit,* and in *my* presence it would be considered ill-mannered even to mention it."

It was Constance's turn to fight tears.

"And how does your brother fare, dear?"

Constance knew the duchess changed the subject to allow Constance to compose herself. Briskly, she said, "He has finally written, and he sounds to be in good spirits. He claims the investigation is making progress. Two Bow Street Runners are engaged now they are so near to piecing the puzzle together. You know Alec: everything is an adventure, and he is always the optimist. However, he does admit to missing England . . . though no mention, mind you, of missing his only sister."

"Young men often find it difficult to speak from the heart, don't they? Except when they are waxing poetically to one another about their latest love interest. But that is not really their heart speaking, I suppose, now is it?"

Constance chuckled. The duchess was as irreverent as Aunt Agatha.

"But speaking of the heart, Constance, what of yours? Any beaux I should know about?"

Lord Havington sprang to mind, and Constance chased him away by concentrating on another spoonful of sugar. "No. I've not thought about socializing since I left town. And as I mentioned, I avoid London like the plague."

"Well, the plague came and went over one hundred years ago, so I no longer think we need to stay away from London to avoid *that*. And you should not be avoiding young men, either, at your age. I may have to insist you circulate with me this coming Season, Constance. It would do you a world of good to get back into the social scene. When is the last time you went to a party? Your great-aunt loved parties!"

Constance remembered the dance of a couple of nights ago and blushed. But this reminded her of the approaching masquerade ball and she colored further. Lady Amelia missed neither, and waited expectantly like a queen at court. Constance was saved from a reply as the remainder of the tea service arrived.

Mrs. Dewberry appeared, curtsying as she beamed at the dowager duchess, having served her many times during her visits at RoseHill Manor. Barrows and a footman followed behind with a heavy silver platter and shuttled the pieces from platter to table. In moments there was a beautiful tea sandwich presentation, and Barrows departed hastily, hurrying the footman ahead of him.

Constance smiled as her housekeeper set the final touch, tiny vases of candied violas. "Thank you, Mrs. Dewberry. When Lady Larissa awakens, will you please invite her to join us?"

"I certainly shall, my La— I mean, Miss Violet." The woman winked mischievously as she left the gazebo.

Constance bit her lip and peeked up to see whether the duchess overheard.

"I feel quite badly you came so far for such a silly dilemma, Lady Amelia. I would have been happy to come to you in London. Though I feared I would be wasting your time in seeking advice over a country comedy."

"I love nothing more than a good comedy. Come, come, out with the tale!" Lady Amelia leaned forward to choose several delicacies.

"Where shall I begin?" mused Constance.

"Let's start with Miss Violet," suggested the duchess, waving a small stuffed fig, "and the other dramatis personae."

"Well. This all started with Larissa — that's Lady Larissa Wakefield, my dearest friend. At least she *was* a dear friend before she ensnared me in her summer scheme . . ."

Before she knew it, Constance was unfolding the story for Lady Amelia, starting with the simple lie, which should have been consummated within an afternoon's interview, and stretching into the ongoing cumulation of fibs and farces.

At several points in her telling, the duchess interrupted for clarification. "But why couldn't Larissa tell her brother she was staying with you, as Lady Constance? That would certainly make more sense, with your brother's title, and your own credibility with her aunt and uncle."

Constance made a face. "What with Alec's scandal, and Lady Larissa's need to enter society unblemished, she feared the earl — her brother — might consider my presence *less than suitable*."

"Harrumph!"

"I hardly know what's the truth anymore," said Constance, "since I'm not who I really am, and this is not my home, and my horse is not my horse." She tilted her head to the side in puzzlement of just how out of hand her world had gotten. "Then, of course, there's the inappropriateness of my character in his Lordship's eyes. At first I thought it was because he expected his sister's companion to be a paragon. But I soon discovered it's his lofty expectations for the entire female population in general. I'm not to enjoy riding spirited horses, I'm not to enjoy fishing. I'm not to converse with my staff, I'm not to enjoy waltzing —"

"Goodness! Is that all?"

"Oh, yes —" Constance remembered indignantly, "— *and* I need to read etiquette tomes. Nor do I dress fashionably, appropriately, or modestly." Constance looked down at her dress. "Though, to be fair, it seems every time his Lordship appears, he finds me in my oldest outfits, or dressed for working in the garden."

"Harrumph!" again from Lady Amelia.

"To top *that* —" Constance warmed up to her subject with heated passion. "— the veriest, most annoying thing of all, is that this . . . this expert on etiquette — this . . . priggish gentleman . . . who sits in constant judgment of what is proper and what is not, was himself raised without a whit of manners!"

"Though he is an earl, you say? Surely, child, he has been raised to suit his station?"

"No, apparently not at all. He is the veriest bumpkin when it comes to social graces. He arrives unannounced, acts boorishly, intimidates my staff, and actually thinks to quote Mrs. Carver to me!"

"Actually, that does sound quite earlish to me. But — Mrs. Carver? I don't believe you've mentioned her yet."

"Oh, she's just someone who wrote a silly book on etiquette. The earl delights in quoting her ridiculous rules to me. As if *I* were the one lacking in manners."

"Constance, I'm not sure I approve of this stuffy earl at all. And how did such a young woman end up with such an elderly brother? Is she the late offspring of a third winter–spring marriage, or such?"

"Oh, no, not at all. His Lordship is twenty-nine years old."

"*Nine and twenty?* Fiddlesticks! The man sounds to be a perfect bore. If he is the only male of the family, then one must regret it will surely signal the end of that dynasty."

Constance laughed, which set Lady Amelia to chuckling at her own wit. They both knew money, land, and title would always win a wife where personableness could not.

A tweak of conscience forced Constance to say, "I am not being totally honest with you, Lady Amelia. Perhaps some of this is my own fault, for I do enjoy plotting things that I know will annoy the earl. And —" Here Constance blushed, remembering how it felt to be in Marcus's arms. "And, he does allow a waltz, as long as he is the gentleman doing the waltzing. He dances wonderfully." A tiny sigh escaped.

Lady Amelia hesitated. "Is this the only familiarity he has attempted with his sister's companion — a waltz?"

Constance looked down, her cheeks noticeably warm.

As if reading her mind, Lady Amelia said, "Agatha and I never kept secrets from each other. It was part of the formula for our closeness."

This decided it for Constance. "I'm so confused, as I find myself at odds with the man. When I'm in the same room with him, I want to kick him in the shins. Especially when I think about his high-handedness. And then, as he moves closer — to within kicking distance, actually — something else takes over, and I experience . . ." She searched for the right word. ". . . feelings?" She discarded that. "Not emotional feelings, rather more like . . . an illness. A physi-

218

cal illness. I feel it in my heartbeat, my breathing, my stomach . . . my . . . my toes!" she blurted in utter bafflement.

The duchess hid a quick smile. "And, does he have these same . . . mystifying physical reactions, do you suppose?"

Constance concentrated, trying to remember if his Lordship had ever complained of a headache or tingling toes while in her company. "I don't believe so."

"Has he been close enough to touch you?" Lady Amelia asked in a casual tone, as if she were asking whether he took jam with his scones, or clotted cream.

Constance remembered the first time they touched, when she'd been crying on the terrace. "Once, he found me crying. It was the first time I sensed any gentleness in the man, but . . . he ended up kissing me," she admitted in mortification. She peeped at the duchess, who said "Mm-hmm" attentively, but waited for Constance to continue. "And there was the dance two nights ago. A local country dance. I was so angry, I vowed not to give him the dance I had promised. But we did, and we touched as we danced. It was a waltz, you see."

"But . . . I thought the earl did not approve of waltzes?"

"He overheard me complaining to his

sister that he did not need to accompany us to the dance, acting as if he were our nanny. I said . . ." Constance hesitated, knowing how churlish this would sound. "I said, if he wanted to go as our carriage driver, or our hired help, then we might permit him to dance," she finished in a quiet voice, looking down at her hands.

Lady Amelia's eyebrows rose. "So. He asked you to waltz with him?"

"There was to be one waltz. Just one, as it was a local dance, and this was all the hostess would allow. His Lordship did not think it appropriate his sister's companion should dance a waltz, so he thought it safer if he bespoke it for himself."

"How very noble," Lady Amelia added drily. "I wonder who waltzed with his sister. But didn't you say you vowed not to dance with him?"

"Yes, and I kept my vow. I did not dance with him — at least, not on the dance floor," Constance said primly, in self-satisfaction.

The duchess's brow wrinkled. "But you said you did waltz? Is that not a dance?"

"Oh, but that happened outside, on the terrace. He followed me, you see, demanding to know my whereabouts. And I *firmly* refused to allow him to escort me to the dance floor."

"I see. So . . . instead, you only allowed him to waltz with you in his arms — alone, on the dark terrace."

Constance missed the gentle sarcasm. "Exactly. And afterwards, he kissed me. Exactly as he did on my own terrace the first time."

"Constance, why did you make a vow not to dance? On the dance floor, I mean," amended the duchess with a quirk of her lips.

"Oh! That is the most important thing I neglected to tell you. It is why I specifically sought your advice. The earl made a most ungentlemanly proposition to me two days ago."

The duchess sat up straight. "By Hades he did!"

Taken aback by Her Grace's swearing, Constance related the meeting at the inn, and Lady Amelia visibly relaxed.

When she finished, the older woman asked, "And this was the proposition you spoke of?"

Constance nodded her head, and did not understand why the duchess smiled.

"Forgive me for smiling, my child. I misunderstood what you first said. However . . ." Lady Amelia put on a stern face. ". . . I must agree with your evaluation. It was wrong of him to expect you to sabotage his sister's plans behind her back. Though I'm not sure the chit does have enough sense to spend the summer with a companion, from what I've heard. On the other hand, she should certainly be allowed to spend the summer with *you,* however, as the esteemed Lady Constance Chambreville."

"What would you recommend I do?" Constance asked, feeling much better as they sat in confidence in the gazebo.

Lady Amelia said, "Let me ponder a moment, child. I do so love this view of the river. Do you know, after tea Agatha and I would set our chairs down at the bottom of the steps . . . just there," she said, pointing, "and we would sit and drink in the sunshine as we watched the river. Would you mind?" she asked, as she stood and began scooting her chair over toward the open end of the gazebo.

"Allow me, Your Gra— Lady Amelia." Constance jumped up to grab the woman's chair, but was waved off.

"I can do this, Constance. You just worry about bringing your own chair."

Wouldn't Barrows and Mrs. Dewberry fall in a swoon, thought Constance, if they returned in time to see the dowager duchess picking up her chair and hoisting it down the stairs? Constance picked hers up and joined Lady Amelia on the grass. The duchess sat and motioned for Constance to place her own chair next to hers.

When both chairs were lined up facing the slow-moving river, Lady Amelia held out her hand, and Constance placed her hand in the older woman's.

The duchess gave Constance's a quick squeeze before releasing it. "Thank you for sending the letter, Constance, and letting me know you needed me."

"It is I who should be thanking you," said Constance.

"Ah, but perhaps I have no advice for you, my dear."

They sat in silence, until Constance noticed Lady Amelia's eyelids lowering. Thinking the woman was about to nod off in the warm sunlight, Constance turned to watch the sparkling surface of the water.

Lady Amelia opened her eyes to announce, "I don't think there's anything you can do about this situation, Constance."

Constance looked over at her. "Then I should not interfere? I should allow her brother to drag her away?"

The older woman kept her gaze on the river. "I'm afraid so, my dear. He is, after all, the head of the family. I cannot think of any way you can persuade him to do otherwise, and you cannot force his hand on this. You cannot think of spiriting her away, either, for that would be an onerous misstep."

Constance chose not to mention her earlier idea of a visit to Bath. "Should I reveal my identity to the earl, if we have nothing else to lose?"

"No, I think not. It would only make him angry at his sister, and she really should be the one to tell her brother the truth. From what you've told me about the earl, I do not believe this would make him any more gracious about letting her stay."

Constance sighed. "I suppose I must agree with you, though it saddens me to be so powerless."

"I believe," added the dowager duchess, "you have already done as much as you can for your dear friend. It sounds as though you've already enjoyed some wonderful days together."

"You are right. It has been a fun summer, in spite of the silliness. Perhaps because of the silliness," Constance realized out loud.

"It is certainly an experience both you and Larissa will always treasure, and laugh about, I am sure. One can only hope her brother will someday look back upon this with as much good humor."

They sat another few minutes, at peace in one another's company, listening to the meadowlarks and watching the water flow lazily.

Lady Amelia interrupted the silence. "Well, about the only advice I have, Constance, is to make sure your friend enjoys this week in ignorance. Make it enjoyable for her, and she'll have enough memories to see her through the remainder of the year."

Constance nodded to herself, knowing she'd reached the same conclusion.

"Is there anything else remaining she has looked forward to?"

"We will still go shopping in London," Constance said.

"Mm-hmm. Please, by the way, do drop in for tea and a visit, if you have a spare moment during your shopping venture. I insist upon meeting this young gel. Anything else?"

"No, not that I can think of." But Constance's blush said otherwise. "Well . . . she did mention she would love to attend a real masquerade ball. She's never had the opportunity to do so."

"And?" inquired the duchess.

"And it seems she never will, as his majesty does not believe masquerade balls are proper for young women."

"Fiddlesticks!" huffed Lady Amelia.

"Yes. The earl most strongly and loudly disapproves of masquerade balls, believing they will lead one to immoral behavior. He has therefore, of course, forbidden his sister to even *think* of attending one."

Another minute of companionable silence followed.

Finally, still staring straight ahead, the dowager duchess asked, "So, when are you planning on hostessing one, Constance?"

"The end of this week, before he returns."

Both women turned their heads to smile broadly at one another.

CHAPTER SEVENTEEN

Marcus strode into his club and was not disappointed to discover Philip sitting in a corner with his newspaper.

"Allermaine."

Philip glanced up with a grin. "I thought you had your nose buried in paperwork, Havington. Thirsty for the unexceptional claret they serve here? Or was it my sparkling conversation you missed?"

"Actually, Philip, I *was* particularly seeking you out." Marcus took a seat opposite. "I have some rather interesting news to share with you."

The duke sat forward, sandy eyebrows raised in anticipation of the latest gossip. "I hope this is more about the saga of your sister. The story delights me and saves me from spending a shilling for a corner novel, which could not be half so entertaining."

"Yes." The earl sighed. "This *is* about my family members . . . and staff." Raising a brow, he added, "And . . . it so happens it now involves yet another family we are both acquainted with."

"Then out with it, man — wait, let's get a bottle, so we can settle in for this fireside tale." Philip laughed, signaling a waiter.

Marcus waited until they'd been served, and raised his crystal goblet toward his friend.

"And to what do we toast?" Philip asked in a jovial salute.

"I haven't the foggiest. How about servitude? To those who know their station in life." Marcus sounded disgusted. "Such as ladies' companions."

"Still stewing about Miss Violet, are you?"

"I can't seem to get the chit out of my mind. She's an enigma, Philip. It's obvious she comes from a noble family, for her diction and her airs of superiority are unmistakable. And yet, owing to her dire situation, one would expect a little more humility. Not to mention modesty. Certainly she ought to have more common sense than to provoke her betters." Marcus crossed his ankles and contemplated the claret. "On the one hand, I'd love to see some of her confidence and carriage rub off on Larissa. On the other, I'm afraid she encourages the rebellious streak that seems to have infected my sister this summer."

Philip drummed fingers on the arm of his chair. "One must naturally wonder, though, how the woman has survived thus far with that haughtiness. One would think a former employer would have set her straight . . . or set her out on her ear, more like it."

"Exactly," Marcus agreed. "My thoughts as well. Which made me all the more suspicious of who could possibly have provided this 'sterling reference' for her in the past. What with Aunt and Uncle gone, I wasn't sure where to begin looking for it. I went through every pigeonhole on my uncle's desk, but it was a fruitless search."

Philip hesitated. "Marcus, if I didn't know you better, I'd think this Miss Violet had bewitched you. You told me you are sending Lady Larissa home shortly. And therefore the companion as well. If Miss Violet will soon be gone, why do you care about this elusive reference? Don't snap my neck for this, but your interest in this companion and her reference begins to border on compulsive . . . don't you think?"

When Marcus didn't snap his head off, Philip added, "And why not simply ask your sister? About the reference?"

"Just so! I sent off a letter to her last week, inquiring and probing, gently. But —" Marcus slapped an open palm on the arm of his chair. "— Larissa's reply gave me no more information than I've received in the past. I believe her exact phrase was 'impeccable, I assure you, so you need not worry further,' but with no other clarification. One would think she avoids the issue."

"Indeed, and why should she not?" asked the duke. "Especially if she is hesitant to have it discovered the reference was not as commendable as one would demand, or — perhaps it does not exist at all. Do you suppose she fleeced your aunt and uncle as well? You have implied in the past they were too lenient where Lady Larissa is concerned."

"Yes," muttered Marcus. "Though that will soon be resolved."

"As will the fate of her companion," Philip reminded him. "I assume you are still planning on sending your sister home?"

"Absolutely."

"And has her companion done as you commanded, and convinced Larissa it is time to end their residency?"

"That I've yet to discover. But I am confident by the time I return she will have seen her duty clear. If no other logic compels her, then the financial implications will. It's obvious from her wardrobe she lives a frugal life. On the other hand . . ." His voice rose slightly in volume. ". . . knowing Miss Violet, she may think to wield power over me by holding out until the last possible moment, just to put me in my place."

Philip raised his glass quickly. "Well, she'll be without a position, surely, within another week, and out of your life for good. Shall we toast to that, my friend?"

Marcus touched glasses and gulped down his wine, then reached for more, wrapped in his own thoughts.

"So, you'll now forget about this damned reference, Havington?"

The earl seemed not to hear him. "Of course, I immediately wrote a second letter to Larissa. And this time I demanded to have a name, or a lead, and I made it very clear to my sister if I did not receive the information posthaste, then she could expect me to arrive in person to extract it from her myself."

Allermaine smiled into his glass and took a gulp. "I must admit that in spite of a gaggle of female cousins, I almost find it unfortunate I have no younger sisters to provide such entertainment . . ." He looked at his friend's set countenance. "Almost, that is. So, this concludes our latest chapter?"

Marcus studied his own glass, catching prisms of light as he turned it slowly. "Not quite. I am deciding how best to deliver the most interesting news of all, Philip," he said, looking at his friend. "Obviously, I frightened the chit half out of her wits, as her response has already arrived by post boy. She must have had the messenger riding all night in fear her loving brother would arrive to pay a social call," he added, his mouth turned down at the corners.

"And? Now I really am curious, my friend."

"Well, they say one picture is worth more than words, Allermaine. Why don't I show you her reply, and let you read it yourself?"

Marcus reached into his vest pocket and extracted a folded lavender sheet of vellum. He kept his eyes on his friend's face as he handed it across the small table. Allermaine took it, still grinning, his eyes on Havington, and then he looked down, unfolded the message, and scanned it.

He lost every trace of the grin on his face. His mouth dropped open, and his eyes snapped back up to the earl's, as he said in disbelief, "The companion's reference came . . . came from the Dowager Duchess . . . of Allermaine?"

Marcus nodded.

"*. . . Grandmother?*"

Marcus replied drily, "I told you it was a family we were both somewhat familiar with."

Philip was speechless; he attempted to say more, but ended up sputtering.

Finally, he blew a breath through his cheeks, and said, "This makes no sense, Havington. My grandmother is the *worst* stickler for propriety. She's a regular dragon in society and intimidates everyone, her own family included. She would not tolerate the airs or the shenanigans you attribute to our little companion."

Marcus looked surprised. "I admit to not knowing your grandmother, as I've been out of touch these many years, but surely my sister would not have lied about the source of the reference? You are definite, Allermaine, in this evaluation of your grande dame?"

Philip looked frustrated, and snapped, "I've known her all my life. Of course I'm definite. The woman frightened my mother so badly, I'm surprised I didn't arrive early. In fact, I'm surprised she didn't die of fright before I was conceived." He must have realized he spoke a little too harshly, for he apologized, "Forgive me — but I've been bowing to Grandmother's lofty expectations

233

my entire life, as has everyone else in the family."

"Of course. Sorry," said Marcus. "But you see this leaves me with only one conclusion: that my sister fabricated the story of the reference." Marcus ran his fingers through his hair. "And how would she have chosen the name? This is damned surprising. I quite expected you to tell me the dowager duchess most likely penned it in one of the forgetful moments of a failing mind, or was tipsy from her afternoon sherry, or perhaps a bit flighty, or . . ." Marcus realized the horrible traits he was ascribing to his best friend's noble grandmother and stopped, coloring to his collar.

Fortunately, the duke was once again his jolly self, and laughed at the very idea. "No. One might *wish* Grandmother would dodder off into senility, but she watches over the family like a hawk, all senses alert and functioning."

Both men sat in silence a minute. As usual, the friends seemed to come to the same conclusion at the same time, as they looked at each other and began to rise.

"Today? Now?" inquired Marcus.

"Why not? Let's see if she is receiving," replied the duke.

■ ■ ■ ■

The dower house was as imposing to Philip as the woman herself — an old castellated structure with the look of a medieval fortress. Towers of grey stone had been added during the second duke's reign, and battlements with heavy stone quoins. It had been the family seat for hundreds of years prior to the building of the graceful mansion now sitting on the hill to the east.

Her butler, Carlton, opened the door. Though Philip rarely attended his grandmother, Carlton registered not one trace of surprise. He bowed them in, with a cool, "Welcome, Your Grace."

"Is Grandmother in, Carlton?"

Carlton coughed into his white glove, saying, "Is she expecting Your Grace?"

When Allermaine merely stared him down, Carlton drew himself up and stated, "I will inquire, Your Grace. May I show you to the sitting room?" He turned without waiting for a response and started down the hallway.

The duke stiffened, saying to Carlton's retreating back, "I know where the damned sitting room is, Carlton. Proceed directly to let Grandmother know I am here, with the

Earl of Havington, if you would."

"As you wish, Your Grace," sniffed Carlton, as he turned a sharp left angle and marched down the main hallway.

"Bloody uppity man," Philip said.

"Perhaps he attended the same school of manners as our Miss Violet?" suggested Marcus.

Upon entering the sitting room, Philip crossed to the cabinet and extracted two glasses and an amber decanter. They had barely filled their glasses and settled into armchairs when Carlton returned with the summons to proceed to the upper drawing room.

Draining their glasses, they fortified themselves to enter the dragon's den.

The blue drawing room belied the coldness of the fortress, with its small feminine chairs and cozy blaze on the tiled hearth. The white wainscoting was elegantly detailed, and a huge bow window dominated the facing wall.

The duchess sat in a tall chair, backlit by warm sunshine from the window. Coming closer, Philip bowed over her ringed fingers, with a simple "Grandmother." She nodded imperiously at her grandson, then arched her eyebrows in his friend's direction.

"Grandmother, may I present my good

friend, the Earl of Havington? Havington, my grandmother, Lady Amelia Thorne, Dowager Duchess of Allermaine."

"Your Grace." Marcus bowed, coming to Philip's side and taking the hand offered to him by the duchess. He looked into intelligent eyes, and he smiled a charming smile.

"Havington." She returned the smile.

Philip should have breathed a sigh of relief, but he found himself just a bit miffed that his grandmother showed diffidence to his friend, while treating her own grandson with her usual disdain.

She motioned for them to sit.

Both men looked very much out of place as they lowered themselves into the tiny tapestried chairs. They may have filled the small room with their tall frames, but it was obvious the short, stout woman enthroned near the window held the power.

Lady Amelia eyed Lord Havington approvingly. She appreciated a fine specimen of a man, and he cut quite a figure with his lean grace and broad shoulders.

She didn't retreat to small chatter, as most matrons would have done, but sat and observed them, waiting for them to state the purpose of their visit. One would not care to challenge the dowager duchess to a game of chess.

Carlton entered with a tea tray, setting it on a cart and wheeling the cart close to the duchess. At her grateful nod, he left. She cleared her throat, pinning her grandson with her gaze, until he came forward to accept the cup she poured. He handed it to Havington, then returned for his own.

The two men tried to wedge their large fingers into the small, dainty handles of the delicate porcelain cups. Marcus finally gave up and wrapped the entire cup in one hand, sipping his tea and cursing women everywhere for their silly rituals.

Philip jumped right in, after his first swallow. "Grandmother, Lord Havington wishes to ask you about a reference you provided, not too distant in the past."

Lady Amelia frowned in concentration. "I cannot think of a single reference I've written in at least the past five years. . . . And the requester of this reference, sir?" She directed her question to Lord Havington.

"Your Grace, the reference was perhaps written at the request of Lady Adamsworth?" Seeing no recognition, he added, "Baron Adamsworth of Cowley? My uncle and aunt?"

She barely shook her head. "I don't believe I've had the pleasure of their acquaintance.

Did your aunt and uncle declare I was the provider? By the way, is this a written reference, or may I assume we are discussing a verbal reference made in casual conversation?"

"Unfortunately, my aunt and uncle are on an extended visit," Havington said. "Thus I am not aware of the details. However, if their names are not familiar to you, perhaps you provided this reference to their niece, Lady Larissa Wakefield?" He quickly amended, "And it would have been a formally written reference."

The name rang a distant bell, but the duchess was nevertheless certain she'd given no written references for at least several years. She again shook her head in the negative.

She noticed the earl's jaw clenching. Someone must have been caught in a lie, using her title without permission. "May I ask, sir, whom this supposed reference named as the recommended employee?"

"You may, Your Grace. This would have been regarding a young Miss Violet."

"Violet? My, I would certainly remember such an unusual name." Something tugged at her memory, but it escaped just as quickly. She looked the earl in the eye. "No, sir. You have been misinformed. I have never known a Violet. Nor have I written a reference for any of the aforementioned parties."

Steel glinted in Havington's eyes. "I must apologize, Your Grace. Lady Larissa is my young sister, and I am mortified she has misled me in believing you provided her with a reference. I promise you I shall get to the *bottom* of this." He glanced to Allermaine. "And I may also attend to a certain companion while I am at it."

Unnoticed by both men, the dowager duchess blinked with a start. A horrible realization began forming in her mind, and the impossible implications and complications if it were true.

Lord Havington began to rise.

"Wait. Sit," she said. "Your sister, you say? And — this reference is for your sister's companion? This Violet, she is your sister's companion?"

"Yes, Your Grace. The young chit's name is Miss Constance Violet."

"Constance. Oh, my." The duchess stalled for time, gathering her wits to her.

How was it she had never once asked Constance the name of her friend's brother? Just knowing he was an earl should have prompted the duchess to ask his name; but the younger generation of lions and cubs no longer piqued her interest. So . . . that young gel, Larissa, having learned of the duchess's visit to RoseHill, had conjured up her name when pressed for the nonexistent reference. Of course there was no reference — because Constance was not really a companion. And how dare Lady Larissa bring the duchess into her Banbury tale!

Lord Havington stared at Lady Amelia, confusion overlaying his stern expression. "Constance," he repeated. "Miss Constance Violet."

"Well," said the duchess with an effort at a shrug and a smile, "why didn't you say her given name is Constance? Of course I know Miss Constance Violet. I was acquainted with her for many years."

"You know the companion by her first name?" asked Havington with obvious skepticism. "But not by her family name?"

The duchess fell back on a tactic that had stood her well her entire life. When put in a losing position of defense, go on the attack. She raised her double chin in the air, and inquired frostily, "And why should I not know her by her first name, sir?"

"Because she is a mere lady's companion." Havington appeared uncomfortable. "Of course, I'm not questioning Your Grace."

"Well, sir, my personal maid is Sally. And my hairdresser is Corinthia. I do not know

Sally's family name. Nor do I know Corinthia's family name." She snapped her eyes to her grandson and challenged, "Philip, do you know Carlton's family name?"

"No, Grandmother. But damn it all, I am not the one who has the argument with you."

"Do not use that language in my presence, Wilbert Arthur Philip!"

Philip, Duke of Allermaine, threw up his hands in disgust, looking at Havington for help.

"Point taken, Your Grace," Lord Havington said. "My apologies. So . . . you do know a young woman named Constance, who may be one and the same as our Miss Violet. Yet you do not know my sister, Lady Larissa Wakefield?"

"Constance herself asked me for a written reference some time ago, but I had no idea to whom it was to be presented." She raised her eyebrows imperiously, adding, "Can you not follow that?" implying the earl was a shade dense.

Lord Havington backed down. "Of course, Your Grace, I understand. Again, my apologies for the confusion." He looked out the window, his expression unreadable, as if sorting out his thoughts. He addressed the duchess. "And the post she sought — did she ask you to recommend her as a lady's companion?"

"Absolutely," responded Lady Amelia firmly, in a tone brooking no argument.

"Could you possibly describe her, Lady Amelia?"

The duchess realized with a second start who Lord Havington was: the dictator! This was the man who was making dear Constance's life miserable. She sniffed loudly, deciding she did not intend to be civil to a man who upset her very special charge.

"And, why are you asking for this description, sir? Are you in need of a companion yourself?"

Havington leaned back at her scathing tone. "Your Grace," he began reasonably, "I am only asking as a brother trying to protect his sister. I simply wish to verify the woman who escorts my sister in society has the credentials to do so."

To question Constance's credentials was not a wise move in this room.

Lady Amelia pursed her lips, furious at this impudent young man who could not recognize a supreme lady when one dropped in his lap. Not that Constance would ever be caught anywhere near this arrogant fool's lap, she amended to herself.

"Perhaps I should ask *you* to describe *your*

Miss Violet," she commanded. Of course, how could she have forgotten that silly name: Violet. Constance had laughed, saying Larissa must have looked about the room that day in desperation, and taken all of two seconds to spy a posy of violets.

Lord Havington cleared his throat. "The Miss Constance Violet I refer to is tall, for a woman. When we waltz, she comes to about — here . . ." He put the edge of his hand to his chin. "Her hair is . . . not just one color. Hard too describe. It's many beautiful colors. I'd say mixed shades of honey and autumn."

He looked to the side, focusing elsewhere as he gave it more thought. Lady Amelia raised eyebrows at her grandson. Philip shrugged with a grin.

"She has a lithe figure. And long, beautiful hands. Graceful hands. Did I mention she's graceful? She carries herself as if she were a queen." Havington snorted. "And she has these very expressive green eyes, which can be gentle and tranquil, but are more likely to flare up in beat with her temper." He paused in thought, then turned to find the others staring at him with looks of surprise. A manly blush crept upon him, and he closed his mouth.

Lady Amelia watched the earl as she chose

how to respond. Well, perhaps this man did care for sweet Constance. And Lady Amelia could not have hand-picked a more masculine and commanding gentleman herself. She found herself softening toward the earl, imagining a perfect future for Constance. Always the matchmaker, her mind worked furiously at the opportunities. Constance and Lord Havington were now the center of her latest romantic bubble.

He chose that moment to elaborate, as if not wanting them to get the wrong impression — that he was smitten with the young lady. He added sternly, "However, it is hard to think she could be the same person you recommended, considering how intractable and willful she is."

Lady Amelia's romantic bubble popped so loudly, it was surprising the two gentlemen did not hear it.

The duchess looked daggers at the earl, saying, "And I, sir, am sure we *are* discussing the very same young lady I did in fact recommend. So it seems your displeasure with her credentials is a reflection on my personal judgment."

Lord Havington looked to be in shock.

Lady Amelia decided he was obviously not the man for her sweet Constance. He was a self-righteous prig. Bad enough he thought to imprison his own sister. Did he think it necessary to bully both women? Was he one of those men who decided women do not have the sense to take care of themselves, or to make a simple decision on their own?

She found herself getting worked into a frothy furor, heaping all the things she disliked about the male species in general upon the earl's broad shoulders.

"And exactly what is the issue you have with Miss Constance Violet, that you think to come here and challenge me on my judgment in having writ a reference for the young helpless gel?" she demanded, in an insulted tone.

"I do not — I mean, I am not — that is, I would not challenge you, Your Grace. I questioned my sister, and I questioned Miss Violet, but I would not question you."

"Do you still question Miss Violet, now knowing I have personally vouched for her impeccable background and respectability?"

"No, Your Grace, I know I should not. I mean, I most certainly do not."

"Then, that will be all. You are both dismissed."

Both men shot up, setting their teacups down as quickly as they could without shattering the fine bone china, then executed quick bows and hastily departed the room, practically elbowing each other in their haste to exit through the narrow doorway.

Lady Amelia leaned back in her chair, exhaling loudly. "Demme, that was the fastest thinking I've had to exert in a year," she said out loud.

She couldn't believe the silly chit, Larissa, had so boldly ensnared her in this tale, as easily and completely as she had ensnared Constance. Now the duchess had an appreciation for just how Constance had found herself making up lies left and right.

She sighed again, and chuckled, "Demme, but that was fun!"

The two men did not even speak until they were in the duke's carriage and the door was closed. They both eyed the castle warily as the carriage rolled forward. They seemed afraid to speak, lest they be hauled back in for more of the Spanish Inquisition.

After they turned the corner and the dower house was no longer in sight, they slumped in their seats and simply looked at one another.

"Bloody hell," muttered Marcus, "why do I feel *I* was the one being interviewed for a reference?"

"And, I believe you failed," added Philip. "Welcome to the family, Havington."

CHAPTER EIGHTEEN

Marcus closed the ledgers with a satisfied snap. The books Hawthorne had dropped off for review appeared to be in order. Actually, to give the man proper credit, they were meticulous. It was obvious his man of affairs was detailed and thorough.

The Earl of Havington enjoyed going over the books, but with so many properties to oversee he had no choice but to trust part of the work to be allocated to another such as Hawthorne. Perhaps he should extend Hawthorne's duties. The young man had proven himself talented and trustworthy.

Marcus pondered giving Hawthorne the outer properties as well. The present estate manager was a good man with the tenants and had a knack for crop production and planning, but was not capable of keeping the types of records Marcus had hoped for. Dividing the duties might be the best solution.

Could Hawthorne begin making the circuit immediately? he wondered. Marcus had sent him on an errand, but would ask him before he departed for the day.

Somewhat guiltily, Marcus realized he didn't even know whether the man had a family to attend to in town or not. He never took the time to learn anything personal about those in his employ. Unlike Miss Violet, he thought, sighing, who thought nothing of getting involved in food fights with the kitchen staff, and bringing freshly baked goods out to stable hands. She knew everyone's name and made sure the earl addressed them as such. He had to acknowledge Mrs. Dewberry when she brought him into the parlour, and he was expected to personally thank Mrs. Eldridge for the exceptional bread they had with their meals. Plus young Tommy at the stables, and his father Old Tom. And one mustn't forget Barrows, the crusty butler who could barely suppress a grin whenever Miss Violet flew up into the boughs.

Marcus smiled; he had just named most of the key staff employed at RoseHill.

Then he frowned. Other than his personal valet, he could not name one other member of his London townhouse staff. And how many were there? He had no idea how many maids and undermaids, cooks and footmen it took to manage his current residence.

It wasn't a home, after all, just a gentleman's city retreat when Marcus was not dining or relaxing at his club. RoseHill felt most like home of all his recent lodgings. Certainly more so than this well-appointed townhouse. Not just because he knew the entire staff at the country domain by name. It was because Miss Violet made everyone feel part of a family. Odd. His sister Larissa was the mistress of the manor, but Marcus could not help but notice how Miss Violet bore herself as a natural commander, and they all looked to her for approval, rather than to Larissa.

His frown deepened. His ears still burned from the severe setdown he had received from the Dowager Duchess of Allermaine.

Did the devious little companion have *everyone* wrapped around her slender finger? How was it Marcus was the only person in the world with the ability to see through her calculated innocence? She had them hoodwinked with her dimples and her caring manner. But the earl saw her true colors. They were right there in her eyes, if they'd only take the time to read them.

His friend the Duke of Allermaine was extremely perceptive. Perhaps Marcus would arrange for his friend to meet the infamous companion. Yes, Marcus relished introducing his observant friend to Miss Violet, feeling the need of a witness to corroborate his opinion about the manipulating temptress. Philip would instantly see through her guise.

And, most likely, he'd see through her indecent blouses and gowns as well, amended Marcus. . . . Perhaps he would not introduce his friend to her after all. Imagine if Philip were to become ensnared by her physical appeal, as this could only lead to disaster for the eligible duke. Allermaine's family would never forgive Marcus if the duke fell victim to her charms and formed a liaison unsuitable to his duty. No, Philip would not suit.

So — whom *would* the companion suit? Perhaps the earl would introduce her to Hawthorne.

They were approximately equal in station. And in age. Not at all in personality, though. Hawthorne was quite the no-nonsense fellow. He would soon have the willful Miss Violet on a short leash. It would be no more than she deserved, justified Marcus, and long overdue. She obviously was too independent for someone of her paltry means. The sooner she realized a woman needed to attach herself to a man who could care for her, the sooner she would realize this meant coming under his full authority as well.

Yes, the more he thought about it, the more he pictured how Hawthorne would deal with the young miss. Hawthorne would not fall into the snare of those green eyes. Hawthorne would deal with her exactly as he tackled his accounting problems:

First, he would slowly and methodically strip away the unnecessary. Hmm, why this thought suddenly bothered Marcus, he wasn't precisely sure, but for a fact it did.

Hawthorne would then expose the most important assets bit-by-bit. Marcus didn't care for the images this conjured up any better, he realized.

Hawthorne was one who tackled a problem physically. He'd roll up his sleeves and spend as long as needed for detailed, careful measurements. Marcus frowned at that annoying train of thought as well.

Hawthorne would then —

A knock on the door announced Marcus's man of affairs, who poked his head around the corner. "Anything else, my Lord, before I depart?" asked Hawthorne.

"Yes!" barked Marcus, as he studied the young, well-built, fair-haired man. "You can bloody well stay away from RoseHill

Manor!"

The Earl of Havington sank into his usual chair at the club and ran a hand through his hair. What the devil was getting into him of late? Every thought led to Miss Violet. Well, in another five days, seven at the most, he would wrap up his affairs in London and would ride out to RoseHill to deal with her, and to deal with his demons as well.

The sooner his sister returned home, and the sooner the companion was dismissed, the sooner she would fly from his thoughts.

He held the brandy snifter to his nose and inhaled appreciatively. He was reminded of the complex florals and herbs unique to Miss Violet. *Enough of this,* he chided himself

As he took a swallow, the fireplace was reflected through the amber liquid, shades of gold and honey shifting and burning. It reminded him of the shades of her hair, and how they shifted like fire when she shook her mane. Enough of that thought as well!

Hypnotized by the nearby fire, he set the glass on the table at his elbow. It was no wonder he was drowsy — he'd not slept well for several nights now, and it was all Miss Violet's fault. He leaned his head back and closed his eyes, allowing the warmth from the fireplace to drift him toward a nap.

"Are you asleep, Havington?"

"Yes," said the earl, without opening his eyes.

"Just as well. You'll need your rest."

Marcus opened one eye, to see Philip patiently lounging against the nearby wall, waiting to see if his friend rose to the bait.

"All right, Allermaine, since you're bound and determined to interrupt the first real sleep I've had this past week, why don't you grab a drink and sit?"

Marcus closed both eyes again, waiting for his friend to settle in and proceed. He didn't have long to wait. He heard the waiter approach, heard the glass clink against the silver tray as Philip helped himself to a drink. A chair was dragged across the floor from nearby.

The duke took a sip and sighed. "Just thought you might wish to do the social rounds with me tonight. I'm in the mood for a little fluff."

Marcus answered without stirring from his comfortable pose. "What's on the billet? I'm not sure I'm in the mood for fluff or otherwise. I'm thinking I'll retire early tonight for a change."

"I'm off to a masquerade ball."

Marcus snorted. Opening his eyes, he

asked, "Since when have *you* enjoyed those silly costume affairs?"

"Since I found out this one's to be an affair of great mystery as well."

Havington reached for his drink and sipped, studying Philip over its lip. "Meaning?"

"Meaning no one has any idea who is hosting it. They only know of a remote address where it's being held. I expect it to be quite a crush, just for the novelty of mystery alone."

Marcus closed his eyes again. "Not interested in crushes. Not interested in mysteries. And especially not interested in masquerade balls," he muttered.

"It's unfortunate you're not interested, considering it's taking place at RoseHill Manor."

Marcus's eyes flew open, and he sat up so fast brandy sloshed out of his glass and onto his jacket.

"Bloody damned hell," he swore. "She — wouldn't — dare."

"Would . . . and has. Of course, if you'd bother to read the betting books, as you were wont to do before you became so preoccupied with tracking down references, you'd have noticed all our rakish friends are betting on who will be the first to unmask the mysterious hostess. Now, you and I both know exactly who is in residence at Rose-Hill. So I wish you to know I saw an opportunity for a hefty return on my bet here, Havington, but I didn't think you'd appreciate it if I put your sister's name in the book. Pity, what we do for our friends."

Marcus was livid. He was already on his feet and swore again, not appreciating Philip's humor. "Let's go."

"Aren't you forgetting something?" Philip hadn't budged.

Marcus spun around, frowning as he looked first at the chair, then the table, then his friend.

"It's a masquerade ball. You can't barge in wearing your usual evening clothes. Come along to my townhouse, and we'll fix you up. I've a spare domino or two. Coach or horses?"

"Horses. If we're to go costumed, let's not announce ourselves with your ducal emblem blazing."

With that, both men hastened out and headed to Allermaine's townhouse.

CHAPTER NINETEEN

RoseHill Manor had metamorphosed into a magical Midsummer Night's Dream. Constance sucked in her breath at the sight. Had winged fairies come flying down from the chandeliers, she would not have been surprised.

Larissa's creative touch was amazing. This masquerade would be the talk of the *ton* for weeks to come. It was a certainty other hostesses would race to imitate this wonderland.

Vines twisted from the chandeliers, their hanging tendrils glittering with sequins. The punch bowl rested upon a piece of Roman column, arranged artfully at just the proper height for serving. In fact, there was no actual buffet table, but rather a "ruin" of odd lengths of columns standing on their ends, serving as round tables to hold the assembled collation. Moss and forest ferns sprinkled the floor around the columns, making them stand out as islands.

The magical forest theme continued along the walls, with dozens of large potted ferns. Exotic fragrant blossoms had been cut and hung on man-sized ferns, redolent of a tropical jungle.

The couples were jeweled butterflies filling the jungle with bright, shiny satins and glittering gauze dresses. Women's faces were disguised behind gold and silver half-masks. Many women wore sheer Roman togas draped gracefully from bare shoulders. Others swirled by in many-skirted gypsy costumes or medieval ensembles with matching silk cones perched upon the head. Even the men were as colorful as parrots, in splendid dominoes of every color imaginable.

She didn't spy Larissa. They had agreed to sneak down the servants' stairs so neither would be recognized as hostess, should anyone be watching. Her friend would be wearing an eye mask of scarlet sequins and sparkling ruby paste gems to match her red silk gown.

Constance wore a white satin half-mask with pure white swan feathers arching high on either side. Her gown was the veriest bit scandalous. Though the neckline was decent by *ton* standards, tight gold threads outlined her breasts. And they hardly needed outlining, since her gown was of the sheerest white silk. Her slippers were white satin, dusted with icy glimmer. She floated like a forest fairy herself.

The invitations had been intentionally mysterious, not mentioning a host or a hostess. The dowager duchess had suggested it — the trick was for no host to appear during the entire evening. It was unheard of, and would be considered quite novel in hindsight, as the *ton* gossip brewed with the morning coffee and tea.

At that moment Larissa slid up next to her, her excitement palpable, hugging herself and practically dancing on her toes. Constance's heart went out to her friend, knowing this masquerade would end tonight, and the other masquerade would end as well within the week. But Larissa needn't know yet; her high spirits would not be dampened this evening.

"Can you believe it, such a crush!" Larissa said. "What if no one asks me to dance? I'll just die, Constance."

Constance arched a brow. "Do not fret. Your weary feet will soon wish that were closer to the truth. Do you regret the anonymity? If our guests knew of your ingeniousness, they would laude you with praise. My congratulations."

"I think a secret is so much more fun. And it was your idea to host a ball, not mine. I admit this has given me a confidence I've never known, thanks to your help." Larissa linked arms. "This has been the most wonderful summer of my entire life."

Constance brushed away bittersweet thoughts. Larissa had tonight's memory to cherish, come what may.

"No hiding, me beauties, we are here to dance." A pair of pirates descended upon the ladies.

Constance and Larissa laughed, curtsying, then placed their hands on the arms of their dancing partners, to be led onto the floor.

As Constance twirled with her pirate, she turned her head to scan for Larissa, but stumbled against her partner as he came to a standstill against an immovable wall.

"If you'll allow me to cut in?" It came out more of a command than a request. Due to the intruder's size, there was no argument from the pirate, who shrugged and then left in search of other, easier treasure.

There was no doubt in Constance's mind just whom that deep, arrogant voice belonged to.

"I thought I was quite explicit that you were to waltz only with me, Miss Violet."

Constance thought to deny her identity. As if reading her thoughts, he leaned close to her ear and warned, "And don't dare think to deny who you are, or I'll unmask you now and deal with you in public. No other lady I know has such a haughty carriage. Not the women of the *ton,* and especially not a governess or companion. And . . ." He leaned even closer. ". . . I would recognize the smell of your hair anywhere."

Constance hadn't spoken, but she feared she might faint in his arms when he whispered the words into her hair. He led her around the dance floor. He held her too closely, and the cloak of his black domino kept enfolding her. She could feel the heat from his body as his chest pressed too close to her thin gown.

When she tried to pull back, his arm at the small of her back barricaded her firmly.

Before she realized where they were, they had spun away from the main floor and were now near a wall, between two large potted plants. Backing her up to the wall, Lord Havington put his arm up, looking as if he lounged in conversation, but effectively trapping her body close to his.

"Silent, Miss Violet? Actually, silence becomes you. Yet I would eventually miss your barbed tongue, I'm sure."

Constance's fog of barraged senses thinned to wisps, chased by the winds of temper.

He chuckled. "Ah, your eyes just gave you away. Even through your mask, they flash brighter than the sequins surrounding them." He clamped a hand on her wrist, and pulled her away from the wall. "And now, Miss Violet, we are going to have a very private discussion." There was no longer any laughter in his voice.

"Where?" She panicked, afraid he would drag her into one of the deserted parlours or — worse — an upstairs bedroom.

But he tugged her along toward the terrace.

Should she dig in her heels and make a scene? She hesitated in her steps.

Lord Havington also stopped, to inform her, "One of the things you should know about masquerade balls — since you chose to hostess one — is that a gentleman may throw a lady over his shoulder and others nearby will glance elsewhere, thinking it all part of the wild reverie. Unless she screams, they will assume she does not wish to be rescued."

She didn't budge. "And what makes you think I won't scream?"

He brought his face close to hers. "Because I am trying to keep my own temper under control. If you did so, I could not answer to the consequences. I merely want to have a private discussion, madam, so — do you attend me on your own two legs, or do I carry you out like a sack of grain, and we cause a scene for Larissa and the guests?"

Sticking her nose in the air, she marched out the French doors. She didn't stop until she reached the stone balustrade. They were dangerously close to the dark, hedged gardens encroaching just down the quarried steps. No other couples were nearby. Constance slowly retraced a few steps, but the earl caught her at the waist, his eyes glittering like hard steel beneath his half-mask.

"I warned you about men in masquerade, Miss Violet. Did you choose this spot because it reminded you of the last time we stood alone on this terrace? You are naive. That innocent kiss was nothing compared to what a wanton woman can expect when she waltzes with masked strangers."

He pulled her into the folds of his cape, and bent his mouth to hers. Constance intended to struggle, but all strength left her with the intensity of the kiss. If Lord Havington expected to teach her a lesson, he must have been shocked, because instead of protesting she went limp and wrapped her slender arms about his neck. Her sheer gown pressed up against his body, and it was Marcus who had to break the kiss.

"Bloody hell, I am not at liberty to take advantage of a penniless companion, and you know it." He held her firmly away, breathing heavily. "And look what you are wearing," he scolded, though it was his fault her breasts now swelled against the sheer fabric.

"This is no more revealing than what half the women of the *ton* wear nightly," she scoffed, unaware it had a particular effect on Marcus.

"But *you* shall not be parading tonight in that outfit. I expect you to cover yourself with a wrap immediately or I shall take you upstairs and assist you to find one myself."

Constance's heart palpitated at the idea of ascending the stairs, escorted by Lord Havington to her intimate dressing room. But the man was dictating again, and she opened her mouth to protest.

He cut her off and deflated the revolution. "If you do not obey my wishes immediately, Miss Violet, I shall seek out my sister and end her party a little earlier than she anticipated. Actually, a lot earlier, considering there's been just one dance so far."

"You are abominable," whispered Constance, knowing it was in his power to do as he implied. She spun away from him and swiftly retreated indoors.

Marcus breathed an internal sigh of relief. He had counted on his trump card. It seemed he would always be able to manipulate Miss Violet through her misguided sense of honor, this loyal concern for his silly sister. Well, all he cared was that she obey. He would rest easier knowing the gentlemen indoors would not be ogling her perfect body.

The shock of his realization hit him like cold water.

He was jealous.

Constance chose a glittery gossamer length of material for a shawl, no more opaque than a spider's web. She draped it artfully, standing and turning before her dressing mirror. Satisfied with the effect, she congratulated herself. If she were to allow herself to be bullied by the earl, it would be on her own terms.

But you certainly didn't make a maidenly protest when he enveloped you in that kiss, Constance chided herself. She looked at her lips in the mirror, touching them where his warm lips had shaped themselves to hers and sucked gently. She could still feel the warm satin lining of his cloak, how it trapped the light, musky smell of his skin. She closed her eyes, her body weak with the memory. Frowning, she didn't understand why. Nor did she understand why the closeness to his bare neck had made her want to put her lips there as well.

Her cheeks coloring, Constance quickly covered her face with her mask, rearranging her hair where it tangled with the white feathers. She reviewed herself in the mirror. The slinky panel of silk seemed to draw even more attention to the shadows of cleavage it was supposed to be hiding. Well, he insisted on a shawl, didn't he?

Did he really think she would come downstairs covered in a hermit's wrap of hair cloth or wool? *I hope he's satisfied,* Constance thought smugly, and once more found herself sneaking down the servants' corridors.

Slipping out into the crowd, it seemed the guests had doubled since the opening strains of the first dance. She should be able to avoid the earl in this crush.

But you don't wish to avoid him, her conscience informed, though she refused to look for his tall figure. *No,* she admitted, trying to untangle these feelings. *I do enjoy his physical nearness. And I enjoy conversing . . . when he is not dictating. And I most definitely enjoy dancing in his arms.*

As Constance filled a glass with punch, she continued to ponder her dilemma: How could a man who was so arrogant affect her sensibilities so? Perhaps — was it possible *all* men caused the same physical reactions? Surely this must be why we are all so well chaperoned. Perhaps *no* gentlewoman can resist a man's advances. Thus we hide behind our duennas and our companions.

That reminded her. She must locate Larissa, to be sure her friend was safe. If Constance herself, a woman of refined intelligence and sensibilities, could be so physically affected by a man such as the earl, then what of innocent Larissa? She might find herself swept away in a flood of desire. Constance was convinced men were attempting to seduce Larissa even now.

In panic Constance began her search within the dense, colorful throng. She was conscious of men's stares, and a few of the gentlemen barely moved aside as she pressed through the crowd. It was as if they chose to force her to brush by, chest-to-chest, as she squeezed through the maelstrom.

Yet the physical contact was quite disappointing. She found it distasteful. What if her theory was wrong about all men?

Perhaps she should test it further. Perhaps she would find a man of bearing and charm and dance with him. Just one dance, to find out if all men could make her toes tingle.

A horrible thought struck her — what if they did not? *Oh no.* Constance groaned. Surely it was not possible that she was attracted only to the earl? Fate could not possibly be so cruel. But they would soon be parted, in a matter of days. Her body might pine, but her head and heart would take charge, and the sensations would disappear with haste.

It took her almost a quarter of an hour to locate her friend. To her relief, Larissa was sipping punch and holding court with three men, each of whom stood a proper distance away. Constance came up and took her friend's elbow.

Larissa giggled charmingly. "I suppose since we are all mysteriously masked, I cannot make any introductions. However, I must warn you: this is my companion, come to chaperone me."

It struck Constance that Larissa was

slightly tipsy. This was something she should have foreseen. In fact, she didn't know if Larissa had ever had a drink before in her life. Constance glared at the circle of men, wondering who had provided the innocent girl with spirits.

All she saw was a sea of bland masks.

"Dear, come walk with me, and take in a bit of fresh air," Constance urged, tugging on her friend's arm. Larissa followed obediently, waving her goodbyes with a lopsided smile.

Constance dragged Larissa to the nearest wall, to a bench hidden behind a large tropical bush, below open windows. Here they would remain unseen, and in the path of a gentle breeze. Constance would visit with her friend unobtrusively, until time and clear air did their trick.

The image of the earl finding his sister thus chilled Constance to her very bones.

Larissa asked, with a silly grin on her face, "Constance, have you danced yet?"

"Yes . . . Larissa, have you seen anyone tonight who looks familiar to you?"

"No, other than yourself. However, I'm not sure I would recognize anyone from the baroness's party under all these wonderful costumes. And I certainly haven't recognized any of the men I've danced with — at least, not by their voices."

"And?" prompted Constance, "have they all been proper gentlemen?"

"Oh, yes. Else, I would not have anything to do with them," Larissa added primly.

Constance felt better upon hearing this. They sat quietly a moment. "Larissa, may I ask you a rather personal question?"

"Of course! We are best friends. You know we may ask each other anything."

"Well . . ." Constance considered the best way to phrase her question. "Do you notice any especial . . . feelings . . . I mean *physical* feelings . . . when you are dancing closely with a gentleman?"

"What sorts of feelings do you mean? Oh, I know! Yes, I notice if their hands feel warm, or clammy. And sometimes I notice their breath, if they've had too many of our garlic oysters. Or if the brandy fumes are too strong." She wrinkled her pretty nose.

"What about in your feet? Do your toes ever . . . tingle?" asked Constance, relieved she could hide her utter embarrassment behind her mask.

"They've definitely smarted a few times," Larissa said, "as my slippers are thin, and some of these clumsy men wear heavy boots. It's quite a bit more unpleasant than a tingle, though."

"I don't mean if they are *stepping* on your feet. I mean . . . when you waltz, and a man holds your waist just a little too . . . closely." She hoped the tipsy Larissa would not remember this conversation tomorrow. "Does it affect your senses? Does it make you feel weak-limbed, and flushed?"

Larissa's clear blue eyes could be seen to widen through the holes in her face mask. "Constance! Are you allowing a man to hold you so closely?" She sounded shocked.

"No. Not intentionally. But some men are stronger . . . and do not seem to have any manners," she finished lamely, thinking of Larissa's brother.

"Then you must not dance with that kind of a man again, for he is *not* a gentleman." Larissa giggled. "Perhaps I need to be *your* companion, Constance. I am not letting you out of my sight again tonight."

Constance hugged her friend and said, "Do not worry about me, dear. I am determined to avoid that gentleman tonight as well."

And she resolved it would be so.

CHAPTER TWENTY

The two friends were careful to remain in sight of one another. Suddenly the gentlemen of the *ton* seemed more like a frenzy of black and white sharks, and the masquerade ball was tinged with a slight frisson of danger.

Constance never spotted the earl again, though she found herself comparing each dancing partner to Lord Havington. They were never as tall, or as strong, or as graceful . . . and not one of them made her toes tingle.

One striking gentleman pulled her closer than was proper, and she allowed it — for just a matter of seconds — as an experiment. She wished to know how her body would react to this charming male of the species. But to her disappointment, there was no weakness; certainly no melting inside, and she found his grip distasteful and annoying. She pushed away a proper length.

Her research followed a pattern of scientific pursuit, yet the results were all disappointing. She couldn't believe Lord Havington — of *all* possible men — should have this affect on her when no others did. It was not fair. She'd always believed in destiny, but resolved at that moment to ignore it in the future.

Perhaps she needed to conduct just a few more experiments? After all, she reminded herself, science was simply a disciplined observation of an ample number of carefully arranged investigations.

Marcus, leaning lazily against the wall, saw the rogue pull Miss Violet in toward his body as they danced. He came immediately away from the wall, bearing down in their direction. As quickly as it happened, however, the man released his partner and completed the steps without further familiarities.

The earl returned to his roost, a spot three steps higher than the dance floor, from where he could keep an eye on both his sister and her companion. He thought it unusually fortunate they stayed so close to one another, but gradually it became obvious their nearness was intentional, as each constantly glanced over to keep the other in her sight, especially while dancing. He smiled. Larissa and Miss Violet stood out like two frightened little rabbits who were out frolicking in the cabbage patch but fearful of every movement.

His smile straightened to a slight frown. The fact they put themselves in this situation displeased him. Once again a direct order of his had been disregarded. He was sure it was the influence of the uppity companion.

Just look at the little minx now: dressed so no bare skin was exposed, yet all the more enticing for suggesting what lay beneath the gauzy, clinging layers. It was a direct counterattack to his explicit orders. *Why does she always have me thinking in military terms?* he wondered. *Every disagreement becomes a skirmish, a battle of wits, a chess game.*

And he loved it. Who was the last woman to challenge his disfavor? Certainly no one of his circle.

When it came time to do his duty to the title, he must settle by necessity on a lady of similar background and nobility — to a dull life. While some lucky young blade with no title, no money, and no land would find his life in constant disarray with Miss Violet, enjoying the verbal sparring and being bossed and finagled by this charming lass.

Life was not fair when one was bound by duty. How fortunate, thought Marcus, were those without title, family, and wealth.

What would Aunt and Uncle say, were he to announce he had decided to court a penniless little hellion, just because she stirred his blood and gave him a joy to look forward to each day — even as she made that same blood boil with her stubbornness and sauciness?

She would have daughters who looked like their mother, who would toss their honey-streaked locks and stamp their imperious little feet.

He shook himself from the daydream. It was not for him. Though the thought of carrying off Cinderella from her drudgery to the palace, and showering her with dresses and jewels tugged at his fancy. Even now, she looked like Cinderella at the ball.

Marcus became aware of someone standing close by. He snapped his head around and found Philip smirking.

"Enjoying yourself, wallflower?" asked the duke.

Below his mask, Marcus's mouth set in a grimace of disgust. "I've been propping this wall up all night, afraid to let those two silly lambs out of my eyesight, with all these wolves prowling."

"Thought that might be so. Myself, I've been prowling." His friend grinned. "However, I thought the shepherd might need a drink, so I brought an extra." He held out a tall, bubbling flute of champagne.

"Thanks." Marcus reached for the glass. "Of course, by the time you decided to come by, the shepherd might have died of hunger."

Philip laughed. "All right. Go forage. I'll keep an eye on the ladies. Which are they?" He surveyed the costumed crowd floating about.

Marcus pointed out his sister, and turned his head to see if Philip followed his direction.

Allermaine's sandy brows could be seen to rise above the edge of his mask, and an appreciative smile lit his face. "*That* is your baby sister? The petite vision in red? The very chit you've led me to believe should still be in the nursery room?"

Marcus scowled. "Keep an eye on her, but do be careful of just how you keep your eyes on her, Allermaine."

Once again the duke laughed. "And the companion?" he asked, scanning the walls for a wallflower, or a woman in matronly colors. "I don't see anyone who might fit the bill."

Marcus turned his friend by the shoulders, and pointed to a group of men. "She is there."

At first Philip could not see where he meant. Then, one of the men shifted, and allowed a glimpse into the center of the circle. An orchid in white — as the forest parted and Titania stood alone.

Philip was not smiling when he whispered, "My God, Havington. No wonder you're infatuated. She doesn't resemble any lady's companion *I've* ever seen."

Marcus searched his friend's face. Allermaine didn't wear a wolfish expression. No, he rather looked moonstruck. Havington cleared his throat.

Philip tore his gaze away. "I sympathize, my friend. I have to admit, I'd wondered about this infatuation you seem to have for the companion. But I begin to understand." He glanced again at Miss Violet, then back to Havington. "Have you thought past the end of next week? Are you willing to give her up?"

There was something in the duke's tone that made Marcus suspicious. "Why do you ask?"

Philip's smile was back. "Because I'm a duke, so *I* don't give a fig what society says on my choice of consort. If you're going to give her up, I want fair notice."

Marcus's jaw clenched beneath the mask.

"I'm having fun with you." Philip laughed. "Bloody hell, you need to come to grips with this situation, Havington. She's eating away at you. Either you give her up, or you pursue. Deal with your devil, man."

If they weren't such close friends, Allermaine thought, he would indeed pursue the forest enchantress. He sighed inwardly. "Now go and get a bite to eat. I'd recommend the garlic oysters myself. Oh, and bring back more champagne?"

Marcus sauntered off and Philip turned back to his two charges. He thoroughly enjoyed dividing his attention between the two misses. *Ahh,* he lamented, *what we do for our friends.*

Then it hit him: neither Lady Larissa nor Miss Violet knew who he was. And Havington would not be back for some time. Why not keep an even closer eye on them?

He walked purposefully in the direction of Larissa's circle. Even in costume the duke was a formidable figure. He'd already caught Larissa's eye. "Ah, the mysterious

Lady L?"

She inhaled prettily, and bit her lip, not knowing how to respond.

The other gentlemen laughed. One quipped, "Well, that's *one* letter of the alphabet. She won't share her secret with us, so we may as well guess."

"One letter of the alphabet is as good as another," agreed another fellow, adding, "will you promise the next dance, madam, to the gentleman who correctly predicts your initial?"

Larissa looked back to the duke, who executed a perfectly graceful bow as the music started up for a waltz.

"As the lady has not disputed the accuracy of my guess, I shall claim her now." He placed her arm on his sleeve as he drew her toward the floor, leaving the others to grumble.

"So, Lady L," he began, drawing her into his arms, "how are you enjoying the night's entertainment?"

She tossed her dark curls. "How, sir, do you know my name begins with an L? I am sure we have never met."

"If it does not, then I confess myself flattered. For it would mean that in spite of my error, you prefer to be here in my arms."

Larissa's blue eyes flew open. "What a

279

roguish thing to say! Pray do not flatter yourself, as it happens you did guess correctly." She put her little nose up, and stared over his shoulder. Actually, she tried to, but to her chagrin she found herself looking straight into his cloak, due to his height.

Philip smiled, enjoying every moment of the little innocent in his arms. It was obvious by her shock she was unused to the empty flirtations of gentlemen of the *ton*. He found the fact appealing.

"You look striking in crimson, Lady L. It suits your hair and your perfect complexion."

He got the response he hoped for as she blushed a lighter shade of her dress.

"And you dance very well, sir," she said seriously, as if politeness compelled a return compliment. "Or — need I say 'my Lord?' I confess, I do not know the proper protocol when one dances with a stranger."

He laughed heartily. *She's even pretty when she frowns,* he thought. "But, my Lady, isn't that somewhat of an oxymoron? How can one honor propriety when dancing with a complete stranger who has not been properly introduced?"

"Now you sound like my brother." She sighed. "He insists I memorize every page of Mrs. Carver's dusty old book."

Philip was charmed. He had a desire to unmask her, to see if her expression matched the oh-so-appealing frown on her lips.

"And what book is that, Lady L? A scandalous romance novel?"

It was her turn to laugh. "I wish it were! But it is only a book of behavior for young ladies. It is *terribly* boring, but my brother believes every young woman should read it several times, from cover to cover." She didn't realize why her partner found this so hilarious, but he did.

"And *have* you?" He smiled down at her. "Have you read it several times, from cover to cover?" She was so refreshingly innocent. Philip did not want the dance to end. And he didn't blame Havington for wanting to protect her from society.

"Well, I was supposed to . . . but the drawing room was quite drafty, so my friend Constance decided the book would serve a better purpose keeping out the draft by placing it on the floor near the doors."

Allermaine laughed harder. Knowing his friend, the earl, this was ten times more enjoyable. Unfortunately, he couldn't repeat the joke, since Havington would decidedly not see the humor involved.

Philip wished he could be an insect on the

wall, watching this charming young miss and her companion and all the mischief they must surely be embroiled in on a daily basis. He was sure Havington did not know the half of it, and this made him laugh again.

Larissa dimpled, obviously pleased to find a dancing partner laughing at her conversation — though she didn't think she'd said anything witty.

The music began to wind down.

"Thank you for the dance," she said in a breathy voice.

"It was my pleasure, Lady L."

"And might I know your name, sir?"

He released her a few feet away from Constance and instead of answering, bowed once more over Larissa's hand. "Until we meet again." He turned her hand over and touched his lips to her inner wrist.

Larissa felt the warmth through her thin glove and bent her head shyly. When she looked up again, he had disappeared quickly into the crush.

Constance touched her friend on the arm. "You shivered. Are you cold, dear?"

Larissa turned, with stars in her eyes. "No, but I think my toes just tingled!"

CHAPTER TWENTY-ONE

As the guests dispersed and the orchestra wound down, it seemed the dawn could not be far away. Marcus yawned, his watch duty finally completed. He and Allermaine agreed to rendezvous at the nearby inn, then Marcus would get back to London to complete his interrupted work. He *should* send Larissa packing immediately, but any remaining risk now seemed minor. The moment his London business affairs were wrapped up, he'd return to collect his sister and escort her home to Amber Crossing. And he'd see the companion sent off as well, to her next destination.

Hopefully the two chits could not get into any more trouble in another day or two. They'd most likely sleep the day away tomorrow.

With the crowd thinning, he chose to slip out by way of the terrace. He'd prefer Larissa and Miss Violet would not spy him crossing the ballroom. Not that he wouldn't mind another glimpse of Miss Violet, the poverty-stricken Cinderella who had mysteriously donned a beautiful, obviously expensive gown and slipped into the masquerade ball. She'd elevated herself beyond her station. He smiled at how she'd deceived everyone there . . . except himself, of course.

He crossed the patio. He'd blend through the hedges, circle around, and collect his horse at the stables.

"Larissa, I see Barrows. Go ahead without me," Constance said. "I wish to have a word with him. I'll see you later, all right? Or tomorrow?"

Larissa nodded, mumbled, "Tomorrow," on a yawn, looking about to fall asleep on her feet.

Constance could not wait to thank the staff on an excellent job. Turning to follow the butler across the vestibule, she heard her name hissed.

She spun in all directions, but saw no one. No. There was someone, a man. He stood stealthily at the edge of a service doorway leading to the patio. His figure looked familiar in the dark alcove: his height, his stance.

He moved, revealing sandy hair above the

half-mask . . . Constance gasped. It was Alec!

The dark figure moved back, stepping into the night. Constance flew to the opening, looked desperately around. Tearing off her mask in order to see better, she spied someone. He stood under a honeysuckle bush that arched over the terrace wall, a small pocket providing darkest privacy along the balustrade.

She picked up her gown and ran to him. "Alec!" she choked on the cry, halfway across the flagstones.

"Shhh! Don't use my name, little one." With a laugh, her brother opened his arms as she flew to him and crashed against his chest.

"Is it really you?" she asked. "I'm afraid to open my eyes." Constance squeezed her eyes tightly shut, but was unable to stop the flow of tears.

"Look at me, then, and no more tears." He tilted up her chin. "I missed my only sister far too long."

"Alec —"

"Listen." Lord St. Edmunds spoke low, quickly. "I don't know how much time I have. You've been brave, Constance, but I must ask you to continue on your own for just a while longer." She shook her head, and he grasped her shoulders with a gentle insistency. "I'm finally close to resolving this — the real blackguards are near to apprehension. But I must remain hidden until everything falls into place."

She took a steadying breath. "Yes, I can do it, Alec. Only — do promise you'll be careful."

Placing a hand on each side of her face, Alec said, "I can't tell you how pleased I was to hear of tonight's masquerade ball. It gave me the perfect opportunity to slip within the walls and have a word with you." He looked around, then back at her. "I'll be able to return — for good — within a fortnight. Or perhaps a matter of days. Just as soon as the Runners get word back to me."

Constance laughed shakily. "Then I'm happy for you, if this will finally be resolved."

He planted an affectionate kiss on the top of her head. "It's been hard being separated this long, little sister, but everything will soon be back to normal. For both of us. I promise." Alec's voice broke and he took a breath. "It seems you've grown since I've been gone. I used to have to stoop to plant a kiss upon you."

She dipped her head, hugging him tightly

again, then raised her eyes to his face. "Be careful, Alec. I know you'll come back just as soon as you can."

"I'm reluctant to leave you, Constance. But I mustn't linger. I cannot be discovered in the area as yet. And — I know I needn't tell you — you must not let anyone know we've met."

Constance nodded mutely, the tears spilling over, even though she fought to block them.

St. Edmunds's face crumbled, seeing her pain, and he hugged her a final time.

Marcus stopped in his tracks as his very real Cinderella lifted up the skirts of her gown and scurried across the terrace, as if terrified the clock would strike midnight and the coach would disappear with the moon.

Where the devil is she running to? It seemed to him the lady needed a companion herself, to be scurrying about in the dark this late.

The answer slammed into him like a cold fist: she was out here for an assignation. She'd been lured by one of the gentlemen who had partnered her tonight.

What did she hope to gain by such scandalous behavior, when *she* had everything to lose? Was she naive enough to think the scapegrace might offer her a secure future just because they'd shared a dance together? Who could it be? If it was that chap who had attempted to hold her so closely while they danced, Marcus would beat him to a pulp.

He had to control every muscle as he watched her run into a stranger's open arms.

The bounder was still in costume. He was tall and lean, with sandy hair. In fact, he reminded Marcus very much of Lord Allermaine in his coloring and his height. Marcus narrowed his eyes, but it was not Philip. He experienced a twinge of guilt to even suspect it could be so.

Marcus's insides were churning. Should he accost the two? Or should he remain and keep an eye on her for her own protection? Or should he finally allow his rage to sever all feelings for the deceitful young lady? So far, her indiscretions had seemed harmless. But this was unacceptable.

He watched with horrid fascination as the man placed his hand under her chin and tilted her head up. He knew the stranger looked into beautiful green eyes. He saw Miss Violet gaze up at him with adoration in her eyes — and in her entire body. It was obvious from where the earl stood.

Witnessing another embrace, Marcus's rage broke. He clenched his teeth and hit a fist against the wall behind him.

Unfortunately, a small chunk of loose mortar flew, and the crumbling grit hit the terrace in a soft shower of sound.

Alec's head snapped to the side at a noise. He broke the embrace and whispered, "Take care, little sister." Taking the balustrade in one graceful leap, he ran off into the deeper hedges.

Constance brought her fist up to her mouth, trying to stifle a cry of frustration that might bring discovery in Alec's direction.

She'd heard the soft sound that had startled Alec. Now she heard the sound of booted feet approaching swiftly. Someone was intent on trapping her brother. Throwing her arms out, she turned, intentionally stepping into the path of the swiftly approaching pursuer.

Lord Havington ran into Constance, almost knocking her down. He stumbled with her, catching his own balance, and swore as he stared into the moonless night.

He clenched her arms a little too tightly. His unmasked face wore its own angry mask. "Who was that?"

Constance panicked. She dared not identify her brother. Especially not to the oh-so-proper earl, who would not hesitate to report his appearance to the authorities.

Yet she struggled inside. She didn't want to lie to Lord Havington; she wanted to confide in him.

In truth, she wanted to crumble against him, find comfort in his arms. The despair of finally seeing her brother, only to be wrenched from him moments later, was overpowering her, and she felt faint. She was miserable and needed a friend.

But it was Lord Havington who had frightened Alec away. And this instead made her want to beat upon the earl's chest in frustration.

"Who was it?" he repeated loudly.

She couldn't take the chance of trusting Havington. Not with her brother's safety. She'd given Alec her word.

Her lips trembled. Without meeting his gaze directly, she shook her head. "I — I don't know."

She felt the cold disdain of the earl. Felt his eyes rake her. If she could admit to such scandalous behavior with a total stranger, he had every right to look at her with such judgmental venom.

"I am asking you once more, Miss Violet. Who was that man? Is he known to you?"

All she could do was hang her head, and

answer dully, "No. I do not know who he is."

Marcus released her, abruptly, as if she were unclean, and stepped away.

Constance turned and ran through the open doors and didn't stop until she was in the service hallway. Once in the dark labyrinth of the servants' stairs, the dam of emotions broke. She grabbed her stomach and folded over, sobbing. Climbing the stairs by feel, through burning tears, she stumbled to her room.

She had not known such despair; not since her great-aunt had died.

CHAPTER TWENTY-TWO

The man and his horse rode recklessly at breakneck pace. He raced as if pursued by a horde of devils, but these were demons he could not elude.

With no moon to light the road, Marcus was unaware of his surroundings until reaching the inn. He waved off the sleepy stable lad, preferring to see to his sweating horse himself. As he curried Gallant, there was no brushing away his own weariness. The repeating scenes haunted him. The sequence was unbreakable. Over and over again he saw Miss Violet running across the terrace into the stranger's arms. Repeatedly he saw the man place a hand under her chin, and later place both hands on her delicate face.

Marcus knew exactly how it felt; he knew what the man had experienced. When the stranger kissed her upon her head, Marcus smelled the herbal scents in her hair. He saw the man's arms tighten around her, crushing her beautiful body to his chest, as if he owned her already. Marcus breathed heavily, wanting to cry his frustration out loud.

But this wasn't the worst of what he helplessly witnessed again and again on the stage before his blank eyes. The worst was seeing Miss Violet's reaction written upon her face. She adored this stranger. This man who had shared only one evening — perhaps only one dance with her — had captured her heart and her hope. He saw her dip her head, place it against the man's chest. Against the man's heart, it seemed. And when she looked up, he saw stars in those beautiful green eyes.

Only a fool could not recognize her feelings as she gladly leaned into the fierceness of that embrace.

He stomped away from the stable, weary from torture. He needed sleep. Chilled by the cold wind blowing through the inn's courtyard, he was chilled inside as well, to his very core.

In reply to his query, he found Allermaine in a private sitting room, reading before a crackling fire.

"Havington." Philip glanced up briefly from his book.

When Marcus didn't reply, Philip looked up again. Marcus stood just within the door, staring at the fire, a haunted expression in his shadowed eyes.

The duke sat up and closed his book. "Are you all right? Havington? Let me get you a drink. Have a seat." He nodded in the direction of the fire as he crossed to the sideboard.

Marcus obeyed woodenly and dropped into the empty chair as Allermaine poured two generous tumblers of brandy. The glass he was handed reflected the fire like a rich amber candle. It reminded him of the color of Miss Violet's tresses.

"Thank you," he mumbled, but instead of taking a drink, he ran his other hand over his face.

"What's wrong? You look like the devil."

"I feel like the devil."

Allermaine sat and waited, watching.

Marcus still had not taken a drink, but turned the glass round and round, hypnotized by the golden highlights backlit by the fire. "I don't know," he muttered. "I'm not sure what I want anymore. Or what I feel." He looked at his friend, finally seeing him. "But never mind that. . . . How did you fare the rest of the evening?"

Philip looked about to say something, then

closed his mouth. He shrugged. "In truth? I thought the ball was a smashing success. You should be proud of your sister, Havington. It will be all the talk tomorrow, you know. It had the earmark of an experienced hostess. And I believe no one was able to discover the identity of our hostess . . . or rather, hostesses, I suppose."

Marcus only half-listened.

"It's rather odd," Philip mumbled, "but I have a feeling the fugitive earl has returned to England."

This seized Marcus's attention. "What's that?"

"It's just that . . . as I left RoseHill tonight, I went to the stable to collect my horse, and heard voices speaking. You know how once you get a voice in your head, you can't shake it, until you recall who the owner is? I tried to catch a glimpse of the fellow but missed him. On the way here, it came to me. I think it was St. Edmunds. You knew him, of course?"

"No. We never met formally. I believe by the time he began circulating, I'd already left for the military. But it's not likely he'd risk returning, is it? What makes you think it was him? Just the voice?"

"That could possibly be enough, if you'd ever spoken with him. But, no, another piece I chewed on was the manner in which the stableman deferred to him. There was no acknowledgment of title, but he answered this gentleman in a deferential tone. Of course, he'd be respectful with any guest. But I noticed the chap seemed downright emotional. In fact, it seemed odd, but he wished him Godspeed. But — you're right. I'm sure he'd face legal implications if he were to set foot on English soil."

St. Edmunds. At RoseHill? Marcus bolted upright. "Good god, Allermaine! My improperly chaperoned sister is residing in that house — the house belonging to a relation of the earl's." He stood and squinted at the clock, which was barely visible in the firelit room.

Philip must have read his mind. "It's almost dawn, Havington. The ladies will be safely abed and sound asleep by now. Besides, the man was riding away on a horse, and he would not be foolish enough to be found out in his own relative's manor. They're safe. And he's gone. At least for this night."

Marcus sat again. He recalled Cinderella's escapade. *Surely* it was too coincidental. "Can you describe St. Edmunds, Allermaine?"

"Easily, but with everyone in costume, my

description may be moot." Philip took a drink.

When he set it down, he found Marcus waiting impatiently, and said, "He's quite tall. A strong build, though lean. Um, light brown — no, more of a dark blond — hair. He used to crop it a little on the longish side. In fact —" Philip laughed. "— when we were together, we were often taken to be brothers. I never saw the likeness myself, of course, but we were always getting mistaken one for the other. I can tell you, though, the thought did make me a bit nervous when all that trouble was going on."

Certain he could not feel any worse, Marcus did indeed feel worse. Ill at heart, his stomach now twisted violently. He believed it was the infamous St. Edmunds who'd captured his Cinderella's heart.

Marcus, who'd always scoffed at the notion of love at first sight, realized he'd been captivated himself the first time he spied the saucy companion standing demurely in RoseHill's library.

And now *she* had fallen in love at first sight. With Alec Chambreville, the Earl of St. Edmunds. If Marcus had not treated her so shabbily — with such high-handedness — it might have been Marcus she looked up to with such adoration in her exotic eyes.

He'd never gained her heart, and now he had most certainly lost it.

He shook himself. His main concern right now should be his sister. The earl might return to the manor in the morning. He would quickly learn no relatives were in residence. And would as quickly discover innocent Larissa, a ripe plum within picking reach.

But Marcus could not help thinking about the lovely Miss Violet also residing in the domain of St. Edmunds.

Had the man confided his identity to her tonight? Was this the reason she allowed his touch so eagerly? Did she really think the blackguard cared a fig for her future? Men such as St. Edmunds had only one pursuit in mind. And she'd made it clear she was available to be pursued.

"Why do you ask his description, Havington? Did you see him tonight?"

"Aye, I saw him tonight. And the companion was thoroughly wrapped in his arms."

"Dancing?" asked Allermaine. "With Miss Violet? I don't recall seeing anyone in her circle fitting St. Edmunds's description."

"Not dancing." Lord Havington looked at his friend. "On the terrace. Alone. After most of the guests had departed. It must have been just before he left for the stables.

I startled them, and the coward ran off."

Philip stared at him with disbelief.

"I left by an outside entrance," Marcus said, "and I spotted Miss Violet running to him. I'm sure it was him, now. Because my first thought was that it was *you*."

The duke raised eyebrows coolly. "I shudder to think of our meeting here tonight if you'd suspected it was me, Havington."

"As you say, if you both are similar in build and color, it must have been him. And if she knows of his title, then one can only assume she thinks she will gain something by throwing herself in his arms. Though when I questioned her, she denied knowing the blackguard's identity." Marcus finally noticed the glass in his hands. He wanted to hurl it against the hearth. Instead, he raised it vertically and let the liquid rush down his throat. He barely swallowed.

Philip looked warily at the clock. "Surely they must be asleep by now."

"Surely," hoped Marcus. "And you said he rode away? You are quite certain of this?"

"Yes. Definitely." Philip breathed a sigh. "At least for tonight, there is no master in the manor."

"Then we had best get a few hours' sleep ourselves."

"I take it you will not be continuing on to

London tomor—"

"Absolutely not," swore Marcus. "Larissa comes home tomorrow morning. Not one day later."

He did not even notice when the duke muttered, "Good."

Chapter Twenty-Three

Larissa carefully spread her toast with gooseberry jam from a delicate porcelain dish. She'd have slept later, but the unexpected rainstorm brought ferocious winds, slapping branches and leaves against her bedroom window, startling her awake.

Even the breakfast room, in spite of tall east-facing windows, was gloomy. She heard the wind whipping around the house, rising and falling in eerie whistling moans. Raindrops would splatter against the glass and then fly off in another direction.

Thank goodness the ball had been scheduled for last night instead of tonight, she thought. This was certainly not a day one would choose to be traveling about.

Hearing a commotion in the hallway, Larissa suspected the approach of another tempestuous storm. Her instincts were confirmed as her brother, glowering, stalked into the room. Larissa wished Constance were here sitting beside her. Her friend's support was palpable when the earl was on a fresh tirade.

Lord Havington did not waste any time on social pleasantries as he crossed the room. "Larissa, I have instructed Barrows to have the coach brought round. You will tell your maid you are to be packed within the hour. Bring only what is necessary for today. I will have the remainder of your belongings sent along later."

Larissa froze, the toast point halfway to her mouth. Her hand began shaking, and she set the triangle down. "What? I . . . I don't understand. I'm not supposed to be going anywhere, Marcus." Her blue eyes were filled with honest confusion.

"I will brook no argument, sister. I am escorting you from RoseHill immediately. We will stop at an inn tonight, as it is too windy to travel along the coast. Tomorrow, from the inn, you shall proceed directly home."

"But — what are you talking about? Aunt and Uncle — and you and I — agreed I would spend the summer here. You promised me two months. You can't yank me away at your whim. I won't go! I won't." Though the words were firm, Larissa ended on a whine.

Where was Constance? Constance could stand up to her brother and make everything all right.

But Constance was ill, according to Mrs. Dewberry. In fact, the housekeeper informed Larissa that Constance had requested only a small pot of tea be sent to her room. When the tweeny returned from her errand, she informed the housekeeper my Lady had wished the curtains be left drawn, and hadn't even responded when asked if the fire should be rekindled. Of course, Mrs. Dewberry had sent the girl scuttling back to quickly rekindle the fire whether her Ladyship noticed or not. It was a dark, chilly day outside, and Lady Constance did not need to catch a cold along with whatever else ailed her.

Larissa guiltily realized she should be upstairs checking on her friend, instead of wishing Constance were here to defend her. But Constance had seemed fine last night. She'd looked in excellent health and spirits when they had retired for the evening.

Now the world was in gloomy chaos. Constance was still abed, ill, without an appetite, and Marcus was an insane man, commanding her to return home immediately to Amber Crossing.

"Larissa, I speak with full authority as

your guardian when I tell you that — you — will — *not* — spend one more hour, let alone another night, in the same house that will likely be occupied in the near future by Alec Chambreville, Earl of St. Edmunds. You will obey me in this, as I know Uncle would have handled this situation in exactly —"

"The earl? Lord St. Edmunds? Are you sure, Marcus?" *Oh, if only it were true!* Constance and her brother to be reunited!

"Aunt and Uncle should have listened to me weeks ago." His eyes narrowed. "Are you saying Miss Violet said *nothing* to you of Lord St. Edmunds's appearance last night?"

"Last night! He arrived last night? After the ball, or during? After I retired for the evening?" Larissa's smooth brow wrinkled. "But she'd have told me if he had."

With a twitch in his jaw, Marcus said, "Evidently St. Edmunds crashed the ball in masquerade. He appeared at the stables and was recognized by a friend of mine, who chose discretion for my sake, thank goodness. And yours," he added pointedly.

Larissa looked toward the door. "Where is Lord St. Edmunds now?"

"I have no idea where he stayed last night. And can only be thankful his identity wasn't revealed. However, news will spread fast now that he's returned, and when it does *you* will be well away from the scandal. Now, Larissa. I am ordering you to move now, and with haste."

Larissa sat very still. It wasn't stubbornness; she was simply in shock at the news.

Marcus must have interpreted it as insurrection, however, and he was already at a breaking point. He strode to the table and, clamping his hands on her arms, lifted her out of her seat and turned her toward the door.

"Lord Havington, take your hands off her this instant!"

Marcus released Larissa in surprise as Constance rushed into the room, face pale and lips pressed whitely together. It was obvious from her red eyes she'd been crying.

"Miss Violet," he said coldly, his eyes staring right through her, "you will also pack your belongings within the hour. As my sister's companion, you shall be ready to accompany her on her trip home to Amber Crossing."

Constance reeled, struck by his fresh anger. It was obvious he despised her, but he'd made that obvious last night. There could never be anything between them. Her heart was traitorous and foolish.

She threw a desperate look to Larissa: surely now was the time to end this charade? Shouldn't Larissa be admitting to her brother that Constance lived here? That she would not be accompanying them home? That the whole last month had been a ruse?

Hadn't Constance done enough for her friend?

Yet Larissa was no help. With a heartbreaking sob she flew from the room, her face buried in her hands. Constance spun around, moved toward the doorway to follow and comfort her. She would convince Larissa the time for truth had arrived.

"Stay, Miss Violet. I would speak with you." After a pause, he added, "If you please," though it was not a request.

Constance stopped in her tracks near the door. Stubbornly, she refused to turn around. She heard him approach, coming very near. Now would be the time to slowly turn around and enjoy the long-promised satisfaction of putting him in his place. Or she could march out. She was lady of the house once more and need take no orders from this man. Ever again.

"And don't you dare walk out," he threatened, as if hearing her thoughts.

She feared he might grab her if she attempted to leave, shackle her arms as he had his sister. She didn't know how her treacherous body would respond to his touch. She hesitated a moment too long on her decision.

"Why was my sister not made aware that St. Edmunds had returned? You were with him last night."

"I didn't —"

"Don't lie! Do not pretend you did not know his identity. How dare you compromise my sister's virtue and reputation by clandestine meetings with him? A man who has proven himself no gentleman."

Her mouth dropped open, then closed as she gritted her teeth.

"You will look at me when I address you, madam." Yet still he spoke to her back. "This home, I believe, belongs to a member of his family. Yet you neglected to warn my sister that she might find herself under the same roof with a man who has been barred from polite society — a defiler of innocent ladies."

Constance turned slowly to face Lord Havington. She quivered with anger, her hands balled into fists against her full skirt. She was so indignant, she could not even form a reply before Marcus closed the two steps between them and came face-to-face with her.

"Madam, whom you choose to dally with is your business, but *not* while you are an employee of this family. You put my sister in a dangerous position by not warning her of the dishonorable bastard."

And with that, Constance swung her hand around and launched her fist into his eye.

Lord Havington clapped a hand to his face and stared at her in shock — a one-eyed stare.

"Well, I suppose there goes my reference!" she hollered. Then she did walk out.

CHAPTER TWENTY-FOUR

Having spent the last ten minutes sobbing her heart out, Larissa sat on the bed snuffling and wiping her eyes. Constance came in, intent on convincing Larissa it was time to end the charade — now, immediately. Instead, she found herself fighting tears of compassion. She sat on the counterpane and when Larissa turned to her, Constance wrapped her arms around her friend.

When weeping subsided to a hiccup or two, Constance retrieved a fresh square of linen from the bedside cupboard. Handing it to her friend, she rested her hand solidly on Larissa's shoulder.

"Th-th-thank you." Larissa inhaled, her breath shuddering and threatening to spill into sobs again.

"Larissa, dear," began Constance, but found no words of comfort.

"Constance?" Larissa's eyes were red and swollen. "Is it true? About Alec? Has he really returned?" She dabbed at her eyes. "I'm so selfish! I did not even think to ask you if this were true."

"Hush, Larissa. You were upset, and with good reason." Constance took up Larissa's hand. "Yes. He was here last night. But . . ." Here her own voice caught. "It was by necessity much too brief. He had time only to say the investigation proceeds favorably."

"Oh!" Larissa gave Constance a hug. "I cannot tell you how happy I am!" She sat back and squeezed Constance's hand with both of hers. "Tell me more."

"He . . . he believes he will be able to return home within a matter of days. A fortnight at the most, he said. With all of this behind him."

"Why did you not waken me?" scolded her friend.

"I would have told you this morning . . . but . . . I was despondent." Her voice trailed off.

"But why? How can you be saddened when you've seen Alec? When you've received his good news?"

Constance couldn't bring herself to speak of the confrontation with Lord Havington last night. Nor of her feelings toward her friend's brother.

She chose instead to tell a partial truth:

"Alec and I had been together only one minute. Someone spied us on the terrace, and Alec feared recognition. He fled quickly. I suppose it was the emotional turbulence of seeing him, finally, only to have him disappear again . . . so soon. It was most difficult for me. I took myself to my room, to cry out my frustration. I'm sorry I didn't seek you out sooner. I — Larissa, Marcus knows of the earl's presence. But not of my identity. Don't you think . . ."

Larissa's eyes opened wide. "Was it my brother who recognized Lord St. Edmunds? Oh, Constance, I hope he was not the one who caused your brother to flee last night."

Constance reassured her with another half-truth. "No, Lord Havington and Alec are not acquaintances. Evidently it was someone else at the masquerade who recognized Alec."

"Yes, I now recall." Larissa sounded relieved. "Marcus did mention it was a friend of his who discovered your brother. Surely St. Edmunds is now safe?"

Constance twisted her hands together. "I have to assume so, since I've heard no news to the contrary. We must hope he remains undiscovered and is given the time he needs to resolve this."

Larissa had finished with crying; her

breathing was regular. Nodding, she said, "Then I'm happy for you. I could not wish it otherwise, even if it does mean my departure is eminent."

Constance smiled. "Thank you."

Both women sat for a moment in thought.

"But —" Larissa was first to break the silence. "— why can't I stay on with you? I mean, once the investigation is successful, and the scandal is no longer attached to your family, my brother can have no quarrel."

"Well, yes, if this scandal were resolved. Remember, though, Alec said this may not happen for a handful of days. In the meantime, I promised him I wouldn't say anything for fear of his being searched for, or tipping their hand in this investigation. Also remember, Lord Havington does not yet know Alec is my brother. He may not appreciate looking the fool when he learns. Still, don't you think it is time to admit —"

"Then I shan't say anything yet either." Larissa puffed her cheeks and blew loudly. "Though, this certainly is perplexing and frustrating, isn't it? If only we had not woven this complicated tale, we would be free to explain the truth!"

Constance had to hide a smile. She longed to remind Larissa just who the tale weaver had been, but said instead, "Larissa, perhaps it *is* time to tell your brother of my true identity?"

The carriage stood ready and servants were busily loading trunks into the boot.

Marcus was not about to sit inside the coach for the long ride, not with two emotional females for company, but preferred instead to ride ahead to the inn.

He wrapped himself in his greatcoat, pulled on his gloves, and went to speak to the coachmen. He instructed them at which inn they would be stopping. The thick rain poured and slanted in great driving sheets. Marcus kept his hat pulled low and his collar up against the drenching, and hoped none could see the purplish bruise making itself known about his left eye.

If, by some chance of nature, the storm should turn, they might be able to continue on their journey to Amber Crossing, but it looked doubtful. In addition, it would be a long, tiring trip for the ladies on the slow, muddy road. Marcus almost wished to force it upon them, if only out of spite.

He reflected on the past quarter hour. His sister had finally reappeared, her small nose permanently stuck in the air. He'd followed her into the sitting room, where she retrieved her work bag. She would not answer any of his questions, and he had narrowly avoided shaking her. He bit out his instructions, and warned her she would not care for the consequences if she and her companion were not in the carriage in the time specified.

Larissa had looked pointedly out the window while he talked. When he moved toward the window, she turned her head toward the pedestal table, intently studying every tiny golden vein of its faux marble surface. When he moved around toward the table, she turned her attention to studiously inventorying every pattern in the hearth rug, ignoring him. He swore and left the room.

His many capes swirling about him, he stalked through the downpour to the horse held by the patient groom, swung up, and galloped away from the manor.

If he'd glanced over his shoulder, he would have seen Larissa at the downstairs window, watching to see when he took to the saddle. And he would have seen Constance peeking out from the floor above, at a window directly above Larissa's.

If he'd been closer, he'd have heard both sighs of relief.

Chapter Twenty-Five

In a black mood, Lord Havington didn't bother to uncross his booted legs as he stretched to reach the bottle at his elbow. A pair of glass brandy snifters waited on the small circular table, but he ignored them. He held the cool, smooth bottle against his swollen eye.

He stared, one-eyed, into the flames. All he could see was Miss Violet running across the terrace to fall into another man's arms. She'd never looked at Marcus with such open admiration.

No, she'd rather punch him in the face than smile at him.

His stomach rumbled. Where was his sister and her companion? He'd been informed their coach had finally arrived some time ago. Marcus reached for the bell rope and gave a tug. Within a minute there was a firm knock at the door, and the innkeeper's stout wife poked her head around the corner.

"Please inform my sister, Lady Larissa, that I am waiting upon her for dinner. And then please begin serving."

"Aye, my Lord." She bobbed, more by bending her thick neck into her large shoulders, and closed the door behind her.

Marcus waited impatiently until he heard footsteps outside the door. The knock was softer, and it was an aproned lad who opened the door wide. A buxom girl came forward, balancing a large tray. She waited while the boy set a linen cloth upon the table, then she carefully lowered her load. Whisking off several lids, which she held out to her helper without a glance in his direction, she eyed Marcus as hungrily as he eyed the food.

"Where is Lady Larissa?" he asked with a frown.

"Her Ladyship be sayin' she has the headache, yer Lordship." She lewdly looked him up and down, and smiled. "Were ye wantin' a bit of female company, then?"

"Where is her companion, Miss Violet?" he asked in the same brisk tone.

"Yer sister wants the other lady should stay and feed her some simple broth. She be sayin' she will see yer Lordship in the mornin', if yer Lordship don't mind."

"His Lordship does mind, blast it, but *that* doesn't seem to matter to my sister, as she only takes counsel from her private advisor," he muttered, knowing how petty he sounded.

The maid motioned impatiently for the boy to leave, and moved forward to serve. Marcus watched her from the deep armchair as she walked around to the other side of the table and spooned the rabbit stew into a deep dish, leaning across the table in his direction as far as possible. Taking a knife, she sawed off thick pieces of bread, hunching her shoulders forward as she did so, to accentuate the cleavage bubbling out. She kept her eyes on Marcus, letting her eyes wander down his body.

"That will be all I need for now." He dismissed her, ignoring the unspoken side dish she offered, and concentrated on the fire until she left.

She frowned and flounced out, and when he heard the door close, he rose from the chair and seated himself at the table to eat.

Alone.

The situation did not settle well with him. He half suspected Larissa was pouting, and not in the least bit ill. He ought to go to her room and see for himself. Damnation, but his sister was becoming less tractable by the day. And he was sure it was all because of that damned companion of hers.

Well, when they were in his territory, the rules would change. He smiled grimly as he speared a piece of rabbit a little too viciously. The gravy splashed upon his snowy cravat, and he cursed Miss Violet.

Knowing he had an easygoing disposition, it was obviously the companion's fault he couldn't seem to keep his temper under control of late.

CHAPTER TWENTY-SIX

"Really, Nigel, this is the last time I shall travel in this turnip cart. I don't know why we still retain it. It has no springs to speak of, and is simply too old for comfort."

The gilded traveling carriage bounced over yet another deep rut in the road, tossing Lady Adamsworth against her husband's side.

"Ah, Maggy, perhaps it's because I enjoy having you bounced onto my lap," the baron laughed as he captured her in his strong arms.

"Sir, you are incorrigible!" she admonished, not without humor.

Looking up into the dimples she so loved, at odds with his craggy face, she surprised him by doing something she considered scandalous: she pushed up off the seat and hoisted herself right upon his lap.

"Madam, consider yourself compromised," he said huskily, bringing his face within a kiss of hers.

At that moment the coach bounced again, causing them to bump foreheads quite painfully. Lady Adamsworth groaned and pushed herself away, settling down upon the opposite banquette. Lord Adamsworth clasped his hands between his knees and looked down in sham penitence, but she caught him peeking up at her with a grin through his thick lashes.

"So you pretend to be contrite, you unfeeling beast?"

"Maggy, my dear, you know how to wound me. However, I will once again admit you are correct. I should have exchanged this crate last fall when we were at Tattersall's." As the coach swayed on a curve, he speculated, "I wonder if we still have a coachman perched atop, or do you suppose they've all been bounced away?"

Lady Adamsworth's eyes flew open in horror, eliciting a rich laugh from her husband. She huffed in exasperation. After twenty years of marriage, the man still played his tricks on her. She looked out the window, feigning disgust, but smiled. They were considered beyond hope by their peers, who believed it gauche for a husband and wife to be actually in love with one another.

Lord Adamsworth saw his wife's smile reflected in the window. He drank in the sight of her delicate profile turned toward the scenery, her copper hair and pink cheeks. She still quickened his heart, after these two decades of marriage. And she still managed to surprise him, as he thought of the hoyden jumping onto his lap. Dwelling on this delightful thought he reached for her, and tenderly pulled her back to his side of the coach.

Nuzzling her ear, he whispered, "How far away do you suppose we are?"

Lady Adamsworth leaned back and arched one aristocratic eyebrow. "Not *that* far, my Lord. And *not* in this bumping carriage."

"Ah, but what's another bump or two? No one would ever notice."

She slapped his hand lightly. "That is very bad of you, sir. Mama and Papa were right. You are a terrible influence on their innocent daughter."

He scowled, reminded of what he'd gone through to court their daughter. Lady Adamsworth's papa had been quite intimidating: a master at interrogation. But — Lord Adamsworth smiled — starting with their wedding night, it had proven worth every torturous inquisition and inconvenience.

"I prefer to think of myself not as an influence, my dearest, but more as a *tutor.*"

Lady Adamsworth blushed. Laughing prettily, she leaned her head on his shoulder and linked her arm through his. "I cannot *wait* to see Larissa's face when we arrive at RoseHill Manor, Nigel. This was a capital idea, thank you. The very thought brings tears to my eyes, I've missed her so terribly."

Lord Adamsworth had already come to this conclusion when he proposed cutting short their visit with Lady Adamsworth's cousin. He knew his wife well enough to see she was homesick, pining for her sweet niece. Larissa was more of a daughter in Lady Adamsworth's heart.

As if reading his thoughts, she said, "I was so happy when you said you were ready to return home. We are so much alike, sir! And to think of coming here unannounced and surprising our dear Larissa. Such a splendid surprise. A perfect end to a perfect trip." Her eyes misted over, and he squeezed her hand where it rested upon his arm.

"Nigel," she began softly, on another thought, "did it upset you that Larissa chose to spend the summer months away from our home?"

"Not at all, madam wife. Did it you?"

"I must admit I had mixed emotions. But I cannot think it reflected on her love for us. When Lady Constance returned from Town to RoseHill, I knew Larissa would be excited to visit her friend. But Constance is so young — to be retiring alone to the country! I still wonder if it was wise to allow Larissa to summer with her."

"But, dearest, immediately we left on our trip, Marcus promised to venture to Rose-Hill himself to check on the two of them."

"I know, darling, but what would Marcus know of the suitability of two young ladies' doings? He has been out of touch with society these past years."

"Precisely my point. He has no use for social silliness. Therefore, if anything, I would expect him to be extra critical in keeping an eye on them." Lord Adamsworth shook his head in amusement. "Even as a youngster the lad was such a stickler for propriety. He chuckled. "I am sure he'd declare Saint Ursula unsuitable to spend the summer with our niece."

"Sir, you blaspheme," Lady Adamsworth said in a prim voice belied by her smile. "Nevertheless, I must agree with your summation of my sister's eldest child. How did two such sociable beings as my sister and her husband produce such a stodgy off-spring?"

After a few moments, she laughed heartily.

"What is so funny, madam wife?"

"Heavens, I just had a realization. I was wondering how the blundering stork had delivered such a serious packet to my sister's doorstep, considering she and her husband were so flighty and fun-loving — more in the pattern of darling Larissa. Whereas picturing our nephew, I see only his ramrod posture, his arched eyebrow, and his frown. Then . . . I had a vision of my father!"

"Good Lord, woman, *please* don't tell me he will be as stodgy as your papa. Is it possible? Lord help Larissa and young Lady Constance!"

Once again, they popped up as the carriage raced over a pothole.

CHAPTER TWENTY-SEVEN

Marcus strolled into the private parlour where he'd dined alone the previous night. It was cozier this morning: the fire crackled and popped tunefully, the table was laid to accommodate his sudden appetite, the smell of smoked bacon permeated from the kitchens below. Even the streaks on the window caused delightful prisms of the morning sun.

Perhaps his own good mood was filtered by the prism of a good night's sleep. He looked forward to breakfasting with his sister Larissa and her rebellious companion. Thinking of breakfasting with Miss Violet brought back sharp memories of generous cleavage exposed in the breakfast room that morning in RoseHill.

Perhaps, he thought, smiling, since she'd packed so hastily, she might once again have forgotten her fichu. Or — now he scowled — she would deliberately discard it along with all his other commands. *If only,* he thought wistfully; it would not really matter why.

He was feeling magnanimous this morning, now he was fully in charge. He would see his sister returned home safely today. The sun had already begun sponging the mud, as morning steam rose from the road outside the inn. Sooner than anticipated they would be in *his* domain, and he most certainly was master of his manor. But what to do with the companion after their arrival? How quickly to send her on her way? To where?

And what of the reference he had promised? He chuckled out loud at her explosive mention of the reference, then winced as he touched his eye. No, perhaps the miss would not receive a written testimony . . . at least, not one she would care for anyone to see.

Lord Havington turned with pleasurable expectation at the knock on the door, hoping to see Miss Violet in another of her scandalous outfits. But, alas, it was only the innkeeper's wife.

"I'll be back in with the mornin's victuals, yer Lordship," she bobbed, and set down fragrant pots of tea and coffee. "This here's tea." She indicated a stumpy silver teapot with an oversized hinged lid, topped with an acorn finial. "And," she said, pointing, "coffee, if yer Lordship prefers." The unmatched brass pot gleamed. She left a white bar towel wrapped around its pearwood handle.

As she moved to leave, Marcus requested, "Please inform my sister, Lady Larissa, that we will breakfast early, as I am anxious to leave."

"Yes, yer Lordship, right away, sir," she nodded herself backward out the door.

The thought of arriving home at Amber Crossing appealed to Marcus. His uncle and aunt would be pleased to receive a letter while at Cousin Ruth's, a report from him. He'd promised to keep an eye on Larissa and felt satisfied his mission had been accomplished. Their choice of companion, however, was deplorable, but he needn't include that information. If it hadn't been for his intervention, Larissa's reputation would likely be in shreds by now.

Thankfully, this nonsense would never be necessary again. Once the Season started, his sister would have a proper coming out and they could turn her over to a husband for future guidance and supervision. Good luck to the man!

Of course, *that man's* job would be far easier than it had been for Marcus — *he* wouldn't have a companion constantly underfoot, undermining his instruction at every opportunity.

Larissa's husband wouldn't have to reprimand the lovely Miss Violet, only his bride.

He wouldn't have to read passages from an etiquette book in hopes of converting the hoyden Miss Violet. Nor would he suffer her snubs, or be tempted with marvelous ways to get even with the lovely devil.

Of course, neither would the man see the sparkle in Miss Violet's eyes when mischief was brewing. And he wouldn't hear her delightful laugh, even when it was at his own expense. Nor would he get a glimpse of her lovely assets in the breakfast room while attempting to concentrate on his morning newspaper.

Yes, Marcus was definitely looking forward to his sister's arrival in the breakfast room. And that of her companion's as well, of course.

The steaming food arrived. And with it, bad news.

"Pardon, yer Lordship, but my Lady says she is 'in-deez-posed,' and will not be able to join ye for breakfast." The woman shifted a cut crystal marmalade dish aside to make room for the baked kippers. "I'll just make up a small basket of muffins and fruit for her, for the journey." She transferred another small dish to the table.

"No, you will not!" Marcus thundered, startling the poor woman so, she had to juggle the porcelain sauce dish in her pudgy hands. "By Zeus, my sister *will* join me, if I have to carry her downstairs myself. You will be so good as to inform Lady Larissa she has exactly *ten minutes* in which to be seated in *that* chair, or I shall come to fetch her. And tell her this includes Miss Violet as well."

With round eyes, the innkeeper's wife waddled quickly out of the room.

Marcus pulled his pocket watch from his vest and checked the minute hand. In exactly ten minutes he would march up the stairs to his sister's room. He folded his arms and brooded on the fire. Checking his watch several times, he noted eight minutes had passed when to his satisfaction the doorknob bell jangled softly.

Larissa stood white-faced in the doorway. Marcus noted her tear-stained eyes, but was determined not to budge from the course he had chosen.

"Come in, Larissa." He stood and made a slight bow.

"G-good morning, brother." She glided

over to take a seat as Marcus pulled her chair out.

He settled her in and turned expectantly toward the door. "And where is Miss Violet?" He checked his pocket watch. He rather relished the idea of going up to her room and hauling her over his shoulder as he had threatened.

"Marcus, sit down, please. I have something to confess." Larissa was twisting her linen napkin so tightly her knuckles were white.

Marcus did not sit. "Yes?"

"The reason —" she began in a tiny voice, "— the reason I did not have dinner with you last night was because I was trying to avoid you." She peeped out at him from under her lashes, as if testing his reaction to this revelation.

Marcus laughed. Though it was not really a friendly, brotherly laugh. "This is what you need to confess to me? You think I did not realize exactly what you and your companion were up to?" Then another thought struck him. "And exactly whose idea was this, dear sister? To avoid me?"

Larissa looked extremely uncomfortable, and squirmed in her seat. "Well, I suppose we both talked about it, and we both thought about it together."

"Mmm-hmm. And . . . ?"

Larissa's clear blue eyes widened innocently. "And what?"

Marcus slid into his seat, and leaned forward conspiratorially. "And where is your partner in crime?" He bared his teeth in a smile. "If the plan was to avoid me last night, it worked."

"Well . . . and also to avoid you this morning, you see."

"Ah, but *that* did not work." His teeth remained bared, but without the smile.

"No," she said, pouting, frowning at her brother. "You were not expected to deliver an ultimatum. I must tell you it was unfair, as it quite ruined the careful plans we had made."

"Mmm-hmm. And . . . ?"

Larissa again looked at him with expectation. "And what?"

"And, where is Miss Violet? Your plan did not work, you admit. And you cannot avoid me this morning. So where is your companion hiding? I find it hard to believe," he added dryly, "that she feels such remorse and guilt about this idea that she is embarrassed to face me."

"Well, we thought if we avoided you this morning, then the coach would be on its way home, and the next time we — I mean

331

I — saw you would be . . . at Amber Crossing."

Now it was Marcus's turn to raise his eyebrows. "I'm not following you, sister," he said in clipped tones, trying not to frighten her into silence.

"Well, . . ."

"And stop saying *well!*" he thundered.

Larissa reacted with a jolt. She brought her napkin up to her face as her lips began to tremble.

"Larissa," he said her name in three slow syllables, "I am not trying to bully you, but I have no idea what you are rambling on about. Now, why don't you explain everything, so we can get on with our breakfast before it is stone cold?"

"Wel —" Larissa caught herself, and began again. "We — Miss Violet and I, that is —"

"Who else could we be referring to, madam?" He asked loudly, his temper at breaking point.

Larissa flinched at his sarcasm and wailed into her napkin.

Marcus ran a hand through his hair. Eyeing the food, which was no longer steaming, he sighed theatrically and chose a different tactic. "I am sorry, Larissa. Please, tell me what you were about to say. You and

Miss Violet . . ." he began softly for her.

She put her napkin down and folded her hands on the table. "Miss Violet and I thought it would be best to avoid you as long as we possibly could."

After several moments of waiting for her to continue, Marcus realized his sister, apparently, was satisfied with this explanation. Feeling ready for Bedlam, he said, "Ah, I see, I'm sure. So you tried to avoid me. And now you can no longer avoid me. Then, that is that."

Larissa nodded, smiled tremulously, as if assuming the inquisition was finally concluded. She picked up a serving dish, ready to fork a fat sausage onto her plate.

Perhaps, thought Marcus, if he were to begin again . . . if he were to speak slowly, nonchalantly, as he poured tea into his cup? As if they were home having a companionable breakfast in the grand parlour, and he just happened to be reminded of an old friend?

"Sister, where exactly is Miss Violet?" Unfortunately, it did not come out as nonchalantly as he had hoped.

Larissa bit her lip, obviously not understanding why they still had to pursue this uncomfortable subject. She set the plate of sausages back down. "I told you, we felt it best to avoid you."

"Ah, so you did." He forced a smile, then dropped it as quickly. He reached for the sugar bowl. "In exactly thirty seconds I am going to rise and retrieve Miss Violet from her room. I assume she is still in her room?"

Larissa froze. She blurted, "Marcus, there is something I promised Miss Violet I would tell you. The moment we reached Amber Crossing."

Marcus dropped a lump of sugar loudly into his tea. "I asked whether she is still in her room."

His sister closed her eyes. "Miss Violet did not spend last night with me." She opened one eye, to look at her brother's reaction. She immediately closed it again.

"You mean . . . she did not spend last night with you in your same room? Or," he demanded, glowering, "do you mean she did not spend last night with you in this same inn?"

"She did not spend the night in my room," said Larissa in a small voice, opening her eyes, but looking down now at her empty plate. "But I promised her I would tell you something the moment we reached —"

"What is this nonsense?" he inquired softly, his teacup halfway to his lips. "Where exactly was Miss Violet last night?"

"She stayed behind at RoseHill Manor."

Marcus dropped his teacup and it bounced on the thick, white linen cloth, splattering hot tea in every direction. Larissa jumped up, whisking her napkin off her lap, and began sopping up the hot liquid.

Marcus's hand shot out and held her wrist. Her face flew up to meet his gaze.

He was flushed. But not from the hot liquid. "Was Lord St. Edmunds to return to RoseHill Manor after you left?" he ground out the words, his voice hoarse and tight.

"I don't know." Larissa's lip trembled, and she looked straight down at the tea stain beneath their hands. "But, Marcus, I need to tell you —"

Marcus released her hand and shoved himself away from the table, knocking his chair over in his abruptness and rage.

CHAPTER TWENTY-EIGHT

After her brother stormed out, Larissa sat frozen in her chair at the breakfast table. She hadn't touched any of the dishes, now cold. She could no longer stomach the idea of breakfasting.

She'd never seen him so furious. Of course, she meant to tell him the truth, she simply hadn't envisioned it being this soon. She had tried to tell him just now, but he hadn't given her the chance.

The careful plot she and Constance hatched allowed for the earl to leisurely find out the truth — sometime later today — when Larissa and her brother were home at Amber Crossing. She and Constance had counted on his proximity to his lands to soften and mellow his mood, putting Larissa's disclosure in a less important light.

Now what would happen? Would Marcus insist they retrace their journey of yesterday, returning to fetch Miss Violet? But there was no longer a Miss Violet. And Constance would not come, of course. She was finally re-established as mistress of RoseHill.

If this were his plan, Larissa could no longer delay telling him the truth. It would be inexcusable to force a ride back, only to disclose at RoseHill's doorstep that Constance did in fact belong there, and they should merrily turn around and head home once again to Amber Crossing.

Perhaps returning to RoseHill would not be his intent. In his rage, Larissa suspected they would continue to their own home, and he would write off the companion as a bad experience best left behind. If so, Larissa thought with relief, she could delay telling him the truth until they were home. He would have had many miles behind him within which to contemplate and cool his temper. Her hopes rose at the prospect of this scenario.

Or — perhaps he intended to send a servant back to RoseHill while he and his sister idled here. If this were the case, then she should let him know the truth before he dispatched a rider.

She rose from her seat and moved to peer out the window onto the courtyard below. She did not see any activity or indications of a horseman being dispatched. Should she seek Marcus out to determine his plans? She continued to twist the napkin in her hand. Larissa was not a pacer, but she found herself flitting to the window, then back to the chair.

Not wanting to confront Marcus until he calmed down, Larissa reasoned he would eventually come to her and make his plans known. The more she considered, she decided if he were to dispatch someone without letting her know, then the unnecessary errand would be his own fault. Yes, it was *his* duty to seek *her* out. In the meantime, she would sit in this private parlour and await him.

She picked up a book from a small shelf, and sat in a cozy chair next to the fire. Concentrating was difficult. After she found herself reading the same paragraph for the fifth time, she sighed, ready to give up.

A knock on the door startled her.

"Yes? Come in." She spoke barely above a whisper.

One of the younger maids bobbed a curtsy. "Miss? John Coachman asked me to tell you he is ready to depart. Shall I send a man upstairs for your luggage?"

Larissa stared at the woman in the large mob cap and hesitated, not sure what to say, what to ask. But the maid would not know to which destination the coach would be bound, let alone which direction it would take when it left the inn's yard.

Sighing, Larissa knew she must now consult Marcus. And, if his destination were indeed RoseHill, she must confess. Now.

"Please, would you tell my brother, Lord Havington, that I must speak to him prior to our departure? Please let him know it is most urgent."

"Yes, mum. And your baggage?"

"Your man will find my trunk ready, just inside the door to my room."

Larissa put the book down and paced to the window. Leaning her forehead on the cold glass, she took several deep breaths to calm herself, watching the fog of exhalation form and clear on the window pane. She stared outside without seeing as she rehearsed her explanation to her brother — depending on his destination, of course. If they were continuing on to Amber Crossing, she might get a short reprieve before she must reveal the truth.

The second knock again startled her. She sucked in her breath and, holding it, came away from the window, waiting for her brother's angry visage to appear as the door swung open.

The same young maid stuck her head in.

"I'm sorry, miss, but they says the earl has already departed."

"But for where?"

"I'm sure I don't know, miss," the young girl apologized.

"Send the coachman to me immediately, if you will."

The girl scurried off and Larissa started sweating. What if her brother had already left, to return to RoseHill? His fury this morning would be nothing compared to when he discovered he'd made the return journey needlessly.

It made more sense, though, that he had opted to continue on ahead of her coach toward home — to Amber Crossing.

Moving once more to the window, Larissa saw her trunk being loaded. The maid looked up at the coach driver, speaking with animated gestures. The man atop the coach secured the leads and hopped down from his perch. As she saw the top of his hat disappear from view beneath her, she turned and waited expectantly for the next visitor to enter.

Booted steps approached the door, and after a quick knock the door opened, and the coachman stood framed in the doorway, hesitant to step inside the parlour.

"Yes, my Lady?" he removed his hat.

"John, I desire to know our destination."

"Yes, my Lady. We are to proceed to Amber Crossing."

Faint with relief, Larissa closed her eyes briefly and whispered a thank you. She would have her wish; she need not see her brother until they reached Amber Crossing.

If Marcus had decided to write off the companion they left behind, then perhaps he'd even see the humor in this whole situation. No, not likely. Anyway, now her plan could proceed as she and Constance had originally constructed.

"Did my brother indicate whether we shall stop and meet for luncheon? Or, is he continuing all the way to Amber Crossing?" *Could she be so lucky?*

"Neither, my Lady. His Lordship is not going on with us. He informed me he has some urgent unfinished business back at RoseHill, and I am to proceed directly to Amber Crossing with you in my charge. We've got your trunks loaded, my Lady. Shall I escort you down now?" The coachman eyed the covered plates on the table. "Or did you need a bit more time to finish eating?"

The room was spinning, and Larissa grabbed the chair for support. *Marcus returning to RoseHill!* And she was being

ordered on ahead, to Amber Crossing.
Constance would need her support. Marcus
would murder Constance! Looking at the
no-nonsense coachman, Larissa knew Marcus would have threatened him to assist her
home in haste if he valued his job.

She clutched at his question to buy a little
time to think. "Yes, please, I do need a little
more time to finish my breakfast, if you
will."

He nodded solemnly and closed the door
behind him.

Larissa dizzily slid into the chair and sat
frozen, still not touching any dishes or
plates. Her mind worked furiously. She
could not desert Constance. What should
she do?

She thought of the many books she'd
read, considered her favorite heroines. What
would each of those brave women have
done? An idea began unfolding in her head.
Nodding to herself, she let it take on a life
of its own, until it all made the most perfect
sense. She jumped up with determination,
and tugged on the bell.

"Are you sure they won't beat me, miss?"
asked the maid in a shaky voice.

"Of course not! My brother is not a
barbarian," huffed Larissa. "He simply likes

to act like one . . . occasionally," she added in honesty, in a low voice.

This did not seem to have the desired effect of calming the young girl who quaked before her wearing Larissa's traveling cloak.

"Now," instructed Larissa, as she pulled the hood of the cloak up over the girl's head. "When you walk out, just look down at the ground. Hold this handkerchief to your face, as if you have been crying. Make sure you step into the carriage as if you owned it. Do not hesitate, or they will become suspicious."

Larissa turned to the table and picked up a parchment sheet, folded it. "Here is the letter I wrote. It says I ordered you to deliver this message for me, and I put you in the coach, but you know nothing else. In this letter, it explains I take full responsibility, and you thought you were only delivering a letter of life-and-death importance."

She tucked the folded letter into one of the large pockets of the cape, then dug in her reticule and pulled out several coins. Putting one into the maid's hand, she said, "This one is yours to keep, regardless of the outcome." She dropped several more into another deep pocket of the cloak. "Remember, if you cannot fool them with this disguise in the next few minutes, then you must return this cloak to me with all of these coins. However, if they are fooled, and the carriage rolls out of the inn yard, then all of these are yours to keep."

As a final thought, she dropped in a few more coins, saying, "And here is enough for a return fare on the post as well."

The young girl's eyes were round as she watched all the coins as they dropped and clinked into the deep pocket, speculating they could soon be hers.

"Have you cleared your absence with the inn?" asked Larissa.

"Yes, mum. 'Tis my aunt in charge today, and she gave me her permission. I offered to split the coin with her," she explained.

At this satisfactory answer Larissa dropped three more coins into the folds of the cape, in generosity to the co-conspirator.

"Now you must go. Remember, don't stop for anyone, and march into that carriage as if all these coins were awaiting you on its cushions inside. I'll watch from this window. Good luck to you!"

The maid bobbed a quick curtsy, and went jingling out of the room.

Larissa moved to the edge of the window and peered out cautiously through the curtains. A new coach was pulling into the yard. Drat! It could not be possible the maid would get into the wrong coach, could it?

But no, she saw her green cloak hurry across the yard and right up to her brother's coach. The door was opened and the young girl, face buried in the handkerchief, practically fell into the coach in her hurry to be up the steps and inside, ignoring the hand offered to her. Larissa had to grin.

She hid behind the curtain until they rolled out of the yard. As the dust settled and the coach was no longer in sight, she released the breath she'd been holding.

Now — there was the matter of how to get herself back to RoseHill Manor. What would the heroine of her novel do?

Larissa squinted, conjuring up a young maiden, destitute and determined. She pictured the lass borrowing a horse from the stables and riding pell-mell along the highway . . . alone . . . pell-mell . . . unescorted on a wildly galloping horse, her mane of hair and the horse's streaming in unison in the wind. Hmm, the last time she had spent more than one hour astride a man's saddle, her limbs had been sore and numb for days. No, perhaps this heroine did not resemble Larissa after all.

She squeezed her eyes shut, picturing a different heroine. One who did not gallop across the countryside. One who carried herself with all the nobility of a young lady of the castle. One who coolly approached the innkeeper, inquiring as to a carriage for hire. One who hinted of a payment commensurate with the long trip and back.

Yes, this heroine suited her. She stood gracefully and, leaving her room, regally descended the stairs, her chin high and her hands clasped together at her waist.

CHAPTER TWENTY-NINE

Constance eyed the tea service. Bless Mrs. Dewberry! She must have sensed her mistress needed extra comfort and pampering this afternoon.

The bottom tier of the crystal server balanced a delicate bowl of spiced peaches, one of Constance's favorites, and a dish of fresh blackberries. Perched on the middle plate were delicate cucumber sandwiches. And on the smallest top crystal tier, thin slices of poppyseed cakes — another of Constance's favorites — alternated with square iced biscuits. Atop the table's snowy linen sat a dish of thick cream and a fragrant pot of tea.

It was then she spied the tiny sherry glass, filled to the brim. This brought a smile. Aunt Agatha had always insisted on a sip of sherry with their afternoon tea. Here was Mrs. Dewberry's way of declaring the true lady of the house was officially back in residence. Constance lifted the liqueur and sniffed appreciatively. And sipped.

Thirty relaxing minutes later Constance dabbed her lips with a starched napkin. The tea was aromatic, a fine oolong.

Oh, my. The sherry had quite gone to her head. She felt a bit drowsy and quietly content, sitting in the early afternoon sunlight. She could almost forget about the Earl of Havington and her poor friend Larissa. All that mattered now was that Alec had returned, just last evening. Everything had finally been resolved and it was a joyous homecoming. Surely she could not be more content.

But if this were so, why did she keep thinking of Lord Havington?

"Hullo, Moppet!"

She looked up to see her brother framed in the doorway. How deliciously surreal: here she sat, relaxing in the sunny parlour, and Alec calling her by the old nickname she used to despise; now it was precious to hear the endearment.

Alec crossed the room and leaned his tall frame down to plant a kiss on top of his sister's head. "I still can't believe I'm here."

"Neither can I. Would you care for some tea or biscuits?"

"No, I just visited the kitchen. Mrs.

Dewberry swears I lost weight while I was gone, and she's on a campaign to stuff me. I could not eat one more bite or I would be banned to the trophy room. However . . ." He swiveled, and spied the liqueur cabinet. "I will have a glass of brandy. Will you join me, sister?"

"I'd love to." She thought to decline, still feeling the effects of her cordial. But it was so refreshing to once again be treated as an equal, as an adult. She would not miss out on the camaraderie.

She watched Alec withdraw two generous snifters. He unstoppered the decanter and filled each glass halfway. She tried hard to imagine it being Lord Havington's back, and to picture the stuffy earl offering her a glass of brandy. She snorted. *That* would never happen.

Alec turned at the sound, raising an eyebrow. "Did you say something?"

Constance was chagrined at the unfeminine sound. Well, she was once again mistress in her own home, and she could drink — and snort — if she so chose. She giggled, and saw Alec looking at her with a bit of concern. *I've got to get control of myself.* She shook her head. "No, brother. Just thinking of someone."

"Pleasant thoughts?"

"Not really," she admitted, picturing Lord Havington delivering a lecture. "Rather a pompous, unpleasant gentleman of my acquaintance. . . . Do you remember my friend Larissa?" Seeing no immediate recognition on his face, she continued. "Anyway, the gentleman I mention is Larissa's older brother — quite stuffy. You and he would absolutely not get along. He happens to be an earl, though he is really cut of a clergyman's cloth. Just loves to lecture people on their behavior. And he puts the fear of Hades into his sister."

"But not you?" he teased.

"He wouldn't dare." She laughed merrily, reaching up to accept the glass Alec handed her.

Marcus strode into the room, Mrs. Dewberry once again flying helplessly in his wake.

He stopped cold when he spied Constance sitting in the corner chair by the window, and then his gaze flew to St. Edmunds, who lounged next to the fireplace.

Alec stiffened. Mrs. Dewberry, out of breath, apologized, "I'm sorry, my Lord. He would not wait to be announced."

"It's all right, Mrs. Dewberry. Thank you," said Alec, watching Constance and Marcus stare at one another. The tension strung between the two across the wide space was a physical thing, a rope twisted so tightly it might snap.

The housekeeper bobbed a curtsy to St. Edmunds, threw a resentful glance at Lord Havington's back, and exited.

Marcus moved across the room until he stood directly in front of Constance, who remained glued to her seat. Her face was pink, and she turned it away from Lord Havington's intense stare. "Has he touched you?" he whispered hoarsely.

Constance was slow in responding; her thoughts were fuzzy. She shook her head, which felt heavy and clumsy. Why should Alec touch her? Alec was her brother. The silly Havington goose! She smiled at her cleverness, and a tiny hiccup escaped. Her eyes widened and she put two fingertips to her mouth in mortification.

Lord Havington's eyes narrowed. He leaned his tall frame down, putting a hand on each arm of her chair, and he put his face very close to hers. Constance blushed furiously, extremely aware of the warmth he exuded, fresh from his ride. She inhaled his smell, which she loved. Marcus sniffed, then straightened abruptly.

"You've been drinking —" He turned to

St. Edmunds, furious with accusation. "She's been drinking!"

"Yes, you can see she has a glass. Of course she's been drinking." Alec tilted his head and frowned at his sister. Her eyes were in fact a little too glazed, and she still had a silly grin pasted upon her face. "Though I confess," Alec muttered, "I didn't believe she had *that* much to drink."

Constance giggled. "That *was* quite a large snifter of brandy, Alec!"

Marcus stiffened further at her familiar use of the man's name.

She picked up the small sherry glass on the tea trolley, and said in a singsong voice, "I also had — a bit — of — sherry." With a lopsided grin, she held the empty glass higher, as if they couldn't see it otherwise.

Marcus came over and reached out his hand. Constance set down the sherry glass and placed her slender hand in his large warm one.

"No, madam," he instructed. "I want your glass."

She handed him the tiny offending sherry glass.

"No. The other one."

She contritely held out the almost-empty brandy glass. Marcus had to pry each finger from the glass stem so he could finally relieve her of it.

Stepping away, he set it on a nearby table, his face an inscrutable mask. Then he turned to deal with St. Edmunds.

"She is drunk," he accused flatly.

"Ppppphhh!" Constance snorted through her lips, though it came out a little more sloppily than she'd intended.

Both men stared at her in surprise.

"I most certainly am not . . . drunk . . . sir! I am an adult, and I shall have a drink . . . if — I — wish," she slurred slowly, the last word leaving her lips as if making a shushing.

She stood up, swaying just a bit, and made a grab at the wingback of her chair. She put her nose in the air, but lost her balance slightly, and pulled herself closer to the chair. She leaned on it and said to Marcus, "And, I do not appreciate being spoken of in the third person, either. You, Lord Havington, shall stop treating me as if I were a child." She emphasized her decree with a satisfied "Humph" and a careful nod.

He crossed the room swiftly.

Constance backed up against the wall as he continued stalking forward. He placed both hands high against the wall, boxing her in, and brought his face to within inches of hers.

"Believe me, it's taking every bit of restraint I have *not* to," he said in an awful tone. "Now, madam." He grasped her arms tightly, brought her forward a few steps, and sat her back down firmly in the deep armchair. "Sit down." He bent his mouth to her ear and added quietly, "While you still can."

Alec could not believe his eyes. *He'd* never had this sort of luck in dealing with his sister's temper. Who was this gentleman? Had Constance formed a tendre for someone in Alec's absence? Though the man certainly wasn't treating her very tenderly, Alec thought with a grin. He lost his smile when he found the gentleman's cold glare upon him.

"You are St. Edmunds?"

"I am. And you, sir?"

"Havington. The rumors were true, then. I heard you'd returned."

"You heard correctly. Fortunately, I am in England to stay. My run of bad luck has been resolved, and I intend —"

"So — having ended one scandal, St. Edmunds, you propose to move directly into another?"

"I'm sure I don't know what you are talking about," Alec said coldly. "Explain yourself."

"Did you spend the night here last night?"

"Of course I did. This is my sister's home."

Marcus did not take his eyes from St. Edmunds as he asked loudly, "Miss Violet? Did you also spend the night here last night?"

Alec spun toward the door, but there was no one there. He turned back to the earl. "Whom are you addressing, Havington? There is no other lady here."

Marcus held murder in his eyes. "There is most certainly a lady here, St. Edmunds. Though she may be a mere servant to you — to use as you wish — she is still a lady. And as it is obvious she did spend the night here — with you in residence — I demand to know your intentions."

"I have no idea what you are raving about, Havington."

"She —" Marcus pointed at Constance, while still staring intently at Alec. "— spent the night here, did she not? I refer to Miss Violet."

"*Wh— ?* She is most certainly not a *Miss Violet*. That is *Lady Constance*." Alec turned and looked at his sister, waiting for her to confirm that this man they had allowed into their home was deranged.

Marcus groaned. "She is in fact *Miss Violet*," he bit out, advancing toward Alec. "If she has passed herself off as a member of the nobility, she has fooled you. But that is now water under the bridge. For the fact is, sir, you *both* spent the night under the same roof, and I demand to know what you intend to do about it. If you have one shred of honor left, you will offer to marry her."

Marcus came within an arm's length of St. Edmunds before he froze. This wasn't what his heart wanted. He wanted her for himself — he realized it with disorienting certainty.

"Marry her! You're stark, raving mad, Havington," said Alec loudly. "This is ridiculous, and furthermore, I demand you leave this house at once, before I have you thrown out."

Marcus lost any remaining control. "And so I shall, St. Edmunds." With that, he planted his fist in St. Edmunds's face, and the earl dropped like a dead stag to the floor.

The room became as deathly quiet as a tomb. Marcus turned to Miss Violet, certain he would find her in maidenly shock.

Actually, the companion was oblivious. Slumped in the armchair, her eyes were closed and she smiled peacefully. Her head lolled to one side. Marcus approached and heard her soft snoring. The lady was passed out.

"Bloody hell!" Marcus reached down and softly shook her, to awaken her.

No response, though she let out the softest of moans.

Coming to a hasty decision, he took her arms and pulled her forward to the edge of the seat. Lifting her lifeless form, he slung her over his shoulder and stalked out.

In the hall he ran into Barrows, who looked in shock to see the inert form of his mistress slung across the earl's shoulder like a sack of barley.

"Order the traveling coach brought round, Barrows," snapped the earl.

"Yes, my Lord. Right away, my Lord." He hastened to obey, not thinking to challenge the earl's command.

Marcus continued toward the entryway, and ran into a mob. All of RoseHill's servants were gathered in a cluster, gossiping and whispering. At the sight of the earl striding forward, they jumped sharply aside. He stood for a moment, with Constance dangling similar to a knapsack.

"Return to your stations," Marcus barked. "All of you."

They scattered quickly in all directions.

After Lord Havington walked past them and on out the door, they came back together in another wave and scampered to peer out the doorway.

"Oh, dear, he's done murdered the missus!" shrieked Ellen, the tweeny.

"Stop yer bansheein'. Of course he ain't murdered 'er," threw in old Tom. "She were breathin', weren't she?" He looked around at the desperate faces. "Weren't she?"

They all crowded closer in the open doorway, watching Lord Havington deposit Constance into the coach.

"We should go get help," suggested Barrows, joining them at the door and feeling guilty no one was moving to assist Lady Constance.

"But, where is Lord St. Edmunds?" queried Mrs. Eldridge, looking around.

"P'haps he's done murdered the master, too!" shrieked Ellen.

"Nonsense!" everyone responded at once, but as a group they all hurried swiftly down the hall to verify.

CHAPTER THIRTY

Marcus's thoughts were in turmoil as the coach rolled along. What had he been thinking, to kidnap Miss Violet from under St. Edmunds's nose? What was it to Marcus if the earl kept her in luxury, to use as he pleased? His jaw clenched. *That* was not going to happen.

He softened as he looked down at her. She slept peacefully, cuddled against his side. At some point during their journey, she'd wrapped her arms around one of his and snuggled closely. He touched her hair where it lay disarrayed on his shoulder and smiled. She was so innocent.

"What to do with you?" he wondered aloud.

And where was his destination? If he returned to Amber Crossing, would she be content to remain with his sister as companion, knowing she could be a nobleman's mistress? Apparently she saw nothing wrong with the proposition; else, why remain behind at RoseHill? Though . . . she had been drunk. Perhaps this was St. Edmunds's ploy. Perhaps he'd kept her drinking since yesterday so she would be disinclined to leave.

Perhaps nothing had happened between them last night. He wished it so, much too violently. He thought of St. Edmunds touching her honeyed hair and had to stop, or he would turn the coach back around and kill the man . . . if he hadn't already. Once St. Edmunds had hit the floor, Marcus had not given him another thought.

It did not matter now. She was fully compromised, whether or not anything had happened between them last night. Her only recourse was to marry, and to marry quickly.

He looked idly out the window, considering. The solution flashed by — it was so simple! If St. Edmunds did not care about her honor, then Marcus would make the ultimate sacrifice: he would escort her to Scotland and marry her there.

After all, the blame for her going astray could be laid at her employer's doorstep. He should have escorted both ladies into the coach before riding off yester morning. The innocent companion had been under his protection. What if it had been his own sister who had been tempted by the licentious earl? He felt immediately grateful it was not Larissa who'd been compromised, then just as immediately felt guilty, looking down at the helpless Miss Violet leaning against him.

It was only fair and just he do the honorable thing. He didn't wish to be married, of course, but this was the only course of action a true gentleman could take. Having her as his countess would scandalize his friends, of course. On the other hand, the woman already carried herself as if she were a bloody princess.

Looking at her again, he was extremely aware of her body against his. Thinking about being married to her and having her in his marital bed sent a delicious thrill through his body.

Perhaps doing the right thing would not be such a difficult sacrifice after all.

Constance awoke slowly. Why was her head so heavy? And couldn't someone do something about all the bumping and jostling? Her skull throbbed dully with every bounce.

She opened her eyes to see Lord Havington's face close to hers. He was smiling, an easy, soft smile; she smiled back. It was easy to respond to the warm regard in his grey eyes. She also liked the smell of his clothes, with her nose nestled so closely against his vest, and his arm wrapped round her —

What? Her eyes flew open and she shot up straight. Instantly she regretted the quick move, her head a percussion instrument. Moving a bit more cautiously, she removed the earl's arm and scooted as far away from him on the banquette as she could. And narrowed her eyes at him. *Where were they going?*

"Where are we going?" she repeated aloud in panic, looking out the window in dizziness as the countryside flew by — countryside she did not recognize.

"We are on our way to Scotland," he began calmly, as if watching her for a reaction. He did not have long to watch.

"Scotland!" she screeched. "Stop! Stop the coach this instant. I demand you take me back to the manor."

Lord Havington's jaw twitched. "Miss Violet . . . may I remind you that last night you spent the night at RoseHill, unchaperoned? And may I also remind you that last night the Earl of St. Edmunds spent the night at RoseHill Manor?" His eyes drilled into hers.

"Of course I spent the night there. I live there."

"You *lived* there, as chaperone to my sister. But that was before the earl returned home. Good God, can you be so unaware of the seriousness of your situation? As of this morning, you have been compromised. Thoroughly. Your maidenly honor is now destroyed. The only way for you to retain a shred of dignity is to marry, and to marry hastily. Since St. Edmunds refuses to do the honorable thing by you, I myself have decided to step into the role."

Constance stared at him, not sure which statement was most shocking, not sure whether to laugh — her instincts told her not to laugh. *Marry?* Was he offering to marry her?

"Do you say you are offering to marry me?"

"Yes. I have searched my soul and come to the conclusion it is entirely my fault you were left helplessly in the grasp of the Earl of St. Edmunds. I should have seen both you and my sister safely ensconced in the traveling coach, and on your way to Amber Crossing. I must now rectify the situation. We will be married as soon as we cross into Scotland. I have only myself to blame for your situation, Miss Violet, and I intend to do the honorable thing, since St. Edmunds refuses to do so."

"Alec? You told Alec he must marry me?" If she couldn't laugh, she feared she might scream.

"Miss Violet, I find it most inappropriate you should use his given name on such familiar terms." His brow wrinkled in horror. "Unless — that is — just how familiar did the two of you become?"

She huffed with indignation. "When I become *familiar* —" She stressed the word, pulling it slowly like taffy. "— with a gentleman, *that* shall be none of your business, my Lord."

"As your future husband, I believe it shall be very much my business."

Constance put her hands on her hips, the picture of discontentment, but just as quickly moved them to hold her pounding head. "And I say you shall never be my future husband — nor any other kind of husband, because I do not intend to become your wife. Now turn this coach around immediately, or I shall scream that I am being kidnapped."

"I have explained quite logically, if you will simply rein in your hysterics, madam. This is the only course you have open to you. If you think it through you will come to the same conclusion." He ran a hand through his hair, a gesture Constance might have found appealing at any other time but this. "I dislike stating the obvious, but — if this is so distasteful to you, then perhaps you should have thought about the implications of your actions last night. *Before* you stayed behind at RoseHill Manor."

Her rebuttal was a sound of disgust. "Stop the coach — *now,* Lord Havington. I am getting out." She placed her hands on the banquette, preparing to scoot toward the door.

"You do not even know where we are." He sounded bored, looking out the window.

"I don't care. I will decipher it soon enough. I said, stop the coach now."

He turned his gaze back to her. "And I said we are going on to Scotland," he said loudly, with anger. "And we are going to be married."

"Such a sweet proposal, my Lord!"

"Love has nothing to do with this situation, Miss Violet, as you well know."

Constance thought furiously. How to get this odious man to turn the coach around without immediately admitting the truth about her identity and her brother? *Let Larissa tell him; I don't owe him any explanations.* "Even in Scotland, my Lord, a marriage cannot be forced. I shall let them know this is against my will, and I shall refuse to participate. They cannot force me to marry you."

He did not budge. She tried another tactic. "If you do not turn the coach around this instant, I shall open the door and throw myself out." Already she was up against the side of the coach, reaching for the handle.

His arm shot out, grasping hers. "Don't be an idiot!"

"Stop the coach now, Lord Havington." Her eyes stared coolly into his.

"Please, we need to discuss this calmly."

"We will discuss this calmly all the way to RoseHill, I promise. Otherwise, I shall scream non-stop, and attempt to fling myself out until I am successful."

Lord Havington swore. He picked up his traveling cane from under the seat and rapped loudly and sharply overhead. Their momentum gradually slowed, and the overhead hatch opened.

"Yes, my Lord?"

"Back to RoseHill," snapped his Lordship, watching Constance to be sure she did not jump out.

"Yes, my Lord."

"I'm sure *he's* not surprised, and why should he be?" Lord Havington said in an exasperated voice. "Yesterday the carriage rode away from RoseHill. Then this morning he took me back to RoseHill. Then this afternoon we ride away from RoseHill. Now we shall return to RoseHill. I'm surprised there's not a bloody rut in the road from my travels to and from RoseHill," he muttered aloud.

Constance could not resist adding, too sweetly, "There most likely is, since your Lordship could never seem to stay away for more than one day at a time."

Despite the fact the coach was now pointed back toward RoseHill, Marcus and Constance did not talk the situation over, calmly or otherwise. A silence as impervious as a stone squatted between them in the carriage.

Marcus was considering just how far he should allow the coach to proceed, for he had no intention of dropping Miss Violet at RoseHill Manor. They needed to engage in a calm discussion of this situation, and soon.

He had hoped to discern by her earlier reactions exactly what had occurred between the earl and the companion last night. As a gentleman, Marcus himself would never take advantage of a lady by plying her with drink. No, he'd have known exactly what to do with the lovely Miss Violet under his roof, without benefit of spirits. Immediately, he chastised himself for these thoughts.

He dwelt, instead, on the woman's abhorrence of marriage with him. She had nothing to her name in this world. Did she not realize the extent of the Havington wealth? She understood the title of countess. She knew he was willing to marry below his station to do the honorable thing.

A dose of gratitude would be presumed by a reasonable man. But no. Miss Violet hadn't even uttered a meek "thank you."

All the time she'd slept, her head upon his shoulder, Marcus had anticipated her awakening. He knew that once he explained his plan — his ultimate sacrifice — she would look up at him with dewy green eyes. A tear or two would escape as she breathed a soft, "Thank you, my Lord." He would dismiss it as "nothing." But the lady would protest; she would insist, "My Lord, this is so, so generous. I shall be in your debt for the rest of my life. I shall strive to pay you every day, in some small way, with my loyalty, obedience, and love."

Ha! Instead, a tigress came awake, and turned into a shrew before his eyes. He was made to feel a cad for rescuing her! She chose to see it as kidnapping, not the noble gesture it was.

Marcus faced forward, with his arms

crossed and his chin propped stubbornly upon his chest. He eyed Miss Violet from the corner of his eye, only to catch her doing the same thing. Swiftly she stuck her nose in the air and turned to stare out the carriage window.

Staring straight to the side out the window, Constance saw nothing. Of course, at this speed, even if she had been focusing as she pretended, she could not have discerned one tree from another as they streaked by in a blur.

Who did the arrogant earl think he was? To assume he could decide her future and her fate for her! Even if she had truly been a penniless companion, it was not for him to pass his lofty moral judgment and condemn her to a life of bondage with a cold-hearted husband.

Constance felt a little guilty at this last tirade, admitting she'd seen a gentler side of the man. She'd spied the teasing beckoning within those grey eyes, knew he could be caring and witty. She smiled her remembrance of their cribbage competitions. Seeing her smiling reflection in the glass, she ironed her lips straight, not wanting his Lordship to see any emotion exposed.

It was important Lord Havington return

her straight-away to RoseHill.

Now was the time to tell him of Larissa's charade. Slanting a glance his way, Constance saw him staring straight ahead, deep in thought. Looking at his stern profile, it was hard to picture him seeing the humor of the situation and laughing in camaraderie. More likely, she realized, seeing his angry visage, he would attempt to use his bloody traveling cane upon her.

She eyed the cane where he had replaced it behind his boots. Perhaps, she thought wisely, she ought to ensure they ended their journey at RoseHill, where her brother would surely protect her, before she need disclose any secrets to the earl.

She glanced over again and caught him looking back. They stared openly at one another.

"So," stated Havington. "You plan to return to RoseHill for a confrontation."

Constance blushed and looked down at the cane at his feet, afraid he might have read her mind. But she was being fanciful; of course he didn't know. She looked him in the eye, and insisted firmly, "I do."

"Why, how easily those two words come from your mouth, Miss Violet! Yet you are loath to say those very same words before a blacksmith priest in Scotland."

"And when *you* say those words, my Lord, will you be agreeing to love?"

"I've already told you my reasons for offering this marriage, and they have nothing to do with love. One —" He held up an index finger. "— it was entirely my fault you were left behind with St. Edmunds."

He continued to tick off rationalizations upon his fingers. "Two, you have shown yourself to be a young woman of pride and honor. I could not forgive myself to see you lose your maidenly honor."

Constance looked down, and he waited until she met his eyes. "Three, your reputation would be ruined, and you could no longer seek employment as a gentle companion to discerning ladies."

He now held up four fingers, as if swearing an oath. "Four, even if I did not give a fig about *your* reputation, there is my sister's to think of. Your ruination would quickly spread to touch her."

Constance had watched his hand as he ticked off his reasons aloud. She waited, holding her breath, but there were no more. Just the four. Four cold, impersonal reasons to take her as wife. A wife he did not even want. A wife forced upon him, due to his overwhelming sense of duty.

Why did she feel on the verge of tears? It

371

must be the sherry or the brandy — or both — making her feel so blue-deviled. How else to explain the turmoil swirling inside?

She could never marry unless it was for love. The earl, on the other hand, would apparently marry anyone, and for all the wrong reasons.

She'd already suspected she was in love with Lord Havington. It was time she admitted it to herself, as she dwelt upon the last weeks. While she vocally deplored his showing up at odd times, she'd been fooling herself. She looked forward to his chance visits and encounters . . . she couldn't remember when those feelings had started.

She thought he was a one-dimensional dictator when first they met. But she'd come to see the many more dimensions to the complex earl. He had a most wondrous sense of humor. Even while annoying her, he enjoyed the game; knew exactly how he played her. She couldn't remember when this realization had finally dawned upon her either.

The warmth and intelligence in his eyes made a lie of everything he tried to hide from her. When had she begun to notice?

She'd thought, when he held her in a waltz, that only her body was betraying its mistress. When had her heart also become engaged? The body and heart then conspired, until this moment, when they finally convinced her brain it was no use pretending it was not so. Ignoring the unwelcome thoughts would not make the facts go away.

She fantasized marriage with Lord Havington. He would be a most interesting life companion. When had she fallen in love with him? And now, how to fall out, since it was clearly a one-sided affair?

She wished she really were just a simple companion. How easy it would be to succumb to his plans and to marry the earl. With a start, she found herself quite jealous of Miss Violet.

But . . . wishing would not make it otherwise. He would have no reason to marry Lady Constance Chambreville, once he learned the truth of who she was. He would have no reason to save her reputation when he learned she had spent the night in her own bedroom, in her own home, under the protection of her brother. He would have no reason to fear for his sister's reputation when he realized scandal no longer clouded the St. Edmunds name. His sister had in fact been excellently companioned by a lady equal to her class.

Certainly, after today's disclosures, Lord Havington would ride away in disgust, out of her life, with relief and speed. Escaping a marriage he did not welcome would only hasten his departure. Most likely they would never meet again.

Never again would she enjoy heated arguments with the man and his audacious logic. Never again would she enjoy a companionable dissertation during the evening meal with Lord Havington, or linger over a game of cribbage, or see the laughter hiding in his grey eyes.

The realization overpowered her. Once they arrived back at RoseHill, she would never see Lord Havington again.

Just this morning she thought she had reconciled herself to the loss of his friendship. And now the fresh scars were torn open.

Her throat constricted at her loss, and grief threatened to overwhelm her. An unwelcome tear escaped, but she ruthlessly shut down all other emotions. She would sort this out later, in private. She was desperate to be home at RoseHill.

Marcus saw a tear roll down her cheek, though she swiftly turned her head to hide it.

He checked an urge to reach out and wipe it away. He was afraid once he touched her, he would not be able to resist pulling her close and comforting her.

It pained him to see her so destitute.

He had to think of an argument to present, to convince her she need not linger at Rose-Hill. He would allow her to pack up her things, while he guarded her from St. Edmunds.

And then what?

CHAPTER THIRTY-ONE

The coach pulled up at RoseHill.

Larissa peeked out while waiting for the footman. She did not see any black wreaths on the manor door, nor black bunting at the windows. Perhaps her brother Marcus had not killed Lady Constance. Yet.

She stepped down and saw Barrows hastening in his crab-like walk down the wide entry steps and across the aproned drive toward her. He bowed quickly to Larissa. She'd never seen the staid butler in such an agitated state.

"Please, come inside at once, my Lady," he implored. "The earl is just now recovering."

"Recovering! Whatever do you mean, Barrows?" What had happened to her brother Marcus, she wondered. He'd been in perfect health when he left the inn that morning.

"He's had a nasty fall, my Lady." Barrows hardly paused; he turned a wide limping circle and started back toward the entry.

Larissa followed. "An accident? Where did he fall? From his horse? On his way here?"

"No, my Lady." Barrows did not turn around. "He was clobbered right solid, he was, if you take my meaning."

Larissa was aghast. "Has Lady Constance done physical harm to Lord Havington?"

Barrows paused to look back at her in confusion. "Why, no, miss. Rather, I shouldn't be surprised if she should attempt to murder the man . . ." He pointed his bony knees toward the door again. "But I'm sure I would not be able to see what's happening. Not from this distance."

Now it was Larissa's turn to look confused. "Distance? Exactly where is the earl, if he's been clobbered?"

"Oh, he's most definitely been clobbered. And he's in the upper parlour, my Lady," explained Barrows over his shoulder, hurrying her back toward the manor.

"Barrows, wait. Then where is Lady Constance?"

"Nobody knows, my Lady. But we conjecture she's most likely on her way to Scotland by now."

"Scotland! But you said the earl is recovering. Did Lady Constance flee from England because she believes she murdered

Lord Havington?" Larissa could think of no other reason why her friend would run away so quickly. "Is this why she chose to leave?"

"She did not know she left, my Lady."

This is maddening, thought Larissa. "Barrows, wait. Please stop! This is not making any sense. How could she be gone somewhere, if even *she* did not know she left?"

Barrows scurried up the front steps. "She was unconscious, my Lady."

Larissa gasped, frozen at the bottom step. "Who clobbered *her?* I thought *she* clobbered the earl, if he is in the upstairs parlour."

Barrows turned at the top step. "And why would she clobber the earl, my Lady?"

"Barrows!" she cried in exasperation. "If she did not clobber the earl, and he is lying in the upstairs parlour, then who did clobber him?"

"Why, your brother did it."

"My brother clobbered himself?" Larissa found herself in the middle of one of those dreams that make absolutely no sense. She would have shaken her head to awaken, but had to focus on the steps as she hurried to the entry, where a footman stood beside the open door.

Barrows turned in the entry, and looked at Larissa as if she had lost her wits since he last saw her. "No, my Lady. Your brother — Lord Havington, that is — clobbered Lord St. Edmunds."

Larissa stopped and gasped again, as his meaning sank in. "You mean the earl who is lying upstairs — it is *Lord St. Edmunds* who is recovering? *From a clobbering by my brother?*" she squealed.

"Yes, my Lady," Barrows once again picked up speed as they hurried down the hallway toward the main stairs. "Quite a shiner he has, but we are hoping he will be fine, other than a bit dazed. We had already sent for the doctor, of course."

They were at the door of the parlour. Barrows threw open the door and stepped aside, allowing Larissa to enter first. She spied a lean man sitting on the floor across the room, looking in a fog and holding a large slab of raw meat over the left side of his face.

Larissa ran up to Alec Chambreville, Earl of St. Edmunds, and leaned down. "My Lord! Are you all right?"

Alec slowly lifted his head and stared. "My word. I didn't know angels had blue eyes. . . . Are there two of you? Twin angels?"

Larissa looked around, but saw no one else. Why was no one in this house making sense? "No, sir, it is only myself. Lord St. Edmunds, I am a friend of your sister's. Allow me to introduce myself. I am Lady Larissa Wakefield." She stood up partway, curtsied awkwardly, then bent close to him again. "May I get you anything?"

"I could certainly use a brandy. It's over in the —"

"Right away, my Lord," piped in Barrows, hurrying to the small cabinet. "I shall fetch it, my Lady."

On hearing the butler's voice, St. Edmunds said. "Barrows, I've changed my mind. If you would, I'd prefer the Macallan scotch in the library."

"Yes, my Lord," echoed Barrows in pleased tones, already on his way out of the room.

St. Edmunds and Larissa were left alone in the parlour, she kneeling, and he sitting next to her on the floor.

The earl looked up at her with his good right eye and said, "You are a friend of my sister's? Can you tell me where she is, then?"

Larissa took a breath. She lifted his hand from the floor without realizing it, and said, "I hardly know how to tell you this, my Lord. But . . . I suppose I must be the one. 'Twas Marcus Wakefield, the Earl of Havington, who knocked you out. Then, your sister revenged you, and she has fled the country."

She neglected to include the small detail that the Earl of Havington was her brother.

"My sister revenged me?" he asked in mortification. "Just how did she revenge me, madam?"

Larissa's eyes filled with huge crocodile tears.

"Please, tell me," he begged, squeezing her hand.

"It appears, from what Barrows has hinted to me, that . . . that she may have murdered him, my Lord."

"What?" St. Edmunds looked about to pass out again. "Where is the earl's body?" he asked in a stunned whisper. "Perhaps we can cover up the murder, before it is discovered."

"I do not know where the body lies, my Lord. I've only just arrived by coach."

The two held silence together until Barrows reentered with two funnel-bowled glasses of scotch.

"Barrows! Where is the earl's body?" asked St. Edmunds.

Barrows leaned down to hand him the scotch, then presented the other to Lady Larissa, who remained kneeling next to his master. Contemplating the earl still sitting upon the floor, he prayed the doctor would arrive soon. Perhaps his master's mind had been slightly impaired by the fall.

"The earl's body, my Lord?" he repeated.

"Yes, man. The Earl of Havington's body. Which room, Barrows?"

"The Earl of Havington's body certainly is not in this house, nor on these premises." Barrows spoke slowly, clearly, as if to a simple-minded person. "Last seen, my Lord, his *body* was departing on a coach, and it was very much alive. His body, that is — not the coach."

"Ah! Then where has my brother gone to?" cried Larissa, flooded with relief.

"Your brother?" echoed St. Edmunds. "The devil you say. Why did your brother plant me a facer, my Lady, if I've never met you before? And by the way, do you know who Miss Violet is?"

Larissa hesitated. Fortunately, Barrows saved her from answering the earl's question by answering her own first. "I'm not sure where Lord Havington has gone to, my Lady. All I can tell you is that he has abducted the Lady Constance and taken her with him."

Larissa screamed, a short high-pitched cry. "Abducted, you say?"

"*What?* Abducted my sister?"

"Yes, my Lady," confirmed Barrows. "Yes, my Lord."

"But, Barrows, didn't you tell me she murdered Lord Havington?" asked Larissa.

Barrows furrowed his brow in concentration, as if trying to recall their conversation on Larissa's arrival. His face lit up. "Ah, no, miss, I said I should not be *surprised* if she attempts to do so. For she will be in quite a temper at being abducted . . . when she gains consciousness, that is."

"Oh," said Larissa with a shuddering sigh of relief. She smiled at St. Edmunds. "I raced back to RoseHill because I feared my brother was going to murder your sister. But thankfully, it now appears no one's been murdered. At least not yet."

St. Edmunds could not follow what the angel was saying. Besides, his head hurt.

The large carriage rattled up the circular drive and rolled to a dusty halt.

No sooner had Lord Adamsworth and Lady Adamsworth descended than the butler appeared upon RoseHill's great porch. Calling for a lad to see to the horses, Barrows scuttled down the steps to greet the visitors.

He appeared flustered. "I am so very sorry to inform you her Ladyship is not home."

Lady Adamsworth was visibly crestfallen, yet forced a smile of politeness. "And when do you expect your mistress to return from her errands?"

"If you would forgive my asking, madam . . . sir . . ." Barrows hesitated. "Your connection to her Ladyship?"

"I am Baron Adamsworth, and this is my lady wife. We've come to visit our niece."

Barrows discreetly wiped his brow with a starched square of cloth. "Might I show you to the drawing room, where refreshments will be in order after your journey?"

As he led the way, Lady Adamsworth touched her husband's sleeve. "Did he say both young women were away, Nigel? He never answered us as to when they would return."

"I would assume they are away together. Surely they will be along shortly, my love."

Barrows bowed them into the finest drawing room on the ground floor. He was about to ring for tea when Lady Adamsworth confronted him squarely.

"You never mentioned when our niece was expected to return."

Barrows looked toward the door. "Perhaps his Lordship will wish to discuss the matter with you," he said in sepulchral tones. "Though he is a bit indisposed at the moment, as he is with the doctor just now."

"Our nephew is here? But with a doctor? Is the earl sick?"

"No, my Lady, not sick," answered Barrows truthfully.

"But, then why is he with a doctor?" she pressed, then demanded, "And why would our nephew need to discuss his sister's whereabouts?" Her voice rose in panic. "I wish to know what is going on." Lord Adamsworth put a comforting hand on her arm.

Mrs. Dewberry hurried in. "My Lord, my Lady, may I bring tea?"

"Where is our niece?" repeated Lady Adamsworth to Barrows, on a near-note of hysteria.

Mrs. Dewberry gasped. Lord and Lady Adamsworth turned to her and she burst into tears. "Oh, 'tis a sad, sad day for all of us at RoseHill. I am so sorry about your niece, my Lady."

Lady Adamsworth turned ghostly pale, and looked about to faint. Lord Adamsworth immediately escorted his wife to the sofa, and insisted she sit.

"A brandy for Lady Adamsworth, if you will," he addressed aloud, not taking his eyes from his wife. He sat next to her, an arm wrapped protectively around her. He faced

Barrows and Mrs. Dewberry. "Now, please tell us the worst, and have it done with."

Mrs. Dewberry looked helplessly at Barrows, who was quickly pouring a tiny glass of spirits for Lady Adamsworth.

Barrows turned with the drink, shaking his head sternly at Mrs. Dewberry. "We should wait for his Lordship to break the news," he said primly.

"Please, madam," cried Lady Adamsworth, petitioning Mrs. Dewberry directly, "have you no children of your own? Take pity upon me, and tell me news of my niece. I cannot bear to wait a moment longer."

Mrs. Dewberry blurted out, "She's been kidnapped, she has!"

And then Lady Adamsworth did faint, right in her husband's arms.

The doctor finished with St. Edmunds; his prognosis was to declare his Lordship perfectly fine. A nasty bruise was already purpling Alec's swollen face, but no sign of concussion could be detected.

Barrows came hustling in, faster than anyone had yet seen him move. "My Lord, if the doctor could spare a moment, we have a guest in the blue drawing room requiring attention. She has fainted."

The doctor picked up his bag and, snapping it closed, he followed Barrows out. Larissa took St. Edmunds's elbow and walked at his side, keeping an eye on him, as they exited much, much more slowly after the others.

As Alec and Larissa entered the room, they saw the doctor bent over his patient. At the same time, Larissa discovered Uncle Nigel staring at her as if he'd seen a ghost.

Both exclaimed loudly in happiness.

"Uncle! Dear Uncle!" cried Larissa, deserting St. Edmunds and flying across the room to embrace the man.

"Larissa! You are safe! You are safe!" he could only repeat these words over and over as he wrapped his arms about his niece in a hug.

"Larissa?" came a faint feminine voice hidden behind the doctor.

"Aunt?" Larissa broke gently away from Uncle Nigel, and stepped around the doctor.

Coming to herself, Lady Adamsworth looked about to faint again. She stretched her arms toward Larissa as she sat up, and sobbed happily, "My dearest Larissa! My darling! You are safe!"

Larissa dropped to her knees before her aunt. The two cried together as Lady Adamsworth gathered her niece and rocked her in a motherly embrace.

Mrs. Dewberry poked Barrows. When he turned to her, she whispered, "Did Lady Larissa just call that woman Aunt?"

"My Lord?" Barrows turned to address Sir Adamsworth. "If I may inquire, exactly who is your niece?"

Lord Adamsworth looked dumbfounded at the question. "Why, Lady Larissa here is our niece."

"*Oh.* My apologies, my Lord, for the mix-up." Red-faced, Barrows nudged Mrs. Dewberry, signaling they should exit. Mrs. Dewberry was hesitant to leave the happy scene, but Barrows pointedly held the door for her, waiting for her to exit, which she did.

Larissa moved to sit on the settee next to her aunt. Both sat wiping their eyes, smiling at one another.

"And, sir? I don't believe we've been introduced." Lord Adamsworth pinned St. Edmunds with a stern gaze.

"I am Alec Chambreville, Earl of St. Edmunds, sir. This is my sister's home." Alec waited.

"My Lord," acknowledged Lord Adamsworth stiffly. "Allow me to present my wife, Lady Adamsworth. I am Baron Adamsworth."

Lady Adamsworth acknowledged her husband's meaningful look, then turned to her niece. "Larissa? But, your uncle and I — we understood you to say the earl would be absent while you were staying here with Lady Constance."

Larissa blushed as she stammered to explain. "Aunt, Uncle, Lord St. Edmunds has only returned to England — well, to RoseHill — last night."

"Last night?" Lady Adamsworth was aghast. "You were here in the manor last night? With his Lordship in residence?" Her eyes were now dry . . . and round. "And where is Lady Constance, Larissa?"

"She is not here," Larissa mumbled.

Lady Adamsworth had to start fanning herself. "Oh, dear. I fear I am about to faint again. And I *never* faint," she said with disgust. "Larissa. I do not comprehend." She kept her voice as even as possible. "Are you saying you stayed in this house — without Lady Constance — knowing the earl had returned?" She shook her head back and forth as she spoke, as if hoping for a denial.

"Oh, no, Aunt, I only arrived this last hour! Just before you did."

Her aunt closed her eyes in relief.

"And where is Lady Constance, then?"

inquired her uncle.

"She has been abducted, Uncle, just this morning," answered Larissa truthfully. She almost blurted out "by my brother," but caught herself in time. Perhaps one revelation at a time would serve best in this situation. After all, no one had specifically asked by whom.

"By whom?" thundered Lord Adamsworth. "Who is the scoundrel? Have the authorities been notified?"

Larissa looked at St. Edmunds, who left it for their niece to answer her uncle's question.

"She was abducted . . . by my brother," she said very softly.

"Did you say your *brother?*" queried Lord Adamsworth with disbelief. "*Marcus?*" echoed her uncle and aunt at the same time.

Larissa nodded.

"That is impossible. Absurd!" declared Lord Adamsworth. "Havington is the most even-headed of gentlemen I know. He would not be capable of such a hot-headed act."

"Is that so?" St. Edmunds could not contain a slight sneer. "Then how do you explain my face, sir?"

Lord Adamsworth and his wife looked at the purple bruise distorting St. Edmunds's face in open-mouthed shock.

"Are you saying my nephew — Lord Havington — is also responsible for this deed?" sputtered Lord Adamsworth.

"Yes, I am. And your niece can confirm it is so."

All faces turned to Larissa, who demurred, "Well, I did not actually witness it myself, you see."

"Lady Larissa," snapped St. Edmunds.

"Well . . . yes, according to the servants, it is as Lord St. Edmunds says," she stated simply.

Lord Adamsworth sighed. "My apologies, St. Edmunds. If you would, sir, I will join you in a drink."

"Make that three," said Lady Adamsworth.

CHAPTER THIRTY-TWO

Marcus was aware of each piece of gravel crunching beneath the wheels as their carriage lumbered to a stop at RoseHill. The return ride had been so silent the last hour, the earl's wits were at a breaking point. He had not attempted to reason any further with Miss Violet, who sat mutely against the far wall, already withdrawn from him.

He'd been crazy to have removed her this morning, yet he would have done it again. He was desperate to reach out to her, to change her mind. But they had resolved nothing; had not even tried.

The moment the horses stopped and the door was opened, Constance shot out of the carriage, not even waiting for the earl to descend and assist her.

"Miss Violet!" called Marcus to her quickly retreating back. She stopped and turned, and he saw her eyes were wet. "Please, may we discuss this? Before you make a decision that will ruin your life?"

"A decision such as marrying *you*, my Lord, in a marriage of convenience and resentment?" she asked with bitterness as he reached her side.

"No, though you could do worse, madam. You know to what I refer." He looked toward the manor. Realizing they were about to have a scene in the middle of the front drive, he implored, "No more of these barbs and retorts. I only ask we both speak fairly and honestly to one another."

She waited.

"Hear me out," he continued, "before you decide. If you pack your belongings, I will put you up at the inn, in their finest room, and you will not be pressured to go with me — or with anyone. You'll have time to think carefully about this, as many days as you need, before you make a commitment to St. Edmunds and do something rash and irrevocable."

"I can no longer prolong this charade," she whispered, almost too low for him to hear. She turned and continued to the manor, leaving Marcus standing helplessly.

Barrows awaited his mistress at the top of the steps. Her distress was visible in the slump of her shoulders. As her Ladyship passed, Barrows closed the door firmly. A little too firmly.

Marcus ran up the remaining steps and banged on the door. He was sure Barrows counted to ten before opening it. Though why Marcus was the despicable villain and not the knight in shining armor, he did not understand. Had he not attempted to rescue their beloved Miss Violet?

Or was it due to a sense of loyalty to their evil master St. Edmunds, now that the earl had returned? But what of their feelings for this sweet, virtuous maiden who had befriended them all during her stay here?

He spied Miss Violet hurrying down the long hall. Her shoes tapped rapidly on the tiled floor.

Marcus ran to catch up to her, calling out, "Miss Violet!" Finally, in desperation, he yelled urgently, "Constance!"

Shocked to hear him use her given name, she spun around — and saw she had an audience.

She'd stopped just in front of the drawing room's wide double doors. Inside was a frozen tableau of listeners: she saw Larissa, Mrs. Dewberry, and Alec. *When had Larissa arrived back at RoseHill?*

She closed her eyes in frustration. It was too late to escape to her sitting room. So —

she must paste on a false smile, and go inside and greet them. Looking down at her skirts, and pretending to shake them out, she strove to gain a few moments to compose herself. *"Bloody hell,"* she muttered under her breath. Then she lifted her chin and, smiling brightly, she glided into the room.

It was then she spied Larissa's aunt and uncle. "Lady Adamsworth, Lord Adamsworth!" Constance warmly greeted the couple who had made her feel part of their family for so many years.

"Lady Constance!" they echoed together; she hurried toward Lady Adamsworth, who welcomed her with open arms. They hugged each other dearly.

Marcus careened into the room and slid to an abrupt halt.

He was dumbfounded to discover the intimate greeting his aunt gave Miss Violet. And now his uncle gave the young lady a quick hug, and she pulled out her handkerchief and dabbed her eyes. But . . . Marcus had been under the distinct impression from Larissa that his aunt and uncle had not met the companion in person prior to leaving on their trip; that they had only perused and approved her references. And why would they embrace a hired companion they barely knew?

Everyone hovered around Miss Violet, completely ignoring Lord Havington as he stood frozen in puzzlement.

And what were his aunt and uncle thinking of, socializing with that cad, Lord St. Edmunds?

And . . . how had Larissa gotten here? He had distinctly ordered she be placed on a coach from the inn. She should have been home at Amber Crossing by now.

This was the precise straw that pushed him over the edge of civility. He cleared his throat loudly.

Everyone fell quiet, glancing his way.

"You are acquainted with this young lady?" Marcus directed his question to his aunt and uncle.

"Of course we are, nephew," Lady Adamsworth confirmed with a warm smile toward Miss Violet. "She is as dear to us as our very own niece." She reached over for Miss Violet's hand, and the squeeze was returned with obvious affection and appreciation.

Marcus considered this a bit over the top for a hired companion. "You've all met Miss Violet, then, in the past?"

The party turned toward the door, expecting to see another person there. All, that is, but Larissa and Constance. Larissa only blushed and glanced away, while Constance watched Marcus dully, as if all her spirit had left her.

"Miss Violet? Where? Who is she?" asked his uncle, looking around.

Constance serenely took a seat on the sofa, waiting for the world to crash.

Marcus looked at each person in turn, wondering why they were being purposely dense. "I refer to my sister's companion."

Again, the others looked from Marcus toward the door, awaiting an entrance.

"Where is this Miss Violet, nephew?" prodded his uncle.

"She sits in front of you," said Marcus with a frown.

Everyone looked at him blankly, except Larissa, who stared intently at the carpet, as if counting the flowers in its weave.

Letting out a loud sigh of exasperation, Marcus stretched out a long arm and pointed at Constance where she sat upon the settee. "This is Miss Violet. Miss Constance Violet, my sister's companion."

St. Edmunds, Lady Adamsworth, and Lord Adamsworth all looked at Constance, and then back at Marcus. His Aunt Marguerite was the first to laugh, nervously, and then Lord Adamsworth and St. Edmunds joined in half-heartedly. Larissa and Constance, it may be noted, did not join in the laughter.

"You are mistaken, nephew," said his aunt. "This is Lady Constance Chambreville. She is Larissa's very dearest friend. A girlhood companion for many, many years, but certainly not a hired lady's companion."

"The lady is indeed named Constance," added St. Edmunds coldly, "but I insist you shall address her as Lady Constance. She is my sister, and certainly not a hired servant. You offend her, Havington, as you offend me."

St. Edmunds's sister . . . Marcus recalled in horror how he had knocked the man out, thinking St. Edmunds guilty of compromising an innocent woman. Now, it sank in: Miss Violet was the earl's sister.

She had not been compromised. She had not spent the night in a strange home with a strange man. She belonged here. She herself was a Chambreville. He turned to Constance. His hurt and anger at being fooled was written clearly on his face for all to see.

Constance, however, sat stonily. When at last she raised her eyes to Lord Havington, she tried to convey her regret, her desperate feelings, with a repentant look. She opened her lips to form an apology. Marcus turned his head abruptly from her gaze, and she felt his rejection as sharply as a slap.

Quietly, they waited for her to speak. To everyone's surprise, she neither confirmed nor denied it. Instead, she rose and announced softly to the room, "Please, if you will all excuse me, I believe I shall now retire to my room." She turned to Marcus, her eyes flashing. "To *my* room. In *my* house," she enunciated clearly to his averted profile.

She nodded specifically to Lady Adamsworth and Lord Adamsworth, adding, "Please forgive me," then left the parlour quickly.

Marcus turned immediately to his sister. "Larissa. I want an explanation, and I want it now."

Larissa's lower lip began to tremble, and her eyes filled with tears. But Marcus would have none of her theatrics, and he was not in a brotherly mood.

"Now," he repeated loudly.

She looked to her aunt and uncle to rescue her from her brother's wrath. While they both appeared embarrassed, it was clear they hoped for enlightenment as well.

She looked to Lord St. Edmunds. He nodded reassuringly, encouraging her to begin an explanation he too desired.

Larissa and her aunt climbed the stairs to their bedrooms, quite drained from the day's ordeal.

Having explained everything to everyone's satisfaction, over and over, Larissa vowed she would never again make up a story for convenience. For the rest of her life. Wouldn't this be what one of her heroines would declare, after all?

As they reached the landing Aunt Marguerite took Larissa's hand. "Larissa, I know your brother is upset, but in time he will get over it. Just know that your uncle and I love you dearly, and we were so very happy to see you here, and safe. Heavens, when I thought you'd been kidnapped —" She choked back a sob.

Larissa quickly put her arms around Lady Adamsworth, leaned her head on the woman's shoulder. "Thank you, Aunt. I'm sorry to have put you through all of this, though it's not Marcus and his wrath that bothers me." She pulled back and looked at her aunt. "I feel I've betrayed my best friend. *I'm* the one who involved Constance in all of this from the first. And she had counted on me to explain everything to my brother.

I feel just terrible she was put through this. To be kidnapped —" Larissa shuddered. "— by Marcus!" She shuddered even more.

"She was much too quiet at dinner," said her aunt. "Not like the Constance we know. Larissa, you don't suppose anything — happened, do you? Surely Marcus would never have . . . taken advantage . . . of the situation." Her aunt blushed just to suggest such a thing.

Larissa, at her door now, shook her head. "Oh, no, Aunt, I am sure . . . nothing could have happened." She blushed and escaped quickly into her room. "Good night, then."

Lady Adamsworth was so deep in thought, she passed her door and had to retrace her steps. Once in her room, her eyes went immediately to the adjoining door to her husband's dressing room. She could not wait to share her observations with him. Lord Adamsworth was an astute judge of character, and enjoyed keen observational habits. Yes, they would have a most productive whispering session about this in their bedchamber later. She could hardly wait for his Lordship to ascend the stairs; he was at this moment enjoying a game of billiards with Lord St. Edmunds.

During their evening meal, Lady Adamsworth had surreptitiously observed all the players at the dining table, attempting to sort out the undercurrents running through the room as thick as cold custard.

Havington and St. Edmunds had closeted themselves prior to dinner. The two men appeared to have resolved their misunderstanding, allowing for such unusual circumstances. Based on a few snippets of conversation that pursued them into the dining room, she understood St. Edmunds's name had been cleansed of scandal's blackened marks, and the earl also seemed appeased to learn his sister's protection had prompted Havington's actions.

Constance, however, having rejoined their party when dinner was announced, acted like a stranger in her own home, other than diligently insisting Lord and Lady Adamsworth should stay the night as her guests — their nephew being pointedly ignored.

The baroness caught her nephew staring at Lady Constance several times during the meal, though Constance did not return any of his glances with affection or otherwise. She appeared to spend more time rolling peas around on her plate than she did eating. In fact, she recalled that all through dinner she had never once seen Lady Constance make eye contact with Marcus, nor participate in a conversation in which he might be involved.

Lady Adamsworth was sure Marcus did not possess a passionate bone in his body. Yet she had unquestionably seen another side of him today, one she had not known existed. It did not make sense: If their stodgy nephew had truly thought Lady Constance to be a hired companion, it was inconceivable he would have allowed himself to form a tendre for her.

When Constance rose at the end of the meal, the others rose. The men prepared to linger for cigars and port, and Lord Adamsworth announced, "We shall see you ladies in the drawing room shortly, I trust?"

Constance had looked at her slippers, for Marcus stared at her intently just then. "Please forgive me, Lord Adamsworth, but I must beg off. I find I still have a bit of the headache, and believe it would be best if I were to retreat to my room."

"*Your* room? In *your* house, madam?" repeated Marcus, a bit too loudly.

Lady Constance ignored this. Lord Adamsworth coughed uncomfortably. "Of course, my dear, do take care of yourself. Do you anticipate we shall see you at breakfast, then?"

"I do," Constance forced a wan, polite smile.

"What was that?" said Marcus. "Did the Lady Constance," he said, with a great emphasis on *Lady*, which none could fail to notice. "Did Lady Constance just say 'I do'? To what was she agreeing so readily?"

Lord Adamsworth frowned at his nephew as if the lad had overimbibed. "She has agreed we shall see her at breakfast, that is all, nephew."

Marcus moved toward the door, having earlier indicated he would take his leave shortly. "Then I am sure you shall be entertained. She loves eggs and curds, and, by the way, she has a striking collection of morning gowns. Do you not, *Lady* Constance?"

Everyone looked most uncomfortable and anxious to quit the parlour. St. Edmunds and Lord Adamsworth decided to forego their cigars, instead rising and following Lady Adamsworth and Larissa.

As Constance moved to exit, Marcus demanded, "A word with you, madam, if you please."

To the other guests' further embarrassment, she glided on toward the door as if she'd not heard one word he said. Lord Havington was at the door in a few steps, and grabbed her by the wrist.

He smiled grimly at the others, who stood

in shock, and said, "If you will excuse us? We will join you shortly, I promise."

Constance did not struggle; she simply stood as one in a trance, while everyone filed out of the room. St. Edmunds hesitated, but only long enough to make eye contact with Havington, who directed a slight nod at him, as if to say that man-to-man they understood one another, and his sister would be unharmed.

Marcus carefully closed the door as St. Edmunds exited behind the others.

Outside in the hall, there was no movement other than raised eyebrows. No one walked away; all lingered, waiting to hear if voices would be raised inside. They did not have long to wait.

Within half a minute, there was a crash, as of china against a wall, and a shouting match was in progress. To their mortification, all were caught out as the door was thrown open and Constance ran past them and up the stairs toward her bedroom. Marcus stormed down the hallway in the other direction, toward the front entry.

Simultaneously, it seemed, they heard the door to the bedchamber above slam loudly, echoed by the crashing slam of the front entry door. Looking at each other guiltily,

all moved as one body toward the drawing
room.

CHAPTER THIRTY-THREE

Lord and Lady Adamsworth stood in the entry hall amid trunks being bustled about by servants, as Constance and Larissa came arm-in-arm down the stairs to join them.

Larissa, looking charming in a smart carriage gown and a matching maroon high-crowned bonnet upon her curls, stopped halfway down the stairs and turned to her friend. "I feel just awful leaving you alone."

"Nonsense." Constance placed her hand on Larissa's arm and squeezed. "I know you wish to be home with your aunt and uncle. And I have a lot of catching up to do with my brother. I'll be just fine."

They reached the bottom step. Larissa peered closely at her friend as Constance pasted a smile on her face and hoped it was convincing. They'd stayed up late last night talking, after Larissa tapped on her door. Her friend said she was surprised to find Constance still awake. If she only knew . . .

Constance had barely slept the entire night.

Lying awake, examining her feelings, she had no regrets regarding Larissa's visit. Memories of delightful outings, quiet evenings of conversation, the charming confusion of her beloved servants dealing with the mix-up, even the shared jokes at Mrs. Carver's expense brought a lilt to her sad smile. No, she did not regret one single day of this summer.

Her life-long regret would be the loss of the teasing, companionable friendship with Lord Havington — all built upon lies. And now he despised her. He idolized the helpless Miss Violet, whom he wanted to marry and take under his protective wing. But he despised Lady Constance.

Barrows directed the staff to remove the luggage to the traveling coach.

Constance hugged Lady Adamsworth, and turned to offer her hand to Lord Adamsworth. He mumbled something, uncomfortably surrounded by three emotional women, his eyes darting to the open doorway and his escape to the traveling coach.

Larissa and Constance stood together, each reluctant to say the word.

"I shall write and find out how you fare," promised Larissa.

"And I shall write and tell you of my

gardening, and of Alec's travels, and . . ."

Larissa hugged her friend to hide her own trembling lips, which were quickly covered by the handkerchief she put to her mouth. "I hate goodbyes," was muffled through her linen mask, and she hastened out the door.

Lady Adamsworth paused at the threshold. "Constance, come to us if you need. Promise?"

Constance nodded her promise, and returned Lady Adamsworth's smile, then watched the door close.

"What is this?" Constance asked when she saw more trunks in the side hallway. "Did our visitors forget these?"

Mrs. Dewberry deposited a brown leather bag next to the trunks. "No, milady, his Lordship requested we make these ready. He is planning on spending a week or two in town."

Constance hadn't imagined she could feel any further crushed.

Alec strolled out of the library to find her staring forlornly at the luggage. "Ah! I hope you are pleasantly surprised, Moppet."

"That you leave so soon?" she spoke so softly, he barely heard her.

"That *we* leave so soon. Constance." He wrapped a brotherly arm about her shoulders, chuckling. "You silly goose, I am not about to leave you alone again." He stepped back, put his hands on her arms. "You are looking too pale of late. I decided you need a little liveliness, so — you and I are going to spend a week or two in the townhouse."

"Alec, please . . . forgive me, but I'm not up to this, truly. I do admit I've been out of sorts, but . . . being here, at RoseHill, and working in the garden is what I need to soothe my nerves."

"I must disagree, sister, and I am prescribing a change of scenery. We are going to have a lively time in London, and I shall keep you so busy with plays and museums, and rides in the park, that you shall not have a moment to dwell."

Constance almost hid her sigh.

"We will hold our heads high," said Alec. "There is nothing left of the scandal broth to shame you or me. Do you worry about it? You mustn't, as it is best we swim among the gossiping fish, the sooner the better." When she didn't answer, he said, "Say you will come with me, Constance. I shan't go without you, so if you are bound on remaining here, then I shall . . . gladly . . . languish here with you." His look of chagrin lifted the corners of her mouth.

Her brother watched her expectantly. /

cannot be so selfish, she decided. I really have no choice. She pasted a false smile upon her face; it seemed she would be relying on this trick many times over the weeks to come. "Yes, it will be fun." She nodded once. "I am convinced. I would love to accompany you. How soon do you wish to depart?"

CHAPTER THIRTY-FOUR

"What? My bid?" asked Marcus.

Smoke rose lazily in the card room, but none from the earl's unlit cigar. His friends lounged in deep chairs, patiently waiting while he chewed on the cigar and stared at his cards. They'd have been correct in their assumptions that he did not see the cards he held in his hands.

They looked aside at Allermaine in good-natured disgust, then back to Havington. It was obvious the earl's mind was elsewhere, as it had been the entire evening.

"Havington, let us retire," said the duke. "I've other plans for the evening, but desire a few words with you first."

"Mmm." It was obvious Marcus was once again not listening. The others grinned at Allermaine, raising eyebrows.

Allermaine tried again. "Havington — I thought it might be fun to have a tea party in the club's cellar. We could even bake our own biscuits, if we build a bonfire. Would you care to grab an apron and join me?"

"What? Oh, fine. Fine by me." Marcus threw in his hand, saying, "Gentlemen?" He stood and made to walk away.

"Your markers, Havington?" prompted Warwick, indicating the pile at his elbow. "Though how one can play with such distraction and still come out ahead," he muttered with disgust, "is beyond my comprehension."

Marcus carelessly pushed the stack into his pocket.

The other gentlemen nodded their adieus, hiding smiles until he walked away. Then all guffawed at once. Allermaine turned toward them while walking backward, smiling broadly. When he turned forward again, alongside Havington, he raised his arm in a backward casual farewell salute.

"What do you suppose has our earl in such a reverie?" Warwick asked his companions as he shuffled the deck.

"Our cool earl? Hopefully a woman. It would be refreshing to think the man has at least one vulnerable chink in his armor."

"A woman? No, not Havington. Most likely a financial puzzle he's piecing together. There isn't a woman alive who could ruffle the feathers of our hawk. I would place a handsome wager upon it."

"Care to place that wager in the book, Warwick?"

The two friends strode out into the night, and Philip hailed a carriage. Marcus did not even question where they were going. He followed his friend in and closed the door.

"Havington, how are things? You seem a bit distracted of late."

Several days ago Philip had found his friend in his cups at their club. Havington had bitterly related the entire escapade of the false companion. Allermaine had been shocked to think sweet, innocent Larissa could have concocted such a tale. He'd said as much to Lord Havington, who eyed him cynically and harrumphed loudly.

It was obvious Lord Havington found it painful to describe the elopement and his foolish attempt at chivalry. Yet Philip had to admire his friend for describing all, with brutal honesty, even though it made him look the fool. Havington described to Philip every insult the companion had subjected upon him, and the additional embarrassment of having to apologize to her brother for having knocked him out cold.

At the time, Lord Allermaine had commented, "But — this settles the matter, then. You should be pleased. Your sister is no longer under the companion's influence, she is safely back home, your aunt and uncle are keeping an eye on her, and you are once again a free man. Havington, you narrowly escaped the shackles of marriage!"

However, the earl had not seemed pleased. He'd been drunk, but not from celebrating.

The duke had persisted. "Is it your pride that has taken a beating, Havington? No one need know about this. It certainly won't go past me. Count yourself lucky, friend. Celebrate. All turned out better than expected."

Eventually the thought struck Allermaine that Lady Constance was no longer a mere companion. She was a lady, and this opened other options. "Shall you pursue her, then?" he asked.

"Ha! She has already turned me down once," Marcus said. "I am not interested in marriage, and I am not interested in giving her the satisfaction of putting me in my place again."

"But you *were* fascinated with her. Deny that! I admit I could never understand why you allowed the lady to get under your skin . . . until I saw her, of course. Though you did seem overly obsessed. Perhaps there's still something more between —"

"Nothing," Marcus snapped at his friend. "I was obsessed with protecting my sister's reputation. That is all. The companion — I mean the lady — is nothing to me. And she made it quite clear I am nothing to her. I am happy to be free of her clutches. Celebrate with me!" he ordered, pouring more liquor into his half-filled glass, and topping off Philip's as well.

Philip's thoughts came back to the present, to his friend in the coach. It was good to see Havington no longer angry and bitter. Yet . . . this new mood was more frightening. The earl seemed depressed and unfocused. Philip suspected Havington was drinking too much, but there was no slur to the earl's speech, and no clumsiness to his stride that Philip could detect.

"Is the Lady Constance on your mind tonight?" he asked his friend outright.

Marcus focused on him for the first time, with haunted eyes. "Allermaine, I'm afraid I've been bewitched. I cannot even seem to sleep anymore."

Philip did notice the earl seemed more bleary-eyed of late, but had suspected it a sign of too much drink. "Are you in love with the lady?"

Marcus shook his head in the negative. "No. If I were, I think I should feel tender thoughts, and hear music in my head. Isn't this what the poets say? I must confess I've no experience of love. But what I feel is more a helpless anger. I think about the Lady Constance being on her own and I worry about her. And then I hear her tart tongue, and I feel annoyed. And if I think of her out in the *ton,* dancing with those wolves, it drives me crazy with frustration. It makes me crazed to know another may attempt to hold her too closely as they waltz."

Allermaine was dazed at this vehement speech. Not knowing himself what love felt like, still he agreed this mix of frustrated emotions bore no resemblance to what the philosophers described love to be.

"Think you this is something the passing of time will heal?"

"It must, or I shall go crazy," said the earl, sighing dolefully.

The duke was not sure what tactic to take. Should he be a patient listener or an advisor? Should he bluntly tell Havington he was better off without the lass? Perhaps cool, objective logic would work best with the earl. "Havington, if I may offer a suggestion . . ."

The earl looked attentively at his friend in the dark carriage, as if he were ready to cling to any length of spar in the ocean to keep from drowning.

Allermaine continued. "Whenever I am in a complete quandary, I find it helps to step back, so to speak, and take stock of the situation. In the same cool objective manner, for instance, one would order one's thoughts around an investment option."

He had the earl's attention. As well, as they had arrived at Allermaine's townhouse.

"Come inside for just a bit. Let's pursue this thought. You have nothing to lose, right?"

This seemed to convince Marcus. The emptiness of his bed was all that awaited him otherwise, and another fitful night of sleepless turning. He nodded without saying anything and climbed out of the coach after the duke.

Philip led his friend to the library and invited him to be seated at the desk. As the duke rummaged for fresh foolscap, he directed one of the servants to light the fire, and sent the other off to the kitchen for strong coffee. Placing paper in front of Havington, he next collected quills and an inkpot.

The duke set duplicate writing utensils and parchment on opposite sides of the desk, pulling up a chair for himself so he faced Lord Havington, who patiently eyed these proceedings.

"Now," Allermaine instructed, taking up his own quill, "first you must draw a line down the center of your page, thus." Demonstrating, he scratched out a fine line dividing his own sheet into two vertical side-by-side columns. He waited while the earl did the same on his own paper.

"Think of this as one of your ledgers, Havington. On this left side, instead of expenses, you are going to list negative items. While on this right side, instead of income, you must list anything we deem to be a good, positive asset."

He looked up to confirm Marcus appeared to be listening to his directions. "This will be a ledger sheet describing Lady Constance," he said. "Now, the idea is thus: By thinking in terms of good traits and bad traits, you shall take all those thoughts jumbling around in your head and keeping you awake at night, and you shall transfer them here, to this ledger. Then, you will find they are still here, safe and sound in the morning, for you to pick up and worry about again the next day. However, at least your head will be empty when you retire to your bed, thus allowing you to sleep."

Marcus frowned, but looked thoughtful.

Then he nodded in understanding. He appeared desperate to try anything. "How shall I begin?" he asked.

"I shall help you. Let me think . . . all right, I distinctly remember you saying Miss Violet — I mean, Lady Constance — dresses immodestly. So put that down on your ledger sheet. Remember, a negative trait goes in the left column."

Philip dipped his quill and moved its point to the left side of his ledger, where he wrote "Dresses Immodestly" on the negative side of the page.

Marcus dipped his quill and paused with feather held straight, long enough to say, "I suppose it is not the lady's fault if today's fashions show off her charms. One cannot deny she *is* beautifully endowed." Marcus moved his quill to the right side of the page, and scratched the words "Beautiful" and "Enchantingly Feminine."

Philip was tilted back in his chair, concentrating on the ceiling, recalling conversations they had engaged in over the past weeks, trying to remember bits of what Marcus had confided about his sister's companion.

"Ah, yes," he recalled, sitting forward and moving his pen to the left of his page. "You had a problem at one time, and you said the young lady is much too friendly with the staff."

"That's true," muttered Marcus. "She would make an excellent estate wife, as she has everyone wrapped around her little finger." He wrote below the two entries on the right, "Charms Everyone, Staff Included."

"I distinctly recall you saying she is much too bossy, with airs of superiority." The duke wrote another entry on his list of negatives.

"She does carry herself like a queen, doesn't she?" Marcus smiled, as he scrawled "Regal" on the right side of his sheet.

"Then there was that horse incident. . . . And don't forget the fishing," reminded Allermaine.

"Indeed. Quite a sportsman herself, unlike most ladies." Marcus wrote "Enjoys Sports. Accomplished" under his growing list.

"What about the gambling?" Philip easily continued expanding his list of negatives.

"Impertinent little baggage, and loves to gloat. But a hell of a cribbage player," admitted Marcus. He wrote "Excels at Games" on the right.

"You mentioned she was not a proper influence for your sister. Remember how she disobeyed your direct order to end

Larissa's summer?" Philip listed "Poor Influence," and then directly below it, "Disobedient."

Marcus nodded to himself. "Yes. I do. I remember how she stood up to me, to protect my sister." He scratched in "Brave," and right below it, "Honorable."

"And it would seem the most serious transgression was the lie about her brother's identity!" Philip was warming up to the topic now, and put "Lies" in large bold letters on the left side of his ledger.

"She certainly did not give him away, though," muttered Marcus, entering "Loyal to Those She Loves" on the right side of his ledger.

"I believe 'impertinence' is a word you used often in describing her?" noted Allermaine, as he wrote out "Impertinent" on his already long list of negatives, noting he'd almost reached the bottom of the parchment.

"Yes, impertinent," echoed Marcus, "with her little nose in the air and her flashing green eyes." "Beautiful Green Eyes" made his list of positive attributes.

The coffee arrived. The duke set down his quill and took a deep sip from the steaming cup. Returning it to its saucer, he glanced at his list. Poor Havington!

This was certainly a lopsided list of negatives. Not a good sign for the lady; nor for the lord she had duped. The sooner his friend got over her, the better off he would be. Allermaine was pleased he had taken this tactic. Not that he meant to shove it under the earl's nose, but a little objectivity was often what it took to face the stark facts. "The sooner noted, the sooner resolved." He sipped again with an audible slurp, quite satisfied they'd been successful.

Marcus sat back and tasted the rich coffee, staring at the list in front of him. Not one negative item! And such a long list of assets. No wonder she had bewitched him. She was indeed a rare find among women. How could he not have seen it before? This exercise made it so evidently clear.

He set his cup down and debated giving his friend a hug. Instead, he stood and put out his hand, pumping Philip's emphatically.

"Thank you! You were right, Allermaine. This was exactly what I needed to do. It is all so very obvious now. I've been a complete idiot. . . . She and I complement each other perfectly."

Shrugging back into his jacket, he grabbed his greatcoat from a nearby chair, and said over his shoulder as he hurried out, "No reason to see me to the door, Allermaine. And thank you ever so much again, friend. I am finally thinking clearly." He smiled cheerfully, then exited.

The duke sat in total confusion. What exactly did he mean: they complemented each other perfectly? He reached across the desk to the paper Havington had left behind, and slid it to his own side of the table, turning it around to read.

The left side was completely blank.

On the right side, he read the scrawled words aloud in disbelief:

Beautiful
Enchantingly Feminine
Charms Everyone, Staff Included
Regal
Enjoys Sports. Accomplished
Excels at Games
Brave
Honorable
Loyal to Those She Loves
Beautiful Green Eyes

Philip stared dumbly at the list another few moments. He picked it up and held his own alongside. His right column was completely blank; the left overflowed with a number of negative transgressions.

424

Scratching his head in bewilderment, Allermaine was not sure what had just happened in this room.

Two things he was certain about, however.

First, the earl had left revitalized, and in a much more positive frame of mind than Philip had witnessed these last several days.

Second, the earl was an excellent shot, and excellent with the sword as well. Philip got up and tossed his own list into the fire.

CHAPTER THIRTY-FIVE

Marcus left the tobacconist and stepped out into the bright sunlight, the little bell above the door jingling behind him. He pulled out his pocket watch, debating whether to walk to his club or hail a hackney. He imagined Philip would not be kept waiting long if he took advantage of this fine weather to stretch his legs.

He soon regretted his decision. Even strolling at a leisurely pace it was a bit too warm — perhaps if he'd not worn such a dark, close-fitting jacket. He unbuttoned the top button as he walked. A few mamas looked down their noses at him, pulling their daughters closer as he passed. Marcus smiled. One would think the lack of a closed button might make the innocent things faint. Well, they'd no reason to fear: these young misses paled in comparison to Miss Violet.

I really must stop calling her Miss Violet, he

corrected himself. Constance. *Lady* Constance. He'd learned she was in town, had attempted to meet with her, so far without success. Having conjured her by daydreams, he was taken aback to see a honey-haired lass cross the road many doorways ahead. He craned his neck, hoping to catch a glimpse of her face in the crowd. Quickening his pace, he passed slower strollers in his haste to keep her in his sights. It looked to be the very same lady's confident stride, but it was difficult to be sure in the frenzy of shoppers.

Twice he lost sight altogether, thinking she'd ducked into one of the shops. Then, he'd spy the soft mignonette green of her gown, or from his height he'd catch the small bonnet, pale green ribbons flying wildly, no more tamed than the wild amber curls they intertwined.

He lost her again. He stopped and was bumped into from behind, but didn't respond. He scanned the crowds ahead with no luck, as he peered with intensity into each shop window he passed. The fifth gave no hint of his prey, but the window was full of books. With a broad smile, he followed his instincts and stepped into the cool interior.

The bells over the door chimed merrily as

the earl closed it behind him. The shop-keeper greeted him cordially, and Marcus nodded amiably.

"Are you looking for anything particular, sir?"

"Yes, actually," said Marcus softly as he was enveloped in the museum-like quiet-ness. "A young lady, so high," he held a hand to his shoulder; pictured her waltzing in his arms. "In a light green gown —"

"Ah! Yes, sir," interrupted the man, point-ing to the left rear of the large shop. "In the fishing section, I believe you'll find the miss. That's what the lady was inquiring about, anyways."

Rolling his eyes, Marcus realized he should have guessed. Walking softly across the polished boards, he stocked his elusive prey. He peeked around each aisle before crossing to the next. In the farthest corner, a young woman bent over to read the titles on the lowest shelf. He recognized that posterior and stood enjoying the view, though he was honorable enough to chastise himself all the while.

Constance grabbed the spine of a book and rose. Sensing a presence, she spun around and discovered Lord Havington leaning against a tall bookshelf, arms folded over

428

his chest, one booted leg crossed over the other.

Her heart gave a leap of happiness . . . then she stiffened. "Exactly how long have you been standing there, my Lord? And how dare you spy upon me!"

"I didn't know with certainty that it *was* you, Miss V— er, Lady Constance."

"Oh? Then you admit you rake your gaze upon just any woman? And in such an ungallant fashion?"

"Not just *any* woman. No, I would not admit to that. You see, not many women strike such a . . . fetching pose," he said with a rakish nod. "Though it did strike me there was something familiar. It brought to mind a certain lad I caught fishing at the river," he said with a slow grin.

She colored a soft pink, recalling he'd seen her in her brother's breeches. "*This* is an entirely inappropriate conversation." She marched back down the aisle and attempted to move past him, with a frosty, "You will excuse me, my Lord?"

Marcus did not budge. "You are excused. Just do be careful while browsing books in the future."

"You know that was not an apology!" she whispered fiercely. "I simply wish to move past you, and you are blocking my egress."

She stood much too close to the earl, could smell the scents she remembered, through the sun-warmed wool. His broad frame filled the end of the aisle most effectively.

Marcus stood still, as if hypnotized by the nearness of her. "Lady Constance," he asked hesitantly, "may we talk? In private?" He looked around, then leaned back to peer down the cross aisle. "And where is your maid? Or your footman? Don't you know a lady should not be shopping without accompaniment?"

The magic spell was broken, as if cold water had been thrown in her face. Of course: *this* was the true earl, the odious beast always criticizing.

"It so happens my shopping companion — *along* with a footman, *and* a maid —" She pointed out. "— is on her way here next. I simply left my friend at the last shop so I might have a little more browsing time to myself."

"Humph," snorted Marcus, in a tone of disbelief. "Does my sister accompany you, then?" He looked into her eyes, to watch if she flinched while telling a fib.

Constance returned his bold look. "Now, if you will excuse me?" She then looked pointedly down at his boots. Could she step over them without coming into contact with his long legs? The thought of her long skirts brushing his legs screamed of intimacy and made her blush. Lately, whenever she thought of his Lordship, her cheeks warmed with these unwelcome images.

Marcus stood to one side without quite relinquishing the aisle. He leaned closer to her. "Miss — Lady Constance." He softened his tone. "I truly do desire a word with you." He looked around again to be sure none were in hearing distance. "I fear I may have lost something at RoseHill, something important to me. It has been causing me many restless nights. And I have come to realize what it is . . ."

Constance held her breath, but he stopped there. *Do not read too much into this,* she admonished herself. Perhaps he meant a closeness to his sister, or a sense of companionship. Or perhaps the relaxed pace of the country life.

She made her best attempt to lighten the mood. "Perhaps his Lordship misses having an impoverished young woman whom he can bribe and bully? Or — oh, I know! — was it more of a favorite possession? I believe, my Lord, you will find Mrs. Carver in the sewing room. Where she belongs."

Marcus stepped back, reacting as if slapped.

Constance experienced a touch of guilt at the expression on his face, yet she used the opportunity to slip past the earl and continue toward the shopkeeper's desk without looking back.

Her heart pounded loudly. Had he been about to import something personal? Was it possible he had feelings for her, after everything she'd done to make a fool of him? Could he be feeling the same as she felt inside? Surely her setdown would make him think twice.

Yet, she decided, if he desires to talk, there are more acceptable venues to seek out a lady's ear than to lurk in a dark shop aisle, having such a personal conversation. *And* he *accuses* me *of scandalous behavior!* She closed her eyes and shook her curls.

The shopkeeper asked, "Shall I have these sent to you, my Lady? Or will you be leaving these for your footman to retrieve?"

Marcus reached past her and picked up the two thick volumes. "Allow me to carry these for the lady."

Constance knew he was behind her; her body responded on its own when he was near. She also noticed that while she had struggled with the heavy tomes, Lord Havington was able to wrap one hand around the ends of both books and lift them from the counter easily.

"I would not want to impose upon his Lordship." She directed this statement to the shopkeeper. She did not acknowledge Lord Havington.

"Consider it an act of kindness, madam," said Marcus. "You do understand acts of kindness? Toward those less fortunate than ourselves . . . such as *companions?*"

She rolled her eyes, then asked the shopkeeper, "Do you, sir, consider it an act of kindness when one person kidnaps another in order to prove how charitable one can be?"

The old shopkeeper looked confused, then shrugged. No doubt used to the odd goings-on of the Quality, he wisely did not offer his opinion.

"An act of kindness," said Marcus between gritted teeth, "is *always* to be commended. Even when the recipient is unaware. Or in a state of over-imbibed unconsciousness." Ignoring her tiny indignant gasp, he continued. "As the philosophers taught us: 'A deed of goodness does not go unrewarded, although it may go unseen.' "

Constance's scowl just as quickly brightened. "Goodness. I believe I do see exactly your point, my Lord." She turned sharply to the shopkeeper. "Sir, do you have any copies of *Mrs. Carver's Hints for Young Ladies*?"

He pushed his spectacles higher on his nose. "Why, yes, I am sure I do . . ." He opened a different ledger, and quickly flipped to the appropriate entry. Raising bushy white eyebrows, he eyed her above the frames. "I happen to have three copies on the shelf. Would you care for one?"

Constance smiled a feral smile. "Excellent! I wish to purchase all three. Please add those to my account." The shopkeeper looked his surprise. "And," she said, focusing on pulling down and then smoothing each finger of her glove. "Tonight I shall toss them into the hearth fire. Where I shall thoroughly enjoy the warmth of the blaze they give. So . . ." She looked directly at the earl. "The young ladies of London will never know the act of kindness I am doing for them: saving them from that odious tome." She inhaled and straightened. "My, you are correct, my Lord. I do feel so much better already."

Marcus's tanned face showed a slight red flush. The chimes over the door, indicating another guest, jangled in the silence.

"It is unfortunate . . ." Lord Havington drawled the last word. ". . . that you and my sister never bothered to learn anything from the book, madam. I'm sure there is an entire chapter on the impropriety of ladies shopping alone." He turned to the merchant. "Since the lady's foolish — or non-existent — companion has left her without proper servants to see to her packages . . . and to her safety," he added pointedly, "please fetch me her other three 'kindling' books, and I shall assist her with the lot."

"No need to, sir," came a voice behind them. "Her foolish companion has finally returned. Thank you, though, for your most kind and gentlemanly offer."

Lord Havington turned slowly and looked in horror at the Dowager Duchess of Allermaine.

Two footmen loaded with packages stood behind her, in readiness to retrieve Lady Constance's purchases as well.

CHAPTER THIRTY-SIX

Carlton opened the door, but could not see who had knocked. All he could see was an armload of long-stemmed flowers, with well-breeched legs and polished Hessians showing below.

"Yes? May I help you?" Not a spot of surprise or curiosity inflected the butler's tone.

"The Earl of Havington wishes an audience with the Dowager Duchess of Allermaine," came a voice behind the flowers.

"Your card, sir?"

"Good god, man! Don't you think if I had an extra hand, I would have presented you with a card?"

Now *this* was a tone Carlton was familiar with. Satisfied this was a member of the Quality, in bored nasals he said, "Please come in, my Lord."

Marcus stepped into the entry hall and thrust the mountain of blooms at the butler.

"Please present this arrangement to her Grace, with my good wishes."

Carlton did not budge. He looked at the bundle disdainfully and called "Deeter!"

A baby-faced footman hurried around the corner. He stopped in his tracks, staring.

"The flowers, Deeter?" Carlton enunciated slowly, belying patience.

"Yes, sir. Right away, sir." The lad opened his arms and relieved Marcus of his bundle. He was hidden behind the mound of flowers and greenery before he thought to ask, "Sir? What shall I do with them, sir?"

"Ask Betty for a large vase, and then bring them to her Grace. You will find her Grace in the lavender parlour, Deeter."

"Yes, sir," piped the footman, and he scampered off, walking sideways so he could see his way without running into a door.

Carlton cleared his throat, bringing a white glove to his mouth. "Is Her Grace expecting you, my Lord?"

"No." Marcus sounded just as bored as the butler.

"Very well," drawled Carlton. "I will see if she is receiving visitors."

He shuffled off, leaving Marcus to look around the hall, remembering his last intimidating visit to the dower house.

Lady Amelia raised her eyebrows at Carlton's announcement. *What on earth brings the earl back here?* According to Constance, "The Farce" had been exposed. In addition, Alec had returned, and all sounded well at RoseHill. She smiled as she thought of dear Constance.

The smile changed to a frown as she thought of Marcus. He would not dare come here to upbraid the duchess for her assistance in the charade. No, she decided. The man could not be so unwise.

Perhaps he was here to apologize for his rude remark in the bookshop the other morning. Her curiosity got the better of her. "Please see his Lordship escorted in, Carlton. I shall receive him here. And a little tea would be nice." The butler slowly shuffled away.

Five minutes later, a parade marched through the lavender sitting room. First came Carlton, announcing, "The Earl of Havington."

Marcus stepped around Carlton and moved forward to bow perfectly over Lady Amelia's hand, murmuring, "My pleasure, Your Grace."

Following Marcus came the housekeeper, with tea service. She carefully set her balanced load upon the table next to the dowager duchess.

"Thank you, Mrs. B," said Lady Amelia with a fond smile.

Lastly came the flowers. Everyone turned as the giant bouquet was carried through the door. The same young man struggled with the heavy crystal vase. "Where shall I put this, Your Grace?"

She eyed the flowers appreciatively. "The round table by the window would be perfect, I think."

Marcus breathed a sigh of relief that his gift pleased the duchess. "Thank you, Deeter," he said. "My compliments to whomever did the arrangement."

Deeter beamed. The duchess raised eyebrows; she did not know many men of the *ton* who deigned to acknowledge staff, let alone by name.

"The flowers," said Carlton in his funereal tones, "are from Lord Havington, Your Grace."

"And they are quite beautiful. I thank you, Havington."

"It is nothing, Your Grace. I can only hope they help to excuse my poor manners of late, and the presumptuous way I seem to appear at your door unannounced." He smiled his warmest, most charming smile.

The smile was not lost on the grand dame. In fact, she wondered how this could be the same man who had appeared with her grandson less than a fortnight ago. And where was the boorish behavior Constance attributed to his Lordship? Hadn't the gel said he was lacking in all social graces and manners? Perhaps she'd not actually used the word "barbarian," but it wasn't far from the image she'd painted.

"If this is your calling card, then please feel free to call on me more often, sir. Will you join me for tea?" Without waiting for an answer, she turned to the service and commanded, "Sit, Havington, and tell me what brings you here."

Marcus waited until the servants had exited the parlour. "Your Grace, I am here to ask a favor. It involves Miss Vio — Lady Constance, that is."

The duchess concentrated on the dark brew streaming from pot to teacup. Her mouth was set in a thin line. "Yes? And what sort of favor is this, Havington?"

"I would ask you to write a reference, Your Grace."

She started, and almost spilled the hot tea. Without looking up or answering, she took great care with placing delicacies onto the small plates. Finally, she shot him a shrewd glance. "Surely you realize by now there never was a reference. As you also realize, none was ever requested. Nor," she said, pinning him with a stern glaze, "will one ever be required in the future. So . . . what is your game, sir?"

"Your Grace, I need your assistance." He accepted a steaming cup, which he set down, followed by a small dish of tea cakes which he distractedly set next to the cup and saucer. "I have found myself coming to . . . care . . . for Miss — deuce take it — I mean for Lady Constance. However, the lady is never 'at home,' at least not to me." He touched neither the food nor the drink. "In her eyes I have become all that is despicable. Nor will her brother receive me — though I'm sure his sister has ordered it so."

"Mmm . . . could this be the same brother you flattened with your fist on your arrival?" she asked dryly.

"Yes." Marcus had the grace to grin sheepishly. "I had no idea. All I could see was the blackguard crushing Lady Constance — whom I believed to be Miss Violet at the time — to his chest the night of the masquerade. And then, when I found out she'd sneaked back to RoseHill and spent the night under the same roof with him, I assumed St. Edmunds had compromised her."

Lady Amelia laughed gustily. Constance had of course written to explain all of this, yet it still tickled the duchess every time she thought about it. She pulled a finely laced square of cream silk from her sleeve and wiped tears of laughter from her eyes.

Picking up her teacup, she asked, "And — does Lady Constance know you have come to care for her?"

Mimicking her motion, Havington did not yet take a drink. "No. Not only will she not acknowledge my calling card —" Frustration clenched his hand on the delicate bone china cup. "— she gives me the cut direct when we meet in public."

"Mmm . . ." The duchess nodded. "I must assure you she has certainly had nothing positive to say about you in our correspondence. In fact . . . while awaiting your entrance, I was tickling my memory, trying to remember the *precise* word she used to describe you . . . was it *barbarian?* No, I think not. Perhaps it was dictator?"

Marcus's lips thinned. "I confess —"

"Draconian! That was it," she practically crowed, pleased with remembering.

442

Marcus cleared his throat, sipped his tea, and continued. "As I said, I confess I am not surprised. It is my fault I've not given her reason to feel otherwise." He sat forward. "But I am determined to make amends, Your Grace. I must orchestrate a meeting. It is *imperative* Lady Constance see me in a better light."

"And, what sort of light might that be?"

Marcus set down his cup and looked her in the eye. "As a suitor."

"But didn't you already try to carry her off to Scotland, sir? She did not seem interested at the time, as I recall." She tried not to smile as she remembered Constance's distinct opinion on the escapade.

"She thinks I only offered to marry her to save her name. And I suppose that's what I believed at the time. But I was fooling myself. Even thinking her a mere companion, my heart was determined to make her my countess."

Lady Amelia's eyes widened at this straightforward declaration from the earl.

"I am still determined to have her," he stated firmly.

The duchess raised both eyebrows further.

"For my countess, that is," he amended quickly, his tanned face flushing becomingly.

Lady Amelia took a sip of tea to hide the tiniest of smiles. However, a loose thread still tickled at the back of her mind. Ah, yes. The reference.

"A reference, Havington? I must say, I still do not understand why you ask me to write a reference. Or is this an attempt to chide me for my little part in the play?"

"No. No, Your Grace. Most certainly not. I have known my sister's follies long enough to understand *everyone* gets pulled in, knowingly and unknowingly. That is no longer here nor there."

"Then what exactly is the nature of this reference you now refer to?"

"I would ask Your Grace to write a reference for me to deliver — in person — to Lady Constance."

She waited for him to expound.

"A reference recommending me for the position of husband," he forced himself to declare without embarrassment.

The dowager duchess raised her lorgnette and stared at Marcus for ten seconds, before smiling and replying, "Demme. This is most interesting!"

Marcus stepped into his town coach. Removing a handkerchief, he wiped his brow.

For the last quarter hour, he'd been

unsure whether his venture would be successful. Gradually, the dowager duchess had warmed to his idea. In fact, it had given her pause several times to chuckle. Once, for no reason Marcus could now remember, she had exploded with one of her gusty laughs.

Still, she'd made it clear she did not write references on a whim. Thus, if she were to agree to provide said reference — *if* she were to agree, she stressed — he must convince her of his sincerity, and his attributes of recommendation.

For instance, she bluntly pointed out, Lady Constance was an independent young woman. She did not need a strong-handed husband, and would resent such.

Marcus quickly agreed he loved the lady just as she was, and was not looking to change a hair on her amber head.

"You may as well know, Havington, that she enjoys certain pursuits. Pursuits that might be frowned upon by *tonnish* standards."

"Such as, Your Grace?"

"Such as gardening, sir. Lady Constance is happiest when she is tending her gardens. There are some in the *ton* who do not consider this to be a suitable pursuit for the lady of the manor. They might allow that overseeing a conservatory be deemed ap-

445

propriate, but would frown upon a countess who goes out into the sun to dig in the soil." She watched him for a reaction.

"I find her most charming when she has a smudge of dirt across her nose," he answered truthfully.

"And she enjoys fishing, Havington. That is certainly not considered a ladylike pursuit by most, wouldn't you agree?"

"She would be free to pursue that hobby." He hesitated, then added bullishly, "But not while wearing her brother's breeches, Your Grace."

Yes, that was certainly one point at which the duchess had laughed heartily. But he did not budge from the concession.

"Horses, Havington?"

"Many ladies of the *ton* ride, Your Grace."

"Oh, did you assume I meant side-saddle?" she asked slyly.

His brows came together, and he paused, then sighed. "Very well, but only on our country estate. Not in Hyde Park."

Following that exchange, they continued to dicker. The dowager duchess expressed a wish that Lady Constance could be here to enjoy the negotiations, but immediately thought better of it.

"Books?" she continued. "Some could

consider the young miss quite a bluestocking."

"I would prefer she collected no more books on animal husbandry," he stated firmly, which met with raised eyebrows and a quirk of the lips from the duchess. When she said nothing further, he added, "Of course, classics are certainly appropriate."

The duchess waited.

"Silly romantic fiction would not be frowned upon," he experimented, but was met with the same patient expression. "Treatises on the sciences are also fine, for a keen mind such as hers."

The duchess sipped her tea. "And?"

He knew he was lacking, but did not know what she wanted him to say.

"And," she repeated, "are there books she would be *expected* to read? Aloud?"

"No, who could command her to — oh." He sipped his tea, thinking how best to phrase his next thought. Smiling, he said, "However, when one insists on betting as a gentleman, one must pay the consequences, Your Grace."

She also smiled. "Point conceded, sir."

And so the bartering went on for some time, until finally the duchess said, "Havington, something is still not clearly connecting in my old brain."

He grinned within, for she was an extremely sharp opponent, and none would ever believe otherwise.

"Lady Constance has painted you as quite the priggish, parsonish gentleman."

Marcus was careful to control his expression, other than a slight lift to one eyebrow.

"I, however," said Lady Amelia, "find you are willing to compromise your strictures where her happiness is involved. So, where is the stubborn man she sees inside of you? Is he pulling the wool over my eyes? Are you one of those men who charm on the outside just until the wedding papers have been witnessed, and then transform into an ogre before the ink has dried? I think not. So, where is the dictator hiding?"

Lord Havington looked down at his hands. He spread them out in a helpless gesture. "I admit I have shown a very narrowly focused side of myself to Lady Constance, Your Grace. However, in my defense, I thought she was merely my sister's hired companion." He glanced up at the co-conspirator sitting across from him, who had the grace to smile. "As such, I had specific requirements of the woman who would chaperone my sister in society."

He stretched out his booted legs, crossing them at the ankles, as he looked the duchess in the eye and said clearly, "However . . . as my countess, I believe she will set her own style, and I dare anyone of the *ton* to take her to task for it."

Lady Amelia nodded in approval. "Bravo. I like your style, Havington. So, no one will dare take her to task." She took her time choosing a ginger biscuit. Studying the assortment, she asked, "And does this include her own husband?" She glanced up.

It was the first time she saw his jaw clench, as he said, "Absolutely not."

Laughing her deep laugh, she dismissed him by saying, "You and she will make an excellent match, Havington." She rang the bell for Carlton. "I must admit I am feeling so very pleased at the prospect."

Marcus stood; the interview was over.

"Therefore," she said, "look for my reference to arrive by messenger before tomorrow evening."

He once again bowed over her hand.

CHAPTER THIRTY-SEVEN

Lord Havington, one hand on the balcony railing, surveyed the resplendent crowd in Lord and Lady Stuffleshire's ballroom. The din of those crushed together in animated conversation rivaled the orchestra.

Elegant in austere black jacket and high, starched cravat, he searched the partiers with unflagging determination. He'd been to every rout, soiree, and ball where he suspected he might find St. Edmunds and his sister. The Earl of St. Edmunds should be easy to pick out among the crowds, given the man's height and light hair, yet this was the seventh affair Marcus perused without success.

Of a sudden, he spotted his quarry. In the midst of a clump of men he glimpsed a halo of honeyed curls. He descended the stairs with purpose, his boots ringing upon the marble.

Sir Douglas and a colorfully dressed man

Marcus did not recognize argued over whose turn it was to escort the lady to the dance floor. As the musicians struck up a waltz, both men gazed imploringly at Lady Constance, who looked about to present her hand to the foppish peacock.

"I'm sorry, gentlemen," Marcus said in a steely tone that contradicted his words, "but Lady Constance has promised the waltz to me." He took her outstretched hand and placed it firmly upon his arm.

"That was most rude of you, my Lord," said Constance, after half a minute of silence as they swirled amid the other couples.

"Do you wish to stop dancing now, then, and be returned to your admirers?"

Constance looked across the room. "No. To be honest, I was bored to tears. They were competing in tales of their favorite hunting dogs. And I think the baron is jealous because my dress has almost as many silver threads as his vest."

Lord Havington laughed and held her away as he glanced down at her white gown with intricately woven silver silken threads. "You look beautiful tonight." He pulled her close again as they spun.

"And . . . ?" she asked, resignation in her voice.

"And?" he repeated.

"Well, his Lordship usually then goes on to inform me that my dress is indecently cut. Or my shoulders are overly exposed. Or the fabric is too thin for propriety's sake."

"You look perfect in this dress, and you know it, minx." His words caressed in a low voice, intimately close to her ear. "Be honest."

Now it was Constance's turn to laugh. "I think I have been *very* honest tonight, Lord Havington." Her eyes shone with mischief. "Did I not admit I would rather dance with you than be bored by the baron?"

"Hmm. Quite a comparison, yes. Should I be flattered by that remark, Lady Constance?"

Constance laughed again, enjoying herself thoroughly. "I propose we make a deal, my Lord."

Marcus groaned. "I do not think so, madam. The last time I made a deal, I had to spend time in the kitchen, getting to know your staff."

"No, this deal ends when the music stops. Just for tonight — while we dance — we shall promise to be honest with one another." She held her breath.

His expression was unfathomable, but she

was distinctly aware of a tingling warmth that started in her toes and spread upward.

"You have a deal. By the way, since we are being honest, did we not have an understanding you were to waltz with no one except me?"

"Oh, no, my Lord. You are mistaken. That was an agreement you made with *Miss Violet.* And, actually . . . I don't recall whether Miss Violet ever even agreed to that outrageous demand."

"Perhaps not. Though Miss Violet *was* a bit of a spoiled brat."

"She was not!" Constance tried to pull away indignantly, but Marcus held her firmly trapped within his arm.

With a deep chuckle, he said, "I am teasing you, Lady Constance."

"And I demand you apologize for that remark, sir."

"Of course. But to whom should I apologize?" He looked over her head, then over to where the duennas sat fanning themselves. "I do not see Miss Violet here tonight, do you?"

Constance saw the humor in her ridiculous demand, and had to smile. "Do you assume every woman who does not swoon at your sweet proposal of marriage is spoiled?"

"I cannot answer that, as I have proposed only once, and my pride took quite a beating."

Constance chuckled as they spun.

"I may even have lost my confidence," he said. "It is most likely I shall never be able to propose to a woman again for the remainder of my life."

"How tragic, my Lord!" Her sparkling eyes betrayed her cry of sympathy. "Then you shall not be able to do your duty by your title?"

"No, I fear the Wakefield line will die out, and a too-distant cousin will inherit the Havington title. A pity, don't you agree? And all because of a saucy little companion."

"And . . . if she had agreed to marry you, my Lord?" Constance asked in a quiet voice, the playfulness slipping away. "You would have married for all the wrong reasons. And you'd soon resent her for shackling you thus, for the rest of your years."

"Perhaps not, my Lady. Perhaps Miss Violet and I would have suited each other . . ." He leaned his head closer, as if he meant to kiss her neck. ". . . extremely well," he added in a low voice.

Constance fought against the shivering sensations sweeping through her as he breathed into her ear. She fought her dangerously reckless mood. There was so much she longed to say, and this might be her last opportunity. The dance would end too soon.

Closing her eyes, she spoke to his shoulder. "If I were to be truly honest, Lord Havington . . . I would have to tell you I've found myself quite jealous this past week."

Marcus looked at her in wide-eyed amazement, but she failed to notice, as her eyes were still closed. "Jealous?" he asked, not without a tinge of annoyance. "But I've been a hermit! I've done nothing, I've seen no one. It seems between drinking bouts at my club, I do nothing but prowl the night scene hoping to catch a glimpse of you — in the arms of other gentlemen. What could *possibly* give you a reason for jealousy, madam?"

"I've been insanely jealous of Miss Violet," blurted Constance. She opened her eyes to judge his reaction.

He surveyed the crowd over her head. "And if I were to be truly honest, Lady Constance, I would have to tell you I have been doing an inordinate amount of thinking the past several days. In fact, I've been driving my friends crazy, as they point out that I've become most rude and inattentive."

"And? Have you come to any conclusions?" Her heart beat too fast.

He returned his gaze to her. "I've a very good friend. He sat me down the other night, and helped me to make a list of . . . well, of things that are important to me."

"He sounds like a wise friend as well."

"Mm-hmm." He tilted his head upon hers. "Actually, he is my closest friend. And he happens to be the grandson of an acquaintance of yours."

"Do you speak of the Dowager Duchess of Allermaine? I recall she has three grandsons."

"Yes. Her oldest grandson, Philip, is my good friend."

"The duke himself? Lord Allermaine?" she asked.

"The very same. Though I must admit that until recently, I had no idea you were acquainted with his grandmother." He cleared his throat. "Other than as a servant requesting a reference, of course."

Constance blushed, her face as warm as her body. She wished this dance never to end.

"Lord Allermaine assisted me with my dilemma."

"And what dilemma was that, my Lord?"

"You," he smiled down at her.

Constance stiffened in his arms. *"You discussed me with your friend?"* she squeaked. "The two of you had conversations about me?"

The music came to a stop. Constance was frustrated. There was so much she still needed to say; so much she needed to know.

As if reading her mind, Marcus gently took her gloved hand in his. "We are not finished with this discussion, my Lady." He towed her to the nearest terrace door.

Neither spoke until they were out of doors. Marcus walked her to an isolated corner, though well-lit by lanterns. She did not think to protest.

"I regret your name happened to come up whilst in conversation with my best friend. However — since we are being honest tonight — I know you can assure me that you and my sister never discussed *me* while I was not in your presence."

Constance did not meet his eyes, but instead picked up a curl and found herself twirling it around her finger. Indeed, they'd spoken of Lord Havington more times than she could recall.

"Constance . . ." He hesitated with a sigh.

It was not lost upon her that he called her by her first name.

"I thought I was being noble," he said,

"offering to marry you. But Allermaine helped me understand why I did it, and how I felt afterwards."

"Yes, your sense of duty . . . and afterwards, I am sure, your immediate regret," she filled in for him, a lump in her throat.

"No, just the opposite! I became mesmerized by the idea of marriage with Miss Violet. I began obsessing over it."

She would not cry. "Miss Violet is gone, Lord Havington. She was never real. That penniless, defenseless young woman who needed protection is gone." Constance looked out at the lantern-lit garden. "You don't know how many times I've envied her, but the reasons you gave for marriage to Miss Violet no longer apply. The fact is, she is gone forever."

"Reasons? Perhaps we should talk about those reasons," he said.

"Ah, yes," said Constance with not a little bitterness. "Your four bloody reasons. Allow me to refresh your memory: One . . ." Constance held up her gloved index finger, exactly as Marcus had done that day in the coach. "One," she repeated, "it was entirely your fault that I was left behind with the Earl of St. Edmunds."

She waited for his response. He did not answer.

458

She answered for him, her finger still held aloft. "Well, as you now know, there was nothing at all wrong with my being left with my own brother. In fact, it was the safest move, and the most correct of all situations. Therefore, no one was at fault."

Marcus reached for her hand. Slowly, he peeled off the thin white glove. "That is one reason," he said, lifting her hand, capturing her index finger, wrapping his fingers warmly about it.

Constance did not know what he was about. Clearing her throat, and steadying her voice to overcome strong physical sensations of his touch, she raised the next finger alongside his fist. "Two, you could not bear to see me lose my maidenly honor."

Again, he did not respond.

She said, "No honor was lost, as we both now know."

Marcus opened his hand and recaptured both fingers within his fist.

Frowning, Constance continued her count, though it became a bit harder to concentrate. "Three, I could no longer seek employment as a genteel companion to discerning ladies."

Raising her eyebrows in question, she waited, but he said nothing.

Laughing nervously, she confessed, "I

459

think we both know I shall not be needing to seek employment. In fact, after this episode, I vow I shall pay much closer attention to my investments and my financial accounts."

Marcus refolded his hand around her three fingers.

"Four," her voice shook slightly, "my evil reputation could have quickly spread to touch your sister. Well, Larissa has escaped unscathed, and she will go on to have the most glorious Season, as pure as a lily in the eyes of the *ton*."

Marcus took all four of her counting fingers in his large hand. She stared at his hand holding hers, wishing this moment could last forever.

But it would not, and she shook herself back to reality with an inner sigh of regret. "Did I miss any reasons, my Lord? I do not think so," she said quietly.

He brought her captured fingers to his lips and kissed the tips. "Yes. You missed the most important one, Lady Constance."

Her eyes filled with tears at his tender gesture. "Yes?" she whispered hoarsely.

"I am in love with you," he replied simply.

Constance froze, afraid she may have misheard.

Still holding her hand, Marcus reached

into his pocket with his other hand and withdrew a note. Wordlessly, he handed it to her.

Constance extracted her hand from his and took the parchment with shaking fingers. She unfolded the piece of paper and tried to focus through her tears. She read aloud:

The gentleman bearing this reference is seeking a post.

He is also looking for a Companion. His needs are simple:

She must be an independent young woman.

She must love gardening. (It is important she not be afraid of getting a little soil under her graceful fingernails.)

She should enjoy fishing.

She will be an accomplished rider, not afraid to ride a spirited mare.

She loves to read, but chooses her own books.

Constance noticed there was a change in handwriting at this point. The entire note had been written in close, flowery script. Yet in the margin at this point, someone scrawled in bold letters:

Books for bonfires are acceptable.

461

She laughed through her tears and continued reading:

She must be a countess who sets her own style.

The gentleman bearing this reference is seeking this Companion for life.

He is desirous of a permanent post as well — that of her husband.

Much later, Marcus broke the embrace. "I will come first thing tomorrow, to speak to your brother."

"I'll be waiting for you." Constance smiled tremulously. "I wish we could remain here all night, together, until tomorrow's dawn."

"In the spirit of honesty, I must tell you that if we remain out here any longer, we will once again be forced to elope." He cupped her face in his large hands. "I'm not sure I can wait to be this close to you again. You cause havoc to my senses, you know."

"Do I?"

He grinned. "You sound pleased at the prospect of my discomfort, minx."

"Well, if I am to be honest in return, I must admit to the oddest sensations when I am near you. It is inconceivable, but — there is a tingling. It starts in my toes."

Marcus kissed her again; she could feel

the shape of a smile upon his lips.

"I confess," she murmured against his mouth, "I do not know what to do about it."

"Oh, I promise you I have some ideas on how we can alleviate it, madam."

EPILOGUE

Constance could hardly wait for the phaeton to come to a stop; she was poised to bounce out of her seat. Marcus cleared his throat and she took his hint, waited for him to alight and assist her.

Putting her hand shyly in his, she matched his sedate pace to the front entrance, though she really wanted to pick up her peach skirts and run to the Dowager Duchess's door.

Carlton peered around the footman at the open entry, with a disdainful look at the earl, but visibly brightened upon seeing Lady Constance.

"Carlton!" Her smile was dazzling. "It is so good to see you again. Is Her Grace receiving guests?"

"I am most sure she will be receiving *family,* my Lady."

Constance dimpled, and Carlton unbent in a tiny bow. "Please follow, and allow me to announce you."

Marcus frowned. Evidently the butler had another speed, reserved for those he approved of. They glided along in the butler's wake. The fact that everyone on the staff acknowledged Constance was not lost on Marcus. Of course, it was the lady's natural charm that bewitched everyone, members of the *ton* and servants alike. It was one of the reasons he loved her.

As if feeling his gaze, Constance glanced up demurely, her green eyes smiling beneath thick lashes. "Oh, Marcus, I am so happy," she whispered for his ears alone, hugging his arm. "Thank you so much for bringing me to see Lady Amelia. She will be thrilled with our news."

"She will also be happy to know her reference did not go to waste," he said with a glint in his eyes.

Both French doors were opened wide by Carlton as he stepped into the parlour to announce, "Lady Constance Chambreville, and the Earl of Havington, Your Grace."

Just hearing the two names together gave Lady Amelia's heart a happy anticipation. Could it be . . . ? She waved the two in, and did not fail to notice their arms were linked.

As Lord Havington bowed over her hand and their eyes met, she nodded in approval.

Constance leaned forward to give her a hug, and the duchess held her a bit longer in her affectionate embrace.

"Your Grace," began Constance, "Lord Havington and I want you to be the first to share in our happy news." Constance looked up at the earl, who finished the announcement.

"Lady Constance has agreed to become my wife." He looked softly down at his betrothed.

Only when the dowager duchess cleared her throat did they both self-consciously return their attention to their hostess.

"I am quite honored to be the first to know, of course," she declared. "Yet those words do not begin to tell you how very, *very* pleased I am. I could not have wished you happier, Constance! And my congratulations to you, Havington, for having come up to snuff . . . finally," she drawled, raising her imperious eyebrows.

Marcus laughed. "I am sure it was your well-written reference that did the trick, Your Grace. I am forever in your debt."

"Then do not forget it, sir," said the Dowager Duchess. "I shall expect to be named godmother to your first child, of course."

"We would be honored," hc said. With a

smile, he added, "The sooner the better," just to see Constance blush prettily.

His bride-to-be changed the subject. "Oh, Your Grace —"

"I am still Lady Amelia, child."

"Lady Amelia," Constance corrected herself, "I received the most *wonderful* bridal gift in the world from Lord Havington! I was so excited to rush over and tell you! It is the best gift I have ever received. In my entire life."

Marcus tugged a finger across the inside of his cravat. "I fear it is not so wonderful as that," he said in embarrassment.

"Oh, but it is!" Constance's eyes argued, filled with sincerity.

"Then you must tell me all about it," said the duchess. "It does not appear to be a betrothal ring," she observed, looking at Constance's hand. "Is it perhaps a piece of heirloom jewelry, Havington?"

"No, not at all, Your Grace, it is just —"

"It is *much* more exquisite than a piece of jewelry, Lady Amelia! I brought it along to show you." She jumped up. "Allow me to run and fetch it from our coach."

Marcus looked dumbstruck, obviously unaware Constance had brought it.

"It was in the ivory box I placed in the phaeton, my Lord. I shall return shortly," she said over her shoulder as she hurried out of the room.

He returned the duchess's look of surprise. "I must say again, Your Grace, it is nothing spectacular." He shook his head in amusement. "It was simply something I ordered to be made, to please Lady Constance. I cannot believe I left her to retrieve it herself." His rambling appeared to cover his discomfort.

"Tut, tut, Havington, I shall make good use of this opportunity to privately tell you I am thrilled. You will make a happy couple. Rather, you *will* make a happy couple, sir! That is an order. I could not bear to see my young Constance hurt again. She has borne too much sorrow for a young lass as it is."

"I could not agree with Your Grace more. It is an order I shall be most happy to carry out."

The dowager duchess pressed Lord Havington to tell her every detail of how Constance responded to the reference and its content. She quite enjoyed her role as co-conspirator.

They were interrupted by Constance's rushing back into the room, out of breath, a large satin-striped box in her arms. Flushed and excited to share her treasure, she stopped at the settee in order to set down the box and open it.

"Well, I see it is too large to be a piece of jewelry," said Lady Amelia, craning her neck to see.

"Marcus had this especially made for me. In Bond Street!" exclaimed Constance as she removed the lid and began sifting through the tissue.

"It was nothing," murmured Marcus again in consternation.

"A wedding dress?" the duchess hazarded a guess, which she expected to be quite accurate. She glanced at Marcus, who looked as if he wanted to sink through the floor in embarrassment.

"Oh, no, something much, *much* more special than a wedding dress," said Constance, tissue flying everywhere.

Marcus shook his head in amusement, no longer protesting.

Constance turned to face them. She held up a buff-colored coat and hugged it to herself as she rushed over to share it with her Grace.

"Just look! It is a fishing coat. Isn't it beautiful? A fustian fishing coat, made just for me." Her eyes glowed as she stopped in front of Lady Amelia and held the material out for her to touch. Then Constance slipped her arms through it and continued pointing out its assets as she modeled it for the duchess. "And just look: it has half a hundred pockets! And this bit of sheep's wool here —" She pointed to a creamy patch just below her left shoulder. "— where I shall place my hooks and my flies." She twirled around so the duchess could see the back. "The other anglers will be so jealous!" Constance could hardly contain her smiles. "And see here, a loop for my pocket knife, and a hook for my line spool."

"I do see," agreed Lady Amelia. "It is definitely a most wondrous gift. And a most thoughtful gift," she said to Marcus, not without amusement and a glitter in her eyes.

Marcus smiled lopsidedly, then looked upon Constance with wonder, that such a simple gift could please her more than jewels.

The duchess must have been thinking exactly the same thing, for she added, "Well, child, if ever there was a doubt, you most certainly are your Aunt Agatha's bloodline."

Constance was busy fastening and unfastening the various pockets.

Lady Amelia Thorne, Dowager Duchess of Allermaine, looked pointedly at Marcus and reminded him of their bargain. "Keep her happy, Havington."

He returned her gaze evenly and promised firmly, "I will, Your Grace."

ABOUT THE AUTHOR

Sharol Louise and her husband live in the Pacific Northwest, where her psyche was born. However, her body was born in downtown Los Angeles, so it took about 25 years for the two to catch up.

As a youngster, she thought people were referring to the dictionary when they said "the good book," as she grew up in the library reading Edgar Rice Burroughs, Mary Stewart, and Sir Arthur Conan Doyle.

She's been known to miss her bus stop when engrossed in a novel and wishes that her books may do the same for you.

The employees of Thorndike Press hope you have enjoyed this Large Print book. All our Thorndike, Wheeler, and Kennebec Large Print titles are designed for easy reading, and all our books are made to last. Other Thorndike Press Large Print books are available at your library, through selected bookstores, or directly from us.

For information about titles, please call:
  (800) 223-1244

or visit our Web site at:
  http://gale.cengage.com/thorndike

To share your comments, please write:
  Publisher
  Thorndike Press
  295 Kennedy Memorial Drive
  Waterville, ME 04901